Charles Biddle

Autobiography of Charles Biddle

Vice-President of the Supreme Executive Council of Pennsylvania, 1745-1821

Charles Biddle

Autobiography of Charles Biddle
Vice-President of the Supreme Executive Council of Pennsylvania, 1745-1821

ISBN/EAN: 9783337117863

Printed in Europe, USA, Canada, Australia, Japan

Cover: Foto ©Raphael Reischuk / pixelio.de

More available books at **www.hansebooks.com**

AUTOBIOGRAPHY

OF

CHARLES BIDDLE,

VICE-PRESIDENT

OF THE

SUPREME EXECUTIVE COUNCIL

OF

PENNSYLVANIA.

1745—1821.

(*PRIVATELY PRINTED.*)

PHILADELPHIA:
E. CLAXTON AND COMPANY.
1883.

COLLINS PRINTING HOUSE,
705 Jayne Street.

THIS work is printed from the Manuscript, in the possession of Judge Craig Biddle, exactly as written, with no attempt to embellish its natural, easy, and simple style. Having been found of interest by the immediate descendants of the writer, it is thought that it may prove so to the large number of persons more distantly related to him. That the period covered by it embraces the American Revolution and the early days of the Republic seems an additional reason for putting these reminiscences in a permanent form.

The original letters appended, from Burr, Wilkinson, and Truxtun, have not before appeared in print.

The family history contained in the Notes has been obtained from the most authentic sources, and is believed to be accurate.

JAS. S. BIDDLE.

JULY, 1883.

1*

ERRATA..

Page 41, line 22, *for* 1763 *read* 1768.
" 110, third line from foot, *for* Sanderson's *read* Simpson's.
" 135, line 6, *for* Cartaret *read* Carteret.
" 315, line 25, *for* 1809 *read* 1807.
" 366, third line from foot, *for* Shewsbury *read* Shrewsbury.
" 370, line 27, *for* Note D *read* Note G.

CONTENTS.

CHAPTER I.

CHAPTER II.

CHAPTER III.

CHAPTER IV.

CHAPTER V.

NOTES.

I was born in the city of Philadelphia the 24th of December, 1745. My father, William Biddle, was a native of New Jersey, grandson of William Biddle,* who came from England, one of the proprietors of that State. My grandfather was a man of very large fortune. He sent my father to Philadelphia, where he was brought up by Mr. Griffiths, at that time one of the first merchants in America. My mother was the daughter of Nicholas Scull,† Surveyor-General of Pennsylvania. She possessed great firmness, and was one of the most amiable and best of women. My father was unfortunate from his first entering into business. Soon after he was married, he became bail for a Captain Turner, in a large sum of money. As he understood he was going off without settling the debt for which he was bound, my father took out a bail-piece. Turner had locked his room, and declared he would put any man to death who forced the door. As the sheriff and his officers knew Turner to be a desperate fellow, they were afraid to go near the door, but called on my father, who was a man of uncommon strength and resolution. He immediately went to the house, and, notwithstanding Turner declared he would cut down the first man that entered, he forced the door, when the villain wounded him with a cutlass in the right arm in such a manner that it was almost useless the remainder of his life.

* See Note A at the end of this volume.   † See Note B.

1

During the confusion that ensued the fellow slipt among the
crowd and made his escape. For him my father had a large
sum to pay; in everything he undertook he was unfortunate.
Although naturally of a mild disposition, his temper became
soured by his misfortunes, which at last he sank under. My
mother gives some account of their situation about this time,
in a letter to her granddaughter, Mrs. Lux, daughter of my
brother Edward, married to Mr. George Lux, of Maryland,
a man who, had he conducted himself with prudence, would
have been an honor to his country. If Mrs. Lux had not
died without children, I would not have mentioned this
letter. She wrote:—

"I am truly sorry to hear you have met with great affliction. If it arises from the behavior of Mr. Lux, as I fear
it does, your prudence and fortitude must be called in to
assist you. I am informed that he cannot dispose of his
property without your consent. If so, and I hope it is, never
give your consent. It is only making him a prey to game-
sters, the worst of villains. If he gives them his bond, and
they should sue him, they cannot recover. When you married, the estate was equally yours, and dearly have you earned
it. I allow that it seems hard that a wife should deny to
pay her husband's debts, but they are not just debts. How
many wives are now suffering the utmost misery by comply-
ing with the wishes of such a husband! I am now writing
supposing your present uneasiness is owing to Mr. Lux.
Whatever it is, there is one will never forsake you. It is,
perhaps, for our advantage to be sometimes afflicted. We
too often forget ourselves. I was married nineteen years,
and at times thought everything that gave me pain a dreadful affliction. But when I really knew what sorrow was, I
looked back on my former repinings with shame. I had
nine children, one at my breast, when Mr. Biddle informed
me one morning that he had involved himself and ruined
me and his children. I was much shocked, but begged he
would settle his affairs, and hoped he would be better off
than he expected. We had an estate in Jersey, which he
sold for two thousand pounds. He could not see his children

without tears. We paid all our debts, and Mr. Biddle entered into partnership with one Jacobs, a man supposed to be possessed of a great fortune. In one year he broke, and we had to pay fourteen hundred pounds for him. This quite sunk Mr. Biddle. We had very little left. My dear Mr. Biddle was taken with a lingering disorder. For six weeks before he died I never slept with my clothes off. The situation of my children made me exert myself to provide for them. Your Uncle James had just begun to practice the law, and this best of sons shared with me everything he could earn. Your father, then but sixteen years of age, went an ensign in the army. Charles and Nicholas, at about the age of fourteen, went to sea. They, as well as your uncles John and Thomas, all were happy in rendering me every assistance in their power. I suffered much at the loss of your uncle Nicholas in the Randolph, but it was a consolation to know that he was one of the best of young men, and died in the service of his country. I am now, with the assistance of my sons, very comfortably situated, and when I look round me, think I have as little reason to complain as any person in the world."

When about eleven years of age my mother sent me to the wharf after wood. Returning along Water, near Market Street, to avoid a dray, I stepped on a pile of wood. There being snow on it, my feet slipped and my left leg came directly under the dray, which had a hogshead of sugar on it. My right leg was nearly in between the spokes; the bone was mashed a little below my knee. When they were carrying me to my mother, I thought it disgraceful to cry, and she, seeing me brought home without making any noise, concluded I was drowned. I was laid upon a table, and one of the most eminent surgeons in the city thought it would be necessary to take off my leg. This was opposed by Dr. Evans, the family physician, by my mother, and myself. It was near six months before I was perfectly recovered. In Jamaica, many years after, I felt some pain where the bone had been broken, but none since.

Before I went to sea, few boys were more mischievous

than myself; two or three of my companions were much the
same—Robert Shewell, Townsend White, Frank Manny,
W. Budden who was some years older than either of us,
S. Hepburn, and Esquire Forman. We were always playing
some pranks. Budden's father commanded a ship. He told
one of his apprentices, of the name of Bowen, who had done
something improper, that he did not believe there was so
wicked a fellow in the city as he was; "Go see, you rascal,
if you can find any one as bad as yourself." He went to our
companion and told him his father wanted him immediately.
They went together, and Bowen says to his master, "Here,
sir, is one that is my match." The old gentleman laughed,
and told him he believed he had found one full as bad as
himself. With White I have frequently gone close to a man
walking the streets and fired one of my brother Edward's
pistols close to his ear; sometimes gone of a dark night with
a rope and tripped up the heels of people. Whenever we
met a person in the night with a basket or tub on his head,
one or other of us would throw it off. Going one night with
him throwing down cellar doors, among others, we threw
down our schoolmaster's, Captain Stiles. He happened to be
just coming out of the door, ran after us, caught me and
gave me a most severe beating. As it was dark he did not
know me, and I was afraid to make a noise for fear he should
find out whom he was flogging and remember me the next
day.

One day Shewell persuaded me, without much difficulty,
to take a very large imported horse, belonging to Mr. Gray,
a brewer, out of the stable. We rode this horse without
anything but a halter up to Chestnut Hill, where we both
had relations, to buy game-fowls upon credit, for we had no
money. Upon our return Shewell, according to agreement,
took the horse back to the stable. The Sunday following we
were in the brewhouse yard, when one of the porters, who
had seen Shewell bring the horse home, caught him, and, notwithstanding all he said about my taking the horse, beat
him very severely. At this time Shewell was not more than
thirteen years of age. I was two years younger.

One evening, pulling off my shoes, I clambered up a board and got into the gallery of the theatre in Southwark through a small opening in the upper part of the building. Just before I reached the opening, one of the attendants of the house caught hold of the board, and threatened to turn it over if I did not come immediately down. At this time some person called to him to let the board alone—the little rascal has run the risk of his neck, let him get in if he can. The play was just over when I got into the gallery; all the actors were on the stage. I thought it a most grand sight. In fact there was no kind of mischief could be proposed but what I was ready to be concerned in. Fortunately for me, my brothers James and Edward heard of one of my pranks. They took me into a room and pointed out to me in strong terms the ruin I should bring upon myself, and how unhappy my conduct made my mother by keeping the company I did. Young and thoughtless as I was, what they said made a deep impression upon me; the thought of giving pain to the best of mothers affected me very much. The lecture of these excellent brothers had an effect on me ever after. I immediately quit the company of my companions in mischief, and associated with those who conducted themselves better. I believe the young people at this time are not so bad as they were when I was a boy.

When I was fourteen years of age, my mother being extremely anxious to put me an apprentice to a merchant, I went for a short time to Mr. William Ball. Although I had not the least reason to complain of this gentleman, I soon was tired of this business, and was determined to go to sea, where I expected soon to make a fortune, or at least do something to prevent my being a burden to my mother and elder brothers. However, after I left Mr. Ball, at the earnest request of my mother, I went with her to Messrs. James & Drinker, eminent merchants that were concerned in shipping, and who from the regard they had for the family wished me to live with them. Not finding either of these gentlemen at home, and falling in with a Captain Robert Grant, bound to St. Lucar, in Spain, who wanted such a lad as I was, he easily persuaded me to go with him, and I believe now, that my going to sea was the best thing I could have done; nor have I ever repented it. The leaving my mother and family was the only cause of regret. Grant was a good seaman, but, what is very uncommon in a seaman, he was a great miser. We went to sea without any poultry, and few stores of any kind. He used to say he did not like to indulge himself in any luxuries, for he did not know how soon he might want. However, I have no doubt that he would have indulged himself if he could have done it without any expense.

Before I went to sea with Grant, I wrote to Mr. McFunn, my brother-in-law, who was then master attendant of the navy yard at Antigua (he had been many years an officer in the navy), to know if he could get me on board a man-of-war. As he was much esteemed by Sir James Douglass, he agreed to take me as an acting midshipman on board his own ship, the Dublin; and I should have gone if peace had not been soon after concluded. I did not want to enter when nothing was to be done. Had it not been for the peace, I should have gone into the navy, and probably remained in it.

We left Philadelphia the 10th of May, 1763, and nothing remarkable happened until the 3d of June following, when at daylight we discovered a large armed ship about three miles to windward with Spanish colors, bearing down upon us, and an English brig almost within hail. There was very little wind. Grant, not liking the appearance of the Spaniard, which he took to be a pirate, or some privateer that had not heard of the peace between Great Britain and Spain, spoke the brig. She was from Jamaica bound to London, and, the captain being of the same opinion that Grant was, we both kept away before the wind. At 12 o'clock it was almost calm, and the Spaniard nearly within gunshot of us. As the brig had a few guns, it was concluded between the two captains, that we should all go on board the brig, and if the Spaniard came up with us, to fight her. At 4 o'clock she was so near as to heave a shot over us, and then all went on board the brig, and fired several shots which fell short,

which convinced us her metal was much heavier than ours.
It soon fell calm and remained so until about 10 o'clock at
night, when upon the appearance of a squall we went on board
our own vessel, and had hardly time to get in our boat before it came on to blow very hard. We soon lost sight of
the ship and brig. About 2 o'clock in the morning the mate
came down to inform Grant that the Spaniard was upon our
weather-quarter and coming up fast. This put the crew in
great confusion, for we all firmly believed she was a pirate,
and we should be treated very ill. Being then a boy and
only wanting to learn my business as a seaman, and having
nothing to lose, I felt as little uneasiness as any one on board.
However, upon the vessel getting within hail we found it
was Captain Betson, who left the Capes of Delaware with
us bound for Madeira. After this nothing material happened
during the voyage. We arrived at St. Lucar on the 20th
of June. St. Lucar is a considerable town, and was said at
this time to contain twenty-five thousand inhabitants. Five
leagues distant from it is Port St. Mary's, and here you take
passage for Cadiz. A few days after our arrival there was a
grand bull-fight, given on account of the peace between Great
Britain and Spain. They had a large circus amphitheatre
with seats arranged one above another to a considerable
height. In a large balcony near where the bulls entered, the
Governor and a great number of the nobility were seated.
They had procured a number of the most ferocious bulls
that could be found in the Province of Andalusia, which is
famous for those animals. Before the bull enters the arena
he is goaded by a fellow placed above with a kind of pike,
so that when he enters he is perfectly mad, and rushes with
great violence at the first person he sees. The men who
fought the bulls behaved with most astonishing courage and
dexterity. Frequently when the bull was rushing on them,
and you would suppose they must certainly be killed, they
would put their hands on his head or neck and jump over
him. Whenever anything remarkable was performed, they
were called to the balcony and money thrown to them.
Notwithstanding all their skill, several were thrown a great

height, and three were so much bruised as to be carried to
the hospital, where it was reported two of them died the
next day. The fight gave great pleasure to most of the
spectators; for my own part, although the novelty of the
fight pleased me at first, I was soon so much disgusted that
I would gladly have quitted my seat long before it was
finished, if I could have done it. But that was impossible,
for we were on one of the upper seats. It was near night
when it was ended, and the mate, who went with me, and
myself were moving off, when we were stopped by some
Spaniards. As we could neither of us speak a word of
Spanish, nor they English, it was not until a person came
up that could speak English, that we found they wanted to
be paid for our seats. We were detained by these fellows
until it was dark. Having paid for our seats we set off to
go on board our ship, which lay about two miles above the
town, but, mistaking our way, we went the road to Seville.
We had proceeded about a mile when we came to a small
hill from the top of which we could see the river, and were
then convinced we had mistaken our road. We determined
to cross the vineyard until we reached the waterside, where
we had no doubt of soon finding our ship. However, we
had not gone far before we were hailed by one of their
watchmen. As we had done a good deal of injury to the
grapes, and expected to be roughly handled, when he halloed we ran, but we were soon stopped by some fellows in
front of us. They were taking us to their watch-house when
we broke from them and made our escape. We now did
what we should have done when we first discovered the
river; that is, go back to town. We did this now, and,
having kept along the river, about twelve o'clock at night
got on board, heartily sick of our expedition.

About two weeks after our arrival I was taken very ill
with the flux, occasioned by my eating too many grapes,
which I believe has been fatal to many not accustomed to
eating them. As I had never been sick before, nor ever
heard of this disorder, I inquired of an old seaman who had
been long on board of a man-of-war, whether he knew what

the flux was. "That I do," answered he, "for I lay two
months with it in the hospital at Gibraltar, and never expected to get up again; many of my ship-mates died of it.
Indeed, very few recovered." While my honest friend was
comforting me in this manner, Captain Grant came on board,
and, the mate telling him of my disorder, he went ashore
and spoke to Mr. David Ferrier, to whom the vessel was
consigned. This gentleman had been concerned in the rebellion in Scotland, and was obliged to leave his country. He
was a very worthy, respectable man. He took me to his
house, and treated me with great kindness. I was also much
indebted to Mr. William Seton, a young gentleman of New
York, who lived with Mr. Ferrier. He behaved as a brother
to me, and it was owing to the goodness and attention of
these gentlemen that I recovered. They dieted me on barley
broth, which Mr. Ferrier thought good for all disorders.

When the vessel was discharged of her cargo, we went up
to the salt-works and were soon loaded. While we lay there,
we had frequent disputes with the Spaniards about the
bravery of the British and Spanish troops. They would
allow that no people fought so well at sea as the British, but
that their troops were better. However, we could always
silence them by telling them of the Havannah, which they
had always supposed it was not possible to take. The
Spaniards are a people very honorable in their dealings, but
very indolent and proud. Captain Hardy, of Philadelphia,
told me of an old woman whom he had known for many
years at Cadiz, a beggar; the last voyage he made there,
when he saw her, she cried very much, and told him they
had taken her son from her and bound him to a cooper, and
that he was the first of the family who had ever been brought
up to a trade.

We sailed from St. Lucar about the first of August, and
nothing unusual happened during our passage home. We
arrived in the Delaware the 20th of September. When we
anchored off Marcus Hook, Grant hired a horse to send me
to inform the owners of our arrival. I was greatly rejoiced
at being sent up, and rode as fast as I could get the poor

animal to go, but, notwithstanding all my exertions, it was at least five hours before I arrived at Philadelphia, and there found Grant, who was there an hour before me, through a fair wind soon after I set off. My joy was so great at getting home that I hardly knew how to contain myself. My mother and all the family were greatly rejoiced to see me. I believe there never existed a family fonder of each other than we were.

As Captain Grant had behaved well to me, the family took a good deal of notice of him, and when he was again going to sea he prevailed on me to go with him. Had I then known the difference between a summer and a winter voyage, I never would have gone in such a vessel. We sailed the beginning of December for the island of Fayal. A few days after we were out, we had a most violent gale of wind which obliged us to lay to. About 3 P. M., the mate desired me to go below and bring him a drink ; I was on the ladder, just going to hand it to him, when a tremendous sea broke on board and cleared the decks of everything upon them but the masts and pumps. There were two men with the mate upon the deck. The seamen had, fortunately, taken hold of a rope the moment the sea struck us, and by that means were saved. The mate was lost. As he was fond of liquor and surly, the crew did not much regret his loss. A coop broke when washed overboard, that had some geese in it ; they appeared atop of the waves to enjoy very much their liberty. A large dog was in the midst of them ; he swam to the vessel and we took him on board. Grant and the watch below were soon upon deck. We put our bark before the wind, and were rejoiced to find she made little or no water. The wind was at northeast, and although out of our course, we were obliged for twenty-four hours to keep before it, and frequently expected our old bark would have been stove to pieces. The next day the gale abated, and at night it was perfectly calm. The wind afterwards springing up from the westward, we made sail and stood our course. Christmas day we made the land. It being thick weather, and not knowing the land, we stood close in with it, when a

boat came off and informed us it was the island of Flora.
We stood for Fayal, and two days after anchored in the road
in twenty fathoms of water. This is a bad, and in the winter
season a dangerous road, being entirely open to the southeast
wind. The weather was boisterous from the time of our
arrival until the second of January, 1764, so that we could
not land any of our cargo, although it was sold, and a part
of it much wanted by Mr. Gathorn, the British Consul, as
about a month before our arrival a transport, with between
two and three hundred of Montgomery's Highlanders, Lieuts.
West and McKenzie (son to the Earl of Cromartie), of the
king's own regiment, and Lieut. Bloomfield of the artillery,
from Quebec, bound to England, had put in here in distress,
and their vessel was so leaky they were obliged to run her
ashore to prevent her foundering.

The evening of the second of January it began to blow
hard, and by midnight increased to a perfect storm. Signals
of distress were fired from all the vessels which had guns, and
they continued firing all night. At daylight signals of distress were made by every vessel in the harbor. In our old
bark we expected every instant to founder. Grant would
have cut and run the vessel ashore, but was afraid we should
all perish. We continued in this situation until about one
o'clock, when we parted our best bower cable, and found we
were drawing on shore. The scene now before us was
enough to shock the stoutest heart. We were drawing fast
upon rocks that the sea broke over in such a manner that
death appeared inevitable. In this situation we did everything that was possible to preserve our lives; we cut our remaining cables, (here every vessel hires cables, especially in
the winter) hoisted a small piece of our foresail to keep her
clear of the rocks, and stood for a sandy beach opposite the
town, where we expected there would be some hopes of our
being saved. Although it blew and rained harder than it
had ever been known before by the oldest inhabitant of the
place, there was scarce a person belonging to the town but
what was on the walls gazing at us. In front of those on
the beach, when atop of the sea, we could see the gallant

Highlanders standing ready to afford us any assistance that could be given. As I swam remarkably well, I was determined as soon as the vessel struck to commit myself to the waves, and swim for the shore. For this purpose, I had stripped myself naked. A young Scotchman, of the name of Daniel Carr, who was one of the men washed overboard when we lost our mate, swam well, and agreed to follow me. Grant, from the quarterdeck, seeing me naked, called to me. He represented to me the impossibility of my being saved by swimming while there was such a dreadful surf. When he found this had no effect, he begged me not to leave him, that a few moments would decide our fate, and that I had a much better chance of being saved by staying with him than by jumping overboard. When I looked at him, I perceived tears in his eyes. This and his request had more weight than anything he could say about the danger of my attempt. As he could not swim, and he knew how well I did, he thought it probable I might be of service to him. This, indeed, was one great inducement for me to stay. His countenance expressed satisfaction when I told him we would live or die together. We were now driving fast on shore, which had a horrid appearance. As soon as the vessel touched the ground Daniel went overboard. He had nothing on him but a handkerchief tied round his waist, with the little money he possessed in it. Twice he was on his feet, and some of the brave troops were very near him; but the undertow carried him off, and he was drowned. He was the most active man belonging to the vessel. Having a great regard for him, I was much affected at his loss. His money prevented our ever finding his body, and possibly occasioned his being drowned. When we first struck, I expected the vessel would have gone to pieces; however, the second heavy sea, after we struck, hove her so far on the beach, that when the sea left her she was almost dry. In this situation we dropped from the end of the bowsprit, and with the assistance of the Highlandmen, we reached the shore in safety. Lieutenant McKenzie distinguished himself in his endeavors to save us, and had very nearly lost his life in the attempt he made to save poor Daniel. This young gentleman, I think, told me he was at his mother's breast when she applied to the king for a pardon for her husband, who was concerned in the Rebellion. We were treated with great kindness by Messrs. Gathorne and McKnight, merchants of this place, and by all the British officers, most of whom had served with my brother Edward, for whom they expressed a great esteem, and on his account were particularly kind to me. All the vessels in the road, being eight, received more or less damage, and two besides our own were totally lost.

Shortly after the loss of our vessel, an English merchant died here suddenly, and was buried near one of the churches. The Portuguese were, or pretended to be, much shocked at a heretic's being laid near one of their churches, and during the time of our walking to the ground and putting the body in the grave, continually pelted and abused us. Had the soldiers been armed, there would have been some bloodshed. At the grave there was a dispute whether the head should be laid to the east or west. This was settled by an old master of a ship, who said, if the head was laid the wrong way, when all hands were called, he had only to turn upon his heel, and all would be right. We were told the inhabitants took up the body in the night and threw it into the sea.

Two nights after this funeral, the Highlanders were determined to be revenged for the insults they had received. They paraded the streets, and insulted and abused every inhabitant they met with. They wounded some who opposed them. Complaint was made the next day by the governor to their commander, Captain St. Clair. He requested St. Clair to have their broadswords taken from them; this he refused, and told the governor that unless his soldiers were treated better, he would give them pistols. After this the people of the island were afraid of the soldiers, and behaved better to us. Many of those Highlanders who had served some years in America, and with English regiments, I was told could not speak a word of English. It was remarkable that none of the officers could fire well at a mark. They pitched upon me to fire against an Italian gentleman, who valued himself much upon his skill. We had several trials, and although I never at home was considered a good marksman, I was fully equal to this man who, one day, took some improper liberties with the officers; but they soon convinced him that if they did not fire well at a mark, they were any of them very ready to take a shot with him, or try him in any way he chose. He was obliged to humble himself very much to prevent being severely handled. It was with difficulty Mr. McKenzie could be prevented from kicking him.

Mr. Gathorn told me that the winter before we were cast away, a ship hove to off the harbor when it blew a gale of wind from the westward. She had a signal of distress, and was full of people. As the water was smooth, he engaged a number of boats to go off to her. They intended to take the people out and run into a small harbor in Pico, but before the boats could put off, the ship made sail and ran ashore upon Pico, where the captain and most of them perished. She was from Ireland, bound to America. Those who were saved said the captain was very drunk at the time they ran ashore. Passengers should be very careful how they put themselves with a drunkard. They had better be in a bad ship with a sober, careful man, than in a good one with a man too fond of liquor.

In the month of February, Mr. Graham, partner of Mr. Gathorn, arrived in a Snow from Philadelphia. The captain and he having differed on the passage, the captain left her at Fayal, and the command was given to Captain Grant. About this time a transport ship belonging to Philadelphia, Captain Dennis,* arrived from Lisbon, and took on board the troops to carry them to England. We parted with the officers with much regret. The Snow was ordered to Charleston, and I shipped myself on board of her. It was the ninth of March before we left this island, which is very pleasant and fertile. By my long residence here in a Portuguese house I had acquired a tolerable knowledge of their language. We

---

* Afterwards commanded a revenue cutter in New York.

arrived on the coast of Carolina early in April. Just off soundings we lost both our topmasts. This was entirely owing to the obstinacy of Grant, for the mate, who was an old seaman well acquainted with the coast, advised him to take in sail long before he would do it. I was going up to hand* the maintop-gallant sail, and was just getting into the top when the topmast went over the side. Great care should be taken to be well prepared for these squalls, for frequent accidents happen by trusting that they will not blow hard. Having a fair wind we arrived a few days afterwards in Charleston. Grant and myself left the snow, and took passage for Baltimore, and from thence went to Philadelphia, where I had the happiness to find the family all well.

After settling with his owners Grant was determined to go to England, and from thence to India, where he had been before, and where, he said, he was sure of making his fortune in the coasting trade. He wanted me very much to go with him, and probably I should have done so, but my family were all very much against it, particularly my mother. He promised to write to me, but I never heard of him after he left England, so that it is probable he did not live long after reaching India.

Lieutenant John Lockart Nesmith, who was a half-pay lieutenant in the British navy, came from London this spring to build a vessel. As he had served with Captain McFunn, who had some time before married a sister† of mine, Captain McFunn agreed to take a third in the vessel he intended building. They employed Mr. John Wharton, who built a snow of a hundred and fifty tons burthen. As I attended very constantly to the fitting of this vessel, and was stout of my age, I was appointed second mate of her. Just before we sailed I was paid for my work on board, and had a month's advance given me. As I had not time to go home after it was paid me, I sent it from the Capes to my mother, and I never disposed of any money that gave me so much pleasure. We left the Capes about the middle of October, and a few

---

* To furl.   † Lydia, eldest sister of the writer.

days after it blew so hard from the southward that we were obliged to heave to. As the gale increased in the night, our chief mate, Mr. Campbell, about eleven o'clock went down to inform the captain and to tell him he thought we had better take in the foresail. As Campbell was waking the captain, the vessel gave a lee-lurch, and the table giving way and making a great noise, alarmed Nesmith very much. He came running upon deck, and hallooed down the steerage hatchway, "Jump up, my brave lads; make haste up, my good fellows, or we all perish;" and some other expressions that showed he was much agitated. These expressions were repeated and laughed at afterward by the seamen. From trifling circumstances of this kind many a brave officer has been thought a coward. There are few gallant men but what will on some occasions behave in such a manner as to be considered wanting in courage. At that time all our ship's company thought him a coward; but he was a very brave man, and a good seaman, that had raised himself by his merit. He afterwards mentioned that just as he was called, he was dreaming that the vessel was foundering. We had a tedious passage of thirty days to Antigua. We soon discharged our cargo, took in ballast, rum, and dry goods, and proceeded for the bay of Honduras. One night while at Antigua, being on shore in the boat by myself waiting for the captain and crew, a drunken fellow, who commanded a drogher, insisted upon my putting him on board his vessel. From words we soon came to blows, and as he was much too strong, I got severely beaten, and probably would have been murdered, but fortunately the captain and crew came down while we were fighting. They hove the fellow overboard.

On our passage down we touched at the Mosquito Shore, and hired one of the Indians they call a striker, that is, a man to supply the crew with fish, turtle, and maniti or pacon, which is excellent eating. One of these men will (or would at this time) supply a ship's company with more fish and turtle than they could eat. We lay here nearly four months, and were daily furnished by this man. The crew were at last so tired of fish and turtle that they would beg for a mess of salt provisions. The inhabitants of the bay at this time were chiefly old seamen or unfortunate merchants. They were very hospitable and generous, would give freely any liquor or provisions they had in their houses. In return they would expect to be treated in the same manner when they came on board your ship. If you did not treat them well they never would purchase or sell to you, and you would be insulted whenever you went ashore.

When loading, and Captain Nesmith up the river, a shallop came alongside with a load of logwood. We had taken but a few tons on board, when Captain Wright, who commanded a brig belonging to New York, came on board and told Mr. Campbell that the wood was intended for him and he must have it. Campbell informed him that as Captain Nesmith was not on board, he could not let the wood go. Upon this Wright attempted to cast off the shallop, and called his boat's crew to come on board and assist him. As soon as they entered a battle ensued, in which several on both sides were much hurt, and George Peters, one of our crew, being knocked from the gunwale of our vessel into the shallop, had his arm broken and lay for some time lifeless. Wright was a remarkably stout man, and after a warm contest he carried the shallop off. That night Nesmith returned, and was very much exasperated when he heard of the behavior of Wright. Early in the morning he ordered the boat manned, and we armed ourselves as well as we could, Nesmith being determined to bring the shallop back or lose his life in the attempt. She was at this time alongside of the brig. As Wright was an old captain of a privateer, and a very determined fellow, I expected we should have a bloody piece of business, but he had been so much bruised the day before that he could not get out of his bed, and we took her without opposition. The baymen at this time would frequently sell their wood to two or three different captains, which occasioned much squabbling and fighting. There being no law but club-law, the strongest always took the wood.

We sailed the beginning of April for Curaçao, and beat for several days to get up as high as Bonacco. This is done

2

by most masters of vessels before they stand to the northward for Cuba. I do not, however, think it necessary to
beat up to this island, for you may go to the westward of
Turneff and between the Northern Triangles and the main,
or to the windward, if the wind will permit, and beat up
when you get into the latitude of Cape Anthony or to the
northward of it. When you beat up to Bonacco, and stand
over for Cuba, you frequently make the land to windward
of Cape Anthony and have to run down. You sometimes
meet with a westerly wind, which if to leeward, would be
a fair wind for you. From December to March you frequently have westerly winds. In the latitude of 20° 50′,
about five leagues from Cape Catoche there is a bank that
I have been upon. You will have on it from twelve to sixteen fathoms. I believe it is not laid down in any chart.
When we first discovered the bottom we were in company
with the ship Sally, Capt. Osman, and it alarmed us a good
deal. Having never heard of this bank, as it was in the
evening when we made it, we could not tell the extent. In
navigating those seas your safety much depends upon a very
careful lookout, and never to run for any of the islands or
reefs in the night if you can possibly avoid it. Thousands
have perished by being too anxious to make a short passage.

Nothing material happened until we arrived in the latitude of Curaçao, which we passed about ten o'clock in the
morning, mistaking it for one of the islands that are to the
windward of it; nor did we discover our mistake until we
spoke a schooner beating up. They told us the island we
supposed to be Curaçao, and for which we were standing,
was the island of Oruba. We immediately hauled our wind,
and inquiring if they could furnish us with a pilot for Curaçao, they, after some consultation, informed us they could.
The schooner was full of men, and Nesmith was under some
apprehension of their being wreckers or some ruffians that
probably would plunder us. He therefore directed me, when
I went on board of her to bring the pilot, not to suffer any
other person to come into the boat, as there were between
thirty and forty men in the schooner, and only four of us in

the boat, and we had no weapon with us but the boat-hook.
I knew if they were determined on it we could not prevent
them; yet, as I was then, and have ever since been, of the
opinion that an officer should always obey his superior's
orders, be they almost what they may, or endeavor to do it,
I told him no other should come into the boat. While we
were alongside several ill-looking rascals attempted to come
in, but when I told them my orders, and that I would drive
the boat-hook into any that came into the boat, they desisted. We understood from the pilot, that the people on
board the schooner had gone from Curaçao to a vessel that
was wrecked in Oruba. We beat here several days, when
being in want of provisions and finding we daily lost ground,
we bore away for Jamaica. The poor pilot, when he found
we were standing for Jamaica, was ready to jump overboard,
for when he came on board he expected to be in Curaçao in
a day or two, and was engaged to be married as soon as he
arrived there. We arrived in Jamaica in a few days. Nesmith, not being willing to take the price offered for his cargo,
stored it. I understood from him afterwards, that it sold for
one-half of what had been offered, and I believe it is better
to sell almost any cargo in the West Indies than to store it.
The expense of storing is great and the result uncertain.

During the time we were at Kingston three of our crew
ran away. I don't know that Nesmith used them worse
than usual, but I am sure he was glad they left us; for they
had several months' wages due them. I have known masters
behave ill to their crew when they had much wages due, to
induce them to run away. This is certainly a most infamous
way of saving money.

We went from Jamaica to the Bay and there took in a
cargo for London. We were loaded and nearly ready to sail
when a vessel arrived from Philadelphia, which brought
letters for Nesmith, ordering him home. As most of the
crew belonged to Philadelphia this intelligence was received
with the greatest joy. We sailed soon after, and arrived safe
after an absence of twelve months.

During this voyage a circumstance happened that I have

been almost afraid to mention, even to my friends, fearing they should doubt it, although they never had any reason to doubt my veracity. It was in March, one pleasant night, when we were on our passage to Curaçao, being at the helm, I thought I saw the apparition of one of my sisters, that I had left sick in Philadelphia, pass and beckon to me. It had such an effect on me that I awoke my brother Nicholas and mentioned it to him, and set down in my journal the time it happened. Upon our return we anchored off the city about ten o'clock at night. I went ashore and was hurrying to my mother's when I overtook my sister Mary. I eagerly inquired after our sister—"She is well, and has a fine boy." "I do not mean our sister McFunn, but Abigail." "My God! have you never heard that we lost her. It is upwards of six months since she died." I found upon further inquiry it was the night I thought she appeared to me. She had been a remarkably hearty girl until one night going to a dance, and, on returning home, sitting for some time in a damp room brought on a complaint that soon hurried her to her grave. The day before she died she requested to be lifted up to see the sun rise, which she said she was sure would be the last time she should ever see it. She died with the utmost composure.

We found that none of the vessels we had spoken during this voyage had published the name of our vessel or captain right. The Snow was called the Ann and Almack. Ann was the name of Captain Almack's sister, who was married to Almack, a celebrated tavern-keeper in London. Most of those who spoke us mentioned their speaking the Snow Almanack.

Captain Nesmith left the Snow in Philadelphia, and bought a small shallop to trade up the rivers in the Bay, and my brother-in-law, Captain McFunn, took command of the Snow. We left Philadelphia in October, 1765, for Jamaica, where we arrived the beginning of November. After we had discharged our cargo, and were taking in ballast, Mr. Campbell sent me one morning in the boat to bring a craft that was becalmed alongside with ballast. We were discharging her when the captain of a London ship came on board. Campbell being in the hold, he addressed himself to me in a noisy, rude manner, and told me the ballast was for his ship, and he would have it. Captain McFunn, who was one of the stoutest, most resolute, and passionate men in the world, was below, and a barber shaving him. Hearing a noise, he called to me to know what was the matter. When I informed him, he came upon deck in a violent rage, and asked the London captain how he dared to come on board his vessel and behave in the manner he had done. Not liking the answer he received, he gave the captain a blow with the back of his hand which knocked him from the gunwale into the water. He very narrowly escaped falling into his boat, which had luckily been just pulled ahead. When he was hauled in his boat he told Captain McFunn that he hoped soon to find him ashore, when he would punish him for his infamous behavior. McFunn immediately ordered the boat manned, and, half shaved as he was, went immediately ashore. However, he was not followed.

A few days after, we dropped down to Port Royal. While here, upon a Sunday, we hoisted a king's jack. A small sloop-of-war sent her boat on board and took it away. Captain McFunn was then at Kingston; when he came on board, and was informed of what had happened, he thought by going on board and informing the captain of the sloop it was hoisted without his knowledge that it would be given up. However, he was mistaken, for the captain of the sloop told him that his being an old naval officer made him more inexcusable, and he should not have the colors. This was very mortifying to McFunn, but there was no remedy. Had he met him on shore he would probably have demanded satisfaction. Fortunately they did not meet, for we sailed the day after for the Bay.

Soon after our arrival in the bay Captain McFunn hired a black man named Marlborough. He was a stout, active young man, about twenty-one years of age, and of his color remarkably handsome. He was a most excellent servant; had been brought up in Bristol; could shave, dress, and was handy and willing to do everything. He belonged to one Cook, who, after he had been on board a month, said he could not live without him, and took him up the river where he then lived. For some crime he supposed the unfortunate black had committed, and which it appeared afterwards was not done by him, Cook cut off one of his ears. Marlborough immediately took a gun that happened to be in the room and shot his master dead. He fled to the woods. A few days afterwards, as our long boat was coming down the river he knew her, and, driven by hunger, he hailed her; and upon Mr. Scull, who commanded the boat, promising not to deliver him up he came on board. As soon as he sat down to eat they seized upon him, and upon their arrival at St. George's they delivered him to the magistrates, who condemned him to be burned, and he was executed the day after he was tried. They bound him to a stake and made a fire round him with empty barrels and brush. Soon after the fire was kindled, in order to put him out of his pain, Captain McFunn kicked one of the empty barrels that was in a blaze close to his head. He was sensible that it was intended to relieve him from pain, and, being unable to speak, he bowed his head to thank him. No man ever suffered with more fortitude than this unfortunate black. Our crew detested Scull so much for his breach of promise to Marlborough that it was hardly safe for him to come on board the Snow. We all thought Marlborough perfectly right in shooting his inhuman master.

At the Bay we found Captain Nesmith, who had provided a great part of our cargo, and the 28th day of December we sailed from the bay for Antigua. We had light airs and variable winds for several days. On the 2d of January, 1766, we were becalmed between the Northern Triangles and the main. At dark we set* the southernmost part of the reef. It bore S. E. by S. from us. It continued calm until about nine o'clock, when we had a light breeze from the northwest. We set all sail and steered S. by W., intending to keep that course until we passed the reef. At 11 o'clock it blew very hard; we were then under our foresail and close-reefed maintopsail. About half-past eleven Captain McFunn told me he

---

* "To set" is to take the bearing by compass.

felt as if a mountain was removed from his breast; that he had been uneasy at not having any insurance on his part of the Snow; that he had never gone to sea before without doing it; that he was sure we had now passed the reef, and were out of danger. It now blew excessively hard, and he ordered me to call all hands and take in the maintopsail, and told Campbell and myself he intended to stand to the eastward under the foresail. All hands were called, and the chief mate took the helm. We were just going to take in the topsail when George Peters, a Scotch seaman, that was looking out from the end of her boltsprit, called out—"Starboard! Starboard! for God's sake, or we are all lost." The chief mate, who was very hard of hearing, put the helm a-port. The man repeating the cry, I ran aft and we shifted the helm, which was not done more than ten minutes when she ran ashore. We were going at the rate of seven or eight knots when she struck. The first stroke she gave was dreadful, and if she had been loaded with any other cargo than mahogany and logwood she would have gone to pieces in an hour. The second sea that struck her carried her within the outer breaker, and fortunately threw her broadside to the sea, by which means our boats could live to leeward of her. We hoisted them out; the long boat was soon lost. The yawl we veered away with a hawser. My brother Nicholas went in her, and did everything he was ordered with as much coolness as he would have done alongside the wharf. We then cut her masts by the board; one of them falling on the starboard, the other on the larboard side. After the masts were cut away I went into the cabin, and, finding the captain's chest driving about, I was lashing it to one of the stanchions when Campbell came down. He told me it was an unnecessary piece of business, for he was sure none of us would ever live to see daylight. This made me desist; however, as my clothes were wet, I opened the chest and took some out, and by this means did not save any whatever belonging to myself. About two o'clock we all went into the steerage, but had not been there long before we found the deck settling, and all hurried to the after part of the quarter deck, which was the only part of the wreck the sea did not make a breach over. Having lost our long-boat, we had nothing but a yawl, and as she would hardly carry us all, we were afraid of one another. Having done everything we could, we all went into the steerage. We were soon, however, driven thence by a heavy sea breaking on board which made the deck crack. We now retreated to the after part of the quarter deck, the only part of the wreck that was dry. We waited with great anxiety for the dawning of the day. When it appeared, we saw the Northern Triangles,* the nearest part about eight miles, and that we had struck on the southern-most part of the reef, so that if Campbell had kept the helm a-port, as he first put it, in a few minutes we should have cleared the reef. He said afterwards, that when he heard a noise forward he suspected what was the matter, and know-ing the reef must be to the eastward, made him put the helm to port. It still blew excessively hard, and we were afraid to venture in the boat. We passed another dismal night on the wreck. The second day the gale abated a little, and the wind hauled round to the northward. We deter-mined to reach the shore, as we thought it impossible to live another night on board. We took with us a small cask of water, a bag of bread, a compass, and a few other necessa-ries. There were ten of us, five at the oars, two lay in the bottom of the boat, I steered her, and Captain McFunn and Campbell were employed bailing, for we took in a great deal of water, so that the poor fellows in the bottom of the boat were almost drowned. Just before we went into the boat, a poor English lad, of the name of John Phillips, who knew how well I could swim, came to me and begged if the boat should sink I would try to save his life. I encouraged him all I could, but thought it very doubtful whether we should ever reach the shore. We had left the wreck but a few minutes when we found the boat was too deep to row. We therefore hove over all our water. For four hours we could not tell whether we gained or not on the shore, and we made every

---

* Off the coast of Yucatan, in lat. 18° 37′ N., long. 87° 20′ W.

possible exertion, well knowing if we went astern we must perish. About eleven o'clock we perceived we neared the shore; this encouraged us, and a little after dark we reached it, almost dead with hunger and fatigue. Notwithstanding our fatigue, we were so much rejoiced that we ran about the island like wild Indians. That night we spent without anything whatever to cover us, the next day we built two huts. The fourth day, being moderate, I went on board the wreck with four hands. We got some flour and other necessaries. We continued going on board for some days, when, having fitted our boat with washboards, and done everything we could to fit her well, we determined to put to sea, and endeavor to get back to the place from whence we had sailed. As the boat would not carry us all to sea with safety, we agreed to draw lots. This was a business we did not feel much anxiety about, for it was expected if the boat got safe those on the island would be saved. If the boat's crew perished, there was little chance of those on shore being ever released. It fell to the lot of Captain McFunn, Mr. Campbell, myself, and three seamen to go in the boat; my brother, an old shipmate of mine of the name of Armstrong, that had been with me when I sailed with Grant, Phillips the boy I have mentioned, and one George Peters, to stay on the island. After taking an affectionate leave of our shipmates, on the 15th of January, 1766, with a moderate breeze, we left the island. It was with great regret I left my brother. At parting, I told him if we did not return in two weeks he might conclude we were lost. The breeze died away when we were about a league from the land, and continued calm all day. Owing to calms and head winds we did not reach St. George's Key until the 20th, in the evening. During this passage we suffered very much. We were all very religious, everything material was done in the name of the Lord until we made the land. The fellow who first discovered it had just stood up to stretch himself, being cramped sitting in the boat; when he saw the land, he halloed out with great surprise and joy, "Damn my eyes, there is the land." We were all overjoyed at the sight. As we drew

near the reef we could see that it broke very high, and we
had nearly perished in crossing it. We kept within the
reef until we landed at the westward of St. George's Key,
and Captain McFunn, who did not know how Nesmith
would receive him, sent me to inform him of what had
happened. When I went to his house, or, rather, hut, he
was mending an old sail. He cast his eyes up as I entered,
expecting to see some person of the island, but when he
found it was me, he stared for some time without being able
to speak one word. At last he exclaimed, "Good heavens!
Charles, where did you come from? I thought you were near
Antigua." I told him in a few words what had happened,
and informed him where Capt. McFunn was. He arose immediately, and asked me to take some refreshment. I told
him I did not want any, and pressed him to go with me directly to the boat, which he did. As we went, I requested
that whatever he felt at the loss he would sustain by the
Snow, to say nothing to Captain McFunn about it, for I was
sure this worthy man was very unhappy both on his own
and his account, and that he must be very certain the loss
was not occasioned by want of skill, or by negligence in Captain McFunn, for there was no man more prudent, none
better qualified to command a ship. Captain Nesmith had
always expressed the most affectionate regard for me. He
told me that he had been uneasy on account of the tremendous gale of wind they had soon after we sailed, but he had
long before he saw me concluded we had escaped it. He
promised he would receive Captain McFunn as an old friend.
Although his reception was not altogether such as I wished,
he behaved with tolerable kindness. I was very glad that
Captain McFunn sent me, for had he gone himself he would
not have been so well received. Being extremely anxious
about my brother, in two days after our arrival I sailed with
Campbell, our chief mate, in a shallop for the Northern Tri-
angle. The northerly winds that generally prevail at this
season made it a dangerous and disagreeable expedition. We
were several times driven back, and I believe if it had not
been for myself, those we left on the island would never have

been taken off. The last time we went out Captain Nesmith was with us in his own shallop. Expecting to save something from the wreck we anchored under Turneff,* and here some Englishmen, who were after turtle, told us that they had heard that a party of Spaniards, who were then at Turneff, had been to the Triangles and murdered all the people we left there. Although I doubted the truth of this report, it made me very unhappy, and I requested Nesmith to let me go with some of the crew and bring the Spaniards on board, that we might carry them with us, and if we found them guilty punish them. After a good deal of persuasion he consented, at the same time telling me he was afraid I would repent it. The Spaniards were about four miles from us. I took three men with me, one of whom spoke Spanish. When I told them of the report they all declared that it was not true, that the turtlers had only mentioned this story because they were afraid of being prevented from getting turtle. They very readily agreed to go on board with me, and I took six out of ten that were on the island. As two of us were well armed we could, and would have obliged them had they been inclined to dispute the matter. The wind and weather being favorable, in three days after this to my great joy we made the island, and soon discovered a fire on it. We anchored near the wreck, and I set off immediately after with the six Spaniards for the shore, taking with us some refreshments. As we approached the land I concealed myself. The poor fellows on shore seeing none but Spaniards in the boat were afraid of being cruelly treated, and therefore prepared, as well as they could, to defend themselves. When we came within a quarter of a mile of the landing, I stood up and called to my brother and Armstrong. Nothing could exceed their joy, they ran up to their waists in the water to get into the boat to embrace me; it was near two weeks we had been absent. I was shocked to see how miserably they looked. The water on the island was so bad that nothing but necessity could induce them to drink it. The island we were

* Lat. 17° 36′ N., Long. 87° 46′ W.

upon is the largest of the Triangles, and is about two miles in circumference. The reef runs near three leagues to the southeast. The Spaniards call it the Devil's Nut. We found some cocoanut trees, and a little animal called a guana. They are shaped like a lizard, about the size of a squirrel, and very good eating; at least we thought so. They are easily caught, for when chased, and got to their holes, they only hide their heads. We lay here about ten days, saving what we could from the wreck. During this time myself, the Spaniards, and one of our crew, had nearly been lost in a gale of wind. Captain Nesmith was ashore with the rest of the crew. He should have come on board before the gale came on, but I believe he thought it safer on shore. When I spoke to him about his staying on shore, he told me he knew I would do everything that was necessary. We parted our cable, and before we could make sail were within ten yards of the reef. It was three days before we again anchored near the wreck. Being all now heartily tired we took our departure from these islands the 22d of March, 1766. Having a fair wind in two days we arrived at St. George's Key. The Spaniards, who had behaved remarkably well, got from the wreck a good deal of old iron, with which they were perfectly satisfied.

Some time after our return from the wreck Captain McFunn chartered a sloop belonging to Jamaica to take a cargo for Charleston, South Carolina. I was then acting as second mate on board a ship belonging to Boston, but at the request of Captain McFunn I left the ship and went on board the sloop as his mate. I did not wish to leave the ship, but could not refuse to comply with any request this worthy man could make, especially as he had been unfortunate. He wished my brother Nicholas to come on board, which he did immediately. This vessel was built at Jamaica upon the plan of the Bermuda sloops, and sat well upon the water, but was one of the worst barks that ever went to sea. We left St. George's Key the third day of July, and had been out but a few days before we were obliged (to prevent her foundering) to throw overboard a considerable part of our cargo. It was the middle of August before we arrived on the coast of Carolina, where we suffered very much for want of provisions and water, and we were obliged to keep one pump constantly going, and in bad weather both. We arrived at Charleston the 20th of August. After we had discharged the cargo Captain McFunn left the sloop and gave me the command of her, which I was then very proud of, although it would have been much better to have gone as a common seaman on board a good ship. She was advertised for passengers to Kingston and the Bay of Honduras. The only passenger we had was an unfortunate black that ran away from his master from Kingston. We sailed from Charleston the fifteenth of September. The twenty-fifth we had a hurricane, and it was wonderful how we escaped. We at length arrived at Port Royal, and soon after we anchored I went up in the boat to Kingston, and delivered my letters to Mr. Jerman, to whom Captain McFunn had written to assist me in anything I should want. We called on the man who owned the black, and he paid for his passage, and I promised to send him up from Port Royal. However, it was a promise not in my power to comply with, for when I returned to the sloop I found the mate had been on shore, and the black had made John Phillips, the boy I have formerly mentioned, believe that he had liberty from me to go on shore, and he went off with some blacks. The next morning I called and informed the owner what had happened, expecting as the black was old and infirm he would be glad to get back the money he had paid for his passage, which I offered him. This he refused, and declared if I did not find him he would make me answerable for his value. I found out afterwards that the black had been guilty of some crime. The fellow who owned him expected he would be executed, and he should be paid for him by government. When this was told me I was very glad the poor devil had got off. Upon consulting with Jerman, he was of opinion as all my business in Jamaica was finished, and my vessel cleared out, I had best get away from Port Royal as soon as possible. Leaving the passage money with him, I set off in the evening in a wherry, determined to sail for the Bay the next morning. When I got on board, to my inexpressible mortification, I

found the mate and all the people, except Phillips and a small
boy about fourteen years of age, had left the sloop. The
mate gave Phillips a letter for me in which he expressed sorrow for leaving me, but declared he did not think it safe to
proceed to sea in such a vessel. Except a negro lad there
were only two boys belonging to the sloop. In the night
Jerman sent me word that the owner of the black who had
run away intended to send the water bailiff after me. Upon
this I was resolved to leave Port Royal early in the morning.
As soon as it was daylight I went ashore to get hands to go
the voyage, for with those on board we could not weigh the
anchor. I could find none that would go the voyage. I therefore hired a few blacks to get up our anchor and make sail.
Before we could do this I saw a boat, in which I supposed was
the water bailiff, coming down from Kingston. Being determined not to be taken, if I could possibly prevent it, I armed
the two boys and negro with handspikes and the fish-gig,
keeping a good pair of pistols myself. They stood after us
for some time, but having a good land breeze they gave
over the chase and stood for Kingston. As it would have
given me pain to have wounded any of the men in the boat,
I was much pleased when they gave over the chase. The
wind was fair for four days when we made the island of
Bonaco, and I flattered myself that in a few days we should
get to the Bay, and be rid of our miserable bark, but before
night the wind shifted to the westward, and blew with such
violence that we were obliged to heave to. The wind for
near three weeks continued blowing from the westward,
during which time we were almost dead with hunger and
fatigue. Everything was in bad order, we frequently had
four, sometimes five, feet of water in the hold before we could
get the pumps to work, and several times owing to the badness of the pumps we expected to founder. That day three
weeks we were driven from Bonaco, we again made it. We
had a fresh gale at northeast, with thick hazy weather, so
that we were very near the island before we discovered it.
Although I had never been in the harbor, and it blew too
hard for a boat to come off, I was determined to attempt

getting in, and went to the masthead where I could see all
the shoals, and soon carried her into the harbor. We found
here a brig belonging to New York, one Johnson, Master, and
three or four small vessels who had come here from the Mosquito shore to shelter themselves from the north winds which
had been blowing for some time on that coast. Soon after
we anchored the boat was hoisted out, and we went on shore.
There was no inhabitant on the island at this time but one
old Frenchman, who lived by fishing and hunting. The
morning of our arrival he had shot a wild hog, a part of
which I purchased of him, and it was the most delicious food
I ever tasted. The island lies but a few leagues from the
Mosquito shore, has an excellent harbor, and there is great
plenty of fish and turtle to be caught here; and the woods
abound with wild hogs. As the island is pleasantly situated,
and, I believe, healthy, it is surprising there are not many
settlers on it. We lay here three days, when the wind being
favorable, we stood to the westward. We had light winds,
and it was not until the next day that we were able to take
our departure from the west end of Ruatan. The next night
we anchored at Key Bokell. The same night a ship from
New York, commanded by Wright, whom I formerly mentioned as abusing Mr. Campbell, the chief mate of Nesmith,
arrived; on board this ship was Mr. Stacy Hepburn, an old,
intimate friend of mine. He was going to the Bay to purchase a cargo for a ship belonging to Philadelphia, which
was to leave Jamaica soon after him. I was greatly rejoiced
at meeting this worthy friend, who came on board as soon as
he understood I commanded the sloop. He brought plenty
of stores with him, and having some difference with Wright,
he continued with me until we came to anchor at St. George's
Key. Owing to the wind being to the northward, I was
under the necessity of anchoring near the River Belize, and
I went from there in my boat to St. George's Key, to inform
the owner of the sloop of my arrival. It was a mortifying
circumstance to him, for she was insured in Jamaica much
above her value. He let me know in pretty plain terms that
he wished her lost before she reached St. George's Key, and

hinted he would make it worth my while if I would run her ashore. I told him he was a villain, and should have exposed him in the Bay but that he was poor and sick. I brought the sloop safe to St. George's Bay, and delivered her up. Upon examining her, the carpenter declared her unfit for sea, and they were surprised at her getting safe from Jamaica.

I had not been long in the Bay before Captain McFunn arrived from Jamaica. After he came to anchor, he went ashore in Captain McCarty's boat, who was here in a sloop belonging to Philadelphia. When rowing for the shore he inquired of McCarty what sloop it was lying aground near the shore. McCarty asked if he did not remember his old sloop—that it was the Kingston, that Charles came in. He told me afterwards he never in his life was more rejoiced, for there were several vessels in Jamaica that had left the Bay three or four weeks after we sailed from Port Royal, and he had little doubt but I was lost, and on his arrival was afraid to inquire for me. I found, in the Bay, Mr. John Scull, a cousin of mine. He was a young man that left Philadelphia with a small adventure, and came to the Bay in hopes of making his fortune. He had been persuaded to go up a river called by the English New River,* by the Spaniards, Rio Mort. The bank of this river, near the mouth of it, was so sickly, that the Spaniards said a child was never raised there to the age of nine years. My cousin being very anxious I

---

* New River is one of the numerous rivers of Belize or British Hondu-ras, and empties into the Bay of Honduras at about $18\frac{1}{2}°$ N. St. George's is a small fortified island off the harbor of Belize, at the mouth of Belize River, in 17° 29′ N., 88° 12′ W. The settlements along the north shore of Honduras proper, the Bay Islands, and the Belize Coast (commonly called British Honduras), were at this time greatly resorted to for their valuable woods, and were, in nautical phrase, all comprehended in the term "The Bay." The English, as early as 1674, had formed settlements about the Belize (see Dampier's Voyages), from which they have never since wholly receded, though often attacked by the Spaniards.

The Bay Islands (Roatan, Bonaco, etc.) were seized by the English in 1742, and were occupied by them during the period embraced in this narra-tive. The whole region was in a lawless condition, perhaps not unlike some frontier parts of our own Western country.

should accompany him up the river, and having suffered so much at sea lately, I agreed to go with him. We went up the river in a craft belonging to my old commander, Nesmith, who had a settlement a great many miles up this river, where he lived retired, with a woman he brought from Philadelphia. After staying a few days at his settlement, we left him, in order to go up a creek called Irish Creek, where, we were informed, the land was good, and that there was plenty of mahogany and logwood near the banks. We had all our fortune in this canoe. It consisted of an old negro man we called Friday, who was a much greater trouble than profit to us, a barrel of flour, a cask of pork, an old musket, a pair of pistols, and a few other trifling articles, the whole not worth twenty guineas. We proceeded, I believe, thirty miles up the creek before we met with a place that suited us. At last reaching a high bank we determined to fix ourselves. Scull, being bred in the country, and a good axeman, soon cut down as much timber as built us a house, which in this country is soon built, four small, forked trees, with a few poles laid on the top and covered with plantain leaves, being all that is necessary. This will keep out the rain, and we were in no danger of house-breakers. We had no household furniture but what we made ourselves, except a tin mug and an iron pot, and this last had but one leg, and there was a small hole in the bottom. However, with this we were contented, which is a happiness seldom, I believe, found in a palace. Our situation reminded me of a saying of one of the ancient philosophers, when going through a fair: "What a number of things are here that I do not want." We continued to work hard for two months, when we paid a visit to our friend Nesmith. During these two months we had not seen a human creature but ourselves, and to human creatures we had not much resemblance, being almost naked, and in all that time had never shaved. Nesmith was very comfortably situated, having almost every convenience of life, and five or six negroes that cut him a great deal of wood. While on this visit, I had nearly been lost. Having taken a gun, in the morning about nine o'clock, I went into the woods after game. It was a clear day, and I knew the river could be easily found by taking notice of the sun. I went in pursuit of game a considerable distance in the woods; towards noon it became cloudy, when I thought it necessary to return. About one o'clock it began to rain. Continuing on for the river, as I thought, as it grew dark I did not know which way to go. It now rained hard, and as it was in vain for me to fatigue myself by endeavoring to get out of the woods, I sat down on a log and began to think I should perish in the woods, as several had before, who, like me, had gone a gunning. After being in this melancholy situation about an hour, I heard a bell. Roused by this agreeable sound I fired my gun, which, as well as my ammunition, I took care to keep dry. Soon after I heard the bell much plainer. It sounded pleasanter than any music I had ever heard. Having good lungs I sang out with a loud voice, which some of the party hearing they answered. Soon after my friends Nesmith and Scull appeared. They had been uneasy at my long stay, and had, with some negroes, come into the woods to look for me. It happened we were not far from the house. This adventure made me cautious of going into the woods.

After staying a few days with Captain Nesmith we returned to our habitation, where we were received with great joy by old Friday, who expected we never intended to return. Want of society soon made us tired of our plantation, and we determined to proceed down the river. We put our little property in a craft and sailed for St. George's Key. We left our old negro with Captain Nesmith, who promised and I knew would take care of him. Had he been young we would have given him his freedom, for I was always averse to keeping of slaves. In the Bay the blacks are treated much better than in the islands, their masters being afraid of their running away to the Spaniards. They allow them Friday and Saturday, and many of them that are industrious make a good deal of money, and all are well fed and comfortably clothed.

When we arrived at St. George's Key we disposed of our wood, and, having divided our stock, I was about entering on board a ship belonging to Liverpool. The captain of the

ship, having buried his mate a few days before we arrived at
the Key, offered and pressed me to accept of the berth, but
my friend Hepburn, being at this time about leaving the Bay,
was anxious I should go to Philadelphia with him. At this
time my returning home was so much a matter of indifference
to me that I tossed up, whether I would go in the ship to
Liverpool or return with Hepburn, when, it happening to turn
up for my returning to Philadelphia, I went immediately on
board with Hepburn. The ship we were going in was called
the King George, one Henry Dunn, master, belonging to
Philadelphia. He was an old man, a good seaman, but much
addicted to liquor. The ship was a very old one, in which my
friend Campbell had served his apprenticeship with Captain
Charles Stuart. He often mentioned that during the rebellion of 1745, they were hailed going up to Leith, " What
ship is that?" "The King George." "Who commands her?"
"Charles Stuart." "Oh!" says the man that hailed, "I wish
to God it was true, that Charles Stuart commanded King
George." We left the Bay the beginning of February, 1767.
Besides Mr. Hepburn, there was a Mr. Crisp, passenger. We
had a good deal of blustering weather, but nothing remarkable happened until we reached the north side of Cuba and
had beat up near the Havannah. Here we had a gale of wind
from the N. W. and stood with a press of sail to the eastward. The next day, the wind hauling round to the eastward, we stood to the southward, to make the land. When
we drew near it, I perceived we were above the Matanzas,
which is the usual place for vessels to take their departure
from that are bound through the Gulf of Florida. I told
Captain Dunn we had better run to the westward till we
made the Matanzas, but he would not, and declared he would
stand to the northward. I knew in the night we must get
upon some of the keys, or the Bahama Bank. Accordingly,
about ten o'clock at night, all hands were called, the bottom
being plain to be seen under the ship. She was immediately
put about. While in stays, I hove the lead, and found we
were in five fathoms. At first, Captain Dunn appeared much
alarmed, but having taken a drop of comfort, he was deter-

mined to put about again and stand to the N. W. This he
did, and I believe we ran for thirty-five hours over the bank.
The weather was fine, and as we had two good boats, and
there was no danger of our lives, I was perfectly indifferent
about the loss of the ship. However, we got safe over into
the Gulf. We had a favorable wind from this time till the
sixteenth of March, when we had a gale of wind from the
S. E. We were then, by our reckoning, a little to the southward of Cape Hatteras, and not more than fifteen leagues
from the land. One of our pumps was continually at work,
and could hardly keep her free. Towards night the gale increased. The ship was very deep, being full of logwood and
mahogany in the hold, and several large pieces of mahogany
on deck. As I knew this must strain her very much, I told
Mr. Wright, the chief mate, that the ship would be much
eased if we were rid of those pieces, in which he agreeing,
we cut the lashings and were soon clear of them. The morning of the seventeenth it blew very violent. At 9 A. M., the
foresheet gave way. Captain Dunn was then standing in the
companion. Instead of having the sail clewed up, he ordered
the helm up, and put her before the wind. Being up most
part of the night, I was at this time fast asleep. The passengers, Hepburn and Crisp, were much terrified—they begged
me to go up on deck. I found her before the wind, and the
foresail blowing to ribbons. Dunn was standing, drunk,
upon the companion ladder. I persuaded him to go below,
and then directed the ship to be hove to. When she was
brought to, I went first upon the foreyard, to hand what remained of the foresail. The crew were so fatigued with
pumping, and being all night wet, that it was with great
difficulty I could get as many up as were sufficient to hand
the sail. Hepburn and Crisp, who were looking up, told me
they never expected to see me come down alive. As I was
upon the lee yard-arm, they thought the sea or sail would
carry me overboard. They both caught me in their arms
when I did come down, calling me their preserver. I, however, had exerted myself *at least* as much on my own account
as theirs. It blew with great violence till about 4 P. M.,

when in a heavy squall it shifted to the S. W. The hardest
gales we have on the coast of America are from the S. E., but
they seldom last long. The wind continuing from the S. W.,
in a few days we arrived safe at Philadelphia. On the passage, Hepburn and myself broke out with what the people
of Honduras call the Bay scrub, which is a very bad kind of
itch. We both broke out at the same time. He accused me,
and I him, of having first had it. We rubbed ourselves for
three nights with tallow and brimstone, drinking, at the same
time, warm tea. This effectually cured us of this trouble,
which may truly be called a vile disorder. To my great joy,
upon going home, I found my mother and family well. Captain Dunn wanted me to go as his mate to Ireland, but I had
enough of him during our passage from the Bay. The ship
was never heard of after he sailed for Ireland.

I had been at home but a short time when Captain Budden
called on me, and offered to sell his fourth part of a schooner
he commanded, and Messrs. Chew, Clayton, and Chew, who
owned the other three-fourths wishing me to command her,
with the assistance of my brother James I made the purchase, and sailed in June for Grenada, having Mr. John
Chew, the youngest partner of the house, our supercargo.*
As he is a very agreeable man, we had a pleasant passage
without anything remarkable. Not being able to procure a
return cargo at Grenada, we sailed for St. Croix. At this
place I was attacked with a violent fever, which with my
own imprudence had nearly destroyed me. From thence we
proceeded on our passage home. We had a gale of wind
from the eastward which obliged us to put into Chincoteague,
a harbor that all the Delaware pilots should be acquainted
with. It was owing to our having a good pilot that we got

---

* The nature of the restriction upon colonial trade imposed by Acts of
Parliament, is shown in the bond required in the case of this vessel, still extant, dated June 18, 1767. The captain, Charles Biddle, of the " Betsy,"
and John Clayton, bind themselves that the iron shall not be landed in any
part of Europe except in Great Britain or Ireland, and that the lumber shall
not be landed in any part of Europe to the northward of Cape Finisterre,
except in Great Britain or Ireland.

in, by which means the vessel and cargo, and probably our
lives, were saved.   At this place I had a foolish dispute with
Mr. Harrison (a young officer that was a passenger with me
from Grenada), that had nearly proved fatal to us both.   I
esteemed him much, and he professed a very great regard for
me; indeed, he afterwards proved himself a sincere friend.
Our quarrel was occasioned by a bet upon two fowls we had
bought ashore.   After they had fought until they were
almost dead, I had them separated.   This, he declared, was
owing to my being afraid of losing the bet.   Upon my using
some language he did not like, he told me I would not treat
him in that manner ashore.   I immediately ordered the boat
manned, and we went ashore armed with pistols.   We fired
at the distance of ten paces and missed, and had agreed to fire
the next shot at five yards, but before we were loaded an old
gentleman, at whose house we had been, came down and prevented us firing a second time, and soon persuaded us to be
reconciled.   This difference with Mr. Harrison was of service
to me afterwards, and it was a caution not to lose my temper
in a dispute with a friend.   The wind being soon after favorable, we sailed for Philadelphia, where we safely arrived the
first of October.   As the owners intended to send the schooner
to Lisbon, it was necessary to put another deck upon her.   It
was December before she was fitted.   We then took in a cargo
of flour and staves, and sailed for Lisbon.   It was the tenth
of December we left the Capes, and I believe she was the
smallest vessel that ever crossed the Atlantic at this season
of the year, for she carried but five hundred barrels.   We
had continued gales of wind, and were thirty days before we
made the Rock of Lisbon, which was on the eighth of January,
1768.   During most of that passage the sea made a continual
breach over us, and there were but three or four days during
the passage that we could cook.   We took a pilot on board
and proceeded up the Tagus as far as the castle of Belum,
where we came to anchor.   The next morning at daylight it
blew a hard gale of wind, and about sunrise we found the
schooner was driving very fast upon a dangerous shoal called
the B——, before we could make sail she struck, and the sea

broke on board with great violence. The pilot, like a pious Christian, went below to say his prayers. As she continued striking very hard, I ordered the mainmast cut away. Thomas Armstrong, who had been shipwrecked with me in the Snow, took the axe to cut the lanyards. Just as he gave the first stroke, a sea broke over us, and he lost the axe. He came aft to me and told me what had happened, saying at the same time, "I believe, Captain Biddle, it is all over with us." Armstrong was an excellent and brave seaman. A young lad who had persuaded his parents to let him make the voyage, hearing it, cried out, "Oh! my mother, what will you suffer!"

I told Armstrong not to despair, that as the flood was coming in, we would endeavor to force her over the shoal. I knew we had no other chance of being saved. For this purpose I had the cable cut, and the jib and foresail set. Although she struck in such a manner that we expected every moment she would go to pieces, I went to the masthead to try to con* her over the shoal, and placed Armstrong at the helm. We at last beat over the shoal. As it blew very hard I kept away for St. Ubes, and set both pumps to work, not permitting the well to be sounded for fear of discouraging the crew. We kept as near the shore as possible, that if she foundered we should stand some chance of being saved. In the evening we came abreast of the castle at the entrance of the harbor, and as I would not anchor for fear of being driven out or foundering (for we had not yet freed her), they first hailed and then fired. The first shot went between our masts. I hoisted a signal of distress, and continued on. Our pilot again wanted to go below, but as I thought his presence necessary on deck, I would not suffer him to leave it. We ran in, and the castle kept firing until we were among the shipping close in shore where we anchored. About nine o'clock we had all the water out of her. The next morning we went ashore where the Portuguese directed us, and after the health officer had examined our papers, were permitted to go to the town. I went to the house of one

* To "con" is to direct the helmsman in the steering of a vessel.

Nicholson, an Irishman, that kept a tavern. He was also a pilot and had lived many years at St. Ubes. He was a kind, generous fellow, and his wife well calculated for her business. The day after our arrival the Portuguese pilot wanted me to pay him much more than I thought, from his conduct, he deserved, and upon refusing, had me up before the consul. There he made me very angry by calling me an impudent boy. I was so imprudent as to strike him. He went away threatening to take my life before he left St. Ubes. This he had nearly accomplished a few days after by attempting to stab me with a knife, when a person present caught his arm. He ran off, and I never saw the ruffian afterwards. Having received a letter from Mr. Daniel Arthur, to whom I was consigned, requesting to see me, I set off with a Portuguese gentleman for Lisbon. We rode on mules, and the man they were hired of went with us. He was afoot, and frequently ran from one side of the road to the other, to beat our miserable animals. The roads are sandy, and the country appeared very poor. I was received very politely by Mr. Arthur, who was one of the principal merchants in the place, and very much respected. He lived very elegantly. Shortly after this he broke, and my owners lost a considerable sum by him, they having sent a large ship consigned to him, which arrived but a few days before his failure.

There is not much improvement since the earthquake. The orange and lemon trees, with the vineyards, make the country about Lisbon pleasant.

The Castle of St. Julian is at the mouth of the harbor. It is founded on a rock, the base of which is washed by the sea, and is a very strong fortification. There is a fort on a small island opposite that defends the entrance of the river.

The fandango which the people, high and low, dance is very indecent—they throw themselves into all attitudes. In the streets you never see the face of a woman—she has a hood turned over and you can only see her eyes.

The streets in Lisbon are narrow and dirty, and the poor live miserably. The merchants live well, and are men of as much honor as those of any country whatever. Their soldiers do not make a very military appearance. Most of their officers are foreigners. I staid in Lisbon a week, and then returned to St. Ubes. In proportion to the size of the place there was much more damage done at St. Ubes than at Lisbon by the earthquake. Immense pieces of the walls were carried from the seaside to the commons back of the town.

While I was at St. Ubes Henry White, one of the seamen that had frequently occasioned disturbances, came on board one night in liquor. A small apprentice boy of mine, Wm. Williams, speaking to him about making a noise, he took up a handspike and threw it at him with such violence that if it had hit him, as he intended, must have killed him. Hearing the boy cry I ran upon deck, and, being informed what White had done, I was determined to punish him severely. When I went forward to take hold of him he jumped into the boat; however, before he could cast off the painter, I had hold of him, and forcing him on board gave him such a beating with the end of a rope as I supposed would be a caution to him not to behave in such a manner again. For several days he pretended to be too unwell to work; soon after he ran away, swearing to one of the crew that he would be revenged of me whenever he had an opportunity.

We sailed from St. Ubes the 11th of February, 1763, loaded with wine, oil, and fruit. The 20th, off Madeira, we had a squall of wind that sprung our mainmast so badly that during the remainder of the passage we could not let the boom out of the crutch. Schooners, from the manner of their being rigged, are more apt to meet with accidents than other vessels. This unfortunate accident, with calms and light winds, made it the second of May before we arrived at Philadelphia. Our long passage occasioned a good deal of the fruit to be spoiled. Some of the boxes of lemons were put into the hands of Mr. Patrick Farrel, an honest Irish cooper (well known in the city from his being concerned in digging for money). He was to separate the good from the rotten lemons. He came on board a few days after the boxes were put in his hands to tell me if I would send him up a case bottle he would fill it with very good lime-juice he squeezed out of the rotten lemons.

The beginning of June we took in a cargo for Fayal, and greatly to my satisfaction my friend Hepburn was put on board as supercargo. We had a pleasant passage to Fayal, and I found Mr. Gaythorn still consul. This worthy man received me with great kindness, and his partner, Mr. Graham, was very friendly. While we lay here, Mr. Gaythorn gave an entertainment at a house he had a small distance from the town. The house not being finished, we had to go up a ladder to get in the dining-room. When he was called away, which I believe was done by his own orders, he placed me in his chair to do the honors of his table. I drank so freely, that I could not tell how or when I got down the ladder. In going to town in the dark, I fell down in a field, and was unable to rise. My friends searched in vain for me. I remained on the ground very quietly until daylight, when I went on board and felt no injury from my hard bed. Never before or since was I in such a plight. No person ever had, or has, a greater detestation than myself against a person addicted to liquor. It renders a man unfit to be trusted with anything. While we lay here this voyage we were much diverted by the masters of two whaling sloops, one belonging to Cape Cod, the other to Cape Ann. The Cape Cod man insisted on it, that the men belonging to Cape Cod were far superior in skill and courage to those of Cape Ann, while the men of Cape Ann held those of Cape Cod in the most sovereign contempt. Gaythorn was highly entertained with these disputes, but he was obliged sometimes to interfere to prevent their coming to blows. A few days before we sailed, a ship from London, bound to St. Augustine, put in here. She had on board Mrs. Farmer, who was going to her husband, Major Farmer. She was a beautiful and accomplished woman. I understood afterwards she kept a lodging-house in London. The day we sailed, a vessel from China, bound to London, put in here in distress. One of the crew had a very handsome set of china which he brought to Mr. Gaythorn's to sell. I wanted to purchase it, and was talking to the man about the price when Mr. Gaythorn came up and told the man he would take it. The manner in which this was done provoked me very much, and I should have affronted almost any other person who had behaved in the manner Mr. Gaythorn had done. When we were on the beach, and I was just going into the boat, he called me aside, and told me he had put the china aboard the schooner. and begged I would deliver it at Philadelphia to his sweetheart, but if I could not find his, to give it to my own. As he had never been in Philadelphia, I found he had purchased the china to make me a present of it. Hepburn and myself were young, but we looked so much younger than we were, that they called us the boy captain and boy supercargo. During the time we were there, Mr. Gilmore, since so eminent a merchant of Baltimore, arrived from America. He was then going, I believe, to Scotland, intending to return and settle in America, which he spoke very highly of.

We left Fayal the last of August. We had a good deal of calm weather, so that it was the fourteenth of October before we arrived in the Delaware. A few days after we had a most violent gale. The owners, Messrs. Chew, Clayton and Chew, having been unfortunate in business had dissolved their partnership, and soon after our arrival, sold the schooner. The purchasers wished me to hold the share I had and continue the command, but finding they intended to send her to the coast of Africa for slaves, I left her, for nothing would have tempted me to go such a voyage. I expressed my abhorrence of this trade in such a manner as to give great offence to the owners, who purchased my part of the schooner, and procured a master who had no objection to go any voyage they thought proper to send him.

During my stay at home this time I saw my friend Campbell, whom I have often mentioned. It gave me much satisfaction that it was in my power to render him some services. He was a very good, but a very unfortunate man. In 1755 he was pressed on board the Northumberland, commanded by Lord Colville. He told me that when he was first pressed, if he had thought he should have been kept six months on board her, he would have jumped overboard. Attempting to make his escape shortly after he was pressed,

he was taken, and so narrowly watched that he could not
get away, and he continued on board until the year 1763,
when the crew were paid off. He said it was a long time
before he could believe he was at liberty to go where he
pleased. Before I sailed he procured the command of a vessel bound to Curaçao and the Spanish Main. Off Carthagena
there was a mutiny among the crew, and poor Campbell
going forward with a handspike to quiet it, was stabbed by
one of the villians, and died immediately. He was too easy
in his temper to command a crew of such ruffians as they
generally have on board these vessels.

In November, Messrs. James and Drinker offered me the
command of a brig called the Ann, belonging to Mr. O.
Eves, who had been an inhabitant of Philadelphia, but at
this time resided in the Bay of Honduras, where the brig
was bound. I accepted the command, and arrived in December in the Bay. Mr. Eves informed me he had a cargo ready,
and we should sail in a few days; however, owing to northerly
winds, it was two months before we got away. I was glad
of this detention, for I did not wish to go on the coast in the
winter.

The brig this voyage was moored at a small key to the
northward of St. George's, called Sand Key. Here Mr. Eves
at that time lived.

During the time we were loading I frequently took a fast-
sailing boat we had, and went to St. George's Key by myself.
Returning one day I went outside the reef, intending to try to
fish. When about half-way to the brig, perceiving a squall coming on, I took in the mainsail, intending to receive the squall
under the foresail. As it approached it appeared as if there
was a good deal of wind, and as I was too near the reef to put
before the wind, I went forward to hand the foresail, intending to heave to until it was over. Before I had the foresail
in the squall took me and blew with great violence. I ran
aft to get her before the wind, but before I could do so she
shipped a great deal of water, and, being ballasted with pig
iron, went down. Fortunately there were two large oars
which I lashed together with a handkerchief taken from my

neck. When the squall cleared away I pushed for the nearest land. It was about ten o'clock when the boat sank. In crossing the reef I was near losing my oars: it would then have been impossible to escape drowning. The current setting against me, it was nearly three o'clock before I was near enough to hail a man walking on the shore. It was Captain Thomas Remington. It was some time before he heard me, and then looked about a good while before he perceived me. When he did, he called and told me I could touch the bottom. This I tried, and finding it only up to my breast, I quit my oars and walked ashore so much exhausted I could hardly stand. Remington received me very kindly. During my being outside the reef I suffered more from the dread of sharks than anything else. I took care after this not to go in a boat by myself.

Nothing remarkable happened until my return to the Delaware. Having anchored in the night, a little below New Castle, about eleven o'clock a boy came from on board a shallop near us, hailed the brig, and begged for God's sake we would come on board, as some men were murdering the captain. The watch upon deck informing me of the boy's hailing, I immediately ordered the boat manned, and went on board. The skipper, who was an elderly man, told me that two fellows had requested a passage from Philadelphia to Reedy Island, where they said their vessel was lying; that soon after he anchored, when he supposed they thought him asleep, they came down and were fastening a hankerchief around his neck to strangle him when the boy hailed the brig. He said the fellows were on the wharf when he brought a bag of dollars on board, and he was now sure they had come on board with an intention of murdering him. The boy, who was son to the skipper, struck up a light, and I went into the hold where the two ruffians were found covered with an old sail, and pretended to have just waked. When they were brought to the light, I found one of them to be my old shipmate Henry White, as pickled a rascal as ever was hanged. He immediately exclaimed to his comrade. "Oh! it is Captain Biddle, we may expect no mercy from

him." I took them on board the brig, and had them lashed
to the pumps, intending to deliver them up to justice when
I arrived in Philadelphia, but fearing I should be detained
and plagued if they were put to gaol, I directed the mate,
the night of our arrival, to let them run.

I sailed again for Port Antonio, in Jamaica, and the Bay in
the month of May. I had a very worthy Scotch planter a
passenger. He told me in Jamaica that when he came to
take his passage he was afraid he should not be safe with
such a boy as I appeared. He was, however, very much
pleased, and wrote to the owners in the highest terms of me.
We had a very short passage to Port Antonio, where we
staid but a few days, when we sailed for the Bay, where we
arrived without anything material happening. While lying
here there was a man tried for the murder of one McCarty.
One of the witnesses swore that the man went to the companion and called out, "Come out here, McCarty." Another swore
that when he called him he said, "McCarty, come out here."
A Captain Arbuthnot, of Philadelphia, who was one of the
jury, gravely remarked to the other jurors that there was a
very material difference in the *eye of the law* between come
out here, McCarty, and McCarty, come out here. He was
always after this called the "oculist, or the eye of the law
explained." This is a saying I have often heard since, but it
arose, I believe, from what I have mentioned.

I had this voyage four masters of ships passengers, Captains
Green, Shewell, and two of the name of Welsh. There were
at this time four Captains Welsh in the Bay. They were distinguished by Long Welsh and Short Welsh, King's Religion
Welsh, and Priest Welsh. The Priest, who was one of my
passengers, was an honest Roman Catholic. Green had a
dispute with one Samuel Jones, of New York, whom he
struck. Jones stuck up an advertisement at the tavern that
Green, presuming on his bodily strength, had struck him and
refused to give him satisfaction. He therefore published him
as a coward and a rascal. As Green was going with me, and
belonged to Philadelphia, I took down the advertisement and
gave it to him. He immediately called on Jones and agreed

to fight him.   They prepared a boat, and, as I was not present, Green spoke to a Captain Sinnot to be his second.   Sinnot was one of the magistrates, but before he set off he resigned his commission.   There was at this time a sloop-of-war, commanded by a Mr. Jackson, lying here, and the boat happening then to be at the Key with Jackson, some person informed him that Jones and Green were just put off with an intention of going to the next Key to fight, and begged he would send his boat and bring them back.   He immediately sent his boat. When she got near and Jones understood their errand he swore he would fire into the boat if they attempted to come alongside.   Finding they paid no regard to what he said he fired a pistol into the boat and wounded one of the boat's crew slightly in the thigh.   They however pulled alongside, and the bowman, if he had not been prevented, would have driven the boat-hook through Jones.   They carried him on board the man-of-war, and he was kept there until we sailed. There were a good many duels fought at this time in the Bay.   Captain Shewell was wounded in the breast by one Brockholst, of New York, and the celebrated Arnold,* who was here at this time, fought and wounded one of the Bay men.   It was said that Arnold frightened his antagonist, who had agreed that he should fix the distance, by naming five yards.   They were more turbulent at this time in the Bay than I had ever known them before.

We left the Bay the last of August and arrived in Philadelphia the latter end of September.   Being offered the command of a ship by Mr. Aspden, an old schoolmate of mine, I left the brig and took the command of the ship.   She was a large old vessel then chartered to carry a cargo to Port au Prince.   In order to make as much as possible by the freight, Mr. Aspden had a great quantity of boards and scantling put upon the ship's deck.   Some of my friends who came on the wharf when we were loading called her a three-decker.   Some of them said they were sure we should be obliged to clear our decks before we were at sea a week.   We left the Capes the tenth of December, 1769, in a gale of wind at northwest.

* Benedict Arnold.

About eleven o'clock at night the chief mate, Mr. Savage, came down and told me they could not get the pump to suck. I ordered him to call all hands and get both pumps to work. I turned out myself and took the helm. It blew so hard that we were scudding under our foresail. Savage had been a schoolmate of Aspden's and mine. He was an excellent officer. He came to me about twelve o'clock and begged I would allow him to cut the lashings of the lumber and clear the decks. I should have consented but for what had been mentioned before we left Philadelphia, of our soon clearing the decks. It was daylight before we had all the water out of her hold. During the night I frequently looked over the side, and thought she was waterlogged. The next day the gale abated, and we had a tolerably good passage.

Port au Prince was at this time in a miserable situation. A few months before my arrival most of the houses had been destroyed by an earthquake, and owing to many dead bodies lying unburied near the town, and the total neglect of cleanliness in their houses and other causes, there were few that escaped the earthquake but what died or were sick. Every house was a hospital. I was consigned to Messrs. Pasquer and Boyay. Boyay died a few days before we arrived, and Pasquer was very ill with a fever. As he was a very worthy man, I did everything in my power to relieve him, by sending from the ship poultry, apples, porter, and some other refreshments. The porter he thought of more service to him than anything he had taken. I also sent my carpenter, who was very handy, to assist in making his habitation more comfortable. He was very grateful for the services I rendered him, and, when we sailed, made me a handsome present. During the time we were here I anchored outside of all the ships in the harbor. This occasioned my being some time longer unloading, but by this means, and not suffering any of the crew to go on shore of a Sunday (at which time they generally get drunk), I preserved the health of my crew, having none of them sick during the time we were here. A few days after my being in this port a brig arrived from North Carolina, commanded by a Captain Gordon, a genteel young man. I was standing on the wharf with Captain Hamilton, of New York, when he landed. After going up into the town and returning, he appeared much disturbed. Coming up to us, he exclaimed, "My God! gentlemen, what a dismal place this is; how sickly all the inhabitants look." After he had left us, Hamilton, who was a rough old tar, swore he was so much frightened he did not believe he would live a week, and he was right, for poor Gordon took sick the next day, and in three days he was committed to the deep.

At this time we expected, by every arrival, to hear of war between Great Britain and Spain, which made me anxious to get home as soon as possible. The last of January, three of the crew who did not like to go on a winter coast ran away. The 2d of February, 1770, I left Port au Prince. The 4th, I went ashore in the boat at Cape Nicola Mole, in hopes of getting two or three hands, but I could not procure any; we, therefore, proceeded on our voyage. I had on board a young Frenchman named Dubois, concerned in the opposition made to an edict directing the planters to perform militia duty. The edict occasioned great disturbances in the island, and many of the planters declared they would oppose it at the hazard of their lives. My passenger told me he belonged to a company, the captain of which was a rich young planter, who raised about seventy men, with which he supposed he should be able to oppose all the force that could be sent against him. About twelve dragoons came from Port au Prince to attack them; when they perceived the dragoons advancing, they deserted their commander, and Dubois acknowledged that he galloped off as fast as any of them. Leaving his horse, he hid himself in a field of sugar-cane. The next day when he came out, the first object that struck him was his late captain hanging on a tree. Many of the unfortunate insurgents were in confinement during the time I was at Port au Prince, and some were sent to France. They were all afterwards pardoned by their humane and generous monarch, who also restored to them their property.

We arrived the 20th of February off Cape May, and I sent the boat on shore for a pilot. The weather was moderate,

4

and we soon procured one. With the flood it came on to blow fresh from the southeast, and before the pilot thought the tide was high enough to get under way, it blew very hard, and the sea ran high. Our windlass, which was old and rotten, broke, and the ship drove; we immediately cut the cable and made sail. After striking several times, we beat over the shoal, called the Overfalls, which is a quicksand, and the next day anchored off Philadelphia.

A few nights before I had sailed on this voyage, my friend Hepburn called to inform me a vessel had just arrived from Hispaniola, and the captain informed him that the plague was in Port au Prince, and had swept off most of those who escaped the earthquake, and he begged me to give up the command of the ship. I told him nothing would induce me to do it after engaging myself. He used all the arguments he could to make me give up the voyage, but finding they had no effect, he told me he would lay a beaver that I would die there of the plague. I agreed to the bet. Upon my return, and calling upon him for the hat, he swore I was not the same man that went out master of the ship Lark, and he would make oath of it before a magistrate. To prove him mistaken, I went before George Bryan, Esq., one of the justices, and made oath that I was the same man who went out master of the ship Lark, and was then alive. Upon producing the certificate of my having taken the oath, he laughed heartily and paid the bet.

The ship having occasion for a good deal of repair, it was the month of May before we were ready to sail. We took out a number of frames for houses, and several carpenters* to put them up. We also carried out a quantity of flour, five hundred barrels of which were for the governor, and in consequence of his having them at a low price, we had permission to land five hundred barrels more, to be sold to the inhabitants. The granting permission to bring flour from America gave great umbrage to the masters of ships and

* Cowperthwait and Jones, two of the carpenters, made a good deal of money. They afterwards settled at New Orleans, and were much respected there.—AUTHOR'S NOTE.

merchants from Bordeaux, who had before supplied the place with flour. Upon my arrival many of them came on board to inquire the quantity we had, and were much exasperated when they found we should not only supply the garrison, but also had to sell to the inhabitants. However, they were afraid to say anything to the governor, and for myself, I cared nothing about them. They told the bakers and others that the flour was much inferior in quality to theirs, which they knew was not true. The bakers pretended it was not as good, but they did not buy of the Bordeaux men while we had any to sell, and gave us the same price they demanded.

It was the beginning of September before we sailed for Philadelphia. On the passage we saw a vessel ashore on Watling's Island. I ran to the leeward of the island, came to anchor, and boarded her. She proved to be a ship from Jamaica, bound to London, the crew of which had left her, and gone to Providence in what was called one of the Moon-cursers or wreckers. We took out of her a few hogsheads of rum and sugar, and some trifling articles. There was under the cabin scuttle an iron bound cask that I labored at for a considerable time, supposing it contained something valuable. When bored, it proved to be a cask of peas. I had it put down again. Captain Shewell, who sailed a few days after me from Port au Prince, told me he was on board the same wreck and worked very hard to get up this cask of peas, supposing, as I had, that it contained something valuable. The appearance of bad weather made me leave the island much sooner than I otherwise should have done. For four or five days we had fresh breezes with cloudy weather: there was then a perfect calm for two days. The third morning about three o'clock we had a moderate breeze from the eastward. About five o'clock the second mate waked me, and told me the sky had a strange appearance, and he believed there was going to be a squall. I went up immediately, and never beheld such an alteration as one hour had made. From being perfectly clear, heavy black clouds appeared all round the horizon, and a wild sky that denoted an approaching gale of wind. We then had every sail set.

I ordered the top-gallant sails in, and the top-gallant masts and yards sent upon deck, the fore and maintop sails close reefed and handed, the sails well secured with double gaskets, the mizzen yard and topmast sent on deck. By eight o'clock we were under a reefed foresail, and before nine were obliged to hand it. Soon after it blew so hard that no canvas could have stood it. For more than thirty hours it blew the most violent hurrricane I ever knew. In an old ship, partly loaded with molasses, the hold not full, we were in great danger of foundering. During the height of the gale I could not make any of the crew hear me without a speaking trumpet. Fortunately we lost nothing. The next day about eleven o'clock the gale abated so much that we set the foresail and topsails. In the afternoon we saw several sail dismasted, and passed near one that was overset, all the crew of which must have perished. Just before dark we saw a brig with a signal of distress out, and about eight o'clock we were close alongside. She had lost her fore topmast, and sprung a leak. As the sea ran very high, and there was some risk in boarding, I went myself in the boat. She belonged, I think, to Pool in England, and was last from Newfoundland bound to Wilmington, North Carolina. The master's name was Rowe. He told me that before they had the height of the gale all their sails blew from their yards, although he had them secured in such a manner that he thought it impossible this could have happened. The mate, who was a very old man, declared he had never been in such a gale. The crew, who were mostly lads, wanted to leave the brig, and as there was every appearance of bad weather, and the brig was a mere wreck, I endeavored to persuade the captain to leave her, which he would not do, declaring to me in a low voice he had made up his mind, which was never to quit her. He begged me to speak to his crew, and tell them there was no danger of another gale. This I would not do. He, however, persuaded them himself to stay with him. Had the crew requested it, I would have taken them and obliged the captain to leave her. I supplied him with provisions, and every article he wanted that we could spare. He gave me a bill upon a gentleman at Wilmington, which was paid, but the brig never arrived. Indeed from the bad weather we had soon after we parted I did not expect she ever would reach any port. A master should never leave his vessel if he thinks it probable he may save her; but in the condition this vessel was in, no man should risk his life and those of his crew by staying on board when they have a good opportunity of leaving her. The wind continuing favorable, the twenty-seventh of September we made the Capes, and the next day arrived in Philadelphia.

My owner, Mr. Aspden, having made a good deal of money in the trade to Hispaniola, in June, 1772, agreed with Mr. John Eyre to build a ship for him. I superintended the building and fitting her. She was launched in October. As Mr. Aspden left the naming of her to me I called her the Charming Nancy, after a young lady of the city, whom I, then thought a charming girl, and now that I am writing in 1802, although she has lost a little of her bloom, she is a charming woman. I left the Capes in this ship on Thursday the third of December, 1772, bound to Port au Prince. The day after we left the Capes we sprung a leak—in a few hours it increased upon us. One of the pumps we could not get to deliver any water, and the other would not keep her free. After hoisting the pump out, which we did with difficulty, it blowing a hard gale, we found it split. We repaired it, got it to work, and in the night freed her. Our American ships are generally very badly provided with carpenters' tools as well as with sails and rigging. Many a ship has been obliged to leave the coast for want of a few necessaries that they always should have on board. An owner much oftener loses than gains by endeavoring to save a trifle in this way. No nation sails their ships with so few hands as we do, which makes it the more necessary they should be well provided with everything that may be wanted. In this ship, which was nearly three hundred tons burthen, I had but two mates, six men, and a boy; and few of our ships were better manned. The ship sailed very fast. The Thursday after we left the Capes we made Turk's Island, a passage seldom made in a deep-loaded ship in so short a time. The 16th of December we anchored at Petit Guave, where Mr. Pasquer had requested the ship should touch to land part of her cargo, which we did the next day, and sailed in the evening for Port au Prince. This part of the island is very sickly. I took an officer of the army from this place to Port au Prince. I think he told me there were only three officers alive that came out from France with the regiment he belonged to, and it was but a few years the regiment had been in the island. This was the more extraordinary as the French officers are generally very temperate. As they have no whipping in their army they hang and shoot a great many of their privates. It is generally for desertion—if a soldier deserted and carried off his arms, and was taken, they hung him, as they considered him a thief as well as a deserter. If he went off without his arms he had the *honor of being shot*. I believe at this time they sent to the island those who had deserted in France. I have heard this mentioned as the reason of so many here attempting to go off. It was hardly possible for any of them to escape. The roll is called morning and evening, and when any are missing they fire a gun for each one that is gone off. This firing is repeated in the country, and numbers are immediately after them, so that very few get to the Spaniards, where, I believe, they are not much better treated than in their own regiments. If they are brought back to the garrison in the morning they are hung or shot in the afternoon; if in the evening they are executed the next morning. If they are to die the executing them so soon is an act of mercy. I was told that at one time there were nearly fifty deserted in a body. They were soon taken, and all of them ordered for execution; when the regiment was drawn out the soldiers all declared with one voice the prisoners should not be executed, and the officers thought it prudent to pardon all of them except a few of the ringleaders. While I was at Port au Prince, and a soldier was to be executed, the Major, when the unfortunate man was brought out, rode in front of the regiment, and with a loud voice pronounced it death to any man who requested the life of the criminal; and I was informed

that this was done on account of what happened on the above
occasion. I was told of another affair that made a good deal
of noise in Port au Prince. A deserter was cut down, and as
his comrades were taking him to his grave, he was found to have
some life in him. They immediately took him to the bar-
racks, bled him, and he was so far recovered in a few hours
that he was sitting up eating some soup, when the officer of
the guard, hearing of what had happened, had him carried
to the place of execution and shot. So seldom did a soldier
get off that it was a common saying in Port au Prince when
the gun fired for a deserter, "we shall have an execution to-
morrow."

Soon after my arrival I had a difference with my old friend
Pasquer, that gave me much concern. I sold fifty barrels of
flour that belonged to myself to a Mr. Peyrobe, who had
formerly lived with Mr. Pasquer as a clerk, but, having some
difference, they parted. Peyrobe was a manly, generous fellow, for whom I had a great regard. After leaving Mr.
Pasquer, he married and set up the baking business. When
Mr. Pasquer understood Peyrobe had bought my flour, he
declared he never would pay me, that he intended to cheat
me when he made the purchase. I told him if that should
be the case, the loss would be mine, but I was under no apprehension about it, believing Peyrobe to be an honest man.
Some person who heard the conversation told Peyrobe, who
came on the wharf in a great rage, and inquired of Pasquer
if he had accused him of intending to cheat Captain Biddle
out of his flour. As Mr. Pasquer gave him no answer, he
struck him a violent blow in the face that brought him to
the ground. He would have repeated his blow, but was prevented by the people on the wharf. For one gentleman to
strike another was what had probably never happened before
in Port au Prince, and therefore made a great noise. In the
evening, Mr. Pasquer sent for me. I found him in bed, complaining very much of the pain he was in. He had a notary
with him, who had drawn up a paper for me to sign. I told
Mr. Pasquer I would not sign any paper without it was in
English. He immediately sent for one of his clerks that

understood the language, and had it translated. I found he wanted me to declare he never had said Peyrobe intended to cheat me. I told him I never had mentioned to Peyrobe, nor any other person, what had passed between him and me respecting this business, but if he would give himself time to reflect, he must know it would be wrong in me to sign such a paper. He endeavored to explain the meaning of what he had said, but as I understood him differently, I would not sign the paper. This occasioned a coolness until I was almost ready to sail, when he behaved with his usual attention.

Peyrobe, I understood afterwards, was almost ruined by a suit that was brought against him for the blow.

As it was thought by Mr. Pasquer there would be no risk in my taking sugar in molasses casks, I took on board a hundred and ten hogsheads of sugar. The day before we were to sail a frigate arrived from France, and anchored close alongside of us. She sent her boat on board to examine our cargo, and happening to bore a cask of triage (or bottoms of the cistern), they thought it was what would condemn the ship. When I went on board in the evening, I found the chief mate very much alarmed. A number of French sailors were in the hold with a lantern sitting on the cask, and the mate told me the frigate's crew had given three cheers, thinking they had a good prize. I was very glad to find they had not discovered what would really have made her a good prize. After ordering the Frenchmen something to eat and drink, I went on board the frigate. What my feelings were may more easily be imagined than described, for the sugar was taken on board without orders from my owner, for whom I had the greatest affection and esteem. I appeared before the captain cheerful and as unconcerned as I could, and told him that what his people supposed to be sugar we had permission to take on board. His boat being at that time going on shore, he sent for a friend, who after having examined the contents of the cask, told him that what I informed him was true. He immediately ordered his men on board. As they had been well treated, they went away very well contented.

Three things happened this voyage that made a great impression on me, and broke me of a vile habit I had of striking with anything I laid my hands on, or heaving at any of the crew that did not move as briskly as I thought they should do. The first was soon after we left the Capes of Delaware. When we first discovered the ship had sprung a leak, I ordered Mr. Corry, the chief mate, to turn out all hands. They were all soon upon deck except John Walsh, a very stout, lazy fellow, that Corry told me was always the last up. I called him myself, but he not answering, I jumped into the steerage with a belaying pin in my hand, and going up to his berth intended to give him a stroke over his back, but being very dark, I struck him on the head. He soon after began to groan, and when I spoke to him, made no reply. Feeling him about the head, I found I had struck him in the mouth, and that it was bleeding. I ordered a light, but as it was blowing a hard gale of wind, it was a long time before they could get one, or at least it appeared a long time to me. During this time I felt the pains of the damned, for I concluded he was mortally wounded. Had they called out from the deck the ship was foundering, it would have added very little to the pain I then felt. It determined me to break myself of the abominable practice of striking with what might endanger the life of a man, and from that time I never gave a sailor a blow with anything but a piece of rope that could do no material injury. When the light came I was greatly rejoiced to find he was not so much hurt as he pretended to be, or as I expected he was. I, however, let him stay below all night, and was glad to find him on deck in the morning. His mouth was tied up, and he complained of some of his teeth being stove in. He was soon well. After this, when all hands were called, there was no occasion to give Walsh a second call. The next thing that made me think seriously about striking, was an accident that happened in Captain Randall's boat. I had dined with him, and, going on shore in the afternoon, as they were pulling off the boat one of the crew happened to touch Randall with his oar. When he spoke to him, and told him to take care what he was about, the man gave him an insolent answer, upon which Randall gave him a stroke on the head with the tiller. He fell immediately backwards, was taken on board the vessel, and died soon after. The affair was not known at Port au Prince, as Randall sailed in two days. Upon his return to New York he was obliged to keep out of the way. Randall had no intention of hurting the man much, and was shocked extremely when he fell back to all appearance dead. He let none of his crew go on shore at Port au Prince after this accident.

The night before we sailed, which was the 28th of March, 1773, I invited several of my friends to sup with me. When at supper there was a great noise upon deck. Upon first hearing it I was afraid the captain of the frigate had put his boat on board, for I still felt uneasy about the sugar. Upon going up I found the noise was made by William Thomas, an Englishman, that was our cook. He was quarrelling with the second mate. Upon my threatening him he was quiet, but soon after, getting more liquor, he struck the mate. The boy telling me this, I went up a second time, with an intention of giving him a severe beating; but, when I found he was very drunk, and recollecting he was a very good man when sober, I did not touch him, but ordered him carried to his berth. In the morning at daylight we got under weigh. About eight o'clock the cook came up and told me he was very sick. After telling him I supposed it was owing to his being drunk the night before, I directed him to go below. The next morning when I went upon deck, the second mate told me he had just been in the steerage, and Thomas was dead. It appeared the poor fellow had fallen from his berth the morning we came out, and probably broke a bloodvessel. Although I was sorry for the loss of this man, it was pleasing for me to think I had not touched him.

We had pleasant weather until we were within ten leagues of the lighthouse on Cape Henlopen, when, the wind being at S. E., and blowing fresh with rain, I ordered the mainsail hauled up, intending to keep my wind until it cleared away. All hands were called, when the cooper, Robert Craig, who

was one of the most active men I ever had with me, coming up
last, I called to him, "How is this, Robert, all hands up before
you?" He made no answer, but walked forward round the
bow of the boat, then coming aft he gave a spring upon the
roughtree, and then for the main shrouds, which missing he
fell into the sea. I was on the quarter-deck and saw him fall.
Calling to him, I told him not to be afraid, we would be with
him in a minute. With the assistance of a French gentleman
that was a passenger, I threw a hen-coop close to him. He
swam to it, and got upon it. At the risk of the masts I hove
the ship round to immediately, cut the boat's gripes, and had
her over the side in a few minutes. But when he saw the
ship hove to, he quitted the coop, and, before we could get to
him with the boat, went down. Had he staid by the coop, we
should have saved him. He was a young man very much
beloved by the whole crew. Although naturally very cheerful, he was, the day he was lost, remarkably so. He had been
four voyages with me, and what made me have a particular
regard for him was the care he took of his mother, who was a
poor widow, that during his absence he left a power with to
receive one-half his wages. No person in the ship lamented
the loss of poor Craig more than Mr. Dubois, my French passenger, who had been much attached to him from the time
of his first coming on board. He rolled about the deck as if
he was distracted; however, if he lamented more at first, he
was the first to forget the loss of him. Grief never affects a
Frenchman long.*

---

* The father, mother, and wife of Count de Noailles were guillotined
while the Count was in Philadelphia. When he first heard of it, he shut
himself up for two hours almost frantic with grief—this was a long time for
a Frenchman to grieve. I saw the Count the day after he received the
intelligence, and if he had not told me of the loss he had sustained, I should
not, from his behavior, have supposed anything more than usual had happened, and yet the Count is an amiable man, and more grave than his
countrymen generally are.—AUTHOR'S NOTE.

The Count's wife, her mother, the Duchess D'Ayen, and her grandmother,
La Marechale De Noailles, were guillotined on the same day, July 22,
1794. The Count's father and mother, the Marechal de Mouchy and his
wife, were executed a few weeks before, on the 27th of June.

We arrived at Philadelphia two days after this melancholy accident. The unhappy mother of Craig never was well after she heard of his death, but died in a few months after him. What ought not to have given her pain afflicted her more, she told me, than his loss would have done had he died ashore: this was his being buried in the ocean. This, I believe, has been the cause of grief to many a one before and since who have lost their friends at sea.

The ship wanting nothing done to her, in seven weeks after we left Port au Prince we were there again. The governor thought it impossible we could be back so soon, and said he was sure we could not have been to Philadelphia, but had landed our cargo at the Mole, a harbor at the west end of the island. However, I soon convinced him by my papers that I had been at Philadelphia. The governor was the Chevalier de Vallier, and a worthy good man he was. I beat the ship from the watering place up to the harbor under close-reefed sails when it was blowing a gale of wind. Most of the inhabitants were looking at us while working up, and Mr. Pasquer and some of his friends told me they expected every time we hove about the ship would have overset.

The Sunday after my arrival, all our colors were hoisted, when the lieutenant of a frigate (the captain being in the country) hailed the ship and told me to haul down my pennant. This I have no doubt he did at the request of a Bordeaux captain who was moored near us, and was then on board the frigate. I answered immediately that I would not haul it down, nor suffer it to be done. They then sent their boat, and the officer who came on board told me a merchant ship could not hoist a pennant in a harbor with one of our own men-of-war, and they would not suffer me to hoist one. I told him I knew very well we had no right to hoist one in a harbor with one of our own men-of-war, but we were not bound by any treaty to show them that mark of respect, nor should it be done by me; that if the governor ordered me out of the harbor, I would go with much pleasure, but would never suffer the flag of my country to be insulted while in my power to prevent it. Finding me obstinate, and not choosing to push matters to extremities, he left us muttering some curses against the English, and wishing they were again at war with them. This I told him he could not wish more fervently than I did. So high an opinion had I imbibed from Lieutenant Nesmith and Mr. McFunn, the two old naval officers that I was brought up under, that nothing but force would have obliged me to haul down my colors, and had they compelled me to do it, I would have gone to Jamaica and complained to the admiral. No seaman should ever suffer the flag of his country to be insulted; it will make foreigners have a contemptible opinion of you, and dampen the spirits of your own countrymen. The captain of the frigate, being sick, was seldom on board, so that the lieutenant, who was a malicious rascal, had it in his power, and did not neglect it, to give me a great deal of trouble by sending his boat frequently on board under pretence of searching for sugar or coffee. A few days before we were ready to sail, a large Guinea ship that lay to the windward of the whole fleet took fire, and burnt with great violence. The harbor was full of shipping, and, as it was said the Guinea man had a quantity of powder on board, there was a great alarm and confusion among the shipping. The frigate fired a good many shot at the ship on fire with an intention, as it was afterwards said, to sink her, but as the water was smooth this could not easily be done. Instead of firing and trying to sink her, they should have gone with their boats and those of the fleet, and towed her on shore, for they knew on board the frigate that there was no powder on board of the ship on fire. As this was not attempted, we knew when her cables burnt she must drift among us, and we therefore prepared to keep out of the way. I had only two men and a boy on board, the remainder of the crew being gone for a load of molasses. I ran out a small anchor to the southward, intending, when the ship drifted, to heave on it if it should be necessary. Just at this time a large French ship carried an anchor out across our bows, which would have prevented me from heaving should I have wanted to do it. I hailed the ship, and told the captain if he attempted to heave upon his cable we would cut it. He answered, " Do, if you dare," and they began to heave in the slack. Immediately we got a slip-rope, and getting the cable over the cathead, cut it, the French captain threatening all the time what he would do. I was quite regardless of what he said, and did not hear his threats without replying. Fortunately the ship on fire drifted clear of all of us. The sight was awfully grand. The next day there was a complaint made against me by the French captain for cutting his cable. I told the governor and intendant (who happened to be present) that I cut the cable to preserve my own ship, and that they had no business, nor any occasion, to carry out their anchor where they did. The French captain told them I had d——d all the French for a set of lubberly b——. The governor gave him a look of contempt, and told him that was a business he should have settled himself. The behavior of the French captain the day after the fire reminds me of what Smollet in his Roderick Random says of the day after the battle of Dettingen : " Every one of them during the fire had performed wonders."

About a month after my being at Port au Prince, a vessel arrived from North Carolina, commanded by Captain Thos. Allen. I soon became very intimate with Allen and much attached to him, and he had the warmest friendship for me. Allen was born in England. Being in the trade of North Carolina, he married and settled in Wilmington. We were so much alike in our persons that we were frequently taken for each other, and had several curious adventures in consequence of these mistakes. One of them had like to have been attended with serious consequences to me. Going one day to a billiard table, after staying a short time, I paid for what I had lost and was going away, when the tavern-keeper civilly requested me to pay for the wine I had the day before. I told him he was mistaken, for I had never been in his house before. He laughed at first, thinking me joking, but when he found me serious, he was very abusive, and at last declared I wanted to cheat him. Upon his saying this I gave him a kick that overset him. When he got up he ran for

the guard who came immediately and arrested me. They
are always ready to come on such occasions, as they generally get something. I requested they would go with me to
Mr. Pasquer, which, after some consultation, they agreed to,
and we proceeded to his house accompanied by a large mob.
Allen happened to be there, and was just leaving the house to
look for me. The tavern-keeper appeared much astonished
when he saw Allen, whom he knew was the man he had
mistaken me for, and who told him he was just going to his
house to pay him. He said he was sorry for what had happened. As I thought the kick was equal to the abuse, I
gave the soldiers a trifle, and we all parted satisfied. If we
had not found Allen, I should have been carried to gaol, and
perhaps had a large sum to pay, for the tavern-keeper would
have sworn I was the person who had his wine, and what
would have been infinitely worse, it would have been thought
by those that did not know me, that I wanted to impose upon
the man. Allen and myself were going ashore one evening
in the jolly-boat, dressed as common sailors, and just before
landing we ran foul of a French boat. The crew were very
abusive, and one of them caught hold of our boat, when I
gave him a shove with the oar, and pushed ashore. We
were walking up the wharf, his arm within mine, when the
fellow who had been struck, coming unperceived behind us,
gave Allen a stroke with a stick on his neck that brought
him to the ground. The sailor immediately ran to his boat
and they put off. It was some time before Allen could
recollect himself, as he was much hurt. We went into the
first house we came to, and I sent for a surgeon who ordered
him bled. The surgeon said if the blow had been a little
higher it must have killed him. The next day he was seized
with a fever, and I was much afraid we should lose him;
however, the fever left him, and in a few days he was able
to walk about. One of the French merchant-men at that
time acted as commodore, and wore a broad pennant, and we
knew the French boat we ran foul of belonged to the commodore's ship. We went on board to demand satisfaction.
The commodore was ashore, and we found him at his store.

He behaved very politely, sent for the fellow, and told us he should be punished in any way we wished for behaving in so base and cowardly a manner. The man declared he took us for two common sailors, and he was hurt by my shoving the oar at him. As he appeared very humble, we thought it best to let the matter drop. Even if there had been no resemblance this fellow might have mistaken Allen for me, for the night was dark.

As the French frigate still lay near us, I did not think it safe to take coffee on board in the harbor, and therefore hired a schooner to carry ninety hogsheads of coffee to Heneaga*, a small island about twenty leagues to the northward of Hispaniola. I left Port au Prince the 20th of September; the schooner sailed with the coffee the day before me. I fell in with her off Cape Nicola Mole, where she was to wait for me, and we stood over in company for Heneaga, but the weather being dark and squally the night we took our departure we lost sight of her. The next day we came to anchor near the west end of the island in six fathoms water, soft white sand with a few scattering rocks. The southwest point of the bay bore S. S. E. The north point N. N. W. distant about four miles. There is fresh water here in a small pond. The road to it is from a small reef of rocks that are close to the shore. But the best watering place is round the north point of the island in what is called Ocean Bight. I staid here three days waiting with great impatience for the schooner. I was preparing the long-boat to go in quest of her, when we discovered her two or three leagues to the westward beating up. I went on board her, and found, in the squalls the night we left Hispaniola, they were obliged to bear away, and had nearly been lost on Cuba. The skipper Nicholo, an old acquaintance of mine, was very much rejoiced to find us, for he was short of provisions and water, and was afraid he should never have found the ship. As I was uneasy at lying here, being afraid of British or French cruisers, we soon got her alongside, and in a few

* Now called Inagua.

hours took out the coffee and made sail from the island. Nicholo told me afterwards they suffered much in their passage back to Hispaniola. We had favorable weather, and arrived without any accident at Philadelphia.

I made another voyage in this ship to Port au Prince, where I found my friend Allen, who arrived a few days before me. Two days before he got in, he was fired into by a ship called the Ville de Paris. The shot went through his boat, but did no other damage. I sailed from Port au Prince the last of February, 1774.

On the 8th of March in lat. 27°, long. 74° 25', Stout, the mate, came down and informed me that it looked squally. Going on deck it appeared as if it would blow hard. I ordered the topgallant sails handed, and the topsails lowered on the cap to reef them. James Gurly, the second mate, was on the main topsail yard, and I was calling to him to take the second reef in the topsail, when, instead of attending to what I said, he let fall the sail, and taking hold of one of the backstays, came upon deck. Much surprised and exasperated, I inquired what brought him off the yard. He appeared much alarmed, and told me he came down because there was a whirlwind in the squall, that he was on board a large ship which was dismasted in a moment by such a whirlwind, and they had all nearly perished although they had only received the tail of it, and that he was much afraid this would prove fatal to us. As Gurly was a good seaman, and of course not easily frightened, what he said made an impression on all the crew. It approached us, and had a most awful appearance. For a great distance the sea appeared to be carried up to the heavens. Observing it attentively for a minute or two, it appeared to me that it was driving to the northward, and that if we wore and made sail to the southward we should avoid it. I therefore immediately wore ship, and as I thought it would make no difference if it took us, whether we were under sail or not, I made sail and stood to the southward. To our great joy we soon perceived it would pass astern of us. I never thought myself in greater danger than when this whirlwind was coming down upon us.

5

It reminded me of one I had heard of that did great mischief in South Carolina. I had two passengers, who, when they saw the squall and heard Gurly's story, went into the cabin, out of which, they afterwards told me, they never expected to go alive. After this we arrived without anything material happening.

My owner, having the offer of a good freight for Bristol, chartered the ship to go there. While we were cleaning her at Mr. Peter Knight's wharf, a schooner belonging to an old friend of mine, Mr. John Duffield, came from Hispaniola and landed her sugar and coffee in Mr. Knight's stores. The custom-house officers had information of it, and sent to Mr. Duffield for the key. I happened to be on the wharf when Mr. Duffield came up with it, and was going to give it to Swanwick, the chief of the gang. As I felt for Duffield, who had a large family, and I looked upon these people as little better than robbers, I was determined to save the property if possible, and for that purpose requested Duffield to give me the key, and go off the wharf. This he very readily did. Upon Duffield delivering me the key Swanwick came up and demanded it of me. I told him he should not have it. Upon this he directed some of his men to get a crow and an axe, and break open the door. I called to Mr. Corry, my mate, and desired him to come ashore and bring some of the crew with him. This he immediately did, and when the custom-house officers came with an axe and crow they were taken from them and hove into the dock. Upon this Swanwick went to his boat in order to go on board a sloop of war that lay in the cove, but I would not suffer him. Just at this time the people from Phillip's ropewalk (rented at that time by my friend Hepburn, who sent them) came on the wharf. The foreman,* who was an Irishman, coming up to me, called out, "Capt. Biddle, who shall we seize?" At the same time an apprentice boy of mine, with a tar brush in his hand, catching hold of Swanwick, begged I would let him paint

* J. Lang, afterwards an officer in the Continental army.—AUTHOR'S NOTE.

him. I made him let him go, and the poor devil was glad to run from the wharf, and his myrmidons followed him. I sent directly for all the draymen that could be found, and we soon emptied the store, putting the sugar and coffee in different stores, where they were safe. When this was done I locked the door, put the key in my pocket, and went to Duffield, who lives now (1802) in the house he then lived in. I found him and his family much distressed until he heard what had happened, when he gave me the warmest thanks. From him I went to Swanwick, and told him if he was going to give an account to the Governor or Collector of what had happened, not to mention my name, as he must know I saved him from being tarred, if not thrown from the wharf into the dock. He said he was very sorry I had not called sooner, for he had already complained to the Collector. I desired him to let me see what he had written. After some excuses he let me see a copy. I found he had mentioned that Captain Charles Biddle, at the head of a mob, had driven him and the rest of the custom-house officers from the wharf. I told him if he did not take care of himself he would be driven from the city. I expected some notice would have been taken of this affair by the Governor or Mr. Patterson, the Collector, as they threatened to do it, but they did not. They began at this time to be afraid of acting in the manner they would have done some time before.

The ship sailed in May, 1774, under the command of Capt. Corry for Bristol. Corry had been my chief mate from the time the ship was launched. He is a native of New Castle upon Delaware, an excellent seaman, and a very good officer. He had only one fault as an officer, and that was his being too fond of striking. This, in a great measure, I broke him of, for I never allowed any one on board to strike the crew. He slept less than any man I ever knew or heard of. I often told him he must have been guilty of murder or some horrid crime that troubled his conscience and prevented his sleeping.

A curious affair happened the last time I was at Port au Prince that I forgot to mention. A man by the name of Benijah Liston, belonging to New England, wrote from Leogane that a person of the name of J. S., whom he had taken in sick and nursed until he got well, had robbed him of some money, a watch, ring, etc., and he supposed had gone to Port au Prince. He gave me an exact description of the robber, and begged I would try to apprehend him, that he belonged to Philadelphia, and probably would try to get there. He mentioned the maker's name and number of the watch. As soon as I read the letter I went on shore, and going to a billiard table frequented by the English, I saw a person playing who answered the description exactly. I went close up to him, and taking hold of his watch chain I drew it out of his fob, and, before he could recover his surprise, opened it, and found it was the one stolen from Liston. I caught hold of him, and told him if he did not go quietly on board he should be put to gaol and punished as a thief. I sent for a boat, and, as I could not go immediately on board myself, directed Corry to come in her. When S. was going on board he jumped out of the boat and attempted to swim ashore, but he was soon taken and carried on board. In the evening when I went on board he was lashed to one of the pumps. I had him loosed and stripped, without finding any of the articles stolen. I was almost tempted to believe the story he told me of his having purchased the watch, when one of the crew going up to him, says to him, " My father was an old thief that used to hide the money he stole under his hat," at the same time knocking off his hat, when out dropped a purse containing the money, ring, etc. I sent for Liston, who was highly pleased at getting his property. J. S. appeared very penitent —he signed a paper acknowledging his having robbed Liston, which was witnessed by Captains Wilson and Kiddel. This acknowledgment I have kept ever since. S. behaved very well, and was a useful hand during our passage home, for which reason I let him go when we got up to town.

After the ship sailed Mr. Aspden purchased a brig for me in which I went to Port au Prince. She was a miserable old vessel, as leaky as a basket. When Pasquer came on board and saw the vessel, and observed the pump almost constantly going, he declared he would never put a cargo on board of her, and begged me to leave her and let her be condemned. But I had Mr. Aspden's interest so much at heart that I would not consent to it. Fortunately we had good weather until we arrived in the river. Had we remained at sea a few days longer it is probable we should have been lost, for we had a violent gale of wind in the river.

I did not think it safe to sail again in the brig, but left her as soon as she was discharged. Upon examining her the carpenter declared she was not worth repairing.

With Mr. T. Yorke I purchased a large schooner, and made a voyage to Cape Francois. During this voyage nothing material happened.

Upon my return we purchased a remarkably fast-sailing brig called the Swift, and loaded her for the Mole. Two days before we sailed, William Johnston, a young man who had been with me on previous voyages, and whom I agreed to take out as my mate, rode out to Germantown and got married. She was a very good girl whom he married, he had long known her, and she had promised to marry him when he could get to be mate of a vessel. As they were returning to town, he stopped the chair and got out to speak to a friend, when a wagon coming by overset the chair, and the wheels went over his wife's breast. A thick pair of new stays prevented her being crushed to death. In the confusion the brute who drove the wagon got off, nor could we afterwards find him. As soon as I heard of the accident I went to see her and Johnston. He was perfectly deranged; she, although in great pain, composed, and trying to soothe him. She died the next day. I was obliged to sail without Johnston. We sailed from Reedy Island in company with a fine brig commanded by Captain Clay, bound also to the Mole. We bet a suit of clothes upon our passage. I had a very short one, and was nearly ready for sea when he arrived. When I went on board, and inquired what passage he had come through, he declared he had made no land until he made Hispaniola, which appears almost impossible. We sailed the last of November from the Mole; the 10th of December we were near the lighthouse, and by the negligence of the mate in not calling me in time when a squall was coming up we had nearly overset. We escaped however, with the loss of our main topmast. That day seven weeks that we purchased the brig, we sold her and settled all our accounts, and made a very good voyage.

A Mr. Gayraud, a French gentleman who had been an officer in Mariagalante, a small island to windward of Gaudaloupe, was introduced to me as a very worthy, good man. He told me if I would join him we could make a great voyage by going to this island, that he could easily get us permission to sell, and bring away coffee. We purchased a brig called the Greyhound* between us, and loaded her with such a cargo as he said would answer. We left the Capes the 28th of February, 1775. As we drew near Mariagalante I found Mr. Gayraud appeared uneasy and expressed his fears that those who were in office when he left the island were dead or removed. This gave me a suspicion that all was not right. I determined, therefore, not to enter the harbor until I was sure we should meet with no difficulty. As we drew near the island I found his uneasiness increase. I then requested he would tell me candidly if he did not think we ran some risk, should we go directly into the harbor as he proposed. He appeared relieved at the question, and honestly declared he felt some apprehension, and agreed with me that we had best let the brig lay off the harbor until we went ashore, and found whether we could be admitted to enter with safety. The 22d of March we hove to, and went ashore in the boat under pretence of want of water. The little island appears a perfect garden. Upon speaking to some of Mr. Gayraud's friends, I found it would not do to come to an anchor, and told him we had better stand over for Ross in the Island of Dominique. He appeared extremely chagrined, and I believe expected he would not be treated by me as well as he was before we landed; but as he was unfortunate, and, I believed, honest, I behaved with more atten-

* Pennsylvania Journal, February 22, 1775. "Cleared Brig Greyhound, C. Biddle to Grenadoes."

tion to him than ever, and he soon recovered his cheerfulness. We touched at Dominique, Mountserat, Nevis, St. Kitts, and St. Eustatia. At the last three islands we went ashore on the same day. Finding the markets would not answer at any of these islands, we sailed for Hispaniola, and arrived at the Mole the 4th of April, and to my great joy found here my old friend Allen. I had this voyage with me Captain Stephen Decatur,* who afterwards commanded a privateer out of Philadelphia, and in 1778, was in the American navy. He came out with a small adventure, and left me here, to command a vessel bound to Europe.

We sold our cargo, and took another for Philadelphia, and sailed the 23d of April, 1775. We left the Mole in company with several sail of vessels bound for different ports in America, who all soon left us, the brig being flat-bottomed and sailing remarkably bad upon a wind. We however, had a tolerable passage, arriving in the Delaware the 4th of May.

* Father of the distinguished officer of the same name.

CHAPTER II.

Upon our arrival we heard of the battle of Lexington, and found the whole country preparing for war. Being young, and considering my country unjustly persecuted, I was as willing to go to war as any man in America. Perhaps my having little to lose was another reason for my having no objection to it. Talking with my old friend Aspden, I found him as much averse to a war as I was for it; and this was not surprising, for he is what is called a worldly man, and had much to lose. I never felt the less friendship for him, nor did I ever feel the least resentment against any man in America for being opposed to the Revolution, where he acted from principle.

The conduct of our people at this time was not *always* correct. A very genteel young man, son of the Collector of Jersey, I believe from Salem, came to Philadelphia to give information respecting a ship from Ireland. He was seized by a mob while at the Coffee House, tarred and feathered, dragged with a rope fastened round his body through the city, and then obliged to jump into the dock up to his waist in water to wait for a boat to carry him to Jersey. I felt very much for this young man, who was only obeying the orders of his father. When in the boat they took him alongside the ship he had come to inform against, and some of the people on board were so inhuman as to heave hot water on him. I was so much incensed at this inhuman behavior that I got in a boat with a few that felt as I did to take him from the wretches he was with. They, however, put off before we could get to the ship, which probably was fortunate for us. They took him to Cooper's Ferry, where he had

medical aid. I understood he was so much injured that he
could never be perfectly well. While he was tied an acquaintance of mine (concerned in the ship informed against) struck
him with a stick, and would have repeated the blow if I had
not stopped him. I never liked this man afterwards. When
Dr. Kearsley and Hunt were afterwards carted around the
town, I did not feel for them. Kearsley would huzza for the
king, notwithstanding his friends begged him to be quiet and
that they would take him out of the cart. The doctor made
a shocking appearance—he had declared he would not be
taken alive out of his house, and when the mob went there
he was sitting in his front parlor with pistols. A young man
broke the sash, and several entered and dragged him out of
the window. His face and head were much cut. He was
prudent enough not to fire, for if he had done so he certainly
would have been killed. Captain Shewell, a relation of Hunt's,
was anxious to get him out of the cart, and would have attempted it at all hazards had I not persuaded him against it;
for it appeared to me that Mr. Hunt was much pleased with
his situation. He was going to England, where he thought
it would be a recommendation to him, and I believe it was.
He was a lawyer when here, but turned clergyman in England,
and had a living given to him.*

Captain Graydon, of Shee's Regiment, and myself went out
one morning about this time to fire at a mark with our pistols.
After we had each fired several times at a piece of paper on
a fence, a man came running up to us, his face as white as a
sheet, and cried to beg we would not fire again; that we had
shot his child. Inquiring where the child was, he pointed to
a house a considerable distance back of the fence. We had
observed the house, but did not suppose it within reach of our
shot. He desired us to go with him to his house; however,
as we thought that might occasion some trouble we refused,
but told him we would call next day. He said it was no

* An account of the carting around the town of the "Tory doctor," Dr.
Kearsley, and Isaac Hunt, the attorney, which occurred in July, 1775, will
be found in Graydon's Memoirs, pp. 111, 112. Hunt was the father of
Leigh Hunt, the poet, and soon after left the country.

matter, he knew Captain Biddle very well. After consulting together, we thought, as he knew me, it would be best to go with him. We found the ball had gone through a pane of glass and struck the child, who was in its mother arms, in the side, but had not entered the body. Probably it would have been killed but for the thick woollen clothes it had on. After expressing our concern, and giving the mother some money, they were perfectly satisfied. I called several times afterwards, and found the child had received no injury whatever. The pistol was fired by me—the ball must have passed through a hole in the fence. The father, whose name was Gilbert, a potter, and a poor man, told me he was at work in his shop when the mother called out the child was shot; and when he ran to us, which he did without going to the child, he expected it was mortally wounded. He was much delighted when he returned and found it not hurt. Graydon and myself felt little less pleasure than the father. He kept the ball, which he said he would preserve for the child, and probably it is still kept in the family.*

I expected the difference between Great Britain and America would not be settled without a war. The first day Congress sat I rode out with my brother Edward, who was a member of Congress, to meet Mrs. Biddle who was on her way from Reading. He then told me that from the disposition of the members, particularly those from New England, he was sure much blood would be spilt before the dispute was settled. He said he would give up his practice at the bar, which at that time was very great, and go into the army, as he had been an officer in the Provincial Army, and was in the prime of life. Brave, strong, and active, esteemed and respected for his talents, he would probably have been next in command to General Washington, but coming to Philadelphia in January, 1775, from Reading in a boat, he fell overboard. I was in the boat with him. We got him in immediately, and went

---

* This incident is told in Graydon's delightful "Memoirs of a Life chiefly passed in Pennsylvania," etc. p. 110. Graydon's father and Judge James Biddle (brother of Charles Biddle) having married sisters named Marks, the author of the Memoirs speaks always of Judge Biddle as his uncle.

ashore to a tavern that happened to be near where we landed. In order to prevent his taking cold he drank a great deal of wine and stood before a large fire in his shirt to dry it. The landlord being a Tory, and saying something about what Congress had done being improper, he beat him severely. With his passion and wine he became ungovernable. He ordered a blanket to be brought in, and although Col. Patton and several of his friends as well as myself tried all we could he would not change his shirt, but laid down in it damp before the fire. The next morning he was very ill, and in a few days broke out all over his body and face large blotches. He had one in his eye that deprived him of the sight of it. Although he lived nearly five years afterwards, he had scarce a day's health. Before this he never was sick.*

My friend Mr. Yorke launched a ship soon after my arrival, which, offering me the command of, I accepted and fitted her for sea. We took in a cargo for Lisbon, but before we were ready to sail I was spoken to by Mr. Mifflin to go to France to purchase powder and arms. As I infinitely preferred this to going in the ship to Lisbon, with the consent of Mr. Yorke I left her, and on the 10th of September, 1775, sailed in the brig Chance, Captain John Craig, for L'Orient. Congress had declared that, if the British Acts of Parliament they complained of were not repealed by this day, they would not, after it, export anything whatever to Great Britain, Ireland, or the West Indies. It was a very fine day. The river covered with ships and the wharves crowded with inhabitants was a pleasant sight, if you could look at it without reflecting on the occasion that drove the country into the measure. Several of the vessels had arrived but a few days before, two or three only the day before. They were unloaded and loaded with great dispatch—they had as many hands as could work night and day. It would, perhaps, have been better policy in Congress to have prohibited any trade to Great Britain or her possessions. We should then have kept many a gallant seaman that sailed in this fleet and never returned to America;

---

* See Note C, at the end of this volume.

for many of the vessels were sold abroad, and the crews not being able to return were obliged to enter into foreign service. The trade should have been stopped, or the owners obliged to bring back the crews they sent out. I went to town, the day after the fleet sailed, on business; the wharf was clear of everything except a few melancholy looking people.

A schooner under the command of Capt. Ash sailed in company with us for Portugal. He was to dispose of his cargo there, and pay the net proceeds to me in France. We were armed so as to keep off any boat or small vessel, and my orders were to speak no vessel, if we could avoid it. Off the Banks of Newfoundland we fell in with several sail, amongst them was a frigate that, about eight o'clock, gave chase to us; she was then near three leagues from us. There was a pleasant breeze, and she gained very little upon us until about ten o'clock, in a heavy squall we found she had gained considerably upon us, they having carried their topgallant sails when we were obliged to take in ours, and lower our topsails. Just after the squall a young man named John Williams fell from the foreyard overboard. He was a Bermudian, and swam like a fish. A rope was hove to him, which missing, he went astern. He was called to, not to be afraid, and answered he was not the least uneasy. We threw him a spar. Craig was of opinion the frigate would pick him up, and was against heaving to, but I had the brig hove to, the boat hoisted out, and we got him on board. We had no right to expect the frigate would heave to when we would not. It was a very trying time to me, for the frigate was coming up fast, and I did not know what would be the consequence of my being taken going on such an expedition. It may be supposed I was very impatient until we made sail. While the boat was out, Craig was comforting me by declaring he was sure our heaving to would occasion our being taken. However, there was no danger of Williams's being drowned, for he could swim to Bermuda. Before we could make sail the frigate was within less than two miles of us. It blew hard in squalls all the afternoon; in the squalls she gained upon us, but when we could carry our topgallant sails we dropped her. Finding she could not come up with us, just before it was dark she hove to and hoisted a signal of distress. As I supposed it only done to decoy us, we paid no regard to their signal; indeed it was pretty evident nothing material could be the matter, for she carried a press of sail the whole day, and left her convoy, or the ships in company with her, in the morning. Before I sailed we had an account of one of our ships being taken by bearing down upon an armed vessel that hoisted a signal of distress. Taking vessels by this infamous method should be forbidden by all nations, for, if made a practice, no one would run the hazard of being taken, let the appearance of distress be ever so evident, and thus many lives may be lost that if this shameful practice was put a stop to would be saved. I was much rejoiced to get clear of the frigate. Some time after in the night we fell in with a brig bound from Lisbon to Cork. The captain inquired eagerly what news? I told him the American army had the advantage of the British in several engagements, and expected soon to drive them from the country. He struck his speaking trumpet with great violence upon the roughtree and swore he was glad to hear it, and hoped we *would* soon drive the British from America. When we were near the coast we passed a great many vessels that from the badness of the weather would not run in with the land. The twenty-second day after we left the Capes we arrived at L'Orient. I found there was no powder to be had here, and therefore set off in a small French coaster for Nantes. The morning we went from L'Orient the skipper fell into the hold, and was so much hurt he thought it necessary to bear away and go into the river Vilaine, where his family lived. The crew all went from the vessel, and there was no one left on board but an old French seaman I brought from Philadelphia, and myself. As it was cold, I ordered him down in the cabin and to shut the scuttle. A short time after, perceiving a fire in the caboose which was in the hold, I told Peter to get up and put it out, but the hasp of the scuttle had got over the staple, and he could not get out, and there was no cabin window by which we could escape. In vain we tried every method to break or cut our way out. Fortunately the fire burnt down without doing any damage. It blew hard, and we remained in this perilous situation for twenty-four hours before the boat came on board and released us. As the wind was ahead, I went on shore. The people appeared to live very miserably, having little but black bread and fish to live upon. We remained here two or three days, when we sailed for Nantes, where we arrived the 10th of October in the evening. The next morning early I took a walk along the ramparts. In looking out I saw the body of a man lying on his face in the mud. It appeared he was an Irish priest, and it was supposed some person in a fit of jealousy had destroyed him. As I was the first person that discovered the body, I was under some apprehension that the people who were assembling in crowds would apprehend me. However, they took no notice of me.

It was a disagreeable and dangerous business I was on, for I was not acquainted with any person in France, and after an article that was prohibited from being sent out of the country. I had some letters with me from my old friend Pasquer, but they were written long before I had any thoughts of going to France. As I knew Mr. Pasquer had an uncle in Nantes, I brought these letters, and with them introduced myself to Mr. Richard. I believe that was his name. He was a very respectable man, and received me with great politeness; and his son, who was an officer in the army, behaved very friendly. They both told me it was a very dangerous business I was upon, and appeared uneasy at my visiting them. I applied to some of the masters of ships I had known in Port au Prince, but they were afraid of me when they knew my business. One of them told me it was highly probable I would be taken up by the officers of the government if I remained much longer. Finding nothing to be done here, I set off for L'Orient by land. The roads are good, but the country not so thickly settled as I expected to find it. The horses were not good. I was determined on my arrival at L'Orient to sail for Holland, where I was ordered if powder and arms could not be had in France. However, it was left in a great

measure to myself to do what I thought best. Upon my
return to L'Orient, Captain Mason, of Philadelphia, was there
in a schooner loaded with saltpetre bound home. He informed
me the merchant who did his business proposed·sending a
ship for Philadelphia, with a great quantity of powder, arms,
and other war-like stores. He told me if I would go in his
schooner he would load the brig and bring her and the ship
to Philadelphia. It was with great reluctance I consented to
leave the brig, but as I could do it consistent with my instructions, and considered it would probably be of great
advantage to my country, as Messrs. Barard Frères promised
faithfully to send the ship if Mason stayed, fully relying on
their promises and those of Mason, I went on board the
schooner. We sailed from L'Orient the 30th of October.
The schooner was a handsome vessel, and had the appearance
of sailing fast, but she did not. Her mainmast worked so
much in the step that I expected we should lose it. We
stood to the southward until we got into the trade-winds.
While we were running down the trades, the main topmast
gave way at the cap while a young man was then at the top
of it, reeving halyards for a royal we intended setting. He
called out the topmast was going, and a moment afterwards
it went away. He had a miraculous escape, having received
no injury. He was a very active young man of the name of
Dickson. He came from the back part of Pennsylvania, and
this was his first voyage. We kept the trade wind until we
were to the westward of Bermuda, when we stood to the
northward. In the latitude of 35° we had a severe gale of
wind from the northwest, during which the mainmast worked
in such a manner that we expected every moment it would
go over the side. Consulting with Captain Patton, whom
Mason had brought out with him as master of the schooner,
we concluded it would not be safe to go on the coast with
the mast in its present situation, and as we had no way of
securing it at sea, that it was necessary we should bear away
for the West Indies. It would not have been safe to bear
away during the gale. When the wind and sea fell, we stood
to the southward, intending to put into St. Eustatia. Two

or three days after we stood to the southward, I fell down the fore-scuttle and hurt myself very much. It occasioned my having a spitting of blood for some time. The first land we made was St. Martin's.* We went in here to avoid a ship we took for a British cruiser. The day after we arrived I went in a small schooner to St. Eustatia for some assistance. Here I found many of my acquaintances from Philadelphia, amongst others, Captain James Craig, brother to the captain who went with me to France. He was very much alarmed at first seeing me, fearing his brother was lost. From them I understood there was no prospect of peace. Having procured what was wanted for the schooner in a few hours, I returned to St. Martin's. A British ship of twenty guns went into the harbor with us and anchored near the schooner. I expected we should have had some trouble with this man-of-war, but she sailed the next day without taking any notice of us. We hoisted no colors and suffered none of the crew to go on shore, so that it is probable the captain of the man-of-war, who I believe was Hawkes, did not know where we belonged to. Upon our arrival the crew had directions to tell any person that inquired, that we were loaded with salt. Still feeling the hurt I received from my fall, and exposing myself in getting the schooner ready for sea, I was seized with a fever that had nearly proved fatal to me. The schooner being now ready to sail, and being myself too unwell to proceed in her, and fearing some accident should she be detained, I sent her home under the charge of Capt. Patton. In a few days, my fever having abated, I went to St. Eustatia, and finding a ship belonging to Boston, commanded by a Captain Adams, ready to sail for Philadelphia, although she was a miserable old vessel, I was so anxious to get home I took my passage in her. A few days after we sailed we were alarmed by a piece of sheathing coming off. As the weather was good, we soon got a piece of board nailed over where the sheathing was off, but from the badness of the sheathing I was convinced if we had had weather on the coast we should

---

* One of the Leeward Islands.

be in great danger of foundering. The fourth of January, 1776, about four o'clock in the afternoon, we struck soundings. We had no observation that day, but by our reckoning we were in latitude 38° 20'. At this time we had a light breeze from the northeast. At dark the breeze freshened with rain. At six o'clock the fore and main topsails were close reefed, the mizzen topsail handed, and we hauled upon a wind to the eastward. At seven o'clock as there was every appearance of a gale of wind the topsails were handed. Hearing them a long time at the pump about half-past eight I went upon deck, and finding it blowing hard, and the ship laboring very much, I told Capt. Adams (who was a good fellow) he had better ease the ship by taking in the mainsail. He said he was in hopes that it would soon moderate, that he was almost perished with being so long wet and cold. Understanding some time before this, from the mate, who was not on very good terms with Capt. Adams, that this was the first time he ever commanded a square-rigged vessel, and as they had no gale of wind before during the voyage, I began to think he did not know how to take the mainsail off her. I therefore told him he had better go below, and put on dry clothes, and I would attend to the ship. He went immediately down, and I had the mainsail handed, mizzen and fore topsails hauled down, and the ship hove to under her foresail. Still finding the pumps had not sucked, I went to Capt. Adams, and told him we had better go in the hold and see if we could discover the leak. When we went down she had a great quantity of water in her, and some of the empty water casks were floating in the forehold. I then never expected to go alive out of the hold. We found the water was rushing in forward, the ceiling* was cut away, and we perceived the leak was occasioned by the sheathing being off. We stopped it as well as possible, but as she still made a great deal of water we concluded it best to stand to the westward and get in shore, that if the leak gained on us, and we could not get into the Delaware, we could run ashore and

---

* The inside planking of a vessel.

6

probably save our lives. It was disagreeable and dangerous
running in shore at this season of the year in a gale of wind
from the northeast, but of two evils this appeared the least.
We accordingly bore away W. N. W. intending to fall in
with Cape May. The next day, happily for us, it was more
moderate. About eleven o'clock we made the land a little
to the eastward of Cape May. At twelve o'clock, seeing a
man upon the beach, we put the boat ashore for him. The
men in the boat were all New England men, who knew how
to manage a boat in a heavy sea as well, if not better than
any other people. With some difficulty and danger they
brought the man on board. The New England men are not
generally good seamen, being seldom regularly bred to the
sea, but they are sober, active men, most of them very stout,
and will endure more hardships than any people I ever sailed
with. This ship had an excellent crew. The man they
brought on board was a Cape May pilot. He soon anchored
the ship off the Cape. I understood from him with much
pleasure that Patton had arrived safe. As there was a good
deal of ice in the river and bay, the ship could not proceed
up. I therefore took my clothes on shore, and with a fellow
passenger hired a light wagon to carry us to Philadelphia.
We arrived at Cooper's, opposite the city, about noon, the 9th
of January. The river was crowded with people skating and
we crossed on the ice. I found all my relations well except
my brother Edward. Mr. Mifflin, who engaged me to go to
France, was perfectly satisfied with what I had done. A few
days after my being at home, Mason arrived. He put into
Morris River and left the brig. I went there, and brought
her up. He and Craig differed, and would not speak to each
other. She had some powder on board, but her cargo consisted chiefly of saltpetre, which was as acceptable as powder.
Messrs. Berard, after having their ship nearly ready to sail,
were afraid to send her.

As all classes well affected to the American cause were
associating, I joined Captain Cowperthwaite's Company of
Quaker Light Infantry. It was composed of men who were
Quakers, or descendants of Quakers. We went out every

day to exercise, and took great pains to make ourselves qualified to act our parts as soldiers when called into the field.
General Harmar belonged to this company. Of him, Baron
Steuben and General Washington both said they never knew
a better, if so good an officer as he was. Several others of
the company joined the American Army and became valuable
officers.

In the spring there was an account came up to the city
that the Roebuck, Captain Hammond, was aground on the
Brandywine Shoal. We had at that time a provision ship
of fourteen guns, fitting out under the command of Captain
Read. It was determined this ship should sail immediately
with two or three of the galleys. Captain Cowperthwait
waited on the Committee of Safety, and offered his company
to act as marines. The Committee thanked him and the
company, but said there was a full company of marines belonging to the ship. I then offered myself as a seaman, when
Captains Souder, Jackson, Potts, and some others of the
company did the same. Our service was gladly accepted,
and we went immediately on board. The ship was fitted out
with great dispatch, numbers of respectable people coming
down to assist in getting the guns, water, and ballast on
board. Although it rained very hard, they never left the
wharf until she had everything on board. When we put
off from the wharf, we had about one hundred and fifty men
on board, but we were very badly fitted. Our guns were a
great deal too long, and our crew were chiefly landsmen.
There were not more than twenty seamen including the officers on board, so that we should have made a bad hand at
fighting. Having some apprehension of being taken, I took
on board only a few shirts and trowsers, being determined if
taken, and the ship came into the river, to endeavor to make
my escape by swimming. However, I was not put to the
trial, for the day after we sailed intelligence was brought us
of the Roebuck getting off the shoal, and the volunteers were
all dismissed. Had Captain Hammond known our intention,
and kept his ship on a heel near the shoal, he could easily
have taken the ship and galleys.

The intelligence of the Roebuck getting off the shoal was brought by Captain Andrew Caldwell, who had been down to the Capes to see in what position the Roebuck lay. When the galley returned and anchored near the ship, Captain Read ordered the barge to be sent to bring Captain Caldwell on board. I went in her as coxswain, and the rest of the masters as the boat's crew. When we got alongside of the galley, I stood up with my hat off, and received him on board the barge with as much ceremony as if we had belonged to the barge of a British man-of-war, and he had been an Admiral. When we were at some distance from the galley, Captain Caldwell, looking at me very steadfastly, exclaimed, "My God, Biddle! is it you?" I answered, yes. He then recognized Potts and some of the other masters whom he knew. When he put the same question to Potts that he did to me, Potts told him that we had been unfortunate, and were obliged to enter before the mast. As he was well acquainted with my family, he seemed much affected; however, he was soon relieved by Captain Read, who wished us to mess with him. This we would not do, for having entered as foremastmen we were determined to act as such.

Some time after this the Roebuck and Liverpool came into the river, and were attacked by the galleys. I have heard that Captain Hammond then said if the commanders of the galleys had acted with as much judgment as they did courage, they would have taken or destroyed his ship.

Hearing the evening before the engagement that the galleys were going down from Marcus Hook, where they were lying, and that it was probable they would engage the Roebuck and Liverpool, I set off early in the morning in a chair with Mrs. Gibbs, a widow lady, at whose house I was very intimate, to see the intended battle. My intention was to go as a volunteer on board one of the galleys commanded by Captain Thomas Houston, a schoolmaster of mine. This I did not, however, communicate to my friend Mrs. Gibbs, who owned the chair, and I was fearful, if she knew my intention, that she would choose some other gallant, for she was attached to the British and I believe wished them success. After we had passed Chester about a mile, as I was driving furiously along, one of the shafts broke. Having kept the reins in my hands, I stopped the horses, so that we took the ground without any injury. Pulling the chair on one side of the road, I made an apology to Mrs. Gibbs for leaving her, and set off as fast as my feet could carry me for Marcus Hook, which was near three miles from where the accident happened. Notwithstanding all my exertions I was a few minutes too late. Not being able to get a boat to put me on board, I returned to Mrs. Gibbs, who was a very enterprising lady. She had with the assistance of some passengers got a rail put alongside the shaft, and was coming down when I met her. As she had a great friendship for me, she readily forgave me for leaving her so abruptly. She told me she was very glad of my being disappointed, that it was very foolish in me to run the risk of my head or *neck* on such an occasion. 'We drove down and soon saw the ships (which were under way) and the galleys firing at each other. It was a fine day, and the banks of the river, out of reach of the shot, were lined with spectators, and every house near the shore filled. Among others Colonel Turbutt Francis was there. Col. Francis was a native of Philadelphia, who had been an officer in the British service.* He had a chair placed on the bank of the river where he sat to see the action. He was so much afflicted with the gout that he could not walk. As his chair was placed where the shots from the ships sometimes passed over him, I requested he would have it removed. He, however,

---

* Colonel Francis, brother of Tench Francis, had also served as Lieut.-Colonel in the Provincial Army. In the minutes of the Provincial Council is the following entry :—

PROVINCIAL COUNCIL, Monday, May 21, 1770.

This day the Governor was pleased to appoint Turbutt Francis, Esq., to the several offices following in the room of Hermanies Alricks, Esq., who resigned, by five separate commissions, under the great seal of the Province, viz. : Prothonotary or Principal Clerk of the County Court of Common Pleas ; Clerk of the Quarter Sessions of the Peace ; Clerk to Register of the Orphans' Court ; Recorder of Deeds ; and a Justice of the Peace, and of the County Court of Common Pleas for the County of Cumberland.

would not, saying there was little danger, and he sat with great composure, observing the engagement.

On the memorable 4th of July, 1776, I was in the Old State-House yard when the Declaration of Independence was read. There were very few respectable people present. General · · · · · · · * spoke against it, and many of the citizens who were good Whigs were much opposed to it; however, they were soon reconciled to it.

Thomas Paine, the author of *Common Sense*, contributed much towards reconciling the people to the Declaration of Independence; and his pieces afterwards published, entitled "The Crisis," had a great effect in rousing the people to arms. The beginning of his first number, in which he says, "These are the times to try men's souls; the summer soldier and the

* This name is obliterated and entirely illegible in the manuscript.

It is remarkable that we have few accounts of this memorable incident from actual witnesses. Until recent times little importance was attached to the exact date of the public reading of the Declaration. Thus it happens that, writing from memory, the author has given the date as the 4th of July instead of the 8th, the latter being doubtless the correct one. Christopher Marshall says, "in the presence of a *great concourse of people*, the Declaration was read by John Nixon." Mrs. Deborah Logan, who was standing in her father's garden at a point which is now the N. E. corner of Fifth and Library Sts., says, "I distinctly heard the words of that instrument read to the people · · · the first audience of the Declaration was neither *very numerous nor composed of the most respectable class of citizens.*" Note at p. xlv. Penn and Logan Correspondence. In this last particular her account is confirmed by the author of these reminiscences.

Upon the reading of the Declaration to the troops in the field, Graydon remarks: "The Declaration · · · was with the utmost speed transmitted to the armies, and when received read to the respective regiments; if it was not embraced with all the enthusiasm that has been ascribed to the event, it was at least hailed with acclamations, as no doubt any other Act of Congress, not flagrantly improper, would at that time have been." (Memoirs, p. 140.)

It is not certain that there was any public speaking on the occasion of reading the Declaration. There had been held in the State-House yard on 20th of May a very large, and not entirely harmonious, meeting to consider the resolution of Congress, of 15th of May, recommending the Colonies to adopt such government as should best "conduce to the happiness and safety of their Constituents in particular, and America in general." At this meeting, doubtless there was warm debate.

sunshine patriot," published a few days before ·the battle of Trenton, were in the mouths of every one going to join the army, and have since been often repeated. Paine may be a good philosopher, but he is not a soldier—he always kept out of danger. He is about five feet nine inches high, thin, and has a sottish look.

In August, being desirous of having a shot at the Hessians, whom I considered as a set of horrid wretches that would hire themselves to commit any crime whatever, I gave up the command of a vessel to go out with the Quaker Light Infantry. Several of those who signed the articles to go, when we were ordered to march, would gladly have stayed behind. Being determined on going myself, I was resolved to get all I could, and, acting as a sergeant, with a small party, took some of those who intended to give us the slip.* We went in a shallop to Trenton, where we encamped for several days.† We had in the tent I belonged to a Captain William Potts. He was a very stout fellow, and would have been thought by many people an excellent hand for such an expedition. He supplied us with plenty of tin cups and small articles of that kind. If he found anything in that way in the camp that he wanted, he would mark it Tent No. 1. If it was claimed afterwards, he would declare it had the mark of our tent, and nobody should have it without fighting him, and this very few would do. We were obliged, however, at last to tell him that he must leave off this practice or leave the tent. He was a brave, good soldier; he now (1802) keeps a tavern in the Northern Liberties. We marched from Trenton to Brunswick, and crossed the river at Brunswick about the 25th of August, a remarkably hot day. We did not get over the river until ten o'clock. We marched to Woodbridge, which

---

* Capt. John Morril was one of them. He got up into a new house and took up the ladder. I got some shavings, and threatened to burn him out; upon which he surrendered. He is a brave, good soldier.—AUTHOR'S NOTE.

† August 11, 1776. Several shallops, with troops for the camp, went from town yesterday, as [others] did also this morning [at] flood.—MARSHALL'S DIARY.

is ten miles, and had just encamped when an express came in from Gen. Mercer informing us that he intended that night to attack the British on Staten Island, and requested those who chose to go on the expedition to march to Elizabethtown. Our company, although much fatigued with the morning's march, being exposed to a scorching sun, turned out to a man. Leaving our baggage, we set off immediately. During the march several of the company fell with the excessive heat. Before sunset we reached Elizabethtown, and were paraded with a body of New England troops. We were just going to march to the Point and embark when, fortunately, a violent gust arose which prevented it. The gust I have no doubt saved a number of us, for we afterwards learned the British were informed of our intention and well prepared to receive us. The next day we encamped at the Point in sight of the British troops. When marching to encamp we went several times round the guard-house at the Point, which I suppose was done to make them imagine we had more men than there really were. We could see the officers of the British army looking at us from Staten Island with their spy-glasses. A few days after we encamped some of Miles' Rifle Company went without any orders from their officers to Staten Island, and with great deliberation loaded their pieces and fired at a breastwork the British had thrown up in the marsh opposite the Point. When the riflemen first fired, a man we took to be an officer ran from the breastwork along the causeway until he was at a considerable distance. His running with so much speed after he was out of all danger set all the camp laughing. The riflemen might as well have fired at the moon as at the troops behind the breastwork. The British fired a long time without any effect. We were all astonished at their firing so badly. They at last killed one of the riflemen. Bateaux then went over and brought them off. This, and some of the troops deserting, occasioned an order from Gen. Mercer that no person should go over in a boat or swim to the island. Frequently before this order, myself, with a number of others belonging to the company, had swam over. Although we went within musket shot of the British, they

never fired at us. In the tent with me was Captain Souder,
P. M. Austin, and several other seafaring men. One night
Gen. Mercer sent to know if we were willing to go upon an
expedition in boats. We informed the messenger we would
go anywhere the General thought proper to send us. About
ten o'clock at night sixteen of us embarked in two small
boats. We expected it was to take some of the British sentinels from Staten Island. The night was very dark, and it
rained hard. About twelve o'clock we anchored near a sloop
of ten guns, and all our company were anxious to board her;
and I am convinced we could easily have taken her, for, not
expecting an attack, and the rain falling in torrents, I believe
there was not a man upon deck, and probably all were asleep.
However, the officer who commanded had his orders what to
do, and would not make the attempt. Just before daylight
we got under way and rowed up to the guard-house. , We
found afterwards we were sent to intercept some Tories that
were expected to cross at this place. When on guard at the
waterside we suffered very much from the mosquitoes; when
off guard we spent our time very agreeably. One morning
we were alarmed by the sentinels calling out that the British
had landed. Potts was the first out of our tent; he d——d
his eyes if there were not ten thousand of them on the shore.
One of the officers of Grubb's Battalion who heard him set
off and ran to Elizabethtown, from whence he went home.
Grubb swore he would advertise him. We were soon under
arms in our shirts. It was, however, a false alarm, occasioned
by some rails put on end along the fence in the night, which,
as the day broke, were taken by one of the sentinels for the
enemy. We remained here until relieved by what was very
properly called the Flying Camp. They did not arrive until
long after the time for which we engaged to serve. Our company was composed chiefly of men who had been inured to
hardships, and I believe would have fought well had they
been brought to action. Cowperthwaite, our captain, is a
brave officer. Humphreys, who has since been a Quaker
preacher, was one of our lieutenants; his looks and manners
are so much altered since his conversion that I can hardly

keep from laughing when I meet him, which, as he lives near me, is very often. He sometimes seems himself inclined to laugh.*

In 1766 some of our committee pressed the horses of Judge Allen, a worthy, respectable old gentleman, who used often to stop me to talk of my father, who was a great favorite with the judge. I had a dispute about taking the horses with one of the committee. They were most of them a bad set of fellows. Mr. Allen used to say that America was the finest country in the world, Pennsylvania the garden of America, Philadelphia the first city of America, and his house the best situated of any in Philadelphia.

Soon after my return I sailed in the brig Greyhound for Port au Prince. We had a pair of swivels and some muskets, being sufficiently armed to keep off a boat. We also had six wooden guns. Nothing remarkable happened until the 18th of September, when, in the evening, we saw two small schooners lying at anchor under the West Caicos. They

---

* A somewhat amusing account of this military episode is given in "Loxley's Journal of the Campaign to Amboy, 1776." Collections of Hist. Soc'y of Pa., vol. 1.

The following certificate refers to the same period:—

PHILA., Feb'y 24th, 1806.

These are to certify whom it may Concern, That Capt. Charles Biddle joined the Quaker Light Infantry, as it was then called, Commanded by the subscriber. He joined it in Jan'y, 1776. Some time after, there was a Report in the City that the Roebuck Man-of-war was aground in the Bay of Delaware, when the Prove. ship Commanded by Capt. Read, was Fitted out to go down & attack her. I went with my com'y and offered to serve on Board as Marines. The Committee of Safety Returned us their thanks and said there was a company of marines belong to the ship, and they only wanted seamen, upon which Capt. Biddle, Capt. Souder, and some other Captains of vessels that then belonged to the said Com'y offered themselves as seamen and went Volunteers in the ship. In the summer of 1776, Capt. Biddle Left a ship he had then the Command of and went with the above named Co. into the Jerseys. While there, at the Request of Gen'l Mercer, he went as a Volunteer on an Expedition in Boats up the Sound and upon Every occasion behaved as a Good Soldier. The above all came under my notice. Given under my hand

JOS. COWPERTHWAIT,
Capt'n at that time.

weighed and stood toward us. As our vessel sailed heavily, I knew it would be in vain to run from them, and therefore hove to as if to engage them. This had the desired effect, for they soon hauled their wind and left us. We stood over all night for Hispaniola, with a fresh* of wind. At daylight we unfortunately fell in with the Antelope of fifty guns, and about nine o'clock were taken. This ship was commanded by Captain Judd, and had been dispatched a few days before by the Admiral to cruise off Cape François. The brig was a valuable prize, being loaded with flour, which was then much wanted in Jamaica. Captain Judd kept my spy-glass, which Lieutenant Cadogan endeavored to get back for me. As he could not, he generously gave me his own, which was much better. They put Lieutenant Harvey, two midshipmen, an officer belonging to some other ship, and ten seamen on board. They left on board belonging to the brig two young men, Messrs. Hunter and Fisher, who were passengers with me, and Goforth, a pilot. As the officers of the frigate Antelope were very negligent of their arms, I determined to endeavor to retake the brig. Upon mentioning it to Hunter and Fisher, they immediately agreed to join me, and, after some persuasion, Goforth also agreed to assist us. It was my opinion, if we could secure the officers below, there would be no difficulty with the seamen, as one of the men they put on board had been a barber in Philadelphia, and frequently mentioned his regret at leaving it. I conversed with him on the subject, and, finding him willing to join us, told him our intention. This man's name was McKenzie; he said he thought the best way would be for him to go below when the officers were asleep and cut their throats with a razor. As he was one of their own men, he could easily have done this; but neither recapturing the brig nor anything else would have induced me to consent to so horrid a deed. It was agreed that Hunter and Fisher should keep the officers below, while Goforth and myself were to manage the seamen, and we were to begin soon after the watch was relieved at eight o'clock. I have

---

* This quaint nautical expression is now obsolete.

every reason to believe that just before the time we had fixed upon Goforth informed Mr. Harvey of our intention, for a little before eight he secured all the arms which before were lying carelessly on the quarter-deck, and took such precautions as put it out of our power to do anything. We arrived two or three days after this at Port Royal, and I was permitted with Hunter and Fisher to go on shore. At Kingston I met with Messrs. Cadwalader and Thomas Morris, Captain Miller, Mr. Daniel Major, and several other of my American friends and acquaintances, and spent my time as agreeably as a man could do who had just been robbed of nearly all his property. The day after my arrival at Kingston I went on the wharf with several of my friends and met Lieutenant Harvey. He expressed himself very glad to see me, and requested I would go on board with him. As he had behaved very friendly, and my clothes were still on board the brig, I very readily consented. When we were a little way from the wharf, he told me the Admiral wanted to see me, and that he had threatened to break him for letting me go on shore. I begged he would let the boat's crew lay on their oars until I informed my friends that they need not wait for me. One of those friends has since told me he never was so much affected in his life as when I hailed them and said they need not stay for me, for he expected, from his knowledge of the Admiral, that he had ordered me to be taken up, and that he would treat me with great severity. I was taken that night on board an armed schooner commanded by Lieutenant James Cotes, a very worthy man. He went the next morning with Mr. Harvey and myself to the Admiral, Clark Gayton, who stayed at Greenwich. Gayton was as great a ruffian as ever was hanged. At this time he was a miserable, sickly old man, much afflicted with the gout. When we went to his house, he was sitting in his balcony with a young mulatto wench. When Lieutenant Harvey informed him who I was, he took up a Philadelphia paper and read an account of the taking of some prizes by the Andrea Doria, commanded by my brother Nicholas. He inquired if I was brother to that *rebel*. I told him that *man* was my brother.

He then began to abuse him, the country, and everything in it: wishing to God he had "the damned Congress" in Jamaica. Smarting under my loss of property, and the ill-treatment of this man, my temper forsook me. I answered that he knew, situated as he at present was, he could abuse my country or me without any danger. Enraged at this and something else that passed, he ordered Mr. Cotes to take me on board and put me in irons. Mr. Cotes and Mr. Harvey stayed with him, while I walked to the boat with the crew. What they said to him must have induced him to change his orders, for I was not put in irons. Mr. Cotes told me afterwards the Admiral said to Harvey and him he was sure by my eyes that I was a rebel. I was informed this man was born in Boston. Mr. Cotes, who behaved with the greatest kindness to me, begged if I was again taken before the Admiral that I would be more prudent. The attention of Mr. Cotes I imputed in a great measure to the friendship of Mr. Harvey. A person going to sea in war times should be careful of having any papers on board that may injure him. Probably the account of the captures made by my brother induced Gayton to behave with more severity than he otherwise would have done. He was, however—rest his soul—a great brute. In the fifth volume of the *Naval Chronicle*, he is mentioned as a good and gallant officer. He may have been a good officer, but, if applied to him as a man, the word "good" would as well apply to Black Beard the Pirate.

There was, at this time, on board the Admiral's ship, a young man of the name of Joseph Crathorne, a native of Philadelphia. He was taken some time before me, and entered on board the Admiral's ship as a midshipman. He came on board the brig when we first arrived, and not having the least suspicion of him, I mentioned several circumstances to him that happened in Philadelphia after he sailed, which, from the questions put to me by the Admiral, he must have told him. I believe this man occasioned the ruin of many of his countrymen by informing against, and having them detained as prisoners.

Lieut. Cotes being ordered on a cruise, I was sent on board

the Antelope, then lying at Port Royal. The officers all behaved extremely well to me, particularly one of the lieutenants, who informed me privately, a few days after my being
on board, that he had orders to search my chest and trunk.
An hour after he had given me the information, when I had
put away everything that could do me any injury if found,
he had me called, and ordered me, in a peremptory manner,
to give him my keys, which, when he received, he made a
most diligent search, turning everything out and examining
every article. I was afterwards told Crathorne informed the
Admiral, if they searched, they would probably find my uniform coat, and, if I had not received intimation of the search,
it would have been found, for I had imprudently taken it
with me. The lieutenant who gave me the information was
as good an officer, and as warmly attached to his country as
any man in the fleet. He knew if a uniform had been found
it would occasion my being ill treated, and answer no good
purpose whatever.

When the fleet was to sail, which was the beginning of
January, 1777, I was informed the Admiral intended to send
me to England in a sloop-of-war that was going to convoy
the fleet. This I was determined to avoid if possible. My
friends from Kingston having liberty to see me, four of them
agreed to come down in a boat in the night and take me off.
This, on their part, was a very hazardous enterprise, for, had
they been taken in the attempt, they would have been punished severely. For two nights they attended, but it was
impossible for me to get clear of the sentinels, who probably
had orders to be particularly attentive to me. Finding my
escape could not be made in this way, I tried several other
methods of escape, without effect—one was, dressed in the
clothes of a mulatto girl. In this dress I should have got
ashore one night but for one of the midshipmen, who was
too inquisitive. Had he known me, he would not have
stopped me. · The evening before the fleet sailed, a small
sloop, bound to Cape Nicola Mole, anchored at Port Royal.
My friends at Kingston informed me of her. She was commanded by Capt. Paxton, a very worthy Englishman, that

had long sailed out of Philadelphia, and would have done anything to have served me. In the night, as upon all such occasions, there was a good deal of noise, and confusion on board, during which a small boat came alongside with two men who agreed to take me on board the sloop. I took nothing with me but the clothes on my back, a little money, a pair of pocket pistols, and under my coat, a cutlass. We soon got on board, and, the land-wind springing up soon after, we set sail, and at daylight were abreast of Rock Fort, which is about [ten] miles from Port Royal. I now concluded myself perfectly safe, and my good friend Paxton appeared as much rejoiced as myself. He requested me, as I had been up all night, to go below and sleep. I laid down in my clothes, and was soon in a sound sleep from which I was wakened by hearing Paxton say, "By G–d! the Admiral's barge is coming after us." It was now perfectly calm. I went immediately upon deck, took up the glass, and could plainly perceive in the boat one Sims, an American that was a Master's mate. As soon as he boarded us, not observing me, he ran below. I was on deck with Paxton, and, advising him to abuse me before Sims for deceiving him, I called to Sims from the deck, and inquired if it was me he wanted. He ran immediately up, and was much more pleased at seeing me than I was him. He requested me to go in the boat, which I immediately did, being now anxious to get away, fearing much they would take Paxton (who acted his part very well) as well as myself. We had not been in the boat five minutes when the sea-breeze set in and blew so strong that if we had received it before the barge boarded us she never could have come up with us. No officer in the ship would have pursued me so far but Sims, for, being himself an American, he was afraid if he did not take me he would have been suspected of knowing my intention and assisting me. He declared if he had not found me he never would have returned to the ship. When we reached Port Royal I was taken to the capstan-house and confined in irons. In this infernal place they kept me some time, during which no person was allowed to see me, nor did I speak five words during the whole time. From this place they took me on board the Antelope, where I was again treated by the officers with great kindness. Poor Hunter came on board to see me, and cried like a child when he understood I had been in irons. All my thoughts were employed in contriving how to make my escape, which I almost despaired of effecting, when one of the lieutenants, who had been a midshipman under Captain Stirling with my brother Nicholas, and who had a great affection for him, advised me to apply to Captain Judd for liberty to go on shore at Port Royal. Judd was very seldom sober in the evening, and one night when he had taken a larger does than usual, and was staggering along the quarter-deck, I applied to him for leave to go ashore. He told me, "yes; go at any time; he did not care a damn about me." The lieutenant, who heard him, immediately ordered a boat to take me on shore, and in a few minutes I had all my things in the boat and set off for Port Royal, where we soon landed. Lieutenant Cotes was then fitting out, and I was determined not to leave Port Royal without seeing and expressing my gratitude to him for the attention he had paid me. When I told him Captain Judd had given me leave to go, he expressed great satisfaction; and when I rose to take my leave of him he insisted upon my spending the evening with him, which I would gladly have dispensed with, being not perfectly at ease, but I could not get off. We took an affectionate leave about two o'clock in the morning. As soon as it was daylight I went in a wherry to Kingston, and from thence to my friend David Major, a few miles from town.

During the time I was at Mr. Major's we had an account of the British marching through the Jerseys and driving our troops before them, and it was one night reported that General Washington was killed. An honest Scotchman who knew the general swore he was very glad to hear it, "for he was too gude a mon to be hanged;" one or the other he thought must be his fate.

While I made my home at Major's I used to come from his Pen to town almost every evening. One night, when I was at the coffee-house, a Frenchman came in, that was taken a few days before on his passage from Philadelphia for Hispaniola. The people crowded round him eager to inquire about the army. One of them asked him if the British troops were in Philadelphia. "Yes." "And what are they doing, hanging up the rebels?" "No," says the Frenchman, "they came there to be put in gaol." He then gave an account of the battle of Trenton, of which we had not heard before. This gave great pleasure to the few Americans that were in the coffee-house, some of whom were so imprudent as to laugh out. For my own part I had suffered so much for my want of caution that the pleasure I felt was kept to myself.

It has been justly observed that what we think the greatest misfortune frequently turns out the greatest benefit. This was the case with me at this time, for I thought when Sims retook me nothing more unfortunate could have happened, but it ultimately proved of great advantage. When I left Philadelphia several people had sent money with me, which I had saved and contrived to get ashore to my friend Major, who wishing to be concerned in a trade to the Mole, purchased a prize brig, which I took part of. We loaded her with salt, got a Capt. Carr, an Englishman, to command her, and sailed for St. Nicola Mole. We had a number of Americans, who had been robbed of their property, on board, and a young woman of South Carolina, of the name of Nelly Rose, daughter of a merchant of Charleston who had come out to seek her fortune. We arrived at the Mole after a passage of six days. The day we went in, a privateer from Charleston arrived. Had we fallen in with her at sea, we should have been a good prize, being under English colors. I soon sent the brig back loaded with flour. Concluding to stay here some time, I wrote to Mr. Isaac Caton, who had a very good house at the Mole, to beg he would let me have it until he arrived. He was then at Cape François, whence he sent me a very friendly answer, giving me the use of his house and stores. I immediately took possession, and several vessels valued themselves* upon me, so that if I could have

* Probably an obsolete expression, meaning that they placed their business in the hands of the writer.

contented myself here, I should have made a fortune; but my anxiety to get home induced me to purchase one-half of a schooner from Captain Bristol Brown, of Virginia. At this time they gambled very high at the Mole, and at the head of these gamblers was the governor. Any person who had money was welcome to the table. They played at what they called vingt-un, or twenty-one. Nothing was allowed to be staked but gold, and every evening large sums were won and lost. The first night I went to look at them, a Mr. Marignolt (a German who had lived many years with Mr. Meredith a merchant in Philadelphia, and afterwards settled in this place, where he had acquired, with a fair character, a handsome fortune) was dealing, which was what few of these gamblers would do, for the dealer bets against all the table, and must therefore risk much more than those who do not deal. He was confused at seeing me, and took an opportunity of telling me it was only by chance he came there, and begged I would not mention to any of the Americans my seeing him there, as it would perhaps injure him. I told him if he would promise me never to go again, no one should know it from me. He readily promised he would not. However, he went soon after, and in two nights lost everything he had. I was informed by several who were at the table with him, that he left it about two o'clock in the morning very much agitated. It was generally supposed he drowned himself, for he never was seen or heard of after he left the table. Thus ended poor Marignolt, who was an honest, friendly man, and, before he took to the gaming table, a respectable merchant. He was one of the last men of my acquaintance I should have suspected of gaming. He was a very sober, quiet, reserved man, and was in a good way of business. It was diverting to look at the countenances of many of these people at the time they were playing; their extravagant joy when fortune was favorable, and their execrations when losing considerably, were expressed in so ludicrous a manner as would have extorted a laugh from any one that saw them.

We loaded the schooner, which was called the Three Sisters, in April, and I embarked on board her. As there were a

number of British cruisers on the coast, I was determined to
get into the first port we could make. The first land we
made on the coast was near Cape Lookout, and the wind
being fair for Beaufort in North Carolina, we entered the
harbor. Beaufort is a pleasant little village on the sea-coast.
Here it was I first became acquainted with Miss Hannah
Shepard, whom I afterwards married. Mr. Jacob Shepard,
the father of Miss Shepard, had been a respectable merchant
of Newbern, and removed here on account of his health.
Taking a voyage to Philadelphia, he was seized soon after his
return with the smallpox. Notwithstanding he was much
beloved by the people here, they dreaded the smallpox so
much that they were afraid to go near the house, so that it
was difficult for the family to procure the necessaries of life,
and impossible to get any one out of the family to nurse him.
Mr. Shepard died in a few days extremely regretted by all
who knew him. His widow, finding this a very healthy
place, concluded to reside here. Her daughter spent her
time between an uncle Smith's near Newbern and her
mother. Having sold the cargo, loaded the schooner and
sent her to Brown at the Mole, I set out, by the way of North
River and Portsmouth, for Philadelphia. At Portsmouth I
called on Mrs. Brown, the wife of Capt. Brown who was concerned with me in the schooner. She was an amiable woman,
and told me her husband had written to supply me with
everything in her power. I took passage here for Baltimore,
from thence to Philadelphia.

I found my mother and all the family had, on account of
the war, removed to Reading. After going there and staying some time with them, the first of July I set off with
Col. Jacob Morgan and Mr. Charles Shoemaker, for Charleston, South Carolina. The intention of these gentlemen was
to purchase goods, mine to see my brother who was there in
the Randolph. When the Randolph sailed from Philadelphia
bound on a cruise, February, 1777, in a gale of wind they
lost all her masts and boltsprit. They were so rotten they
went over the side, notwithstanding the yards and topmasts
were down. It was very difficult to refit her here. She had

two mainmasts put in that were shivered to pieces with lightning. After staying some time with my brother, who was very dear to me, I went to Beaufort. A few days after my being there, when at the house of an acquaintance a little way from the town, a man came from Beaufort and informed me the Three Sisters was off the Bar. I hurried down and found her standing from the Bar towards a vessel to leeward of her. It surprised every one on the beach; however, the mystery was cleared up at night, for the schooner's boat came on shore with all her crew. It appeared the vessel to leeward was a cruiser from New York, who had hoisted a signal of distress, and by that infamous contrivance induced the captain of the schooner to go down and speak her. Although I was very much enraged at the captain when he came on shore and informed me how he was taken, yet, when I considered he could have gone to speak her only from motives of humanity, I was reconciled to him. Col. Morgan joining me at this time, we set off for Philadelphia. Nothing in the country at this time had the appearance of distress; the people everywhere as we passed appeared cheerful and contented. The day we arrived at Baltimore, the British Fleet appeared in the Bay. The town was in great confusion, and every one that could do it was moving out, expecting the British would land and take the town, which they could very easily have done. As it would have detained them a very little time, and they could have done much mischief to many an innocent person, it is surprising they did not land, for at this time, driven about as they were, they could expect nothing but what they could get by plunder. At the tavern where we stopped a company was collected of very fine young fellows. They had chosen a foreigner for their captain, because they supposed he was better acquainted with military matters than any other they could get. As soon as the fleet was in sight, he sent in his resignation. The company deliberated what they would do with him; several proposed hanging him, and had he come amongst them at this time, if they had not hanged him, they would have treated him with some violence. They afterwards obliged him to leave Baltimore, and he now resides in Philadelphia. He is a quiet, inoffensive man, very unfit to command a company of high-spirited young men. Mrs. Lux, a lady who lived adjoining the town at this time, showed as much love for her country, and fortitude, as was ever done by any of the Roman matrons. As soon as she was informed the fleet was off the town, and the troops would probably land, she went into the town where her only son, Mr. George Lux,* of whom she was doatingly fond, was sleeping. She awakened him, and, having his accoutrements brought, told him to hurry down and join his comrades in defending the town. I knew Mrs. Lux well. She was a very amiable, pious, good woman. We remained in Baltimore until we found the fleet intended to go up to the head of Elk. We then left it, and went to Reading, from thence I went to Philadelphia, and there engaged to go in an armed brig belonging to some of my friends to France. She was built by Mr. Eyre, for a privateer, but I was determined never to go privateering, considering the crew of a privateer little better than a band of robbers.

The British having landed at the head of Elk, I went to our army with Captain Barry and some others. The roads at this time were continually crowded with people going to or returning from the army. We saw the British Army near Brandywine; our troops were in high spirits, and I was in hopes whenever attacked would give a good account of the enemy. Being anxious to get the brig to sea, and not expecting an engagement soon, I returned to Philadelphia. We could distinctly hear the firing at this battle in Philadelphia, where prayers were offered up for both parties. There was an awful silence most of the day. People were coming in every minute from the scene of action, scarce any two of whom agreed in their account of the battle. We soon, however, found that our troops were worsted and retreating towards the city. With some others we wanted to form an artillery company, but I soon found nothing could be done.

* Mr. George Lux married the daughter of Edward Biddle. the writer's brother.

Some that promised to join went to take care of their families. A remarkable circumstance took place at the action.
A brave young man of the name of Scull, a cousin of mine,
who commanded a company in Hampton's Regiment, was
going to make an attack upon some troops that were advancing towards him. When he was going to fire, one of his
company, deceived by the uniform, called out they were
Americans. The officer who commanded them, hearing
what was said (for they were very near), with great presence
of mind called out, "Don't fire, we are your friends;" and,
advancing close to Captain Scull, gave his fire, which proved
fatal to most of the company. Captain Scull escaped unhurt.

As the owner concluded to send the brig up the river to
Trenton, I took on board every person that applied to go up
until we had as many as we could stow. Many of these unfortunate people who were leaving the city knew not how
they were to subsist. Some of them had wives and children
without a morsel of provisions to give them. The day after
we left town, we anchored off Bristol.* I landed there, and
found the place full of people flying from Philadelphia, many
of whom were my acquaintances. I furnished my passengers
provisions while they remained on board the brig. We lay
off Bordentown. A number of vessels followed us up,
amongst others the Washington and Effingham frigates.
As my brig was armed, I lay in the stream to prevent any
shallop going down without a pass. At this time Mr. Riché
lived at an elegant place opposite to Bordentown, and Mr.
Kirkbride near him. Before the war they were intimate
friends, but, taking opposite sides, Riché being a Tory, and
Kirkbride a Whig, they became inveterate enemies. They

---

* A few days before I left the city, having more hard money than I had
occasion for, I buried, in the cellar of the house where I lodged, thirty half
Johannes in a bag. After my return to Philadelphia in 1784, I went with
Capt. Chas. Craig to the house, then inhabited by Mr. Hugh Lenox. Finding there was a new cellar door, I told Craig it was a bad sign, as it was
probable they had been searching the cellar. However, I went down and
soon found the money, loose—the bag, as may be supposed, was entirely
rotten.—AUTHOR'S NOTE.

were both hospitable men, and I often dined at their houses; however, as Mr. Riché had a number of fine daughters I was much more at his house than at Mr. Kirkbride's; and Mr. Riché was always glad to have me with him, as my being there often prevented his being robbed or insulted. The daughters I frequently took over the river to see Mrs. Field, their aunt. This gave great offence to Kirkbride, who, after expressing his surprise that I could take any pleasure in the company of Tories, informed me it was contrary to law to take them out of the State, and that he must stop my boat if I attempted again to go over the river with them. I told him the law was certainly not intended to stop young ladies from crossing the river, and if he attempted to stop the boat I would bring the brig's guns to bear upon his house and beat it about his ears. After this he was so much offended that he never spoke to me. Some time after this Mr. Riché's daughter Mary* went into Philadelphia to see some of her friends, and it was asserted that when the British sent up troops to destroy the shipping at Bordentown Miss Riché requested the officer who commanded the expedition to burn Mr. Kirkbride's house. The house was burnt down by the British, but I do not believe she ever made such a request, for although she detested Kirkbride (and with good reason, for he had her father taken when ill of the gout, and confined in Newtown gaol), she was of too amiable a disposition to make such a request. It is probable that the officer who went on this command had heard from some of the refugees in the city, of Mr. Kirkbride's ill usage of them.

The day after the battle of Germantown I set off for Reading. On my way I stayed two days with our army. They were very badly provided, but in good spirits. Many of the officers were of opinion they would have got into Philadelphia if they had not attacked Chew's house. After remaining some time in Reading I set off with Mr. Collinson

* See "Inscriptions in Christ Church Burial Ground," p. 14. Mary Riché married Charles Swift, and was the mother of Mr. Charles Swift Riché and of Mr. John Swift, Mayor of Philadelphia.

Read* for Charleston, South Carolina. Mr. Read was going to purchase goods, in which I was concerned. When we left Reading I went in a sulky, he on horseback. Before we reached Lancaster he begged I would let him ride in the sulky as he was fatigued a horseback. As I knew the road for a considerable distance was very bad for a sulky, I readily consented. When we exchanged I kept ahead of him to Fredericksburg, where, being over the worst part of the road, I waited for him, and it was two days before he came up with me. He was so heartily tired that he declared no consideration whatever would induce him to ride another day in it. I now took the sulky, and we proceeded on. Coming one evening late to our stage, I found a number of people at it, and was fearful we should have a bad lodging, so as Mr. Read came up to the door I told him to pretend to be very ill. This he did, and getting him near the fire, I inquired if he thought it was the smallpox he had. At mention of this many of the men started, but when he said he had some breaking out and was fearful it was the smallpox, we soon had a clear house. We were obliged to inform the landlord of the trick, or he would have run off with his guests. He was angry at first, but we soon pacified him. We proceeded on without anything material happening. One day when I was a good way ahead of Mr. Read in North Carolina, he said he heard a great noise in the woods which alarmed him and frightened his horse. When he came up to what occasioned the alarm he found it was the wheels of a cart loaded with tar, one spoonful of which would have eased the horses and prevented the disagreeable noise.

At Charleston I found my brother Nicholas, who had been out on a short cruise during which he took a sloop called the True Briton, of twenty guns, and some other vessels that were under her convoy. The captain of the True Briton, when leaving Jamaica, expressed a wish that he might fall in with

* Collinson Read was a member of the bar of Philadelphia, and married, in 1773, Mary, daughter of Captain Wm. McFunn, so frequently mentioned in this narrative. Capt. McFunn married Lydia, sister of Charles Biddle, Dec. 3, 1752.

the Randolph, which ship he heard was cruising off Carolina. When the Randolph was bearing down upon him he kept up a constant fire, but when the Randolph got within pistol-shot, and fired a gun, she struck her colors. Captain Shaw, who commanded the marines, a gallant young officer, was a remarkably thin man. He told me he never thought himself in any danger from a shot until one of the True Briton's carried away a mizzen-shroud of the Randolph's. He then thought himself in some danger. When I arrived in Charleston, they were fitting out some vessels that were to sail with the Randolph to attack two frigates that were off the Bar. The day after my arrival Mr. Drayton sent me a note informing me he had authority to offer me the command of a ship called the Volunteer. I returned him my thanks, and accepted the command. I went on board on Monday, and the fleet was to sail the Saturday following. At the time appointed for sailing we had not more than fifty men, and few of these seamen. Under these circumstances I wrote to Mr. Drayton, that manned and fitted as she was I could not acquire any honor to my country or myself in going out in her, and would therefore prefer going a volunteer in the Randolph. I accordingly gave up the command of the Volunteer and went on board the Randolph. The British frigates sailing away from the Bar before we could get over, I took an affectionate, and as it proved to be a last, leave of my brother, and returned to Newbern, where I had engaged to take the command of a ship called the Cornelia, take a concern in her and fit her out.

During my being at Charleston this time, there was a dreadful fire happened that destroyed a great part of the town. The night of the fire a company of us supped together, and we were sitting up when they began to cry fire. Had there been any engines, it would have soon been put out, but, as no water was near, the people did not know what to do. In the house where the fire originated, a woman was brought out just as we got there, but she was burnt in so shocking a manner that she expired in a few minutes. Finding the flames spreading very fast, I went to the house of the sailing-master of the Randolph, who lived near where the fire began, in order to assist his wife. I found her busy in removing her goods from her shop, in one corner of which I saw a small cask with the head put loosely upon it. Thinking it coffee or tea, I took it in my arms and carried it out. Just as I went from the door a servant girl told me to take care, it was a cask of powder I had under my arm. The fire was then falling very fast near me. I covered it as well as I could with my coat, took it to the waterside and threw it in. If the girl had not informed me it was powder, I should certainly have been blown up. The fire after raging a great while was at last stopped by blowing up several houses. Upon my return to Newbern, I found it necessary to take out all the lower masts and boltsprit from the Cornelia. This, in a country where you could scarce get a seaman, was a very troublesome business, and obliged me to be almost constantly on board. The hull also wanted a good deal of repair. While fitting out this ship, we had an account of the loss of the Randolph. It is impossible to describe what I felt on this occasion. I could get no sleep for several nights, and, as some of the fleet had returned to Charleston, I was determined to go there and inquire into the particulars of the unfortunate accident. I set off from Newbern in company with Major Lucas, who was going to join his regiment in Georgia. During the journey I had many melancholy reflections; it was very different from my last, when I went to see and enjoy the company of a much-loved brother. I arrived at Charleston in the evening, and went to Mrs. Dennis's where I had formerly lodged. She was a native of Philadelphia, and knew my brother and the family well, and always expressed a great regard for my brother as well as myself. As soon as she saw me she took me into a private room, and told me she was extremely glad to see me, that an affair had happened that had given her a great deal of pain, that Capt. Morgan who commanded a State brig, and was out in the fleet with my brother, had given a toast that reflected very much on him. I felt a gloomy pleasure at the thought of calling him out; but I immediately sent a message to him by Major Lucas, desiring he would meet me

with his friend and a pair of pistols, and told Lucas to get
him to fix on as early an hour as possible. In a short time
Morgan called on me with Major Lucas. He told me the
toast he had given was, "More wisdom to those at the head
of our navy;" that he meant it for those who fitted out our
ships; that no man ever loved and esteemed another more
than he did my brother, and that he would at any time have
risked his life to have served him; that, if I wished it, he
would give me from under his hand what he now asserted to
be true. As I knew Morgan to be a brave, good officer, what
he said was perfectly satisfactory. I had some reason afterwards to suppose that Morgan had displeased Mrs. Dennis
by not marrying a relation of hers, to whom, it was said, he
had paid his addresses. Had I known what was long afterwards told me respecting the conduct of Sullivan, who commanded the ship General Moultrie, I should have sent Lucas
to him. It appeared from the testimony of Mr. Davis, formerly of South Carolina, who now keeps the Red Springs in
Virginia, and was one of the Randolph's crew picked up by
the Yarmouth, that they first discovered the Yarmouth about
one o'clock P. M., to windward standing for them. At three
o'clock she approached so near that they took her for a ship
of the line, and one of the Randolph's crew that had deserted
from the Yarmouth, said she was a ship of seventy-four guns,
and that it was her bearing down upon them. As soon as
my brother was certain that she was a ship of the line, he
hove out a signal to make sail, which was instantly obeyed
by all the fleet but the General Moultrie, who lay with her
maintop sail to the mast, so that Captain Biddle was obliged
to engage the Yarmouth or sacrifice the General Moultrie.
It is probable he expected to cripple the Yarmouth, which
he in some measure did, and very likely would have effectually
done it but for the unfortunate accident that happened. One
of the men picked up by the Yarmouth (which took four of
them off a piece of the wreck three days after the action) sailed
with me from Baltimore. He told me he was stationed at
one of the quarter-deck guns near Capt. Biddle, who early in
the action was wounded in the thigh. He fell, but imme-

diately sitting up again, and encouraging his crew, told them
it was only a slight touch he had received. He ordered a
chair, and one of the surgeon's mates was dressing him at
the time of the explosion. None of the men saved could
tell by what means the accident happened. Mr. Davis told
me that the Randolph fired four broadsides to the Yarmouth's
one, and that she was in a perfect blaze from the time the
firing first began until the explosion. Captain Morgan told
me he thought it was the ship the Randolph was engaged
with that had blown up, and he bore away to inquire how
Captain Biddle was, and had the trumpet in his hand, going
to hail, before he found his mistake. Thus fell in the twenty-
eighth year of his age one of the best and bravest of men,
and as gallant and well-disciplined a crew as ever sailed the
ocean. My brother was brought up to the sea. In 1770,
when a war was expected between Great Britain and Spain,
he went to London and entered as a midshipman with Captain Stirling. When the difference was settled between the
two countries, although Capt. Stirling was unwilling to part
with him, being anxious to go on the expedition under
Commodore Phipps, he left Stirling and entered before the
mast. He was afterwards made coxswain of the barge.
Upon the breaking out of the American war, he came out
and entered into the service of his country. He was a remarkably handsome young man, and very cheerful and entertaining. I believe he never drank a quart of liquor in his
life. The following certificate I received from Mr. John
Davis, of Virginia.

"I, John Davis, at present keeper of the Red Springs,
Botetourt County, Virginia, do hereby certify, that in February, 1778, I sailed in the ship General Moultrie from
Charleston in company with the Randolph, Captain Biddle.
That, on the 7th of March following, at one P. M., we discovered a sail standing for us, when the Randolph made a signal
to heave to. About four P. M., Captain Biddle hove out a
signal to make sail. We then spoke him, and Captain Biddle
told us that one of his crew had deserted from the British
ship Yarmouth of 74 guns, and he knew the ship to wind-

ward to be her—and from her appearance he had no doubt it was her; notwithstanding which, Sullivan did not make sail, and the Randolph was obliged to engage the Yarmouth or sacrifice our ship. The Yarmouth hailed us as he passed. We answered, 'the Polly, from Charleston,' and that our convoy was ahead. They then hailed the Randolph; and immediately after engaged. The Randolph appeared to fire four or five broadsides to the Yarmouth's one, until she blew up, when Sullivan hauled down his colors, and we should have been taken but for Captain Blake, who commanded the marines. He insisted upon our making sail, and such was the confusion on board the Yarmouth, or she was so much injured during the engagement, that they took no note of us. To the truth of the above I am ready at any time to make oath.

(Signed)   J. DAVIS.

We, the subscribers, lodgers in the house of Mr. Davis, heard him declare the above account of the engagement between the Randolph and Yarmouth, and of the conduct of Sullivan, to be true.

(Signed)   RICHARD MYNCREEFF,
ROBERT C. LATIMER.

Aug. 21, 1801."

The following lines upon Captain Beauclerk, killed at Carthagena, would apply as well to Captain Nicholas Biddle.

> " Sweet were his manners as his soul was great,
>   And ripe his worth as immature his fate ;
> Each tender grace that joy and love inspires,
>   Living he mingled with his martial fires.
>
> " The blast that nips my youth will conquer thee ;
>   It strikes the bud, the blossom, and the tree."*

---

* " Nicholas Biddle was the ninth son of William Biddle, of New Jersey, who had removed to the city of Philadelphia previously to his birth, and where this child was born in 1750 [Sept. 10]. Young Biddle went to sea at thirteen, and from that early age appears to have devoted himself to the calling with ardor and perseverance. After several voyages, and suffering

After a short stay in Charleston, I returned to Newbern, and applied myself diligently in fitting out the ship. Owing to many disappointments, I could not get her ready to go down the river until the month of August. I had six iron and fourteen wooden guns, and seventy men, not more than five of whom could be called seamen. I lay three weeks

much in the way of shipwreck, he went to England, and by means of letters was rated as a midshipman on board a British sloop-of-war, commanded by Captain, afterwards Admiral, Sterling. He subsequently entered on board one of the vessels sent toward the North Pole, under the Hon. Captain Phipps, where he found Nelson, a volunteer like himself. Both were made coxswains by the commodore. This was in 1773, and the difficulties were coming to a head. In 1775, Mr. Biddle returned home, prepared to share his country's fortunes in weal or woe.

"The first employment of Mr. Biddle in the public service was in command of a galley called the Camden, fitted out by the colony for the defence of the Delaware. From this station he was transferred to the service of Congress, or put into the regular marine [Dec. 22, 1775], as it then existed, and given the command of the brig Andrea Doria, 14. In this vessel he does not appear to have had much share in the combat with the Glasgow, though present in the squadron and in the expedition against New Providence. His successful cruise to the eastward in the Doria has been related in the body of the work, and on his return he was appointed to the Randolph, 32, the vessel in which he perished.

"In the action with the Yarmouth, Captain Biddle was severely wounded in the thigh, and is said to have been seated in a chair, with the surgeon examining his hurt, when his ship blew up. His death occurred at the early age of twenty-seven, and he died unmarried, though engaged at the time to a lady in Charleston.

"There is little question that Nicholas Biddle would have risen to high rank and great consideration had his life been spared. Ardent, ambitious, fearless, intelligent, and persevering, he had all the qualities of a great naval captain, and though possessing some local family influence perhaps, he rose to the station he filled at so early an age by personal merit. For so short a career, scarcely any other had been so brilliant, for though no victories over regular cruisers accompanied his exertions, he had ever been successful until the fatal moment when he so gloriously fell. His loss was greatly regretted in the midst of the excitement and viscissitudes of a revolution, and can scarcely be appreciated by those who do not understand the influence such a character can produce on a small and infant service."—Cooper's Naval History, vol. i. p. 120. See, also, Portfolio for October, 1809, and Sanderson's Eminent Philadelphians.

See note D.

down the river exercising the crew in working the ship, sending down the yards and topmasts, and doing everything I could to make them useful and prepare them for action. I had a tally upon all the running rigging, with what it was called written on it. By this means they were soon useful. As there were several cruisers off the Bar, I wanted to be prepared as well as it was possible before we left Newbern. I told Mr. Singleton, one of the owners, that, at the season of the year we were going to lie at Ocracock, it was probable we should have a gale of wind, and he had better get a new cable. He told me he thought what we had would do very well, and, as he was going down with me to attend the loading of the ship, I said nothing further to him about it. When we anchored in the Road, which is an exceedingly bad one, there was every appearance of a gale of wind. The pilot requested I would let him go on shore, as he had a family, and could be of no service if an accident happened to the ship. I readily consented, but, when Mr. Singleton was going into the boat, I stopped him, and reminded him of what passed in Newbern, and told him, if the cables were good enough for me and the crew, they were for him, and he should not go on shore. He was much surprised, and endeavored to persuade me to let him go with the pilot; but, as I thought he had behaved wrong in not procuring a new cable, I was determined he should not go on shore. It blew very hard in the night, and poor Singleton suffered so much that I was sincerely sorry for having detained him. The next day, the gale abating, he went on shore, and, although we were detained here, for the remainder of our cargo, upwards of twenty days, he never came on board. It is a bad Road, and dangerous at the season of the year we were there, especially with bad cables. I never went on shore, being fully employed exercising my crew, as I expected to be attacked as soon as I went over the bar.

While I was fitting out the ship, a gentleman of the name of O'Neal arrived from France. He came to America to enter our army. He took up his quarters at the house at which I put up (Mr. Rainsford, an honest seaman, who kept the best

house in Newbern). From his name it would be supposed
he could speak good English; he spoke, however, very little.
The first night he came, finding at supper that he had a difficulty in calling for something he wanted, I spoke to the servant and told him what it was. O'Neal, finding I understood
something of the language, came round the table and seated
himself next to me. He expressed much pleasure at finding
some person in the house who could understand him, and
then he gave the history of his life and adventures. He
was one of the most incessant talkers that ever lived. If he
had spoken slowly, which few of his countrymen do, I should
not have understood one-half of what he said, but he talked so
fast that I did not understand one word in ten. I was sorely
grieved that he had heard me translate his French to the
servant. Recollecting that the State of North Carolina was
raising a regiment of foreigners, most of the officers of which
were Frenchmen, and anxious to get rid of O'Neal, I mentioned this regiment to him, and told him I would introduce
him to the colonel, who was an acquaintance of mine. He
was delighted at hearing this, and begged I would go immediately with him. It was about eleven o'clock when we
went to the colonel's lodgings. Knocking at the door, a window was opened by him, and he inquired what we wanted.
I told him there was a gentleman just from France, who
wanted to speak to him on business of great importance.
He hurried on his clothes, and was soon down stairs, when
I introduced O'Neal, and immediately went away, leaving
him to explain the motives of our visit, and congratulating
myself upon my escape, and laughing to think how Mr. Chariot (the name of the colonel) would be plagued with his countryman. O'Neal, however, was not to be done with me, for,
after staying some hours with the colonel, he came back to
the tavern, and, inquiring of the servant that sat up for him,
for my room, he came to me and awakened me out of a sound
sleep to tell me that the colonel had promised to use his interest to get him a commission, and desired him as soon as he
got to the tavern to speak to me to use my interest for him.
This, I had no doubt, he told him, to be up with me for dis-

turbing him so unseasonably. He kept talking to me until
I pretended to be asleep. The next day I saw Chariot, who
was a very pleasant, good fellow. When he came up to me,
"Ah! Mr. Biddle! where you pick up Mr. O'Neal?" I found
he had been as tired of him as myself. As I was the only
person in the house that could speak a word of French,
whenever I came in O'Neal fastened on me. Chariot soon
after procured him a commission, and I have no doubt he
was a good officer. My friends in Newbern used to say I
wanted to get O'Neal appointed a general officer, that he
might make me one of his aids.

We sailed from the Bar the 22d of September, 1778, in the
afternoon; a pleasant breeze and moderate weather. Just
before midnight I directed the chief mate to call me and
mention aloud there was a ship under our lee bow he believed to be a cruiser. Immediately all hands were called,
and I was much pleased to find how readily they went to
their quarters. It convinced me they would fight well if
brought to action. The marines were commanded by Captain
Ward, who had most of them been before in an independent
company belonging to the State of North Carolina. Having
served the time for which they enlisted they entered with
him on board the ship. With fifteen of these men Captain
Ward boarded and took a privateer of eight guns and fifty
men. It was in the night when she was lying at Cape Lookout. The commander of her, when at Beaufort, said if he
had not been surprised in the night, a hundred of them would
not have taken her; and that he should be glad to meet
Ward when they were upon an equal footing. Ward took
no notice of this at the time, but the fellow remaining in the
country, and getting naturalized, Ward sent him a challenge,
and as he had not courage to meet him, he chastised him
very severely with a whip, which he bore with Christian
patience.

Knowing that exercise is an excellent remedy for sea-sick-
ness, and wishing to make the young men on board learn to
go aloft, whenever the weather was fair I had the hand
pump taken up to the head of the main top-mast and there

8

lashed, and every one of them that wanted a drink of water was obliged to go up, bring the pump down, and after they had taken a drink, carry it up again. For the first five or six days many of them would come upon deck, look up wistfully at the pump, but rather than go aloft would go down again. However, they were soon reconciled to it, and I believe it was of great service to them. During our passage, one morning at daylight, we fell in with two ships that I took to be British Letters of Marque bound to America. We were not more than two miles from them, yet we took no notice of each other. My object was to go safe, and I was determined not to be taken if I could possibly avoid it; nor was it my wish to take anything. When we were off St. Eustatia it was calm, and the current going to the windward we were drifted close to St. Kitts. There were then two privateers lying there, one a ship, I believe commanded by a Capt. Phillips, and a schooner. I made all the show we could with our men and wooden guns, hoisted our Jack, ensign and pennant, filled the tops with men, and prepared to engage should they come out. However, fortunately for us, they did not, and the breeze springing up about ten o'clock we soon reached St. Eustatia. The captain of the privateer was laughed at for not going out and attacking us. He said he took us to be a Continental ship of twenty guns, and expected to get nothing but hard knocks; that if he had been in a king's ship he should have acted differently; if any one doubted his courage he would try them. About noon we anchored at St. Eustatia, and I went on board Admiral ———* ship, and told him if he could return it I would fire a salute. He behaved with great politeness, but informed me he could not return the salute. As I lay near him we manned the yards and gave him three cheers, which he returned. Admiral ———* was killed soon afterwards. When the British took St. Eustatia Admiral Rodney sent the Monarch in pursuit of the Dutch Admiral, when an engagement ensued and he fell. During the time we lay

* The name of the Dutch Admiral is wanting in the MS.

here it came on to blow one night very hard. It was expected we should have a hurricane, and I intended at daylight to go out of the Road. There was at this time a heavy sea rolling in. When I was below the chief mate ordered one of the crew in the maintop. He fell from the futtock shrouds overboard, and it was with great difficulty that he was saved. This man's name was Samuel Rogers, a drunken fellow, and the only one of the crew that was so. A few days after he ran from the ship; had he applied for his discharge I would have given it him, and paid his wages, for on a drunkard you can have no dependence. We sold our cargo well, and took in a valuable one. As there were a good many small privateers cruising off St. Eustatia, I purchased a pair of six pounders, and then thought myself a match for any of them. Seven or eight sail of us, bound to different ports in America, sailed together, and although several privateers were in sight they were afraid to come amongst us. The next day we saw a sloop to windward which I took to be an Anguilla* privateer, and hoisted English colors in hopes she would bear down upon us. As soon as our colors were hoisted she did as I expected, and made preparations to engage us. As I found she intended to get upon our weather quarter, I had two of the guns loaded with grape run aft, and all the marines lying on quarter-deck with a bullet and two buckshot in their muskets; and as her crew were entirely exposed in coming up, which they did with their drums beating, I expected to make great havoc among them; but just as we hauled down the English colors, and hoisted our own, and were going to fire on them, they hoisted American colors, and we found she was a privateer from Charleston, I believe commanded by a Capt. Milligan. The captain came on board, and told us he was as much disappointed as we were, for he thought us to be an English Letter of Marque. Nothing material happened until we were off Cape Lookout, when at daylight we fell in with a small British cruiser, which we stood for and expected to

* Anguilla is a small island off the north coast of Cuba.

engage, but when near she made sail from us. In carrying
sail after her we sprang the head of our foremast. From the
appearance of the weather, expecting a gale of wind we
stood for Beaufort, and anchored there about twelve o'clock
the 16th of November, having been just eight weeks on our
voyage. When we were going to salute the town I directed
Mr. Sumeral, the chief mate, to draw the wads and unshot
the guns. When he told me it was done I gave orders to
fire. Hesitating to fire his gun, I went up to him and asked
him if he was afraid to fire, and intended to take the match
from him, but upon my speaking he fired, and the gun burst
into a hundred pieces. A large piece went through the boat,
another through the foretop-sail. A splinter of the carriage
scratched one side of my face, and the same piece tore the
ensign all to pieces. Poor Sumeral had his thigh broken in
two places, and many of the crew were slightly wounded.
Considering the gun was loaded with grape shot, and the
decks full of men, there being many on board from the shore,
it was surprising more were not injured. Sumeral lingered
a great while before he died, and I believe if we could have
procured a good surgeon he would have recovered. He told
me he was really afraid to fire the gun; he had tried to draw
the wad but could not. Had he mentioned this to me the
accident would not have happened.

When I went on shore in the evening, to my very agreeable surprise, I found Miss Shepard. She had just come
down from her uncle's on a visit to her mother. We were
engaged to be married as soon as I returned to Newbern,
which I did not expect, when I sailed, would be before the
beginning of December. The meeting here was entirely
accidental; Miss Shepard, hearing of her mother being
unwell, had set off the morning of my arrival, and rode fifty
miles on horseback that day. The springing of my foremast
(which at the time I was very much concerned about, and
which in the evening I was much pleased had happened) was
the occasion of my being at Beaufort. As it was uncertain
when I should be at Newbern, I persuaded Miss Shepard to
be married here, and, as there was no marriage settlement to

be made, the 25th of November, 1778, we were married, and I can now (January, 1812) say with truth, what with truth *all* married men cannot say, that it was the most happy circumstance of my life, and that she has been everything to me I could wish.

Shortly after my marriage a large sloop anchored near the Bar. We took her to be an English cruiser, and prepared to attack her if she should come near the town. However, at night, the pilot came on shore and brought with him the owner, who, I found, was Mr. William Hodge, an old schoolmate of mine, and who was very much rejoiced to see me. Having been long absent from America, and anxious to get into any port on the continent, and Beaufort being the first port he made, was the reason of his putting in here. Mr. Hodge had been for a long time in France, where he was concerned in a privateer that had taken a packet and some other vessels belonging to the British. The English Ambassador, being informed that Hodge was concerned in the privateer, applied to the French Court to have him confined, and although they were then privately giving every encouragement to the Americans they basely complied with the Ambassador's request, and had Hodge arrested and carried to the Bastile. He told me he was fencing with a master who was teaching him, when two well dressed men came into the room, inquired if his name was not Hodge, and when he informed them that it was, they told him he was their prisoner, and, desiring him to step into the carriage, they also came in and carried him immediately to the Bastile. He was confined there in a room by himself for six weeks, and probably would have died there but for the favorable turn in our affairs. During his imprisonment he never spoke a word to any person whatever. Mr. Carmichael, who lived with Dr. Franklin, frequently wrote to him, but he never received but one of his notes, and that he found in the plaits of one of his shirts. It fell out as he was putting the shirt on. He was very much rejoiced at getting it, as it informed him he would soon be released.

Mr. Hodge left the sloop in my charge, and went to Philadelphia to consult with his friends what he should do with her. He soon returned and fitted her out to cruise. He wanted me to command her, but as I disapproved of commanding or being concerned in a privateer, he gave the command of her to a young man of the name of Simpson (son of Captain Simpson, of Philadelphia), who came with him from Cadiz. I never knew a man whose attachment was so strong to his native place as Hodge's. He thought a man's being born and brought up in Philadelphia was a sufficient recommendation. This must have been his motive for giving the command of the sloop to Simpson, for there were several at that time in Newbern much better qualified, who would gladly have taken the command of her. Simpson was a good young man, and brave, but totally unfit for a privateersman. The best officer belonging to the sloop was John Harris, of Boston. He was a man of uncommon size and strength, very active and brave. Going off with him one day, there was a Spanish seaman behaved with insolence to Harris; he struck him,—the fellow immediately took out his knife and, if one of the boat's crew had not caught his arm, would have plunged it into Harris. Harris took no further notice of the fellow than taking the knife, until we were all out of the boat but himself and the Spaniard, whom he made stay with with him. As soon as we were on board the vessel he took the Spaniard, who was a stout fellow that valued himself for his strength, by the collar and hove him overboard, and, notwithstanding all his prayers and entreaties, put his head under water until he was almost drowned. He several times brought his head above water to let him breathe, and then thrust him down again. He then hauled him on deck, more dead than alive. The fellow, after this cold bath, behaved extremely well. The sloop soon got her complement of men, and sailed on a cruise. She had a brush with a privateer from New York the day they left the Bar. They soon parted, and the Eclipse, as she was called, went off Charleston, where they took a brig and sent her to Beaufort. Soon after they were chased and had a narrow escape from a British frigate. Nothing saved her then but getting into shoal water. They returned without taking any other prize than the brig.

I fitted out the Cornelia, and sent Captain Cook, of Philadelphia, master of her to St. Eustatia. A few days after they left the Bar she lost her main-mast in a gale of wind. She was chased by a privateer near St. Eustatia. The captain told Captain Cook, in St. Eustatia, that he knew the ship and was acquainted with me, and did not think it prudent to come alongside, and so she arrived safe in St. Eustatia. On her return she was taken by one of the Providence privateers.

I moved about a month after my marriage to a small house belonging to an uncle of Mrs. Biddle. We went to Newbern during the winter, which we passed very agreeably. We were entertained at Newbern with great hospitality by the families of Jones and Singleton (where we made our homes), by Governor Nash, Mr. Blount, and some other respectable families there. During my stay at Newbern I attended the trial of a cause for my friend Hodge, who was at Philadelphia. It was about the prize brig sent in by the Eclipse. She was claimed by some merchants of Charleston as American property. I employed the Attorney-General, Avery, who had all the trouble of preparing for the case. When the trial was coming on Mr. Avery advised me to speak to Mr. Nash (afterwards Governor), which I did. He was an eminent lawyer, but very negligent, and did not come into court until after the jury were sworn, and did not speak half an hour. When the jury went out, I called at my lodgings and placed five hundred dollars, Continental money (equal then to about one hundred and fifty dollars specie), in a paper to hand to Mr. Nash. We dined together at Mr. Savage's. After dinner, intending to set off for Beaufort, I called him out, and presented him the money. Inquiring how much it was, I told him five hundred dollars, the same as given to Mr. Avery, and with which that gentleman was perfectly satisfied. He returned the money, telling me he would rather compliment me with his services than take such a fee. I took the money, made a low bow, thanked him for his politeness, and went away. He was a good deal mortified afterwards when he found I had taken him at his word, and gave me several hints about the business, but I took no notice of them, and never gave him a farthing. I would have given him something, but he shamefully neglected the business.

After the condemnation of Clifford and Wells's ship, they applied to Council for the half by law coming to the Commonwealth. At the trial it was clearly proved that the owners were in no way whatever concerned in the smuggling, yet the jury, as the law stood, were obliged to condemn the ship. Council had power to remit fines and grant pardons, but could do nothing in case of forfeiture, a fine being a commutation for a corporal punishment, a forfeiture a resumption of property lost to the owner by breaches of the *municipal* law of society, which has in consequence of such breaches been passed from the owner to the community.

I had some time before this a difference with E——. He wanted me much to command his privateer Bellona. To induce me, he said he would go with me, and near where he formerly lived in Ireland he could load the brig in the night with linen from the bleaching yards. I told him no man but a thief would think of making money by such base means.

In the spring Mr. Stanley, of Newbern, fitted out a ship and several small vessels, of all which he offered me the consignment if I would take command of the ship, but as I found Mrs. Biddle was very much averse to it, and having no great inclination myself, I was easily persuaded to stay at home. I was afterwards sorry I had not gone, for they made a short voyage, sold their cargoes well, and arrived home to a great market.

One morning in April I was reading in the parlor, when a person looking in at the window, exclaimed, "By G—d, that is Biddle!" Looking up, I perceived it was my old friend, J. Allen. It gave me great pleasure to have this worthy man under my own roof. He had put in to get a supply of provisions, and inquiring who lived in the place, he was greatly surprised when he was informed I was one of the inhabitants. He stayed with me several days, and then went to

Wilmington. Poor fellow! he was much altered; he had lost a favorite child, which had almost deprived him of his senses. Although it was upwards of a year before the time he was with me, he could not mention it without being greatly affected. I did not then, but since have known, what he must have suffered.

In July Mr. Hodge concluded to send the Eclipse to the West Indies on freight. Some of my friends soon loaded her with tobacco for St. Thomas, and I agreed to join her. When we were nearly fitted a brig appeared off the Bar, which was said by some person on shore, that pretended to know her, to be a Letter of Marque belonging to New York, that had been before off the port. In expectation of bringing her in or driving her off the coast, I intended to go out in the Eclipse, and was waiting the tide to run at the Bar, to go over it, when Mr. Hodge returned from Newbern. He immediately sent off to request that I would not go out; if I did, and any accident happened, he should look to me for damages. This cooled me, and I returned to the old anchoring ground. We were afterwards informed she was one of the stoutest privateers belonging to New York, who, in all probability, would have carried us there.

When we were nearly ready to sail a small privateer was brought into Newbern by the privateer Bellona, belonging to that port. The crew were confined in gaol. Going to Newbern soon after, and wanting seamen, I went to gaol to see if any of them would enter on board the Eclipse. Thirty-seven, chiefly Irishmen, agreed to go with me. When I was taking them to the wharf on their way to Beaufort, Mr. John Owens, an honest Welshman, then a merchant of Newbern, who came with me from St. Eustatia, stopped me and informed me that one of the men going with me, of the name of Henderson, had agreed to go in a small sloop of his, and begged I would let him go with him. I told him Henderson had been a petty officer on board the privateer, understood navigation, appeared to be a fellow fit for anything, and probably would take the vessel from him, while with me he could do no mischief if inclined to do it. He said he was not the least afraid of that, upon which I let him go. It was my opinion that Owens had a passport or some protection from the British, for he was remarkably timid, and if he had not a protection would hardly have risked taking such a man as Henderson. The sloop was commanded by Capt. Gourling, now of Philadelphia. The day they went over the Bar, when about six leagues from the land, Henderson went aft to Owens and Capt. Gourling, who were on the quarter-deck, and told them the sloop was his, and they might go into the boat. He was followed by seven of the crew who had agreed to join him. They attempted to expostulate with Henderson, but he told them that it was in vain to say anything, and if they did not get immediately into the boat he would pitch them in. Owens and Gourling were obliged to go in, and they had like to have perished before they reached the shore. Just as they were pulling off Henderson called to them and told them he believed Capt. Biddle to be a clever fellow, that he therefore wished them to inform me that the men I took out of gaol had taken an oath that they would kill me as soon as the sloop was over the Bar, for that they did not expect they could get the sloop without putting me to death. It was expected Henderson would have gone into New York with the sloop, and Owens got a flag to go there, but she was not in New York. It was afterwards reported they went to Ireland; however, they never could hear any certain accounts of them. As soon as Owens reached Newbern he sent an express to inform me of the intention of my gaol birds. As I knew well that seamen generally, as well as other people, were they once well treated soon change any bad intentions they may have had, and as I had marines, who were most of them young men of respectable families, born about Beaufort, very stout, active, and resolute fellows who had been with me in the Cornelia, and would risk their lives for me, and knowing what discipline would do, I felt not the least uneasiness. If Owens had not sent to me, the manner in which I obtained these men would have made me cautious of them. The day before we sailed I had them all called aft, told them if they behaved well and did their duty cheerfully, they should be well treated and have everything that had been promised them, but if I found the least murmuring, or intention of making any disturbance on board the sloop they should be punished in the severest manner; and at the same time I ordered the marines that if any man when called to quarters was the least backwards, or did not do his duty in action, instantly to shoot him. As they knew this would be done it had a wonderful effect. Then ordering a drink of grog, they were dismissed; they gave three cheers, and swore they would do their duty faithfully. I believe it very seldom happens that there is a mutiny in a ship, or any disturbance, but the fault is with the officers. If the crew are not ill-treated, or, what is equally bad, too much indulged, are given what they are entitled to, and made to do their duty, it will seldom happen that a crew behave ill. From no men was less to be expected than from those I had taken from gaol, yet no men behaved better. When called, they were the first at their quarters; and if we had been brought to action I am convinced they would have fought well. From their behavior I believe they knew I was informed of what they had intended.

We sailed from Beaufort the 10th of August, 1779. The sloop drawing a great deal of water we struck hard upon the Bar, and I expected, as she was very weak in her bottom, she would have been stove. However, we got off without receiving any injury. We had the prize brig and some small vessels under our convoy. Near St. Thomas we fell in, at different times, with two or three small privateers, but none sufficiently strong to engage us. We arrived at St. Thomas without any accident. I sold my cargo to the Royal Danish Company, which at that time was just established. When I came to discharge it, to my great mortification, I found that a good deal of the tobacco was very much damaged, which could not have happened on board the sloop, for she did not leak. The company sent me word that as the tobacco was not merchantable they must return it. I waited on, and told them I was very sorry to find the tobacco not so good as it should be, but that it would be very bad policy in them, as I was

the first American from whom they had purchased, to dispute
about the cargo, that the Americans would then be afraid to
deal with them, whereas if they behaved generously and
friendly it would induce them always to give the company a
preference. After some consultation they agreed to take it.
I never went on the wharf when they were examining the
cargo, but it made me ashamed to think what trash I had
brought, and if the company had not purchased, it would not
have been sold. They behaved extremely well.

While lying here Mr. Bull, an inhabitant of Tortola, a
native of New England, who appeared warmly attached
to his country, came down to see if any of his countrymen
would engage to go upon an expedition against Tortola. He
complained of being ill-treated there because he was an
American and wished well to their cause. I inquired if he
had never given any occasion for being ill-treated. He declared he had not, but that he did say there and everywhere
that he wished well to the American cause. He reminded me
of a German servant woman of my mother's, who complained
of being beaten by her husband. My mother, knowing her
violent temper, said to her, " And, well, Katy, did you say
nothing to provoke your husband?" "No, Mistress, indeed I
did not. The worst words I said to him were that he was a
good-for-nothing scoundrel." Mr. Bull was of a warm temper,
and probably his ill-treatment was brought on him by his imprudence. Mine being the strongest American vessel in the
port, Bull was very desirous of my going. He said there
was hardly any person in the fort, that we could land a few
men and get possession of it, and then should command the
shipping. When I considered that Tortola was a place of rendezvous for privateers, and as I believed it could be very easily
taken, I had a great inclination to go, and for two or three
nights could not sleep for thinking of it. My officers were
all eager to go. However, when I reflected it would be
exceeding my instructions, and if any accident happened it
would be a great injury to my friend Hodge; and that setting such a crew as I should be obliged to take ashore, would

probably occasion the ruin and perhaps murder of some innocent people, I determined not to go.

The day before I sailed two of my gaol birds getting
drunk, deserted, and enlisted in the garrison. As we had
rather too few for our guns before, and there was a privateer
off the west end of the island said to be waiting for us, I
waited on the Governor, who had treated me with great politeness upon a former occasion, to endeavor to get the men back ;
but when he knew my errand he told me they should not be
delivered up, that they were not my countrymen, and they
had a right to enlist. It was in vain to argue with him. I
therefore shipped two others. When cleared out and ready
for sea I dropped down abreast of the fort and hoisted American colors. This was what they had refused to allow us,
and we were obliged to hoist a white flag. They soon hailed
me from the fort, "Haul down them colors." Upon my
refusing they threatened to sink me ; but I knew their guns
were out of powder, and therefore disregarded all they said,
keeping my colors up and drum a-beating until the afternoon,
when we weighed and stood out of the harbor. When
almost clear of it a black Curaçao man, whom I had shipped
in the room of one of the men who had deserted, jumped
overboard and swam on shore. I made some of the marines
fire ahead of him to frighten him, but he dived, and seemed
to regard their firing as little as I did the threats of the
officers in the fort. Off the west end of the island we discovered the privateer said to be waiting for us. She was
close in with the land, and did not show any inclination to
come out, with which I was full as well pleased as I should
have been to see her bear down upon us.

Nothing material happened until we got on the coast, when,
on the 17th of September, we had a violent gale of wind, or
rather hurricane, in which we all expected the sloop would
have foundered. She worked very much, and we could
hardly keep her free. Two days after this, we made the land
a few miles to the southwest of Beaufort. In the afternoon we
could plainly see the town. As the wind was ahead and we
could not get in that night with the sloop, I was resolved

to go ashore in the boat. Notwithstanding Captain Tucker
and some other passengers begged me not to attempt it, that
I ran a great risk of being lost with all that were with me,
finding several of the crew, who lived in Beaufort, as anxious
to go as myself, I picked out five that could swim and row
well, and put off in a whaleboat. The passengers took leave
of me as if they never expected to see me again. As we
drew near the shore, we found there was a dreadful surf.
We stood some distance to the southward, to try to find a
better place to land, but it was tremendous everywhere.
And now I believe every man in the boat secretly wished
himself on board the sloop; for my own part, I most fervently
did, but we were so far to leeward, that had we attempted
to reach the vessel, we could not have done it before night,
and it was mortifying to think of it. Finding it in vain to
stand further to leeward, and night approaching, with dark,
cloudy weather, I pretended to see a smooth place abreast of
us, and pushed in for the beach. Expecting we should have
to swim, when near, I ordered them to lie on their oars, and
pull off their jackets, and did the same myself. Just as I
had my jacket off, and was taking hold of the oar to steer her,
a sea broke with great violence on board, and filled the boat.
It was some time before I could recollect myself, when looking around, I could see the people hanging on the boat. I intended at first to swim to them, but seeing a heavy sea coming,
I put before it, and was so long under that I never expected
to rise. It threw me on the beach, but so much spent that
it was with great difficulty I could scramble out of reach of
the sea. The boat's crew staid by her until she reached the
shore, one of them so far gone, that it was with much difficulty we could get him out of the surf. We had now seven
miles to walk before we came to a house, and were obliged to
help the young man who was so much exhausted. When
we reached the house they had nothing to cross the sound in
but an old canoe. It is from here, I believe, near eight miles
to Beaufort. Taking three of the stoutest men with me we
embarked, and about two o'clock in the morning reached
Beaufort, almost dead with hunger and fatigue. We lost

our boat, oars, and jackets.   At daylight I was awakened by the sloop firing a salute.   She had got up with the Bar in the night, and the tide answering, she came in as soon as it was broad daylight.

The day I sailed for St. Thomas, Mr. Hodge set off for Philadelphia, and did not return for some time after my arrival.   He brought me the first account I had of the loss of my brother Edward.   Mr. James Read, then a member of the Supreme Executive Council, and who knew him from his infancy, gave a character of him in Dunlap's paper of the 9th of September, 1779, which he justly merited.   He says:

"On Thursday last, after a very lingering illness, died at Baltimore, in the forty-first year of his age, that great lawyer, the Honorable Edward Biddle, Esqr., of Reading in this State.   In early life as a captain in our Provincial forces, his military virtues so highly distinguished him that Congress designed him to high rank in the American army, which, however, his sickness prevented.   His practice at the bar for years having made his great abilities and integrity known, the county of Berks unanimously elected him one of their representatives in Assembly, who soon made him their Speaker and a Delegate in Congress.   And the conduct of this patriot did honor to their choice.   As in public character very few were equal to him in talents, or in noble exertions of them, so in private life, the son, the husband, the father, brother, friend, neighbor, and master, had in him a pattern not to be excelled.   Love to his country, benevolence, and every manly virtue, rendered him an object of esteem and admiration to all that knew him."

The 6th of October, 1779, Mrs. Biddle was delivered of a son, whom I called after my brother Nicholas.*

At this time, being every day liable to an attack, I persuaded the people of the town and neighborhood to build a small fort.   We all worked at it, and soon made a tolerably good one.   There were four six pounders belonging to the United States which we mounted in it.   Mr. Ellis, the Con-

---

* This child died in infancy.

tinental agent, when he heard these guns were mounted, sent for them; but as I knew they were wanted much more at Beaufort than at Newbern, I refused to let them go until we had orders from the Board of War.* Ellis threatened to sue me, but upon my writing to him he thought better of it.

Mr. Hodge having agreed to send the sloop as a flag of truce to New Providence, a great many prisoners were sent from Newbern to go in her. These people, with the English and Irish seamen belonging to our vessels, were frequently making disturbances, and we had one inhabitant of the place as bad as any of them. This man, under pretence of his being afraid of an attack, had a pair of four pounders mounted in his piazza, and frequently in the night, when drunk, would fire them off to the great disturbance of the peaceable people of the town. I spoke to Col. Bell, and told him, as he commanded the militia, he should put a stop to Capt. Gibbons's firing; that if I had the command of the militia, the town should be kept in better order. Bell was a very worthy man, but of too easy a temper to command such a man as Gibbons. He said he did not know what to do with him, he had often talked with him, and he had promised to behave better; but when drunk, there was no doing anything with him, he was a perfect madman. He would, however, try again what could be done. The method he took to try again "what could be done," was to get me appointed captain of the town company of militia. Although this was an appointment by no means agreeable to me, knowing myself not qualified for it, yet after what had passed between Col. Bell and myself, I was determined not to shrink from it, but to do everything in my

---

* The Secretary of the Board of War, Richard Peters, Esq., is an old friend of mine, and remarkable for his wit. The Board wanted to remove Robert Morris, Esq., from the office of Financier, and Col. Grayson, one of the Board, requested Peters to join them. After reading the memorial, he told Grayson if they would strike out one word, he would sign the paper. They were much pleased, and declared they would alter, not only any word, but any paragraph he objected to. "Well," says Peters, "in this memorial you very often have, 'this Board complains,' strike out the word 'board,' and put in the word 'shingle,' and I will sign it directly."

power to prevent any further disturbance in the town. I therefore accepted the commission, and having mustered the company, most of whom were very orderly men, who were pleased with my being their captain, and who I believe recommended the matter to Bell, I told them that in the exposed situation we were in, it was necessary for preservation that we should live in harmony with each other, that everything in my power should be done to promote the peace of the town, and if any disturbance was made, the person or persons who made it should be punished as far as I could punish them, whoever he or they were. After enlarging on our situation, I gave them a drink and dismissed them. Soon after I called upon Gibbons, and told him he would oblige me by taking the guns out of his piazza. After some persuasion he agreed to it, but with a very ill grace, and when I left him did not appear satisfied. In the evening, going by his door, he called me in. Believing the man capable of attempting anything, I was upon my guard, and as at that time we were under some apprehension of an attack by the prisoners, I never went anywhere without pocket pistols. When entering the house, I drew one so far out as to let him see it. There was a pair of large pistols on the table, which convinced me he had some bad design, and I was determined if he took up one of them to try for the first fire. His wife (who was a Miss Robinson, a very good young woman, who was frequently in the night obliged to run out of the house, when she always came to my house for protection, which perhaps was one cause of his dislike for me) was sitting by the fire. He ordered her in a surly tone to leave the room. Having no confidence in the man, I then expected we should try our skill, and I wished some person present to see fair play. He was about half drunk, and perceiving that I watched him narrowly, he appeared sullen and confused. After some time he roused himself, and asked me to drink some gin, declaring at the same time he had a regard for me, and as we were the only masters of vessels in the town, we should live in friendship with one another; that he knew I thought myself much above him, but he would

9

sooner die than be treated with contempt by any person
whatever. I told him it would give me pleasure to be on
good terms with him, that it depended entirely on himself
whether we were, or were not; that he had no reason to suppose I considered myself above him, or treated him with
contempt. After some further conversation we parted, to all
appearance on better terms than we ever had been. The
next day there was a disturbance on board one of the vessels
in the harbor. The captain fearing, as he afterwards said,
he should be murdered, had secured himself in the cabin,
from whence he hailed a coaster lying near him, and begged
the master to inform the people on shore of his situation.
Upon hearing of it, I took some of the company and went off.
When we were near, one of the crew hailed us and swore we
should not come on board. I ordered the boat to row alongside, and told the fellow that hailed, if they made any resistance
they should have no quarter. When I went on board the crew
were mostly drunk. The one who appeared the ringleader,
coming up behind me would have struck me with a handspike, and probably killed me, but for a stout young man
who caught hold of him and took the handspike from him,
declaring at the same time in broad Scotch, that no man on
board should hurt Capt. Biddle. Hearing us upon deck, the
captain came out of the cabin, when the crew and captain
began to accuse each other of behaving ill. Upon inquiring
of the young Scotchman, whose name was Smith, I found the
captain had not behaved well, and the crew worse. After
going into the cabin, and giving my advice and opinion to the
captain, speaking to the crew, and taking the fellow who
attempted to strike me, and who the captain said was the
occasion of all the disturbance, I went ashore.

Returning home one very dark night from a neighbor's
with Mrs. Biddle, we met several of the prisoners armed
with clubs. Having a servant with a lantern, I knew one
we met to have been a lieutenant of a privateer, of the name
of Rankin. Calling to him by name, I told him it was time
he was in his hammock. In an insolent manner he answered,
" Yes it is, and time you were at home." When we got into

the house I found one of my company. He told me he believed the prisoners intended to do some mischief. I sent him with orders to bring as many of the company as he could. We soon mustered about a dozen well armed. We then sallied out, and one of the first men we met was Rankin, who, with a few others, was secured and put in gaol. The rest dispersed. Two days afterwards, in the evening, one of the inhabitants came running into my house much alarmed, and told me a large mob of sailors were collected on the shore and were marching up towards my house. I directed him to go up in the town (mine being the first house as you entered from the eastward) and desire all the men he met to get their arms and come to me. As soon as the sailors came about my house I observed at the head of them one Knox, one of the fellows I had taken out of the Newbern gaol to go to St. Thomas's. Going up to him with a pair of pistols in my hands, I inquired what they wanted. He told me they did not intend to injure any person, much less me, but they wanted Lieutenant Rankin, and the others who were put in gaol with him. While I was in the midst of them telling Knox, who was a good-tempered fellow, the consequences of what he was about, as he was considered as an American, Gibbons fired twice. I believe his intention was to have hit me; however he did no injury. Many of the town company collecting, and seeing me among the seamen, came up and Gibbons with them. The sailors then threw down their clubs and surrendered. As many of them were drunk we concluded it would be best to put them all in gaol for the night and in the morning let them all out but the ringleaders. Among the sailors I was much surprised to find Smith. Inquiring how he came amongst them, he declared he only came with them to try to prevent their doing any mischief, and he begged I would not let him be sent to gaol with such a set of wretches. Having a particular regard for the lad from his behavior before, and believing what he said true, I sent one of the company with him to my house, and desired him to stay there until my return. After seeing the sailors in gaol, and a guard placed over them, I returned home in

company with Gibbons, who declared he thought the sailors
had made me their prisoner or he should not have fired.
But nothing he could now say could do away with the suspicion I entertained of him. When at home I sent for Smith
and found, on conversing with him, he was a sensible, intelligent young man. Inquiring how he came to know me, for
he had called me by name the first time I recollected seeing
him, he told me he had seen me on shore, and from the likeness to my brother Nicholas inquired who I was. He said
the name of Captain Biddle was very dear to him, he never
heard it without bringing to remembrance my brother, who
had taken him in a ship from Scotland with troops when he
commanded the Andrea Doria; that my brother took him
and another lad, Daniel McCoy, as his cabin boys and treated
them with the greatest kindness; that Daniel was a fifer, and
not wishing to go to sea, my brother had him bound, with his
consent, to a house carpenter; that he left the Andrea Doria
and went in a merchant vessel and had continued in one ever
since until he heard of the loss of the Randolph. He had
always been wishing he had continued with my brother,
whom he should ever remember as being his best friend.
What he mentioned respecting Daniel I knew to be true, and
I had no reason to doubt anything he told me. His narrative affected me very much and increased my desire to serve
him. Although greatly fatigued when I lay down, which
was about ten o'clock, the thought of what Smith had mentioned of my brother—that brother who was so dear to my
heart—kept me from sleeping. About eleven o'clock, hearing some person go out of the back part of the house, I
called to know who it was. Smith answered me; he told
me he had left some things in the boat, and, as all was now
quiet, he would go and get them, for he was afraid in the
morning they would be stolen. I desired him to make haste
back, and half an hour after he was gone, hearing a violent
noise at the front door, I inquired who was there and what
was the matter. A man answered he was "Fuller" (this
was one of the company that knew Smith), that he came to
inform me Gibbons had shot Smith, who begged to see me.

I went immediately to the gaol, without waiting to put on my clothes, and found it was true. I had him taken from the gaol to the nearest house, and sent for an English surgeon who happened to be at Beaufort. It appeared the ball had gone in at his breast and lodged in his back. It was cut out, and the surgeon gave me some hope of his recovery. Poor Smith did not think there was any. Upon inquiring how he came to be in gaol, he told me that returning from the boat to my house he unfortunately met Gibbons, who was going on guard at the gaol. Gibbons inquired where he was going. He told him to my house. Gibbons said he lied, and should go to gaol. He requested Gibbons to go with him to my house, which was not a hundred yards away, and he would be convinced that what he told him was true. Gibbons swore he would not disturb me at such an hour, and, being armed, made the poor fellow go with him. When Smith was in gaol he told Gibbons that it was very hard a quiet, peaceable man should be put in gaol by him who was continually disturbing the town. Gibbons swore if he repeated what he said he would shoot him, and upon Smith saying what he had said of him was true the cruel ruffian shot him. Business obliging me to go the next day to Newbern, before my departure I called on Smith, who appeared better. I gave directions that he should want for nothing during my absence. He told me he did not expect ever to get up, and that he considered Gibbons as his murderer. When I looked at the young man, and considered the manner in which he had been brought into a situation that if he lived he could hardly expect to be a hearty man, I could not help execrating Gibbons. He heard of what I said of him from a relation of his wife who was present, and, just as I was setting off sent a note informing me he was unwell or he would have called on me, and begged to see me; that he could convince me that he was not only justifiable but right in what he had done. I sent him word that only *one message* from him would induce me to see him; nothing he could possibly say would alter my opinion; that his conduct was unmanly and brutal; that upon my return from Newbern he or myself must leave Beaufort. After being two days in Newbern I had an account of the death of poor Smith, who went off with great composure. Upon my return to Beaufort I found Mr. Parrot, father to Gibbons's wife, had managed to get himself and some of the crew of Gibbons's vessel and a few poor people, who I have no doubt he bribed, to be a jury for the coroner, and had a verdict returned of accidental death. Being determined not to let the matter pass in this manner I had the body taken up, and respectable people put on the jury, who brought in their verdict, wilful murder. Gibbons, hearing this, and that I was applying for a warrant to apprehend him, went off and did not return to Beaufort. This murder broke up his family and ended in his ruin.

At this time many of the young men who had been to sea with me, with their relations and friends, called upon me to know if I would serve in the Assembly. They wanted to leave out Col. Thompson; who had long been their representative, as he was thought by them not to be so much attached to the Revolution as he should be. I told them that as it was not my intention to go to sea soon, if they elected me, I would serve. A meeting was called for the purpose, and my friends having proposed me, they unanimously agreed to run me, and I was elected by a very large majority. Mrs. Biddle and myself had a very pressing invitation from Mrs. and Mr. Jones, of Newbern, to stay with them during the sitting of the Assembly. Mr. Jones was a native of Pennsylvania, but had been settled for some time in Newbern, as a merchant. Mrs. Jones was born in Carolina; her maiden name was Blackledge, and a more amiable, worthy woman never lived. We were received by them, and treated during our stay with the utmost kindness and hospitality. The evening we got there, Mr. Jones had a number of his friends to sup with him, among others, Mr. ———, the Speaker of the House of Assembly. When Mr. Jones introduced me to him as his friend, who had come to attend the sessions, he asked me what county I was from. This was what I could not tell him, and was obliged to apply to Jones to know. This, as may be supposed, caused a good deal of laughing, not only in the company, but all over the town and with the members of the House, for the Speaker took care to tell the story wherever he went. Living in the town of Beaufort, I thought it was the County of Beaufort that I represented, but the county in which Beaufort is the county town is called Cartaret.

Shortly after the sessions began, there was a report of a British privateer being within the Bar, and doing a good deal of mischief. I was dining with Governor Nash (my lawyer in the case of the prize) when it was first mentioned. I told him if the report was confirmed, I would fit out one of the vessels at the wharf and go down, and endeavor to bring her up. There was at the table a large company, a good many of whom declared they would go with me. Early the next day we had a confirmation of the report. I immediately waited on the Governor and had his directions to fit out a sloop and a schooner. As they did not want much, and we had a good many hands, by four o'clock in the afternoon they were both ready to sail. I then sent a note to each of the gentlemen who had promised to go with me, but they all, except Mr. Spaight (afterwards Governor of North Carolina) and Mr. Blackledge, made excuses. Some were sick, others had particular business; one of them, who had always behaved like a brute to his wife, sent me word she would not consent to his going. He was the only one I sent a second time to, and that was to inform him that I would call up and endeavor to persuade his wife to let him go. Fearing that I would, and knowing his wife would readily consent to his going anywhere, so that she was rid of him, he rode out of town. As there were a good many vessels in port, I went round to them and soon procured as many volunteers as I wanted. In the evening we went down the river. Going down at night, I was telling an honest Irish friend, Mr. Michael Falvey, who went with me, about the promises made at the Governor's table, and mentioning the persons who had declined going after giving their word that they would. From his long residence in Newbern he knew them all, particularly the one who had sent word his wife would not let him go, which he laughed very much at, declaring he knew he had several times beat her, and that she detested the sight of him. "Faith," says he, "I wish you had told me all this before we set off. The devil a bit of Falvey would have come. What the devil business have you or me upon such an expedition when these people decline. We have nothing to lose by the privateer, let her do what she will. In my opinion we had better go back." I told him, probably we had better not have embarked, but as we had, we must do what we could to clear the coast of this robber, who otherwise would plunder, and perhaps murder some of the innocent people on the coast. He was not altogether reconciled, but he knew he could not get back. However, as he was a cheerful, good tempered fellow, he soon was satisfied, or at least appeared so. I have generally found the Irish generous, friendly, open, candid, and sincere; warm in their attachments, and active in support of their friends. You will seldom find one that is a coward, or a miser, but most of them make bad husbands; they are too fond of rambling, negligent of their affairs, and their hospitality frequently occasions their drinking when they are not dry. However, I have known many who were the best of husbands, of fathers, and friends.

The day after we left the wharf, early in the morning I had all hands mustered to quarters and exercised them, when to my great surprise I found among the crew that belonged to the vessel before my taking the command of her, my old acquaintance, Henry White, the identical Henry White who ran away from me in Portugal, and whom I afterwards caught attempting to commit a robbery and murder in the Delaware. Going up to him I inquired where he had been since his adventure with the shallop-man. He had a patch on one side of his face, and I believe expected I should not have recollected him, but so strong an impression had his former behavior made on me, that I should have known him in any disguise. He requested to speak to me by myself. When alone, he said he must acknowledge he had been a very bad fellow, that too much indulgence from the most affectionate of parents had been the cause of his behaving so ill, that he had often wished he had followed the advice I gave him when he went with me to Portugal; he had suffered severely for his misconduct, which he begged me not to mention, declaring I should never hear of his acting improperly again, that no man in the vessel would do more to serve me than he would. Although I had not much confidence in what he said, but as mentioning his tricks would injure him, and perhaps drive him to the commission of some crime, I told him it depended altogether upon himself; if he behaved well, nothing would be said by me against him, but he must be on his guard, for if I discovered his doing or attempting anything wrong, he should be punished with the utmost severity. I inquired about him of the captain he had been last with, who was then on board. He told me he had been with him for six months, and behaved very well. He was very thankful for my promise, and declared for the future he would do his duty and behave to my satisfaction. In the afternoon we spoke a pilot going up. He told us the privateer was a small sloop, had but six guns and twenty-five men, that she was commanded by a Capt. Slough or Slow, an old privateer's man, and belonged to New York; that Slough was a very daring refugee. As our sloop sailed heavy I was determined to send her back, and only take the same number of hands in the schooner that the privateer had. Taking no more than twenty-five was very wrong, but it was the wish of Spaight, Blackledge, and some others, and I was determined to indulge them. I picked my men, they were all young, stout, active, and resolute. Notwithstanding all his promises White was not numbered among the picked men. Falvey being anxious to be at Newbern I let him return in the sloop, although it was with reluctance I parted with him. As to White, in case of coming to action, I should have been more apprehensive of him than of an enemy.

After sending back the sloop, we proceeded to the Bar, and cruised near it for several days without gaining any intelligence respecting the privateer. We, however, at last discovered a vessel coming out of Neuse Harbor, that answered the description we had of her. As our vessel was a coaster

I intended, if possible, to deceive them, therefore putting some lumber on our guns, of which we had but two, and sending all hands below but one man and a boy, we stood on as if bound into the harbor expecting she would run alongside without being prepared. My crew sat about the hatchway, each well prepared for boarding. When we were within half a mile of her, a squall came on and lasted a considerable time. When it cleared away we could see nothing of the privateer. We stood into Neuse Harbor, where we lay that night. A day or two afterwards we went to the Bar, where we understood that Slough being informed that some vessels were fitted out against him, had gone over the Bar. We then returned to Newbern, having been absent about two weeks, during which time we had an agreeable cruise, excepting one day that it blew hard and we had nearly been lost. We received the thanks of the Governor, which was certainly a sufficient reward.

A short time before we left Beaufort to come up to Newbern, Mr. Joseph Biddle, son of my eldest brother, James, came to my house. He was a lad his father had sent with me in the Charming Nancy, intending him for the sea. He had gone from Philadelphia in a sloop for Hispaniola, and was taken. On his return, near Cape Hatteras, they put five hands on board, leaving none belonging to the sloop but himself and a boy, and, in fact, he himself was only a boy. They had a gale of wind the day after they were taken, which drove them in sight of land, and but for the wind suddenly shifting to the northwest they would have been wrecked. Here they beat for several days, when one very cold morning, watching an opportunity when the prize crew were all below but a lad that was at the helm, they secured them down, took possession of the sloop, and bore away for Ocracock, intending to go in there, but at 1 P. M. they fell in with a cruiser. Finding they had no way of escaping but by running on shore they stood in for the land, and a little to the northward of Ocracock, about three o'clock in the afternoon, ran her on shore. The first thing they did was to let out the prisoners, the next the young captain did, was to get his chest, in which he had concealed a sum of money, on shore. In this he was assisted by the inhabitants who had come down to the beach when they saw the sloop chased on shore. The privateer stood very near the land, intending probably to board the sloop. She fired a number of shot, one of which went through my nephew's chest as he and another person were carrying it up the beach. This was all the mischief their firing did. In the night it came on to blow hard, and in the morning the sea ran so high that they could not board the sloop, and before night she went to pieces. Being loaded with sugar they saved none of her cargo. What little of the stores and rigging that were saved my nephew sold to the people that assisted him, and who had behaved exceedingly well. He got to Newbern, and having remitted to his owners the proceeds of what he had saved, came to me at Beaufort. I was very glad to have it in my power to do anything for the son of such a brother, particularly for him who had sailed with me, and whom I knew to be a very good youth. To get him the command I took a concern in a fine schooner that had made a voyage in company with me when I went to St. Thomas in the Eclipse. Upon my going up to Newbern to take my seat in the Legislature, I left him to fit her out. Some of those who had been in her before, telling him the foremast was too small, he had a new one made. This was put in green from the wood, and was much too large. The size I did not know until she sailed, or she should not have gone out with it. I went to Beaufort when she was near ready, and was there when she sailed, bound to St. Eustatia. It was a fine pleasant morning, the wind fair and moderate. The crew were all sober men, belonging to the town, all of whom had been with me, either in the Cornelia or Eclipse. They went from before my door in high spirits, expecting to be back in a few weeks, but none of them ever returned. I suppose that all of them perished that night in the Gulf Stream, for although the wind was fair, it blew hard in the night. The wind continued fair for several days after they sailed, and we concluded they would have a fine passage. While their friends and relations were rejoicing at the con-

tinuance of the fair weather, they, I suppose, were all buried
in the deep.

About a month after the sailing of this schooner, another
son of my brother James (William) came to my house. He
was a very different lad from his brother — he was stout,
active, and strong. He valued himself upon his strength, and
being of a fiery temper, I found he had been in a good many
scrapes. The war having prevented my brother from settling
him to any business, he had contracted an acquaintance with
some young officers, with whom he had been guilty of an imprudent act, which his father threatening to punish him for,
he set off from Reading with some young Carolina officers,
and came with them to Newbern, and from thence to me at
Beaufort. He very ingenuously confessed to me that he had
behaved improperly, and was much affected when I spoke to
him about leaving his parents in the manner he had done,
when he must have been well assured, had he requested it,
they would have consented to his coming to me, and furnished him with everything necessary for his journey, and as
there was nothing dishonorable in his conduct, would soon
have forgiven him. The officers with whom he had travelled
were anxious he should have joined their regiment, and had
he wished it, I would have endeavored to have procured him
an ensigncy, but he preferred the sea, which I thought much
the best for him; for in any country I considered the army
as a poor employment, and in no country worse than ours.
Had our army been in want of officers, I should, from regard
to my country, have advised him to have gone into it, but
we were in want of privates. William sang remarkably well,
which I believe was one cause of his getting into bad habits.
I have known several very promising young men ruined by
their singing well. Their company will always be courted,
and if not very careful of themselves, they will become dis-
sipated and worthless.

Having at this time a concern in a sloop nearly ready to
sail, commanded by Capt. Hunter, who was married in, and
belonged to, Philadelphia, William wished to go in her, and

knowing Hunter to be a very sober, careful man, and a good seaman, I consented. They were bound to Curaçao, and were to go from thence to Philadelphia, where I expected to meet her. But nothing was ever heard of the vessel or crew after she sailed from Beaufort.

The very slight manner in which our small vessels were built at that time, particularly in the Southern States, occasioned the loss of many lives. Many of the vessels that were sent to sea were not sufficiently secured to sail with safety in a river.

Before the sessions ended, Mrs. Biddle went to her Aunt Smith's, on Swift Creek, about four miles from Newbern, to spend some days with her. While she was there, Mr. Smith sent every evening a servant with a horse, to the ferry on Neuse River, to wait for me. One evening before we landed, it began to thunder, and a gust coming on, the servant not perceiving me in the ferry-boat, and supposing, as it was late, I would not cross that night, set off with the horse. As he was in sight when we landed, I ran after him about a mile, when the rain coming on, he galloped off as fast as he could. Finding it to no purpose to continue the chase, I gave it over, and walked towards the plantation. The running had put me in a great heat and profuse perspiration, but the heavy rain soon cooled me. When about a mile and a half from Mr. Smith's, there is a path that takes off to it, and shortens the distance considerably. This path I took, and continued on it for some time, but before I could reach the gate, it came on very dark, with repeated and heavy claps of thunder, and the rain fell in torrents. After wandering about a considerable time, finding myself groping about to no purpose, I sat down under a large tree, laying my hanger down at a distance, fearing it would attract the lightning. In this disagreeable situation I remained from half past eight until near three in the morning, when the rain ceasing, and the moon, which had risen a little before, shining out, I got up and looking round me, perceived the gate that led to Mr. Smith's house close by me, the branches of the tree I had been sitting under all night spreading over it. Sitting with my back to the gate prevented my seeing it when it lightened. The gate was not a hundred yards from the house. During the night the old proverb was brought to my mind, that "the farthest way round was the shortest way home," and I made up my mind to be very cautious of taking short cuts. Had I continued in the great road, I should have got to the house before nine o'clock, with only a wet skin; which, if a person is well rubbed and dried, I believe to be as wholesome, or perhaps more so, than any other cold bath. An old friend of mine, who is a remarkably healthy man, will frequently put on old clothes, and walk in the rain until he gets wet to the skin. I have known him walk in his yard when it rained hard, without his hat, from which he thought he received great benefit.

Being naturally active (so much so that it was a remark of my friends, that they could never get me to sit for half an hour), sitting so long as we did in the Legislature was a most disagreeable thing to me, and what made it much more so than it otherwise would have been, was the frequent disputes between the members from the western and those from the eastern parts of the State. This I believe to be the case in all the States in the Union. Those from the westward look upon the people in any of the commercial towns, as little better than swindlers; while those of the east consider the western members as a pack of savages. In their debates, instead of using the language of persuasion, which should always be done in a Legislature, they were continually abusing each other. A stranger hearing the debates would never have supposed they were sent there to serve the State. Before we adjourned, we agreed to emit a very large sum of paper money; and so much of it was in circulation before I left Newbern that I was obliged to give two dollars of this money for one Continental dollar. Every person of reflection must at this time have been convinced that the paper money would cease passing very soon. A good old Tory, that lived near Newbern, and whom I frequently jested about his attachment to England, a country he had never seen, and knew very little about, told me, when we adjourned, that this was the best time he ever knew, for he could get a dollar for an English half-penny. I never felt the least angry with any of these people for their attachment to Great Britain; on political subjects every man has a right to enjoy his own opinion, and provided he does no mischief, should not be disturbed. A number of people at this time, afraid of being drafted in the militia, pretended to be Quakers, and joined the Meeting. As this was likely to be attended with serious consequences, we were obliged to put a stop to it, by suffering none to be excused that did not belong to the Meeting before the war. Several about Beaufort had been received into the Meeting that were the most profligate fellows in the country. In Virginia, I believe, the Quakers were not excused from militia duty, and even in Philadelphia I have seen some of them dragged up with the troops; but it answered no good purpose, for nothing that could be done to them would make them learn the manual exercise, much more make them fight. It is very cruel to force such men to the field.

At this time several of my old friends and acquaintances passed through Newbern on their way to join the army in South Carolina, among others Major John Stewart (who was known in the army by the appellation of Crazy Jack Stewart) and Major Lucas. Stewart was a native of Maryland, son of a respectable ship builder on West River, who had spared no expense in his education. He was in Smallwood's Battallion at Elizabethtown when I was there in Dickinson's Regiment. It was here we became first acquainted. He afterwards distinguished himself at the Battle of Long Island and at the storming of Stony Point.* He told me that at the attack of this place they were directed where to enter by the fire of the British, and that if the British had not fired a shot the fort would never have been taken. He was a stout, handsome man. A tailor who lived at this time in Newbern had given great offence to many of the inhabitants by his insolent behavior. As he was a strong man he thought he could say

* Stewart led the forlorn hope at the taking of Stony Point, and received a medal from Congress for conspicuous gallantry on that occasion.

anything with impunity. Stewart sent his servant to this
man with some cloth to make a coat. The tailor, who had
before measured him, sent word there was not enough.
Stewart sent the servant back to inform him that he had a
coat made in Philadelphia with less. The tailor told him to
tell Major Stewart he did not believe him. I was dining
with Stewart when the servant delivered this insolent message. "Go back, William," says Stewart, with great calm-
ness, "and tell him as soon as I have dined I will call and
horsewhip him." After dinner, taking a horsewhip in his
hand, he walked down, perfectly cool, to the tailor's, and,
hauling him out of the house, with one hand held him, and
with the other whipped him until he roared like a bull, to
the great diversion of a number of people that his cries had
assembled, not one of whom offered to interfere. After he
had tired himself, he left the poor tailor, advising him in
future to behave with more complaisance to the officers of
the army, a piece of advice I believe he took care to observe.
He intended to have sued Stewart, but, as some of his
acquaintances told him if he took out a writ against Stewart,
he would certainly shoot him, he thought it best to drop it.
I admired Stewart much. When speaking he had more the
air and manner of an Indian warrior* than any person I ever

---

* I have ever had a favorable opinion of the Indians. They are accused
of cruelty, but I have been told by many of the commissioners that were
employed to treat with them, that when accused of any act of cruelty, they
would tell of some act of cruelty committed by the whites that occasioned it.
Mr. McClay, one of the commissioners, told me that when he mentioned to
one of the chiefs his cruelty in burning Col. Crawford, "Why, yes," the
chief said, "that was very cruel; but," continued he, "a party of these
people came to the town where I lived, when all the men were away hunting, they drove my wife and nine children into my house and burnt them.
This was cruel too." Would not the mildest Christian torture wretches
guilty of such a crime? I believe in this business Col. Crawford was not
concerned. My brother Edward, who had been a considerable time among
the Indians, had a very good opinion of them. When they promise you
their protection they will suffer any death to prevent your being injured.
My brother, when in the army, was sent on an expedition with an Indian
warrior. He was dressed and painted as an Indian. They were one day
in danger of falling into the hands of the enemy. The chief told him, with

met with. His speeches at this time were made to induce
the people here to assist their brethren of South Carolina.
This young man (he was not more than twenty-five years of
age), after being in all the considerable actions fought this
war in America, in a frolic in South Carolina rode down a
hill that it was thought impossible he could have done, without killing both himself and his horse, without receiving
the least injury. On the day after, he was riding slowly on a
level piece of ground and good road, when his horse stumbled
and he fell with such violence that he fractured his skull
and died instantly. He often told me he hoped never to
live to be an old man.

Although very anxious to be in Pennsylvania, to see my
relations and friends there, particularly my mother, who
wrote in the most pressing manner for me to visit her, I
thought it would be improper to go without taking my chance
of being drafted in the militia ordered out to join the Continental army. I therefore went to Beaufort and drew with
the captains of Col. Bell's regiment, determined, if the lot
fell on me, to go wherever we should be ordered. Our names
were all put in a hat, and the first drawn were to march with
the men drafted from the regiment. Fortunately my name
was not among the first drawn, and now having nothing to
prevent my setting off, I took leave of my friends at Beaufort, and about the last of May left it for Newbern. Mrs.
Biddle and myself were in a chair. Our child we left in the
care of its grandmother. We had two servants, one of whom
rode in a good chair, the other upon a good saddle horse, so
that we could change occasionally, and this is a very good
way of travelling. If we had been in a carriage we should
have been plagued crossing the creeks, where the bridges are
frequently carried away. About a mile from the town, hearing a noise behind, I looked round and found it was made

every token of regard, "not to be the least uneasy about being tortured, for
the moment you are taken, I will tomahawk you."—AUTHOR'S NOTE.

Colonel Crawford, who commanded in the unfortunate expedition to San-
dusky, in 1782, was made a prisoner, and after being cruelly tortured was
burnt at the stake.

10

by a little sister of Mrs. Biddle, about eight years of age, who was crying and running after us. She was almost fainting when she came up. She declared she could not part with her sister, it would be the death of her to take her from her sister. As we intended to stay a few days at her Aunt Smith's, I thought it best to take her with us, and indeed we could not do otherwise. We took her in the chair, and sent a servant back to inform her mother. At Newbern, among others, I called on Governor Nash to take leave of him. When I was going away he put into my hands a paper which he said would probably be of some service to me on my journey. This I found was a certificate, which is now by me. The following is a copy of it:—

STATE OF NORTH CAROLINA, *ss.*

I do hereby certify to all whom it may concern that the bearer hereof, Charles, Biddle, Esquire, hath upon all occasions during the present war distinguished himself for his bravery and attachment to the cause of America; and having occasion to go to Philadelphia, I do by these presents recommend him to the notice and protection of the citizens of the United States. Given under my hand and private seal at Newbern, this 31st day of May, Anno Domini 1780.

A. NASH.

This was saying too much, and what I did not expect from Governor Nash, as we had not been on very good terms after the trial of the Eclipse prize cause.

On the first of June, 1780, we left Newbern for Pennsylvania, intending to return in five or six months; however, we have not yet, June, 1802, made up our minds when we shall return. We went from Newbern to Col. Smith's, Mrs. Biddle's uncle. The third of June we left his hospitable house, and the next day went to Col. Blount's, father of Mr. William Blount,* who made so much noise afterwards, when he was

---

* William Blount became Governor of the territory south of the Ohio in 1790. In 1796, he was elected U. S. Senator for Tennessee, and in 1797 was impeached by the House of Representatives on a charge that he was im-

a Senator of the United States. This son, with several others, was then at home celebrating the marriage of a relation of theirs with Mr. Richard Blackledge, who had been with me in the Cornelia, and cruising with me for the New York privateer. His sister, Mrs. Jones, Major Stewart, and Lucas, were also here. At this time no family were more respectable than Col. Blount's, and I believe Mr. William Blount would never have acted in the manner he did, if he had not been very much distressed and embarrassed in consequence of his land speculations. He had married a very amiable woman, who was at this time with him. Stewart rendered the same service to many of the neighbors here, as he had before done to the citizens of Newbern with the tailor. A man who kept a ferry in the neighborhood behaved very rudely to almost every person that had occasion to cross. He was hated by every one who lived near him. Unfortunately for himself, he offended Stewart, who, as the ferryman was a militia officer, sent him a challenge by Lucas, and on his refusing to accept it, he gave him a severe beating. We spent two days here very agreeably in dancing and riding about the country. The third day we intended to set off, but there fell a very heavy rain that detained us two days longer, all the small bridges being carried away. From Stewart I received letters of introduction to his friends in Virginia and Maryland, and by all those we could call on we were treated with great hospitality. At Petersburg we met the Baron de Kalb. going to the southward. Here the certificate from Governor Nash was of service to me, for they were pressing horses for the army, and I believe if it had not been for the certificate, I should have had one of my servants dismounted. Meeting here with Mr. Bowie, an old acquaintance of mine from Philadelphia, he introduced me to Col. Banister, who

plicated in a plot to surrender a part of Louisiana to the British. The Senate, however, decided that he was not liable to impeachment. "By these proceedings against him," says Hildreth, "Blount's popularity in Tennessee had been rather increased than otherwise, and nothing but his sudden death prevented his being elected Governor."

invited us to dine with him. Baron de Kalb* was one of the guests. The Baron was a tall, raw-boned man of about fifty. He was a military looking man, and had a fine body of men with him. In the evening we left Col. Banister's and proceeded on our journey very rapidly. Two days before we arrived at Baltimore, we overtook Mr. Wiley Jones and his wife. He was a member of the Assembly during the time I was, had been lately chosen a member of Congress, and was on his way to Philadelphia to take his seat. In point of talents he was one of the first men in America, but, like most Southern gentlemen, was too fond of horse racing and cards to attend much to business.

When we arrived at Baltimore, I went to Mrs. Lux's. Her son had married a daughter of my brother Edward. Both the elder and younger Mrs. Lux were very amiable women, and from them we had the kindest reception. The elder Mrs. Lux was a very religious lady, every morning and evening she had all the family assembled to prayers. This sometimes occasioned her son George a good deal of vexation. He was very fond of backgammon. When playing, and desired by his mother to have the family assembled, if they did not hurry in he would get into a violent rage, and bawl out, "You black devils, why don't you make haste to prayers." When they were all in the room (the old lady would not let him begin if one was absent) he would read over the prayers as fast as he possibly could, and the instant he was done, would hurry back to his game. We staid a week to refresh ourselves and our horses, and then set off by the way of York and Lancaster for Reading. It is a saying of the people of

* When this officer and the Marquis la Fayette first landed at Georgetown, I was there with Col. Morgan, on our way to Charleston. Morgan, hearing that two French officers (for the Baron, although a German, was called then a Frenchman) had just arrived, requested me, as I spoke a little French, to go with him, and speak to them; but I had seen and heard so much of the French officers who came over to enter into the American service, that I had conceived a very unfavorable opinion of them, and told him I supposed they were only barbers or tailors, and would not go with him. They were, however, both officers of great merit.—AUTHOR'S NOTE.

Maryland that in travelling from Pennsylvania to the southward, the first countryman's house you stop at where the
landlord behaves with politeness to you, you may be assured
you are out of Pennsylvania.   On the other hand, the Pennsylvanians say, that in going from Maryland to Pennsylvania, the first farm you come to where you see a good barn,
the fences all up, and in good order, you may be certain you
are out of Maryland.   The fact is, in Pennsylvania, the people are generally industrious and seldom take notice of
strangers.   In Maryland, they are very hospitable, but indolent.   Upon our arrival at Reading it was with infinite pleasure I found my mother and the rest of the family well.

CHAPTER III.

I CONTINUED in Reading the remainder of the summer. In the fall I went with Mrs. Biddle to Philadelphia, and would have gone thence to North Carolina, but as it gave my mother much pain whenever our journey was mentioned, I gave it up, and after remaining in Philadelphia all the fall, returned in the winter to Reading, where we had at this time very good society. Besides the inhabitants, Col. Butler's* Regiment was quartered here, most of the officers of which were very worthy men. Lieutenant-Colonel Mentzger, who commanded in the absence of Butler (who was from Reading most of the winter), was one of the very few foreign officers that were valuable to us. He had been a Prussian officer, came here very young, and was of great service, being a well-informed, attentive officer. There was a Captain Bowen† in the regiment, an excellent officer, but he had a failing that occasioned

---

* Colonel, afterward General Richard Butler, one of the most distinguished Pennsylvania officers of the Revolutionary army, and the eldest of five brothers designated by Washington as "the five Butlers, a gallant band of patriot brothers." General Butler was in continuous service throughout the whole war, part of the time as lieutenant-colonel of Morgan's famous rifle regiment. He distinguished himself especially at Saratoga and Monmouth, and led one of the two storming parties at the taking of Stony Point. He was present with his regiment in the operation on James River, and at the capture of Cornwallis. He was appointed second in command under St. Clair in his expedition against the Indians in 1791, and was killed in the disastrous fight on the Miami River on the 4th November of that year.

A great granddaughter of General Butler, Miss Eliza Irwin Butler, of Pittsburgh, married, in 1877, Nicholas Biddle, a great-grandson of Charles Biddle.

† Now settled in Charleston, as a printer, 1804.—AUTHOR'S NOTE.

some disturbances. He often took offence when none was intended; he fought a duel with the major of the regiment, who declared to me he could not conceive, at the time he went out, in what way he had given offence to Bowen, who did not mention it in his challenge, and the major would not inquire. They fired a shot, and Bowen had one of the buttons shot off his coat; after which, the seconds-knowing them both to be very brave men, persuaded them to talk over the matter, when it appeared the major was walking with some girls the night before, and they burst out laughing just after Bowen passed them. Upon explaining the cause of their laughter, it seems it was occasioned by the major telling them of his and Bowen's being at a dance the evening before, and the blind fiddler breaking one of his strings, the landlady took a candle and held it for him while he was fitting a new string. The mentioning the story, which the seconds had not heard before, set them laughing, and they all returned in good humor. Bowen was a seaman before he entered the army, and had a particular regard for me, and paid more attention to what I said than to any other person, by which means I had it frequently in my power to prevent his quarrelling. He was appointed Town Major, and one evening, soon after, I was playing backgammon with him, when Capt. Bower, who belonged to the regiment, came in, and addressing himself to Bowen, said, "I hope you are very well, major." Bowen immediately started up, "Don't major me, sir! None of your majors! You know I am not a major, sir! What do you mean, sir?" Bower, who was and is a gallant officer, did not know how to behave; he, however, declared he did not intend any offence. Bowen begged me to walk into the next room with him, and then inquired if I thought he ought not to challenge Bower. I told him in my opinion a man that would not fight on some occasions was not fit to live, nor was a man fit to live who was always quarrelling. I took him into Bower, and made them shake hands. Bowen's warm temper was of service to the regiment in one respect; it occasioned all the officers to behave with great politeness to each other.

In February, 1781, Mrs. Biddle was delivered, at the house of my brother James, of a son, three days after which the house took fire, and she and the child had nearly perished. It was discovered just at daylight. I then lodged at the house of a female friend, who, living in a lonely part of the town, was afraid of robbers, and begged me to sleep at her house during the time Mrs. Biddle was confined. I was soon awakened by the cry of fire. Without waiting to dress myself, I ran to Mrs. Biddle, and taking her in my arms carried her out of the house to my friend Dr. Potts. There was at this time a deep snow on the ground, and it was excessively cold; however, neither mother nor child received any injury. We stayed at Dr. Potts's three or four weeks. I then rented a house, and not being of a disposition to remain idle, I went to Philadelphia, and purchased a quantity of wine, upon which I made a handsome profit. I continued doing business in this way until the fall of the year, when being anxious to make a voyage I engaged to go from Philadelphia in a Letter of Marque brig, called the Active, to St. Thomas. We had eight four pounders; the crew consisted of ten men and four boys, besides the two mates and myself, with Dr. Valentine Standley, a passenger. We left the Capes in company with a large fleet the 15th of November, 1781.

My old shipmate, Captain Decatur,* went out in company with us in a privateer of twenty guns called The Royal Lewis. The night we left the Capes it blew hard from the northeast. The brig made so much water going upon a wind that we could hardly keep her free. About 10 P. M. I hailed Decatur, who kept near us, and told him we must keep away to the southward. He said he had an account the day before he left Philadelphia of two British frigates being cruising off the Capes of Virginia. I answered that I must bear away or the brig would founder, and accordingly I bore away. Decatur kept his wind a few minutes, and then followed us. At daylight we made the two frigates right

* Father of the gallant young man who burnt the Philadelphia at Tripoli. —AUTHOR'S NOTE.

ahead, not more than two miles off. They immediately gave chase. Decatur hauled his wind. I stood in shore, determined to run ashore sooner than be taken. Decatur was taken about 12 o'clock. We made our escape.

Standley, whom I have mentioned above, was a handsome young man, a very good surgeon, and of a respectable family. His mother now (June, 1802) lives near me. He unfortunately fell into bad company, and, when he sailed with me, was addicted to gaming and drinking, either of which soon brings a young man to ruin. Had he behaved well he would have been a valuable man ; he was a surgeon on board one of the galleys at the time the Hessians under Count Donop made the attack upon the fort at Red Bank, and after the battle was appointed to attend the wounded. He declared whenever he was called to a Hessian wounded in the leg or arm, whether necessary or not, he immediately amputated it, to prevent their doing any more mischief. Although at the commencement of the war I was much prejudiced against these people, yet when I knew many of them, and considered they were a set of poor wretches, obliged to go wherever they were ordered by their prince, my opinion respecting them was much changed. Many of them captured with Burgoyne were at Reading, and were very useful to the farmers in the neighborhood, who hired them and found they were hard-working, industrious fellows. I know several who have become men of property and behaved well; one of them, J. A. Lewis, has been with me eleven years, and was in the office several years before it was held by me. He has a wife and five children, lives in a good house of his own, and is a very useful, industrious man. He was at the battle of Long Island, and at all the principal actions fought in America. He says, when he first came to America, he and all the Hessians firmly believed that if they were taken by the Americans, they would be roasted and eaten. Had the Hessians been ever so bad, the conduct of Standley would have been inexcusable. His own account disgusted me so much against him, that I would not suffer him, after he had mentioned this affair, to eat in the cabin. We had a good passage, and fell in with nothing until we made St. Thomas, when we saw off the harbor a brig, which we found was a British cruiser. It was early in the morning when we first discovered her; she was beating up, and we were going before the wind. Finding as she drew near that we could have no chance by fighting her, I determined to go into St. Johns, if we could get there. We were both becalmed off the west end of the island, and we got out oars, and rowed for the harbor. They got out their boats and towed their vessel to cut us off. I had been in this harbor with the Eclipse, and knew they had a single fort. They got within gunshot of us several times, and would have taken us, if they had not been too eager. When within shot, they pulled around to give us a broadside, by which means we got a considerable way ahead. They did this without doing us any injury whatever. Had they continued rowing without firing a shot, they would have been alongside before we could have reached the harbor. They kept firing (and many of their shot reached the shore), until I hailed the fort to know why they did not fire. They then fired a shot which struck the water under her boltsprit. She then hauled off. We learned afterwards that she was a King's Brig. The master of her deserved to be broken for not taking us. My crew behaved very well, except one man whom I thought before this day, was afraid of nothing. He, however, endeavored to get down the fore scuttle. Whenever the brig pulled round to fire, my crew gave them three cheers, and were anxious to return the fire, but I knew if we broke off any of the men from the oars, we must be taken, and therefore would not suffer it. I went from St. Johns the same day in my boat to St. Thomas. Mr. Mitchell, an old friend, settled here, told me to be careful of the Governor; if he knew it was me who had insulted their fort he did not know what would be the consequence. I found here my friend Falvey. He was in partnership with a Thomas Reilly, under the firm of Falvey and Reilly. I sold my cargo, which consisted of flour and tobacco, to Mr. Lisle, a native of Philadelphia, who was married and settled in Tortola. Mr. Mitchell was his surety. After delivering the cargo, he was to have returned and paid me in four days. He was gone ten. I was very uneasy, and Mitchell more so, fearing he would not return. However, he came the tenth day, and paid me honestly. He had been detained collecting the money, which was in new half Johannes, which I at first thought he had been coining at Tortola. I purchased some rum at St. Johns, and having procured what dry goods I wanted, sailed from St. Johns the 13th of December. Just before we sailed, Standley applied to me to take him back, but he had behaved ill on the passage out, and during the time we were at St. Thomas, and as I thought he would plague his good mother in Philadelphia, I would not take him. There were several privateers off the harbor; however we escaped them all. Two or three days after we left St. Johns, a fever broke out amongst the crew. For several days after they were taken, they grew worse, and more were taken down with the disorder. They complained of violent pains in their heads, and they were frequently delirious, so that we were obliged to confine them to prevent their jumping overboard. Upon inquiry of the second mate (the chief mate, Mr. Lecroft, was at his own request discharged at St. Thomas) what could be the cause of their disorder, he informed me that the people had filled the casks with water from a pond at the back of the fort, and perhaps it was owing to that. Upon questioning one of those employed in getting the water, he acknowledged, that finding it difficult to get to the watering place, they had filled the casks out of the pond, and that one of the inhabitants told them not to fill the casks with that water, for it would kill them. Knowing how very unwholesome bad water is, I had no doubt but the fever was occasioned by the water, but we had now none other to use. I was determined, if we had any heavy rains, to start the water we had, and fill our casks with rain water. The fifth day after we were out, we buried one of the crew, and had six so ill that they could not come upon deck. I had the sick removed forward, and everything made as comfortable for them as possible. We had a fine wind from the time of leaving St. Johns, and I was in hopes the cold weather we now had would abate the fever, but it had not that effect, probably owing to all the crew being infected with the disease before this time. The sixth day the stoutest and heartiest man we had on board, Leonard May, a young man born in Philadelphia, whose parents now live here, was taken unwell. As it was cold and rainy when he complained to me of being sick, I desired him to go below, but not to go forward among the sick. However, he found the place they were in, the warmest in the vessel, and went there. The next morning we found him dead; he appeared as if he had been strangled. I was much concerned for the loss of this young man, for he was a very good seaman, and did whatever he was ordered with cheerfulness. He was telling the second mate the day before he was taken unwell that he wished the sick would all make a general will and leave him their heir.

The eighth day after leaving St. Johns, about one o'clock in the morning, the wind shifted from the southeast to northwest, and blew hard. At daylight we saw a large ship to windward of us, lying to under her foresail. She so soon made sail after us that I was convinced she was a man-of-war. I therefore immediately bore away to the southward. At this time there was not a man belonging to the vessel, but the second mate and myself, but were sick or had died. We were then by our reckoning about twenty-five leagues from the Capes of Delaware. We had three passengers on board, and with their assistance made sail. At eleven o'clock, the weather being more moderate, we got up our topgallant yards and set the topgallant sails. At noon, while taking an observation, the chase fired a shot over us. I then hove our guns overboard. We were now going ten knots, and there was so little difference in our sailing that it was three o'clock before she got so near as to oblige us to strike. Being then within pistol-shot, and with no possibility of escaping, I hove to. They fired one of their forecastle guns after we had hove to, when they were close alongside. The shot went over the quarter-deck, just above our heads. I was glad to see them fire the first shot, and was in hopes they would have luffed up, and given us a broadside

as the brig had done, but they only fired from their forecastle.
During the chase, as it was a fine day, I had several of the
poor fellows who were sick helped upon the quarterdeck,
and dressed in some uniform coats I had on board, of red
and blue, in hopes they would take me for a British vessel,
and leave off the chase. Some of the officers told me afterwards that they did take us for an English packet, and, had
they seen any other vessel, would have given up the chase.
We found the ship that captured us was the Chatham of
fifty guns, commanded by Andrew S. Douglass. She had
chased a vessel the day before to the westward, which occasioned their being so near the land. We were all taken on
board the man-of-war except four, who were too ill to be
removed. A circumstance that happened a few days after
we were taken, gave me a very unfavorable opinion of this
Captain Douglass. The sick belonging to the brig complaining to me of their being badly accommodated, I wrote a note
to him. His servant told the person I sent it by, that Captain Douglass* had ordered him never to take a letter to him
from any of the prisoners. I suppose this *great man* thought
it beneath his dignity to attend to an unfortunate prisoner.
Upon speaking to the second lieutenant he had everything
that could be of service to the poor fellows done for them.
I found the cooper of the Chatham (Merit Brown) was a
man that had made several voyages with me. He was a
native of Philadelphia, and married there. He was a smart,
active fellow, and told me he had been impressed, but I
believe he got drunk and entered. He was, or pretended to
be, very anxious to get home. They had also Abraham
Wilbank, one of our Delaware pilots, who was a refugee,
and left Philadelphia with the British. Two days after we
were taken we had a hard gale of wind from the northeast.
About one o'clock A. M., finding the ship to labor very much,
and the pumps constantly going, I went upon deck with

---

* I have seen a letter in the Naval Chronicle, from Captain Douglass, to
his uncle, Captain Hammond, wherein he says, " no man in his senses, well
out of active service, would wish to come in again, for it is made up of envy,
hatred, and malice."—AUTHOR'S NOTE.

Mr. Potts, one of the passengers taken with me. The ship was lying hove to, there were but few men upon deck, and I saw no officers but the sailing master, who was an American, one or two midshipmen, and the pilot. I gave it as my opinion to the sailing-master that the ship would lay to much easier if the mizzen staysail was set. He said no canvas would hold in such a gale. I told him I had been lying to on the coast with canvas set when it blew harder. He made me no answer, probably thinking it impertinent in me to give my advice. I soon went below with Potts, telling him as we went down that we were in danger every moment of a sea breaking on board, and, as the ship was old and crazy, it would send us to Davy Jones's locker. I had not been off the deck but a few minutes before the master had the mizzen staysail set, when the ship lay to much safer and easier. The officers then belonging to the ship were men less qualified than any I had ever sailed with. I doubt whether there was a ship in the British Navy that had officers so little experienced. It is customary for officers in the British Navy to undergo an examination before they receive their commissions; how these men did I cannot tell, but possibly they may have received their commissions while in America, without having undergone an examination. The officers of the British Navy that I have sailed with, or met with, were generally the best of seamen; and brave, generous, and humane. I received so much kindness from Cadogan, Cote, Harvey, and others, that I never see a British naval officer without wishing it may be in my power to serve him. The officers of this ship, except the captain, were worthy men, and perhaps I should have had a better opinion of him had I known him better. He talked at one time of going into Delaware Bay, and anchoring in the Road. Had he done so some of the prisoners whom I consulted were determined, if we should have an easterly wind while there, to cut her cables if possible, and let her drift ashore. She was so old and crazy that if she took the ground there, she would never have got off. But Douglass thought afterwards he had better not go into the Road.

We cruised on the coast until the first of January, 1782, when we stood for Sandy Hook with a fair wind. Two days before, we buried John Shute, a fine lad that was taken with me. A cousin of his, of the same name, was left on board the brig. He was so bad the day before we were taken, that we were obliged to confine him to prevent his jumping overboard. It gave me great pain to use the violence we were obliged to use to this valuable young man, who had been an officer in the American army. He went to sea, expecting through the interest of his friends to do better than he could do by staying in the army. When we were tying him I was much affected with his calling out, "Oh! Captain Biddle! my dear Captain Biddle! will you stand by and see me treated in this vile manner?" Finding his entreaties could do nothing, he swore I should fight him as soon as we landed. Poor fellow! it was his fate never to reach the shore.

The 3d of January we anchored off Sandy Hook. Captain Douglass, who was married a short time before to an American lady, went up to New York in the cutter. About nine o'clock at night, while I was in the ward-room with the lieutenants and officers of marines, who were playing cards, one of the midshipmen came in as pale as death and cried out the ship was on fire. All hands were immediately called, and orders were given to heave water down the fore-hatchway, where a great quantity of smoke came up, and under this hatchway the poor American prisoners, to the number of sixty or seventy were grated down, and all the water thrown down went on them, without doing any service whatever. I never saw a man so much alarmed as the first lieutenant, Dalby, was. He was in a situation that any one must have felt very sensibly; but he appeared perfectly incapable of giving directions what to do. I begged he would give orders for the American prisoners to be let out of confinement, that they might have a chance for saving their lives, but he was too much confused to attend to me. The unfortunate prisoners were earnestly praying to be let out, but they prayed in vain. As the water was smooth and not very deep I told him he had better let the prisoners up, point some of the twenty-four pounders down her hold and sink her; there would then be no danger of our lives. He would perhaps have paid some regard to my request and advice, but it was now reported that the Americans had set the ship on fire; and I believe Dalby thought the improbable tale true, and therefore paid no regard to what I said, but looked on me with a suspicious eye. The second lieutenant, whose name, I believe, was Lyons, was asleep when the alarm was first given. As soon as he was awakened, and could recollect himself, he went immediately down into the boatswain's store-room, adjoining the magazine, where the fire originated. In the mean time, as I thought it very probable the ship would blow up, five or six of us got a large spar, and as soon as the exertions to put the fire out were given over, or we thought they could not succeed, we determined to heave the spar overboard, and jump after it. We should have had but little chance of saving our lives, as the wind was at northwest, and very cold, but it was the best method in our situation we could take. There was a ship of twenty guns lying about a mile from us, and a merchantman near her, and I was much surprised that signals of distress were not fired from the Chatham. They would probably have come nearer to us; at any rate they would have been ready in case of an explosion to pick up some of the men that might survive her blowing up; but Dalby knew not what to do, and the second lieutenant was below. It was about half an hour from the time of the first alarm until it was all out. The ship would, I believe, have blown up if it had not been for the second lieutenant. The crew was an excellent one, but where the commanding officer is confused little can be expected from the crew. There was no order among them until Lyons came on deck, he soon restored order, and they passed the water to him as regularly as they could have done on shore. After the fire was over, and the officers again assembled in the wardroom, Dalby candidly confessed he was very much alarmed, which he imputed to what he had suffered formerly by a fire. This fire was occasioned by one of the boatswain's mates going into the storeroom, and snuffing his candle there. He was soon put in irons. I was once before this time on fire at sea; it was when going from Jamaica to the Bay of Honduras. The mate had been boiling tar over the fire, when it boiled over, and we had nearly lost the vessel before it was put out. When the noise brought me upon deck the mate, instead of endeavoring to put the fire out, was going to get out the boat. I said so much to him for this, and for his boiling the tar without my knowledge, that when we arrived at the Bay he ran away.

The day after the fire, the cutter returning from New York, we made sail to go up. We took the ground going up, and I expected the old ship would have beaten her bottom out, which, as there was no danger of our lives, was what I should not have been displeased at. We, however, got safe off, and the next day anchored in the East River opposite New York. We had been at an anchor but a short time before I was told a gentleman wished to see me. Going immediately up, I found it was William Austin, an old, intimate friend, who had been in the tent with me when out in Cowperthwait's Quaker Company. As soon as he saw me he exclaimed, "My unfortunate Prince,* how are you?" and, shaking me very cordially by the hand, expressed great satisfaction at seeing me, and obtaining leave for me to go on shore with him. He took me to his lodging; and, being a good-tempered, friendly fellow, he did everything in his power to serve me. I went with him to Mr. Shoemaker's,† who had formerly been Mayor of the city of Philadelphia. He behaved very kind, and offered me any assistance in his power. I was much pleased with a circumstance he mentioned to me, which was, that he had advanced large sums

---

* When we were out in Cowperthwait's Company he had named all in the tent from one of Shakspeare's plays. Me he had called Harry, Prince of Wales; he was called Pistol. Upon his calling me Prince the officers of the Chatham all stared at me, not knowing who I could be.—AUTHOR'S NOTE.

† Mr. Samuel Shoemaker, Mayor of Philadelphia 1769–71, who adhered to the Royal cause. His kindness to American prisoners is mentioned by Sabine (American Loyalist), and is confirmed by the above statement.

11

on loan to the Americans who had been brought in prisoners, particularly to those belonging to Philadelphia, all of whom, except one, had remitted what they had borrowed, and this one had died going home.

The day after my being on shore I obtained leave to go on board the Jersey Prison Ship to see the remainder of my unfortunate crew. Much has been said about the cruel treatment the Americans received on board this ship. From what I saw and heard from prisoners whose veracity could not be doubted, they were certainly treated with great inhumanity. When I first went on board the remains of two of the prisoners were lying on the gratings,—they had died the evening before. Upon inquiring of a young lad that had been with me, of the name of Eckert (son of Col. Eckert, of Berks County), the reason of these not being buried, he said they were waiting until they had a boat-load. He may have possibly been misinformed. It was at this time reported, and generally believed, among the Americans, that the prisoners were poisoned. I believe it was only by their having unwholesome provisions, and cooked in coppers not cleaned, that they were poisoned. It was greatly to the honor of the American character, that, notwithstanding they were in want of everything to make their situation comfortable, and every method was tried to induce them, there was hardly an instance of a native American entering on board their ships. I never heard of any but Merit Brown, cooper of the Chatham; nor am I certain he he did so of his own will. Had the prisoners in New York been treated with the same indulgence that those who were taken by General Carleton at Quebec were, few would have entered into the American service after their return home. His kindness had a great effect upon the officers, most of whom resigned as soon as they returned to their families. All my crew died except the second mate, now Captain Art, who, with great difficulty, I got exchanged with me. The brig never arrived, nor was she heard of after we left her, so that I have no doubt she foundered in the gale of wind we had two days after we were taken. She was injured by carrying

sail the day of our capture. All the sixteen men and boys
that went with me from Philadelphia were very hearty
when we sailed,—the eldest of the men was not more than
twenty-five years of age. It was melancholy to reflect that
none of them ever returned to their relations or friends,

After my return from visiting the Jersey, I observed two
Hessian officers looking at me very attentively, one of whom
at last exclaimed, in broken English, " By Got, it ish Captain Bittle," and, advancing, expressed great pleasure at
seeing me. I found the one who spoke was Captain Baum,
and his companion another officer, who with him had been
a prisoner in Reading the year before, and had been lately
exchanged. They begged me to go to their quarters, which
I did, and was treated with great kindness by these gentlemen. During the time the Hessians were in Reading the
conduct of one of the privates occasioned a good deal of
laughter, although it was on a melancholy occasion. A
Hessian officer of rank, whose name I do not recollect, was
fishing in the Schuylkill, in a canoe, when he fell out. A
servant on the shore, instead, it was said, of alarming the
people at a house near, ran to inform the commanding officer,
and before he came down the officer was drowned. Had the
fellow called the people of the house the officer could have
been easily saved, for the water was not deep. They saw
the body at the bottom, and hauled it up, but it was too
late; they tried in vain to restore him to life.

I waited on the Honorable Major Wallop, who had been a
prisoner in Reading. By this *gentleman* I had sent into New
York two bills of exchange for twenty pounds sterling each,
one drawn by Lieutenant Batus, on Coxe and Meir, the other
by Lieutenant Wilmot, on Ross and Gray, London. These
bills, Mr. Wallop told me, were not paid, but as a great favor
he advanced me ten pounds on account of them. I afterwards found this Mr. Wallop had sent the bills to England
by Captain Dillon of the Mercury Packet, who received the
money for the bills, and gave orders to Mr. Vanhorn, his
agent, to pay Wallop, and Mr. Vanhorn sent me Wallop's
receipt for the money. This money of mine advanced by

my brother from motives of humanity (abstracted from every interested view) to those British officers in captivity, when every other source failed them, was lost ; for, although I frequently wrote to this Major Wallop (who is brother to Lord —— [Earl of Portsmouth], he has never answered my letter. By the advice of a friend I also wrote to Sir George Young, Secretary at War, who never thought proper to answer my letter, which he should have done, for the case was not a common one, and I was justified in my application to him. If he had any regard to the honor of his country he would not have let me have been a loser when he could have obliged Wallop to pay me ; if he had been a gentleman he would have written me an answer.

After being a few days at New York, I was sent on my parole to Flat Bush, where at this time there were a good many American prisoners. We spent our time as agreeably as people in our situation could do. The Dutchmen here, at this time, began to think the British army would not be long in New York, and therefore treated the prisoners with great attention. They declared privately they wished General Washington success, and one night, late, our landlord and some of his friends returned home from New York, waked us all up, and begged we would drink something with them. I believe some of the guards had affronted them, for they were very noisy, abused the British Army, and repeatedly drank success to General Washington, declaring if he was to come on Long Island they would immediately join him. In the morning, when sober, and our landlord was informed by his wife of what he had said, he was a good deal alarmed for fear we should mention something of what had passed, and that some of the British officers would hear of it. He, therefore, begged us, for God's sake, not to mention what had passed the night before, and considering himself in our power, as in fact he was, he would have done anything we requested him to do. As we considered these people a set of mercenary creatures, who cared for neither Americans nor British, but who would do anything for money, we were determined to plague them. We one day got a friend to come down from New York, who pretended he was sent by the commissary, Sproat, who, he said, had been informed that our landlord, and some others, had spoken disrespectfully of the British Government, and that he was authorized to offer liberty and a hundred guineas reward to any of the prisoners who would inform against them. Potts, my passenger, immediately after he heard him, called him to one side, and our landlord, who was present, supposing it was to relate what had passed, slipped out of the room, and, if I had not followed him, would have fled from the island. No poor wretch going to the gallows suffered more than this man. It was with great difficulty I could persuade him we were in jest. It had one good effect, I never saw our landlord drunk afterwards. Before this he frequently drank too much apple toddy, a drink at that time very common on the island.

I went at one time as far as Jamaica to see Mr. John Potts, brother to Mr. Potts taken with me. Mr. John Potts was one of those unfortunate men who being attached to the British cause had left Philadelphia with them. It was at this gentleman's table I first heard of any complaint against General Washington. A British officer dining with us, talking of the general, said he knew an instance of his acting very improperly. I told him that having never heard any complaints against him, I should be glad to know in what manner he had behaved improperly. He said that after the surrender of York, a number of the British, American, and French officers were invited to dine with Count de Rochambeau, and that General Washington kept them waiting an hour, and when he came made no apology. I told him it gave me pleasure to find it was nothing worse he had done, but as General Washington was allowed to be a well-bred gentleman, he possibly was mistaken about his not making an apology. During all the time of my being a prisoner I never heard the name of General Washington mentioned but with respect, except by this officer, and he had nothing to say but what I have mentioned.

After remaining about three weeks at Flat Bush, I was

exchanged. Taking leave of my landlord, who was very
attentive, I went to New York, and after taking leave of
some gentlemen who had behaved very kindly and friendly
to me, I embarked with a number of other prisoners, for
Elizabethtown. On the passage we were detained all night
by the deputy commissioner of prisoners, Robert Lenox,
going on shore with two ladies. I was much exasperated,
but some of the prisoners' were much more so, and when they
returned on board I was obliged to interfere to prevent their
being very roughly treated. They deserved to be punished,
for at that season of the year our situation was dangerous;
but I could not stand by and see women who appeared
respectable abused without taking their part. They were
very thankful for my speaking in their favor, and supposing
from it that I would serve them further, wished me when we
got to Elizabethtown Point, to claim a few things they had
in the boat; but this I refused, not thinking myself justified.
At Elizabethtown five of us hired a light wagon to carry us
to Philadelphia. At this time there was a set of fellows who
undertook to examine the baggage of every person from New
York for what were called "run goods." It might have been
proper to do it on the lines where people made it a business
to go in and purchase goods, but to search an unfortunate
prisoner, who, with the small pittance he had saved from the
wreck of his fortune, had purchased a piece of linen, or some
such trifle, it was abominable. These wretches robbed many
prisoners of what the British had left them. There were two
wagons of us set off at the same time; I was in the hinder-
most. When we came near the tavern at Woodbridge I
heard a very stout man that was walking the piazza, say in a
loud voice, "I'll be d——d if any man shall search Capt.
Biddle's baggage." Looking at him, I found it was Ezekiel
Furman, an old friend that served his time to a merchant in
Philadelphia. With Furman I had been acquainted when
boys, and in our boyish expeditions he always headed us.
(It was not General E. Furman, him I did not know.)
Although I had nothing that could be taken, I was very glad
to see Furman, and to find him the same honest fellow he

had ever been. Some of those in the wagon ahead of us had told him I was in the wagon coming up, and he waited to see me. If the people here had any intention of searching us they could not have done it. Furman was as brave as he was stout, and he had several friends, and none in the wagon would have suffered a search without resistance. I was very sorry to hear from Furman that he had been unfortunate, and much more so to hear since that his misfortunes had made him intemperate. He married a Miss Wikoff, of a respectable family. Taking leave of this good fellow, we arrived safe in Philadelphia.*

Being extremely anxious to get home, after waiting upon the owners of the brig, I borrowed a phaeton and horses from my friend Hepburn, and early in the morning of the 31st of January, set off for Reading, intending to get there that night. When I reached Perkiomen Creek, twenty-five miles from the city, the rains and melting of the snow had raised it so much that they told me it was impossible to cross. Being determined to try, I drove into the creek expecting to swim the horses over, but finding, that owing to the rapidity of the stream, it was necessary to enter the creek higher up, I put back and entered some distance above, expecting to reach the

* In August this year (1812) I went to Long Branch. At Edentown, near the Branch, I heard that my old friend Captain Furman lived there (the person who was at Woodbridge and swore none of my baggage should be searched when I came a prisoner from New York). When he came to the tavern I knew him immediately, although it was upwards of thirty-one years since we had met. He did not know me, but when I told him who it was that was conversing with him, he was greatly rejoiced to see me. Agreeably to his promise he came the next day to the Branch. He is a very hale, hearty man, and rode down on a race horse, which he mounted and managed with great ease. He has a large, respectable family. Upon some disgust he joined the British army, and being taken in arms would have suffered an ignominious death but for his relation General Furman, and some other powerful friends. He told me that after the war he lived near Frankford, and a report of some of his friends, that he could beat any man in America, had occasioned him many severe battles. It appeared to me that few men now could beat him. He has a small pension from the British Government, to which government he is warmly attached, and has as much hatred to the French as any man in America.—AUTHOR'S NOTE.

shore abreast of the tavern. This I should have done had
both the horses swam, but before they were half over one of
them turned on his side, and they both would have been
drowned if two men had not come off in a canoe, and assisted
in keeping their heads above water. We got back with difficulty. Finding it would be impossible to get over this way,
I took the horses out, and getting two canoes, with great
labor carried over the phæton. By the time it was over I
was almost perished with cold and fatigue, being up to the
waist in water when swimming the horses. After procuring
some clothes of the landlord, and refreshing myself, I hired
a pair of horses and sat off with an intention of sleeping in
Reading, but they were a pair of steady wagon horses that
paid no regard to my impatience. Beating or cursing them,
with all my exertions I did not get to Pottsgrove until after
night. Pottsgrove is thirty-seven miles from Philadelphia;
Reading, fifty-five miles. Early the next morning I reached
home, and found Mrs. Biddle, William, and all my friends well.

A few days after my return I was seized with the same
kind of fever that proved so fatal to the unfortunate crew of
the brig, and it brought me to the brink of the grave.
Nothing but good nursing and having everything necessary
to stop the progress of the disorder prevented me going into
it. When at the worst, and little hopes were entertained of
me, a profuse perspiration broke out on me, and recollecting
what Smollet mentions in his novel of Roderick Random,[*]
I covered myself up in blankets, which brought on so profuse a sweat, that my shirt and bed-clothes were as wet as if
they had been just taken out of the river. I felt myself
better immediately after, and in a few days was perfectly well.

In April I went with Mrs. Biddle to Philadelphia, on a
visit to our friends. While there Mr. John Ross and Mr.
Lecan, of the house of Lecan & Mallet, called on me to
know if I would take the command of a large ship they
had fitting out at Baltimore, intended for Cape François,

---

[*] Reading Roderick Random first gave me an inclination for the sea.—
AUTHOR'S NOTE.

and from thence up the Mediterranean. As I had at this time acquired some property, and had suffered a good deal the last voyage, I did not intend going to sea soon ; however, as they offered me the consignment of the cargo, I agreed to go, provided the mate they sent out with me, or some person sent out on purpose, should take the command of the ship after she was loaded, and ready to sail from the Capes. This they agreed to. As the vessel wanted a good deal done, and the owners were anxious for my going down, I set off immediately for Baltimore. I found the ship was a very large, flat vessel, built by the British to attack a battery. She had twelve eighteen pounders on her gun deck, and sixteen nine and six pounders on her upper deck, forecastle, and quarter deck. She was, when in the British service, called the Sandwich, had been scuttled, and sunk by the British at York just before Cornwallis surrendered, afterwards raised, and purchased by Mr. Ross, Lecan & Mallet, and some other gentlemen. They proposed she should carry all her guns, and one hundred and twenty or thirty men. After making out a list of everything she would want for the voyage, and seeing her in some forwardness, as the owners were not now in a hurry to send her to sea, I went the middle of May to Reading to see my family. Here I staid until the first of June, when Mr. Ross wrote me that the owners wished the ship out as soon as possible. The second of June I proceeded to Baltimore, and used every exertion in my power to get the ship soon manned, and ready for sea. At this time it was very difficult to get men for any ship, much more so for the Friendship, as it was known she sailed very heavy. When we entered a man, we were obliged to send him immediately on board, and keep him there, so that before I had my complement of men, the sailors and people at the Point called her the prison ship. However, by the 20th of June I had all my crew on board, and waited with great impatience for orders to sail, which I expected every hour, when, instead of orders to sail, the owners wrote me that two ships commanded by Curwin and Earl, that had sailed but a few days before from Baltimore, were taken,

and that the coast was so full of cruisers they concluded it
best not to send the ship out, and ordered me to discharge
the crew. This, after the trouble I had, was a disagreeable
business. However, as there was no remedy, I discharged
them all, and had proceeded about fourteen miles on my way
home when an express came down from the owners to Baltimore, who, finding me gone, came after me; they desired
me, if I had not discharged the crew, not to do it, as they
were determined to send the ship out as soon as possible;
that if the crew were already discharged, to get another as
soon as I could. This was a very mortifying thing to me,
and I would gladly have quitted the ship, and would have
done it had she been in Philadelphia, but as I thought my
leaving her at this time would be injurious to the owners,
who, although capricious, had behaved well to me, I returned
immediately, and opened a rendezvous at Fell's Point, and
there was one also opened at Philadelphia, so that in about
three weeks I again had the ship manned. Several seafaring
men, and one carpenter living at the Point, frequented the
rendezvous to dance and drink every evening; some of them,
when half drunk, signed the articles without any intention
of going in the ship. The night before we sailed I went
with a party of marines, and took all these people on board.
The next morning the carpenter's wife, who, by attempting
to drive the marines out of the house, had got some blood
on her clothes, came like a fury to my lodgings, and was
very abusive, calling me every vile name she could think of.
No fishwoman that I ever heard could equal her. After
hearing her for some time, without taking any notice of her,
I called up the boat's crew, and ordered them to take her
down to the wharf, and duck her; I had, however, no intention of letting them do it. The moment they took hold of
her she fell on her knees, and was as submissive as she had
before been insolent. Upon her telling me they had children,
I sent the boat off for her husband and two others, who had
families. The rest, being single men, I kept. Taking these
married men on board was of service to them; it prevented
their going to taverns and getting drunk. Several officers

who had been in the American army, and who were left
out of service, came down to go with me as volunteers. I
represented to them that they could receive no advantage as
volunteers on board such a ship; however, as they wished
to go, and the owners had no objection, I agreed to take
them. Among these was a Captain Wilson, who, I believe,
belonged to Carlisle, Pennsylvania. He had been a very
promising officer, but, being intemperate, had become almost
useless. Understanding his character from my friend Colonel
Craig, who gave him a letter to me, I told him the first time
he was the least intoxicated he should go on shore. Finding
him drunk a few days after, as soon as he was sober I called
him into the cabin, and represented the ruin he was bringing
on himself and the disgrace it was to his family. He left
me, much affected, and going to his cot, was seized with a
fever which soon carried him off. Although the death of a
drunken man is scarcely to be lamented, I felt concern for
this young man, who was gentlemanly in his behavior, and
who, had he taken care of himself, would have been an honor
to his country. There came down also a Dr. Draper,* a little
Irishman, who had been in the army. He was recommended
by a relation of mine, to go as surgeon of the ship. He was an
exceedingly good companion, but I had soon an opportunity
of knowing that, as a surgeon, he was a very ignorant one.
There were at this time in Baltimore two very hospitable
merchants, who entertained a great many strangers. They
were Mr. Hugh Young, a native of Ireland, and Mr. William
Hammond, a native of Baltimore. These gentlemen often
had large parties to dine with them, and it was very difficult
to get from either of them sober. Draper was often with

---

* Soon after the peace poor Draper went out surgeon of a ship from
New York to China. Upon the passage home, after they had received a
pilot on board, he heard a piece of news that affected him very much; and
while standing up for the town with a fair wind, and every person on board
but himself in high spirits, as they generally are when coming off a long
voyage, he went forward, and jumped overboard and drowned himself. I
found afterwards that he had acted very imprudently before he sailed from
New York.—AUTHOR'S NOTE.

them ; he told me he loved those men, they always gave him cool wine, and enough of it. As they were concerned in a ship going out with and consigned to me, I was obliged to be with them sometimes, but I always took care to have some one to call for me soon after dinner upon pressing business. Capt. Charles Craig,* brother to Col. Craig, was to come down and go with me as captain of marines. As he did not arrive at the time appointed, I gave the command of them to Capt. Whitehead, who had been a lieutenant and adjutant to one of our regiments.

Just before we sailed the celebrated Count de Benyowsky†

* Captain Craig was a very brave, excellent officer. He commanded a troop of horse on the lines when the British were in Philadelphia. General Washington, and every person who knew him, was fond of him. He left the army at the request of Marks Bird, of Reading, and married his daughter. After the marriage, he wanted Craig to retract something he had said about him. This Craig did not think, as a man of honor, he could do. On his refusing, Bird did everything in his power to injure him. Craig declared several times to me, before I left Reading, that Bird had used him so ill he had a great mind to shoot him. Having spent all his money, and being bred to no business, he thought if he was gone Bird would take home his wife and infant child. He therefore determined to put an end to his own existence. He told his servant boy, who had been with him in the army, and had no idea of disputing any orders he gave him, to stay in the entry, and if any person came for him to tell them he was lying down. As there was a person asleep in the room where his pistols were, he pulled off his shoes for fear of waking him ; he put the pistols between two pillows, for fear he should be met in the entry, and going into his own room, he lay down on his bed and shot himself through the head just at the moment his brother, Col. Craig, put his foot into the house. I never knew a more amiable man than Capt. Craig. I received the account of his death just before we sailed. It is said to be a cowardly act, but I have been acquainted with four persons, who had all been officers, that shot themselves. They were Capts. Craig, Pry, Lockwood (of the British navy), and Lieut. Morgan. They were all men of undoubted courage. It is, however, a shocking act, and nothing can justify it.—AUTHOR'S NOTE.

† The life of Count Benyowsky was one of extraordinary adventure. Born in Hungary in 1741, he died in 1786. His father was general of cavalry in the Imperial Service, and he himself served in the Seven Years' War. After visiting Holland and England, he engaged as colonel of cavalry in the Polish Service, and, being captured, was banished to Kamschatka. Escaping thence (carrying with him the Governor's daughter), he reached

came to Baltimore to go out with me. He brought letters to me from Mr. Holker, who was one of the owners of the ship. He had with him three foreign officers, and as I thought they all would be of service in case of our coming to action, which they promised they would, I took them. We sailed from Baltimore the 15th of July, 1782, having on board one hundred and thirty men and boys. My orders were to proceed from Baltimore to York in Virginia, and there put myself under convoy of the Sybil French frigate. When we arrived at York, I went on board the Sybil taking with me Count Benyowsky and a French officer that had been in our army. I told the captain of the frigate that as we were in a strong armed ship I expected, if we took any prizes during the passage, we should have a proportional part of them. He declared in presence of the gentlemen I took with me and of some of his own officers, that I should. It was the first of August before we went out of the Capes. In going from York, owing to the misconduct of the captain, who thought he knew the channel better than the pilot, the Sybil took the ground, and had like to have beat her bottom out, which after our arrival at the Cape and their cheating us of our share of prize money I wished she had done. There were near thirty sail under convoy of the Sybil and my ship. The night after we left the Capes we fell in with two ships which we at first took to be British cruisers. All hands were called to quarters and every preparation made to engage. Count Benyowsky I stationed at the colors, the officers who came

Formosa and Macao, and, proceeding to France, was placed at the head of a projected colony in Madagascar. He arrived at Madagascar in 1774, and met with promise of success, but being discountenanced by the French Government, he returned to Europe, and again engaged in the Imperial Service. He distinguished himself in the battle of Habelshwerdt in 1778. Still faithful to his Madagascar subjects, he visited England and America in search of assistance; he was kindly received in this country, especially in Baltimore. In 1785 he again reached Madagascar, and in the following year was mortally wounded in an encounter with French troops sent from the Isle of France. His memoirs, originally written in French, have been published since his death in many languages.

with him, among the marines. The Count appeared pleased with his station, and drawing a monstrous sword, he swore nobody should haul down the colors without my orders. He appeared very cheerful, saying "Hah, Captain! presently a fine battle." I believe he was perfectly brave. The ships proved to be Americans bound home.

I believe there never was a vessel sailed worse than the Friendship. When we had a pleasant breeze and every sail set, some of the convoy would play round us under their fore-sails. The Sybil could at any time go ahead of us with the foretop-sail upon the cap. I do not believe there was a day while we were out that I could not have swam round her. However, as we had plenty of stores, an agreeable company, excellent accommodations, and were well fitted to fight, we passed our time very pleasantly. The officers wished to play cards, but this I would not suffer. It never should be suffered on board an armed ship.

During the passage we took two prizes; one was a ship from St. Augustine with naval stores and skins, bound to London, the other a sloop from Barbadoes bound to New York with rum. The day we crossed the tropic several of the crew were ducked, and we had the usual diversions that take place on those occasions. After one of the marines, whose name was Clagget, a native of Maryland, had been ducked, he came aft and told me he had not only been ducked but treated very indecently by some of the forecastle men, and wished to know if he could not have satisfaction. In-quiring into what they had done, I found he had been very ill-used, and as he was a stout, active fellow, I asked him if he was willing to fight any of those who had behaved ill to him. He replied, yes, he would fight them all, one after another, and it was what he wanted. Upon this I made him go forward and challenge any one of them. Immediately one Jim Ryers, who had learned to box in Dublin, stepped forward, and stripping himself, said he was ready for him. Clagget was much the stouter man, and was as soon ready. In order to give them room I made them come aft on the quarter-deck. Ryers at first took the advantage of the rise

of the quarter-deck, but after the first fall I made them take
it in turn. The second fall Clagget put his thumb out of
joint; however, he was so powerful that he broke down all
Ryer's guards, and closing with him, gave him two or three
such falls that I thought he would have broken his ribs. He was
obliged to give out, declaring Clagget too strong for him. I
made Clagget challenge the rest of the forecastle men to fight
him; this, several were ready in a moment to do, but I was determined there should be no more fighting; indeed, I thought
it wrong to suffer this, and would not have done it, but expected it would prevent in future any abuse of the seamen to
the marines, of which they were frequently complaining.
After this affair I never heard of any complaint. The Sybil,
when the battle first began, was a good way to windward of
us, and seeing so many of the crew on the quarter-deck, they
supposed there was a mutiny, and bore down and hailed us.
It must have been a strange sight to a crew of Frenchmen.
In fact I was very much ashamed they had seen it.

Count Benyowsky had frequently abused Congress and the
Board of War, which, as he always behaved with great
politeness to me, I did not say anything to him about, although
it was disagreeable to me to hear him. But two days before
we arrived at the Cape, after dinner, when he was a little
heated with wine, he spoke disrespectfully of General Washington. This was what I could not hear without taking
notice of. I told him there were a great many foreign
scoundrels went to the army under General Washington, and
when the general found them ignorant and good for nothing
he sent them away, and they then abused him: that if he said
another disrespectful word of the general, I would put him
out of the cabin. He turned pale with rage; he said I was
now on board my own vessel, as soon as I arrived at the Cape
he would make me answerable for insulting him. I told him
if he ever spoke disrespectfully of General Washington in
my presence, be it where it would, I would insult him.

We arrived at the Cape François after a passage of thirty-
five days, which with the winds we had would have been
made in a fast sailing vessel in one-third of the time. I

found at the Cape a great number of neutral vessels, and the price of flour had fallen from forty to seven or eight dollars a barrel. Upon examining mine, I found that from the length of time it had been on board it had got full of weevils. This was a very disagreeable circumstance, but I never let anything of this kind make me unhappy. A man when he finds himself in difficulties should never give way to them, and make himself miserable by thinking he could have avoided them, but should act with firmness and do everything he can for the best. My orders were after selling the cargo, to load the ship and send her to Europe, neither of which could be done. All the proceeds of the cargo would not have paid the crew their wages, and those who wanted to ship would prefer a neutral ship to ours; and I found during the voyage that the ship was not only a heavy sailer, but that her stern post was loose, and that she was otherwise unfit for a voyage to Europe in the winter season. Being ordered in case of any difficulties to advise with Mr. Gaultier, a respectable French merchant, upon what was best to be done, I stated to him the situation of the ship and cargo, and told him Mr. Robert Smith (son of Mr. William Smith, at present a merchant in Baltimore) had offered me fifty thousand dollars for the ship and cargo, to keep the crew, and pay them all the wages then due, and all the expenses the ship had been at since her arrival. He advised me by all means to take his offer. I therefore agreed with Mr. Smith, who had a contract with Count Galvez, the Spanish General, to supply the Spanish army with flour, and wanted the ship to go to the Havannah. This was a good sale for me, and probably not a bad purchase for Mr. Smith. I understood that by his contract he was to receive twenty dollars for every barrel of flour wanted for the use of the army. Mr. Smith was a great favorite with the Count; indeed, it was said by some wicked fellows at the Cape, that he was concerned with Mr. Smith, and received one-half the profits.

Count Benyowsky left the ship without speaking to me. As he was in my debt for some stores purchased for him by my steward, I called on him at his quarters. I expected a very cool reception, and indeed felt some uneasiness for fear he should remind me of what had passed on board the Friendship, but I was agreeably disappointed, for he received me in a very friendly manner, paid me immediately, and offered to go with me to Governor Bellecombe, who, he said, was his intimate friend, and would oblige him in anything. I thanked him for his friendly offer; there was nothing the Governor could do for me without it was to give me a permission to sail for the Havannah (I had not then sold to Mr. Smith), which, as the embargo was just laid on all the vessels in the harbor, I did not expect he would grant. He said he would try that, and dressing himself went with me to the Governor, who treated him with great respect, and when the Count mentioned that he was under obligations to me, the Governor granted me permission to sail. This, if I had not afterwards sold to Mr. Smith, would have been of great importance to me. The Count, I believe, was much gratified at my seeing the interest he had with the Governor. It appeared from what passed that they had served together in the East Indies. During the passage he had frequently mentioned his serving in India as a brigadier-general, and of his being concerned in a great many adventures. From his account he was engaged with General Count Pulaski in aiding to carry off Stanislaus Poniatowski,* King of Poland, and he told many anecdotes of what passed on that occasion. At first I paid great attention to him, but when I found he would indulge himself in saying anything at all I would not listen to him. Knowing him to assert many things respecting the American army that were not true, I paid little regard to what he said. He was no doubt a brave man, probably a good partisan officer, but from his conversation with Capt. Whitehead, our captain of marines, who was an excellent officer, about manœuvres of an army, he did not suppose the general had much military knowledge. He was a few years

---

* If this statement is correctly reported, Benyowsky must have drawn a very long bow indeed. King Stanislaus was seized and carried off on 3d Sept. 1771, when the Count was in Formosa. See his Memoirs.

12

afterwards killed at Madagascar. The Count, when with me, said he was forty years of age, he appeared much older. He was about five feet eight inches in height, clumsily made, a sallow complexion, a determined, ferocious countenance. I never saw him smile, and suppose he never laughed in his life. He was very different from Dr. Franklin, who laughed heartily at any moment.

At the trial of the two prizes taken during our passage, I put in my claim to an equal share, and appealed to the captain of the frigate whether he had not agreed to my having it. He answered that he had agreed to it. The judge requesting to see my orders, after reading them, told me that I was directed to proceed to York, and go from thence under convoy of the Sybil, and that by the laws of France no convoy was entitled to a share of any prize, and therefore I could receive none, that the captain of the frigate could not alter the laws of France. I used every argument in my power to try to convince the judge that there was a great difference between my ship and a French Letter of Marque, but all I said had no effect. If my owners had made use of the word "company" instead of "convoy," they said I would have been entitled to a share, but had this word been in I have no doubt but what they would have found out something to have cheated us of our share. I was sorry afterwards that I did not write to Dr. Franklin, then Minister at the Court of France. The crew of the Friendship were much enraged when they understood the decision of the court. They would have been guilty of some act of violence, if they had not been restrained, and were continually cursing the whole French nation.

About ten days after our arrival, the Friendship sailed for the Havannah. The following morning Mr. Smith requested I would breakfast with him, and he would pay me. While we were at breakfast, he received a letter which, after reading, he handed to me, saying at the same time, "such a letter would take away some people's appetite." On reading the letter, I found it gave an account of the loss of the Friendship. The day she went out they discovered a sail a considerable distance in the offing, standing for them. They were then not more than three or four miles from the land, which they immediately stood for. The vessel in chase came up so fast, that by the time the Friendship struck the ground, the enemy was within gunshot, and fired at them. However, they did them no injury. The vessel was lost, but the cargo and most of the stores were saved. We understood afterwards that the ship that drove the Friendship on shore was the London man-of-war. Mr. Smith paid me in dollars, which I had carried to the treasury, and received government bills for them, which I remitted to the owners.

There were at this time continual quarrels between the French and Spanish officers and the soldiers. They appeared to hate each other most cordially. I dined frequently at the mess of some Spanish officers with Mr. Smith, and I never saw a French officer at the table. I believe they very seldom associated together. The Spanish officers often told Mr. Smith and myself that they were much more afraid of the Americans disturbing them in their possessions in America than ever they had been of the British, and I believe they all would have been glad we had not been independent of Great Britain.

After the Friendship sailed, I purchased a brig built in Philadelphia, called the St. Patrick. When I purchased her, she was under Danish colors. Of this brig Mr. Smith took one-half, I held a quarter, and Mr. Ceromo held the other quarter. Not being able to get a commission as an American, in order to arm her, I was obliged to get a French commission as a letter of marque. This there was no difficulty in obtaining. We sent on board eight iron and six wooden guns, and loaded her with molasses and rum for Baltimore. At this time there was a large fleet in the harbor ready to sail for France, and a week before they sailed an embargo was laid on all the American vessels. I thought this very unjust, and particularly hard upon some that had been ready for some time, and had waited on purpose to go with the fleet; I therefore requested a meeting of all the American masters, in order to get them to agree to a memorial to the

Governor. We drew one up, and requested the interpreter
to translate it, and go with us to present it. After reading
it, he said if he was to go to the Governor with such a memorial, he should be afraid the Governor would have him
thrown out of the window. We, however, got it translated,
and as I understood a little French, I agreed to hand it to
the Governor. Captain Darby and some others were appointed to go with me. Being anxious about the business, I
walked fast and was soon a good way ahead of my company,
when Darby, who commanded a ship belonging to Baltimore,
called after me, "Biddle! the captains won't go." Looking
round I found there was only one with him. When he came
up, he said those who had gone back had been talking with
the interpreter, and they were apprehensive the Governor
would give them a disagreeable reception, and therefore
would not go. I told him if he was apprehensive, he had
better go back with them, but I would go, if no one went
with me. He swore he was no way uneasy; the Governor,
let him do his worst, could only hang him, and that he did not
regard. When I handed the Governor the memorial, he read
it, and then addressing us with great politeness, said he had
nothing to do with the embargo, that it was a business of
the admiral's. As the admiral was at the other end of the
room, I begged the Governor would have the goodness to speak
to him; upon which he called him and gave him the memorial. After reading it he said he thought the embargo necessary for fear some of the Americans should be taken and give
information to the British respecting the fleet. Upon my
observing we were all in fast-sailing vessels, and not so liable
to be taken as the French merchant ships, he said he understood all our vessels were not commanded by Americans, and
they might run to leeward and inform the British. I told
him that could be easily prevented by our keeping close to
the men of war; he, however, thought there would be some
risk, and would not consent to our going with the fleet, but
seeing we were much discontented with our being detained,
he and the Governor both assured us the embargo should be
taken off in two or three days after the fleet sailed, and the

admiral said he would send us a frigate to convoy us clear of the Keys. With this assurance we left them.

Whitehead, who came out captain of marines with me in the Friendship, and left her in order to continue with me, was about this time arrested by his tailor, an English renegade, who had deserted from the British army, and found his way here. They had some dispute about the account before the arrest. Whitehead had told him he must be a worthless scoundrel to desert his country. He declared to me he had paid the account, that, as it was but a trifle, he would pay it again, but he could not think of being imposed upon by such a rascal. Taking a respectable old merchant, Mr. Mernier, with me, I went to the judge, and told him Mr. Whitehead had been an officer in the American army, that I knew him to be a young man of strict honor that would not say he had paid the tailor without he had really done it. The judge, who knew the tailor to be a bad fellow, immediately ordered him out of the house; and thus the business was ended. I thought this an excellent way of settling a law suit, and if we could always rely upon having an upright judge it would be a much better way than leaving it to an ignorant or partial jury. A friend of mine, Mr. Collinson Read, that had a cause to try in Northampton County, told me that upon hearing the evidence, he found he could say nothing in favor of his client, he therefore just observed to the jury, that the cause was so plain he would give them no trouble. When the jury returned he was much surprised to find they brought in a verdict in favor of his client, and as he went out of court the foreman took him to one side, saying, "Mr. Read, I know the verdict should have been in favor of the plaintiff, but you did my son a great favor, and so I was determined to be your friend, and therefore persuaded the jury to give a verdict for your client."

Mr. Mernier, whom I have mentioned, was a very worthy man, who had been settled many years at the Cape. I had letters to him from an old friend, and he insisted upon my staying at his house. We frequently disputed about the liberties enjoyed by the people of France and America. He had been in America, and said we had too much liberty, that there was not so much respect paid to gentlemen of rank as there should be. The lower orders of people behaved as if they were on a footing with them. He allowed it was a very fine country, but thought the government not by any means so good as theirs, that the French had as much liberty as they ought to have. I told him that in America perhaps there was not that respect paid to the officers of government there should be, but that in France they certainly wanted much reformation; a poor man hardly ever knew what it was to have a good meal, nor could he call anything his own. He replied, it was no matter, they were contented. He, however, soon altered his opinion. Governor Bellecombe one day sent an order for him to be taken to the fort, where he had this good man, who was near seventy years of age, confined for a week without any of his family or friends being permitted to see him; and the only reason given for it was, that he, who was an officer (I believe in the militia), had come upon the parade without pulling off his hat to the Governor. This was the reason expressed, but the true reason, Mr. Mernier said, was that the Governor wanted to borrow some money of him, which he knew the Governor would never repay, and he had, therefore, refused him. Poor Mernier never said anything to me after this of our having too much liberty in America. He said he would, and I afterwards understood he did, send a memorial to the King, complaining of the conduct of this Governor, who received a reprimand for his usage of Mr. Mernier. The behavior of this Governor Bellecombe, so different from that of the judge, convinced me that it was dangerous trusting a man with too much power, for the Governor was generally esteemed a good man.

The embargo was taken off in three or four days, but the frigates did not return. Darby and myself determined to sail together, and, should we fall in with any cruiser, to stand by each other. He was in a ship of eighteen guns and seventy-five men. I had in the brig, including passengers, forty men. I had also as passengers two French women, a mother and daughter, going to see some relations in Baltimore. The daughter was a sprightly, brown girl of sixteen; the mother a swarthy dame, about forty. We sailed from the Cape the 25th of September, 1782. I was mortified when we got out to find that the brig did not sail well, and that she was very crank. We had good weather until we struck soundings a few leagues to the southward of Cape Henry, when the wind shifting to the southeast it became cloudy, and looked as if it was going to blow hard. About ten o'clock, the moon breaking out, we saw two sail, a ship and a brig, standing after us. At twelve o'clock they were still after us, although they were not much nearer than at ten o'clock. At one o'clock we had a squall which did not clear away until near two o'clock, when we discovered the two sail had neared us very much. Darby and myself were not a cable's length from each other, and both prepared for action. We neither of us had been off the deck from the time we first discovered the two sail. At two o'clock Darby hailed me: "Biddle, do you see these pirates are coming up with us?" I replied that I did, and that we had better heave to and engage them, or oblige them to sheer off; which he agreeing to, we immediately hauled up our foresail and hove to, and Darby did the same. We were determined to have the first broadside if we could; however, as soon as they perceived we were lying to to engage them, they hauled off upon a wind, and we soon lost sight of them. As soon as we hove to I had the two female passengers, who were a good deal alarmed, taken into the cockpit, and, as the old one had been very troublesome, kept them there a considerable time after we bore away, which we did as soon as the two sail were out of sight. Before daylight we anchored in Hampton Roads. The next day a flag of truce came in, who had been boarded by the two vessels which chased us. They were a ship and brig, privateers from New York; the ship commanded by a Captain Hazard, an old acquaintance of mine; however, I was glad we did not at this time renew our acquaintance. He was a native of Rhode Island, one of the stoutest and best tempered men I ever knew, but no

seaman. Considering himself ill-used in not being exchanged
when he thought he should have been, he joined the British,
and was very troublesome on the coast. They, fortunately
for us, took Darby's ship for a French frigate that was said
to be on the coast.

After obtaining some refreshments we proceeded to Baltimore, where we arrived the 8th of October. A French
corvette lying at this time at Baltimore, seeing us under
French colors, sent her boat on board. They were much surprised to find there was not one on board could speak a word
of French, for I had just before gone with the two French
women on shore. The ladies went to their relations, and
soon after the younger had the good fortune to attract the
notice of Mr. ——, the French Consul, who, a few days
after our arrival, married her. Dining at Grant's with a
large company, a person called to me and told me my passenger was going to be married. I inquired to whom, when
he informed me to the French Consul. I said it was very
well; had it been to an American I should have forbidden
the banns. One of the consul's friends called on me the next
day to know what was my meaning. I told him it was
spoken in jest; that, however, he was at liberty to put any
meaning he pleased on what was said. She was a lively girl,
who, when it was cold, would put on any of my clothes,
dance on the quarter-deck in them, and perform some other
monkey tricks which I suppose she thought there was no
impropriety in. Custom reconciles most things.

My French ladies disgusted all the other passengers, as
well as myself, the first night they came on board. We
supped on the quarter-deck, and after supper they squatted
down before us and wet the quarter-deck. This I had heard
and read of as being common, but I had never seen it before.
The most common street-walker with us would not have
done thus.

As soon as the brig was ready for sea I sent her out under
the command of one Atchison, who had come in as my mate.
Being convinced we should soon have peace, I sold my share
of the brig to Mr. Smith at the rate of six thousand

pounds (six months after she would not have sold for as many hundred), and set off for Reading, being very impatient to see my family. Mrs. Lux wishing to see her mother, we sat off together. When we arrived at Reading we had the satisfaction to find our friends all well. In the month of February, 1783, Mrs. Biddle was delivered of a son, whom I called James, after my brother.

In the spring of 1783, while calling in the coffee-house, Captain Budden called me out. He told me that Crathorne* who had behaved so ill in Jamaica, was just arrived from Providence, and that his vessel was lying at Market Street wharf. As I considered this man the occasion of my long confinement, and of the death of many an American, I was anxious to see him. Going immediately with Budden on board his vessel, we searched every part of her without finding him. I stayed in town four or five days, during which time diligent search was made for him, but without effect. Had he been found I was determined to cut his ears off, for which purpose I had borrowed a penknife at the coffee-house. Many years after he died miserably in the bettering-house.

Going to Philadelphia soon after, I agreed with a relation, Mr. Clement Biddle, and with Mr. James Collins, to go to New York, and there charter two or three British vessels for the West Indies. I obtained permission from the Supreme Executive Council, and went to New York. At this time New York was crowded with Americans from all parts of the continent, who went in to speculate, or to see their friends. A story was told at this time of a New England man, who occasioned a good deal of laughter. He had some dispute about his permission, when the British officer refused to let him enter. "Well, I vow," says the Yankee, " you are very bold, considering you are a conquered people."

New York was at this time a very disagreeable place to me. Many unfortunate Americans who had joined the British army were now extremely anxious to return to their former places of residence, among others, my unfortunate

---

* See pages 93, 94.

brother John. He had been in the British service before the war, and remained attached to them. I felt much pain for these unhappy people, for whom the British Government, to their honor be it said, provided generously.

I chartered a ship and a snow by the month, to proceed to Philadelphia, and there load for the West Indies. As I had a good deal of unsettled business in Hispaniola, I was determined to go out myself and settle it. The ship and snow* were sent to Cape François. I took my passage in a small French schooner commanded by Capt. Le Faure, an old acquaintance of mine, bound to Port au Prince. A short time before we sailed I had an account of the death of Mr. Robert Smith at Cape François. He had purchased a mulatto girl, who lived with him, and imprudently informed her of some provision he had made for her at his death. Although there was no proof, it was strongly suspected she hurried him out of the world. He was an amiable young man, and I believe left a handsome fortune, but having no person about him to take care of the property, the family recovered little or nothing.

We sailed from Philadelphia in June, 1783. There were besides myself, two or three French gentlemen, and Mayer Polonois, a poor Jew, passengers. I do not mean poor as to money, for probably he had more than any other person on board, but unfortunately Le Faure took a dislike to the man, and treated him very roughly. One day at dinner, the Jew saying something disrespectful of the French army, Le Faure started up in a rage, threw the Jew's plate, with his silver fork, and all that was on the plate, into the sea, and, if I had not interfered, I believe he would have thrown the Jew in after them. He never after this would permit the Jew to dine in the cabin. Except the disputes with this poor devil, we had an agreeable time. As I had some business to settle with Messrs. Musculas & Rondineau at the Mole St. Nicolas, Le Faure who was very friendly to me, put in there and

---

* Perhaps it may be as well to explain that the "snow" was a two-masted vessel rigged very nearly like a brig. The term is obsolete.

waited a day for me. He afterwards landed me at Leogane, where I also had some business for a friend. After landing me he proceeded to Port au Prince. I stayed two days at Leogane, which if it was not sickly would be an agreeable place. From here I went to Port au Prince by land, where I found that most of my former friends, Mr. Pasquer, Mr. Peyrobe, and others, were dead. Barère, the interpreter, was still here, and in business, and gave me a very friendly reception. Barère was a native of Bayonne, but had lived for some years in Boston, where he married. He had one son, who at this time was in France.

Polonois called on me to consult me about suing Le Faure. I should have advised against it, even if LeFaure had been a man I had no regard for, knowing, as he had mentioned the French navy and army with disrespect, and spoken very favorably of the British, he would be treated as badly by the court as Polonois was by the captain. He was, however, persuaded to bring a suit. He wrote me afterwards that he wished he had taken my advice, for the suit went against him, and Le Faure in turn sued him for his passage and stores and recovered; although in consequence of his loading the vessel Polonois was to have had his passage free.

After settling my business at Port au Prince, I was determined to go by land to the Cape. This was an undertaking my friends at Port au Prince, as well as those at Leogane and the Mole advised me against, but as I was anxious to get to the Cape, and knew it was very uncertain when I could get there by water, they could not alter my intention. They represented it as a journey, at that season of the year, very disagreeable and dangerous. I took letters from Barère for several persons on the road, and had letters from other gentlemen. The first place I stopped at, after leaving Port au Prince, was St. Marks, where I was again advised to give up my journey by land. They represented the country as very unhealthy, and liable at that season of the year to be overflowed; but having made up my mind before I left Port au Prince, nothing they could say made any impression on me. From St. Marks Barère's friend sent me in his carriage a few miles, and I was sent in carriages or on horseback from one plantation to another, until I reached the Cape. The journey, on account of the excessive heat, was very disagreeable, but not so bad as it had been represented. The planters to whom I had letters behaved with great politeness and attention. My speaking a little French was of much advantage, and a packet from the Chevalier de la Luzerne to the Governor was of service to me. Some of those who saw the packet offered to send it to the Governor with more expedition than I could take it, but I represented it to be of too much consequence to be trusted to any person they could send. My having the packet was owing to my requesting my friend, Gen. Mifflin, to procure a letter of introduction from the Chevalier to the Governor. At the Cape the letter was of service. A person going to any distant place, but particularly to a foreign country, should carry letters of introduction, if he can procure them. They are sometimes of great service; if you have no occasion for them, they give but little trouble.

I found at the Cape the ship discharging her cargo. After settling my business here, and providing a cargo for the ship, I took my passage in a brig bound to Wilmington. We left Cape François the 13th of August, 1783, and without anything material happening, we arrived off Cape Henlopen the 27th. It was night when the pilot boat came alongside. I inquired what news. Instead of answering the question he desired to know who it was speaking to him. I told him Captain Biddle. "Captain Biddle!" he exclaimed, " I never hear that name without being greatly affected." When he came on board he told me my voice was so much like that of my brother Nicholas, that he was quite astonished when I hailed him, and, if he had not been certain of his loss, he should have supposed it was him who was speaking; that he had been a master's mate on board the Randolph, and was put on board a prize the day before her loss. He spoke of my brother as one for whom he would have sacrificed his life. The 29th of August I landed at Wilmington, and went up the same day in the stage to Philadelphia, and the next to Reading, where I found my family all well.

Mr. James Collins, with whom I was acquainted while a prisoner in New York, had come from there, and settled in Philadelphia. During my absence he married Lydia Biddle, daughter of my brother James. He was a genteel man, of a good family, and was strongly recommended to my brother as a very worthy man by Mr. John Maxfield Nesbit, and several other respectable Irish gentlemen of Philadelphia. Mr. Collins entered into partnership with Captain Thomas Truxtun, under the firm of Collins & Truxtun. They opened a large dry goods store, which they wished me to join them in, but I was always averse to entering into any partnership. Without you can place the utmost confidence in the honor, integrity, and prudence of your partner, your mind must be always uneasy, for it is in the power of a partner to ruin you. It was very fortunate for me that I did not join in this partnership. Being just before the close of the war that they commenced business, they set up a ship to carry twenty guns, and sent for a large quantity of goods. At the peace these goods fell considerably, and the ship, which cost them nearly sixteen thousand pounds, sold, I believe, for four thousand, so that they were soon obliged to stop payment, and, but for the honorable conduct of Captain Truxtun, several of their friends, as well as myself, would have been considerable losers by endorsing their notes. Collins not having the means of doing anything for his creditors, took the benefit of the Bankrupt Law; but Truxtun would not do this. He went commander of a ship to India, declaring that not one of the endorsers should be a loser by him, and he was as good as his word, paying the endorsers every farthing due from the house. Such conduct will always make a man esteemed and respected, and every one will endeavor to push him forward in the world.* The practice

---

* Commodore Truxtun, after seeing much service during the war of the Revolution in command of different armed vessels, was, on the re-organization of the navy, in 1794, commissioned as the fifth captain on the list. Whilst in command of the Constellation he captured the French frigate L'Insurgente, and in February, 1800, off Guadaloupe, he had a fierce and bloody night engagement, lasting five hours, with the French frigate

of endorsing notes was little understood here at this time.
Many persons would endorse notes for a thousand pounds
for a friend or acquaintance, who would not trust them to
the amount of five pounds in money, supposing the endorsing a note to be a mere matter of form; however, the matter
of form proved a matter of substance to many who were
ruined by it. The directors of the Bank of North America,
at this time the only bank in America (without probably
intending to do wrong), did a great deal of mischief. If a
note was refused being discounted, they would tell the man
who offered the note, go and get such a one, naming some
friend or acquaintance, to endorse your note, and it shall be
done. By this means many a worthy man was ruined.

This fall I received a letter from my old friend Capt. Thos.
Allen, who wrote me he was just leaving North Carolina for
Philadelphia in a fine new ship, to fit her completely, and
charter her. He expressed great satisfaction at the pleasure
he should have in seeing me, and a wish that we should be
settled in the same place; and that when he saw me he would
endeavor to persuade me to return to North Carolina, but
that if he could not, it was probable he should remove his
family to Philadelphia. I was in daily expectation of seeing
him, when we had an account of his loss, the ship having
overset in a heavy squall. A schooner that was about a mile

La Vengeance. The two ships were of equal force. The contest ended by
the French ship sheering off, and finally escaping, owing only to the loss of
the Constellation's mainmast.

Truxtun was an excellent seaman and an officer of the highest spirit and
courage. In 1802 he left the service, owing, as he always maintained, to
a misconstruction put upon his letter giving up the command of a squadron
to which he was appointed. The Secretary of the Navy insisted (very
strangely, considering Truxtun's high reputation) that the letter was a resignation from the navy. This view prevailed, to Truxtun's great indignation.
The Commodore was a good hater, and denounced the Secretary to the day
of his death; in fact, was anxious to hold that gentleman personally responsi-
ble, after the fashion of the day.

He was subsequently elected High Sheriff of Philadelphia, and died universally respected in 1822. He is worthily represented in the navy at this
day by Captain William T. Truxtun, distinguished in the war of 1861-5.

to leeward of her, saw her overset and founder, without being able to afford them any assistance. The whole crew perished. It was with great pain I heard of the loss of this worthy man, for whom I had the affection of a brother.

I employed myself during the fall and winter in keeping a small store of goods with which I made as much as maintained my family, but intending to enter more largely into business I thought Philadelphia would answer me better than Reading, and therefore intended in the spring to move there, but some of my friends in Berks wishing me to remain in Reading until the fall, when there was to be an election for a member of the Supreme Executive Council, which they wanted me to be elected to, and as I knew my being a member of Council would not prevent my entering into business, I agreed to wait until the fall. I had two powerful German competitors: Beltzer Gehr, one of them, had for several years been a member of the Legislature, and also colonel of a militia regiment; the other was the sheriff of the county, P. Kreemer, whose time as sheriff expired at the election. The Germans are generally a very honest, industrious people, and if treated with kindness, and you render them any services, no people are more grateful. This I have had many instances of. If they find any of their neighbors proud and haughty, they will do anything to injure them. There was one descendant of a German, Nicholas Rossious, who went to school with me when I was a small boy, and with whom I had had many severe battles. He was a warm, active, and influential man at the election, and used every means in his power to serve me. I had also another descendant of a German my friend on the ground, Henry Wertz, who had sailed with me. He came to the wharf just as I was putting off in the Charming Nancy, and inquired if there were oranges where we were going. I told him, "Yes! plenty," "Will you take me?" "Yes, jump on board." He did so, and made the voyage with me. I afterwards found the lad had left his father's wagon and horses in town, and gone off without his knowledge. He came to me some time after we had been at home and begged I would write to his father, and inform him that he had been to sea with me; for, he said, notwithstanding he carried him a bag of oranges his father would not believe he had been at sea, but supposed he had remained in Philadelphia. At the time of the election he went to the court-house, where the election was held, swore he knew Captain Biddle, that he had "been to sea mid him, and fought mid him many times." During the time this honest fellow was with me we had not a gun on board. Several other Germans were active for me at the time of the election, which shows they are not so much devoted to their countrymen as has been said. As a sheriff was to be elected, and there were several candidates, we had a large election. I had more votes than both my competitors. The result was not known until late at night, when some of my friends, who had been sitting up, came to inform me of it. With difficulty I persuaded them, particularly Col. Lutz, a very stout man, from parading about town with a drum and fife.*

I was a good deal affected, a short time before I left Reading, at the fate of a young man who lived near me, of the name of Welsh. He had entered the American army at the commencement of the war, and served during the whole of it. For the first two or three years, being a boy, he was employed as a waiter to Major Scull, a cousin of mine. At the peace, he married and settled at Reading, near which town he was born. Coming home one evening he overtook a lame countrywoman carrying a large bundle. Welsh, who was a good tempered fellow, told her he would carry it for her. She thanked him, and gave it to him. At this time I believe he had no intention of committing a robbery, but finding there was a handkerchief with nine dollars in the bundle,

---

* This election was in October, 1784, John Dickinson being then President, and General James Irvine, Vice-President of the Council. By the Pennsylvania Constitution of 1776, the executive power was vested in a "Supreme Executive Council," consisting of members who were elected (but not on a general ticket) by the counties. The members of the Assembly and the members of the Council met together once a year, to choose from the Councillors, by joint ballot, a President and a Vice-President. This system continued until the adoption of the Constitution of 1790.

just before they entered the town he, unobserved by her, took them out, and gave her the bundle. When she got to her lodging, she missed the dollars; and from the description she gave of Welsh, he was suspected and taken up. When before a magistrate, he immediately acknowledged he had taken the money, but said he only did it to frighten her, and intended to have called and given it to her, and he returned every dollar. The magistrate sent him to gaol. At his trial, several officers with whom he had served, happened to be in Reading, all of whom appeared in court, and gave him an exceedingly good character. He had able counsel assigned him, who endeavored to persuade the jury it was only a breach of trust. The charge, however, from Chief Justice McKean, was against him, and the jury brought him in guilty, and he was executed. I doubt whether in England a man would have suffered death for such an offence, but the war was just over, and it was expected that many of the soldiers would infest the roads; otherwise, I believe poor Welsh would not have suffered. To the honor of the American army, I believe this was the only soldier tried for robbery. I saw Welsh several times after sentence was passed on him. He was perfectly resigned to his fate. He said the day before he overtook the woman, from whom he had taken the money, that he had been obliged to sell a sickle to buy a fowl for his wife who was sick; that he was willing to work, and did work whenever he could get any to do, but it was not in his power to maintain a sick wife and himself. I asked him why he had not informed me, or some other gentleman in Reading, of his distress. He replied, that as he was a hearty young man, he could not bear the thought of begging assistance, that death was less terrible to him. It would have given pleasure to many in Reading, besides myself, to have relieved the poor fellow. The morning he died, I went to see him, and found he was out of his dungeon. He was a very handsome young man, clean, and neatly dressed, and ready to proceed. His wife and several of his friends were with him, but there was not one in the room but what was much more affected than Welsh, who was perfectly com-

13

posed, and behaved with great propriety. The minister who
was to attend him went in with me, and was much
shocked at seeing that the executioner (a Hessian) had his
face blacked, and declared he should not go in that condition. Welsh told the minister that the man's being blacked
could not possibly do any injury, and probably would prevent his being ill-used by some of his comrades, and therefore begged he would let him go as he was. He requested
to walk to the gallows, which was more than a mile from
the gaol. Being Chief Burgess* of the borough, I attended,
and rode near the prisoner, who marched with great firmness.
There was an immense crowd,† the people for fifteen or
twenty miles around having brought their children to see
the execution, thinking it would have a good effect. I
should suppose it would rather be an injury to them. The
hill near the gallows was covered with men, women, and
children. When we drew near, Welsh looked towards the
hill, and said to me, "Mr. Biddle, that is a grand sight, but I
shall soon see a much more glorious one." He continued to
the last moment to behave with the same firmness. A poor
wretch was executed with him, for house-breaking; but he
appeared stupid, and said nothing from the time he was
brought out of the dungeon.

I left Reading the 20th of October, 1784, for Philadelphia,
where I had rented and furnished a house. Several of my
friends rode with me to Pottsgrove. I was now entering
into a scene of life very different from what I had been accustomed to, or expected. At the time I took my seat, the
celebrated John Dickinson was President of the Supreme
Executive Council, and General James Irvine was Vice-Presi-

---

* I was elected Chief Burgess while in Philadelphia, and contrary to my
wish or expectation. Had Welsh been brought before me, after hearing the
parties, and giving the woman her money, I should have dismissed him.—
AUTHOR'S NOTE.

† It was said an old woman walked near seventy miles to see this execution. Being fatigued with her walk, a little before the execution she fell
asleep and did not wake until it was over, when she cried most bitterly.—
AUTHOR'S NOTE.

dent, both of whom I knew, but had no acquaintance with
either of them.   Mr. Dickinson was an intimate friend of my
brother James, who gave me letters to him, and he received
me in a very friendly manner.   Gen. Irvine had served with
my brother Edward, for whose loss he expressed the greatest
regret.   I found Council nearly divided between what were
then called Republicans and Constitutionalists.   From the
knowledge the Republicans had of my brothers James and
Edward, they expected I would join their party, but coming
from the county of Berks, most of the inhabitants of which
were Constitutionalists, it was expected I would vote with
them.   But I went into Council with a firm resolution not
to suffer any party views to influence my conduct, and this I
adhered to.

The winter after my election there were a number of applicants for the office of Prothonotary for the county of Dauphin,
a county just before erected.   Among the applicants were
Col. Atlee and Capt. Graydon.   They were the only two who
had any chance of succeeding; both had served with reputation in the American army, and they both were of the
Republican party, who just at that time had a majority in
Council.   Capt. Graydon and myself had a dispute just before
I left Reading, and nothing but the interference of our friends
prevented our fighting.   At the time he came down to make
his application we did not speak, but he brought me a letter
from my brother James, who wrote me that I could not
render him a more acceptable piece of service than assisting
Capt. Graydon to obtain the office.   This letter from a brother
so dear to me, determined me to use all my interest for Capt.
Graydon.   I introduced him to the President and all the
members of Council in town, with none of whom was he
before acquainted.   When I introduced him to Mr. Dickinson he desired, when the election should come on, that I
would remind him of Capt. Graydon.   Col. Meason, one of
the members, mentioned something like it.   Both these
gentlemen were the intimate and warm friends of Col. Atlee,
who the year before had been with them in Council.   A few
days after this the Republican party, having a majority,

determined to bring on the election. I was much displeased; however they had a majority, and there was no preventing them. There were at this time thirteen members, seven Republicans, five Constitutionalists, and myself. The five Constitutionalists had promised me they would vote for Capt. Graydon; and in fact I knew they would vote for any one set up in opposition to the one proposed by the Republicans. When the election came on Col. Atlee was in the committee room, having been brought there by his friends, who entertained no doubt of his succeeding. The custom then in Council was to set up the candidates, one after the other, and whoever had the greatest number of votes (if a majority of the members present) was the officer. We drew who should be first voted for. The ticket was either yes, or a blank. It happened Atlee was the first voted for; he had seven votes. When Graydon was voted for I went up to the President, and telling him he had requested me to remind him of Capt. Graydon, said I must therefore beg he would oblige me by putting in a vote for him, and gave him a ticket, which I saw him put in the hat. I then went to Col. Meason and desired he would do the same, which he did. By this means Capt. Graydon had eight votes. The President and Meason were almost distracted when they found Graydon had a majority. They both thought when they gave us their votes for Graydon that it would gratify me and be of no injury to Atlee. After musing for some time Mr. Dickinson said he did not think any appointment good without the approbation of the President. I told him if he did think so, he was the only member who did. Before I left Council I sent for Graydon, had his sureties approved of, and his commission made out and signed by the Vice-President. When I afterwards saw Col. Atlee he told me he did not blame me the least, but said he lamented that a brother of Edward Biddle, whom he loved and esteemed more than any other man that ever lived, should have opposed him. But he never forgave Mr. Dickinson. Indeed it was unpardonable in him. Mr. Dickinson is a very worthy good man, but frequently was persuaded to do what he knew he ought not to do. This affair was reported at the time much against Mr. Dickinson; it was said I forced him to vote for Graydon, but it happened just as I have related it.*

In October, 1785, the time of the President, Mr. Dickinson, and the Vice-President, General Irvine, expired. It was, therefore, necessary an election should be held among the members of Council to chose a Vice-President until the meeting of the Legislature. I was unanimously elected,† and thus, for a short time, was the Chief Magistrate of Pennsylvania. It is not from vanity that this is mentioned, but as an uncommon circumstance that a man brought up to the sea, and who, from the misfortune of his father, was left

---

* Of this election, Graydon himself gives the following account:—

"In the year 1785, I had the good fortune, through the warm exertions of an influential friend, to obtain an appointment to the prothonotaryship of the Dauphin County Court. By a combination of circumstances working together to my advantage, I obtained, contrary to expectation, the suffrage of the Supreme Executive Council, of which Mr. Dickinson was then President. The Republican party possessed a majority in the Council, and Colonel Atlee, who belonged to it, was designated for the office. He was conspicuous as a party man, and, if I mistake not, at the time a member of the Legislature; and on the score of services and character no one had better claims." . . . . . . '. "To keep out Atlee, the Constitutionalists were disposed to give their votes to any one of his competitors. Of course, I had all their strength; and by adding to it two or three Republican votes, I acquired a greater number than any in nomination. As the mode was to vote for the candidates individually, there was no physical, or perhaps, moral impediment, to each of them receiving the vote of every member. A promise to one was not broken by also voting for another, unless it was exclusively made. The President had, probably, given a promise to Colonel Atlee, as well as myself; and considering me, perhaps, as too weak to endanger his success, thought he might safely gratify my friend, who pinned him to the vote, which, on coming to the box, he seemed half inclined to withhold." . . . . "Mr. Dickinson, for his want of decision, as it was called, was bitterly inveighed against by his party; and the next day at the coffee-house when receiving the congratulations of some of my acquaintances, Mr. Michael Morgan O'Brien, who chanced to be present, and to whom I was then introduced, asserted it as a fact, that the President had suffered his hand to be seized and crammed into the box with a ticket for me; 'but no matter' said he, "you are a clever fellow I am told, and I am glad that you have got the office.' "—GRAYDON, page 309.

† October 10, 1785.

without a fortune, should so early in life be raised to such a station.

In September, this year, Dr. Franklin arrived from France. He was received with great joy by his fellow citizens. All the officers of government, and the different societies in the city, waited upon him, and congratulated him upon his arrival. In October he was elected a member of the Executive Council for the city. A few days after the election, October 17, 1785, I waited on him, and went with him to the meeting of Council at the State House. Thinking there was an impropriety in my sitting as President of the Board when the Doctor was a member, I proposed, at the meeting next before the one when he came to the Board, to elect him President, which was agreed to, and he was accordingly chosen.

The Doctor, being at this time very much troubled with the stone, seldom attended Council; nothing, however, of any consequence was done at the Board without consulting him; and I called on him almost every day to see if he had anything to propose.

When the election for President and Vice-President came on in the Legislature, some of the leading members of the Republican party, not having found me their thorough-paced devotee, had a meeting for the purpose of preventing my being re-elected, but finding themselves too weak, declined the attempt. Dr. Franklin was elected President, and I was elected Vice-President, almost unanimously.* I believe there were only two votes but what were for me, and but one that was not for the Doctor. My friend, General Mifflin, who was then Speaker of the House, and who counted the votes, was much mortified when he found the election was not unanimous, particularly on account of Dr. Franklin. He was rising to say something on the subject, but sitting near him, and judging his intention, I stopped him. I walked with the Doctor to the old Court House, where we were proclaimed; from thence we went back to the State

* October 29, 1785.

House, where we had to wait until the members of the Council, and the House of Representatives congratulated us upon our election. It was a severe business for the Doctor, who told me that day the stone gave him uncommon pain. He, however, was very cheerful, and, in fact, I hardly ever knew him otherwise. The streets were much crowded from many people in the city having never seen the Doctor. As we passed the door where Baron Steuben stood, he pulled off his hat, which the Doctor thought was very improper to a person walking in a procession. I believe the remark was occasioned by his feeling some pain in taking his arm from mine to pull off his hat. He was very much rejoiced when he reached his own house.

In the spring of 1786 a young woman was condemned at Chester for the murder of her bastard children. Her name was Elizabeth Wilson, and she was of a respectable family in Chester County. Her brother, William Wilson, came with a petition to Council for a respite. He was a sensible young man, and of a very good character. He declared, when he handed me the petition, that he would not have interested himself for her, if he thought her guilty of the murder; that when she was first condemned he believed she was, and therefore would not go near her; but he was now convinced she was innocent, and he had no doubt but that the story she told him was true. She said one D——, Sheriff of Sussex County, New Jersey, visited her when she lived in Philadelphia, that under a promise of marriage he seduced her, and was the father of the twins for the murder of whom she was condemned; that when the children were six weeks old he came to see her at the house she boarded at in Chester County, persuaded her to take a walk with him, saying he intended to put the children out to nurse; that when they got into the woods, he took them from her and laying them on the ground, the inhuman monster put his feet on their breasts, and crushed them to death. He then threatened to murder her if ever she mentioned a word about what he had done, bid her go home, and tell the people she lodged with that he had taken the children to Jersey to nurse, which the dread she was

under of his murdering her, made her comply with; that she
would, at the expense of her life, have endeavored to save the
children, but that she had no suspicion of his diabolical intention until it was too late to save them. The bodies of the
children were found a few days afterwards by some dogs,
which led to the discovery of the murder. Council immediately upon the petition being read, agreed to a respite for
thirty days, and young Wilson set off the same day for Jersey.
He there found the Sheriff, who declared he never knew his
sister, and said he had not been in Philadelphia for two years.
Wilson after making some inquiries, rode back to his sister,
and getting further information from her, went again into
Jersey. He found a person who could prove D—— had been in
Philadelphia and lodged in the house with her, and was in
expectation of obtaining further proof against him, when he
was taken sick in Jersey. Finding the time draw near, sick
as he was, he set off for home in order to get a further respite.
It was late in the morning when he reached Chester, when to
his great surprise he was told that the time granted her was
out that day (he thought it was not until the next) and that the
Sheriff was preparing for her execution. He was very unwell,
having suffered much both in body and mind; he, however,
galloped to Philadelphia as fast as it was possible, and unfortunately went to the President's where, notwithstanding all
his entreaties, it was some time before he could get to see him,
and when he did, he staid endeavoring to persuade the Doctor
to give him a line to the Sheriff, which the Doctor, thinking
it improper, refused, and directed him to me. I was just
leaving the Council chamber when he came, all the members
but myself having gone. I immediately wrote, " Do not ex-
ecute Wilson until you hear further from Council," and directed it to the Sheriff. I well knew the Board intended to
grant a further respite, but had it been a doubt with me, I
should have written to defer the execution, for putting it off
a day could be of no consequence. Wilson set off the instant
I gave him the paper, carrying it in his hand. He rode down
in an hour and a quarter, a distance of fifteen miles, and the
road at that time excessively bad. His sister had been turned

off about ten minutes. What a dreadful sight for an affectionate brother! They immediately cut her down, but although every means were used they could not restore her to life. She persisted in the same story to the last moment of her life, which she resigned with great fortitude, being perfectly calm and composed. The only thing she seemed to regret was the trouble she had given her poor, sick brother, and the pain he must suffer on her account. Just before the cart drove away she looked attentively towards Philadelphia to see if her brother was in sight. For my own part, I firmly believed her innocent, for to me it appeared highly improbable that a mother, after suckling her children for six weeks, could murder them. The next day when Council met, and we heard of the execution, it gave uneasiness to many of the members, all of whom were against her being executed, at least until her brother had had full time to make his inquiries, and I am sure, if he had not been successful, there was a large majority would have been for pardoning her. It is strange, considering the chances this unfortunate girl had, that her life was not saved. It was extraordinary that none of the members of Council, the Secretary, nor his deputy, should have recollected that the time granted was expired; that herself, the clergyman who attended her, nor none of her family or friends, should have applied before, or that the Sheriff, who was a very good man, should not have called or sent to Council before he executed her, and lastly that her brother, who knew Council were sitting at the State House, should pass them, and go to the President. Had he stopped at the State House, she would have been saved. He supposed, if he stopped at Council, there would be some time taken up in debate, and that the President would immediately have given him a letter to the Sheriff. I understood afterwards that he soon followed his sister to her grave.*

* A full detail of the unhappy event will be found in a tract entitled, " A Faithful Narrative of Elizabeth Wilson, who was executed at Chester, January 3, 1786, charged with the murder of her twin infants. Philadelphia: Printed for the purchaser, 1807." 8vo. pp. 23. A rude wood-cut of the final scene ornaments the title page ; a troop of light horse surrounds

Perhaps the punishment of death is too great for an un-married woman who destroys her child. They are generally led to it from a fear of being exposed. It is, to be sure, a shocking crime. If confinement for life, or for a term of years, at the discretion of the court, was the punishment, more would be convicted, and it would tend to put a stop to the crime. While death is the punishment, a jury will sel-dom find a verdict against them. If death is the punishment of the mother, what punishment is too severe for the villain who seduces, and afterwards abandons the wretched mother.

I never was present but at one trial for this crime. It was at Reading. The daughter of a wealthy farmer was tried for the murder of her child. My brother James was employed as her counsel. It appeared perfectly clear from the evidence, that she hove the child into the Schuylkill soon after it was born; but there was one circumstance which had great in-fluence with the jury, and made them doubt the evidence that was given against her. It was, that when the constable broke open her trunk, after she was confined, he found a quantity of ready made clothes for an infant. This induced the jury to believe she did not destroy her child, or made them doubt it, and they acquitted her.

Council were nearly equal at this time, with respect to par-ties. The Republican members were: Messrs. Neville, Hill, Muhlenberg, Ross, Willing, Boyd, and Elliott. The Consti-tutionalists were: Messrs. McLene, Whitehill, Smilie, Find-ley, Watts, Smith, Dean, Hoge, and Martin. The distinction was, that the Republicans wanted an alteration in the Consti-tution. They wished to have a House of Representatives

the gibbet; and hard by is an open coffin and the corpse of her children. The wretch for whose crimes she suffered called himself Joseph Deshong, and first met her at the Cross-Keys tavern, in Chesnut Street, Philadelphia, where she then lodged. The murder was committed in East Bradford Town-ship, Chester County. Her trial came off on the 17th October, 1785, before Judge Atlee; the respite did not reach the ground till twenty-three minutes after she was turned off. There is no doubt that the poor girl was innocent. A copy of this rare pamphlet was in the possession of the late Mr. Winthrop Sargent.

and a Senate. The other party thought no alteration necessary. My brother Edward, when living, was at the head of
the Republican party. Much could be said on both sides.
If a single branch sometimes does wrong, they are (where
there are two branches) often retarded in their business, and
sometimes prevented from doing right. I believe, however,
that, upon the whole, it is better to have two branches.

We had frequent and violent disputes between these members upon political subjects, but they were of little consequence then, and can be of none now. The best informed
man of either party, and the readiest at business, was Mr.
Hoge, but he was so diffident a man, that if we had a full
Council, he could never rise to make a motion, or even to
second one. He was a worthy, valuable man. McLene,
Whitehill, Smilie, and Findley are all sensible men; they
would not be the least embarrassed in speaking before any
assembly whatever. Smilie and Findley are natives of Ireland, the former was brought up a house carpenter; the latter a weaver. They are both men of talents, and if they had
received a good education would have made a figure in any
legislative body. McLene and Whitehill are Pennsylvanians.
These four had been leading members of the State Legislature.
They are all now, May, 1803, living. Whitehill is one of
the Associate Judges for Lancaster County. He, as well as
Smilie and Findley, were elected to Congress. McLene has
retired from public business.

When I first took my seat in Council, not having been
acquainted with any people from the Western country, I
thought from their conversation that McLene, Boyd, Smith,
and Whitehill were Irishmen. It was some time after I
had been in Council, that I found they were not. Talking
one day with Smith (who had as much of the brogue and
look of an Irishman, as any one that ever came from Tippe-
rary) about being at sea, he told me he never was at sea in
his life. "And how, my honey," says Dean, who was sitting
by me, and who also thought him from Ireland, "did you
get to Philadelphia?" "Why I rode here." "And, arrah,
honey! did you ride here all the way from Ireland? I never

heard of a bridge between the two countries." "Devil a bit of me," says Smith, "was ever out of Pennsylvania." And this I found was true, and that McLean, Whitehall, and Boyd were all born in Pennsylvania. People who live in an Irish settlement, or who are much with the Irish, generally affect the brogue. When I sailed from Philadelphia, in the ship Lark, my second mate and most of the crew were Irishmen; on my return, I had as much of it as any of the crew. Landing at Newcastle, while dining with several gentlemen from Philadelphia, one of them asked me if I was not born in Philadelphia. Upon my answering in the affirmative, a man who was sitting in a corner of the room, started up and exclaimed in a great rage, "By J——, I hate a fellow that denies his country." I felt angry at first, but looking at the man, and seeing he was old and feeble, I was disarmed of all resentment, and could not refrain from laughing heartily, in which I was joined by all the company, except the old man, who was much displeased with our mirth. He looked at me with rage and contempt. However, I soon pleased him by speaking favorably of the Irish, and drinking prosperity to Ireland, we became good friends.

John Boyd, one of our Senators, commanded a company on the frontiers, and was an excellent partisan officer. During the war he was wounded and taken prisoner by the Indians. Having killed a number of them before he was taken, they were determined to burn him. For this purpose he was stripped naked and tied to a stake, and expected every moment to suffer death, when he was released by the intercession of one of the squaws who had had her husband killed in the engagement with Boyd. His life was probably saved in consequence of his being a stout, well-made man.

Dean was from Bucks County. It was said he obtained a seat in Council by telling some of the men who make themselves busy at elections, that he would get them appointed officers.* He had been an officer, and a braver never went

* A gentleman who was unpopular in Berks County, got into the Legislature by laying boots, hats, and clothes, with some of the leading men at the election, that he would not be elected.—AUTHOR'S NOTE.

into a field of battle. He is a man of a great deal of humor, and has many good qualities, but is too fond of taverns and keeping improper company. While in Council he had a dispute with a Dr. Linn, who said Dean had promised him his vote for some office, and afterwards voted against him. This by an officious friend was told Dean, who swore he would get a cowskin and whip him until he drove all the molasses* he had in him out. The Doctor hearing of this, challenged Dean. The first notice I had of the affair was Dean's calling on me for my pistols. Upon hearing what the dispute was about, I told him it was a foolish thing to fight about, and it should be made up. He told me it was in vain to preach to him, for fight him he would. They accordingly went into Jersey in the morning. By agreement they were to stand at the distance of ten paces from each other, and fire at the word of command, "make ready, present, fire." This they did the first time at the same instant, without effect. The second time, at the word "present," the Doctor fired. The ball would have killed Dean, having struck him on the groin, if it had not been that he had on a pair of leather breeches, with a thick band. It just penetrated the band, and made a black mark in his groin. Dean supposed himself to be mortally wounded, and although naturally cool as brave, being extremely exasperated, he fired, and then threw his pistol at the Doctor, both which missing, he went up, and before the seconds could prevent him, knocked the Doctor down with his fist. Captain Symonds, the friend of the Doctor, declared he had behaved shamefully, and refused to cross the river in the boat with him. I believe, however, what the Doctor said was true, that the pistol went off by accident. He acknowledged Dean had never made him any promise.

About this time an Indian of the name of Mamachtaguin was tried, condemned, and executed for the murder of John Smith and Benjamin Jones. This poor fellow could not be persuaded to plead not guilty. Notwithstanding all his counsel could say, he persisted in declaring he had killed the

* The Doctor was a native of New England.—AUTHOR'S NOTE.

men, that it was rum made him do it. I believe the Indians who do not associate with the whites seldom or never tell an untruth. A short time before the execution of this Indian a wretch of the name of John McDonald was executed. It appeared that he was left to take care of the house of one Krayman, a farmer of Bucks County. The evening Krayman left home, the villain got into the chamber of Mrs. Krayman, and attempted to get into her bed. Finding she resisted him the inhuman monster murdered her with a hatchet he had taken upstairs with him. He then killed her infant son, set fire to the house, and made off. Upon application to Council a proclamation was issued, offering a reward for apprehending him. He was a remarkable man, being not more than five feet four inches high, and very stoutly made. A few days after the proclamation was out, going down Market Street, I saw a man sitting upon one of the stalls who appeared to answer exactly the description given of McDonald. I immediately went up to him, and putting some questions to him, I had no doubt in my own mind, but that he was the man who had committed the murder. I obliged him to stay at a friend's house until I sent for the description given of McDonald by the unfortunate husband. He answered the description as to size, age, country, and in every other particular, except his hair, which was of a different color. The fellow was so much confused when examined, and so rejoiced at getting clear, that I strongly suspected he too had been guilty of some crime, for which he was afraid he should be confined. The real McDonald died game, as it is called by such wretches, that is, like a hardened villain. A gentleman present when he was led pinioned and put in the cart for execution, observed he believed he had seen him before, wheeling oysters about the streets of Philadelphia. "Yes," says he, "you may have seen me before, wheeling oysters, and if you will wait until Jack Ketch has done with me, I'll turn round, that you may see me behind and know me better at our next meeting."

For many years there had been disputes between the States of Pennsylvania and Connecticut respecting their boundaries, and a good many people lost their lives in consequence of those disputes. Commissioners were appointed by Congress in pursuance of an Article of the Confederation, who sat at Trenton, in 1782, and after a long hearing gave a decree in favor of Pennsylvania. In order to give the citizens of Pennsylvania quiet possession of their lands, the Legislature passed an act for raising two companies of infantry. The command of these men was given to Col. James Moore. Shortly before the time for which they were enlisted expired, they marched a number of the Connecticut families (said by Col. Moore to be very turbulent) out of the settlement, and a few were sent to Easton gaol.* These people complained of being treated with great barbarity. From my knowledge of Col. Moore I do not believe he would have suffered them to be treated with cruelty. When the troops were disbanded, the Connecticut people returned to their former habitations, and fresh disturbances soon ensued. Upon complaint being made to the Executive Council, some militia were ordered out from Berks and Northampton. Gen. John Armstrong,† the Secretary to Council, was appointed to command them. After remaining some time in the county, finding the settlers fled as he advanced, and that he could not bring them to action, he entered into a treaty with them and they delivered up their arms.

In September, 1786, a new county was erected called Luzerne, in which county most of the lands in dispute lay. Colonel Pickering, since Secretary of State, applied to be Prothonotary of the county, and was appointed. It was expected, as he was a native of New England, and a man of great respectability, that he would be able to keep the settlement quiet, and that those who held under Pennsylvania would have peaceable possession of their lands; this, however, was not the case. The Connecticut people drove off the commissioner sent by the Executive of the State to

---

* At the trial of one of these people at Easton, he said he was in a tavern at Wilkes-Barre, when Capt. Ball, who commanded one of the companies under Moore, came in and called out, " Where is that damned rascal, S. Y—— ?" "And I immediately answered and said, here am I."—AUTHOR'S NOTE.

† Afterwards Secretary of War under President Madison.

endeavor to settle their disputes, and soon after obliged him
to leave the settlement, treating him with every mark of
indignity. About this time John Franklin, who was considered the principal leader in all these disturbances, wrote
to Council that if he could appear before the Board in safety,
he would come down and state the injustice that was done
to the Connecticut settlers by the commissioner and others
sent amongst them. Council were surprised at receiving
this letter; however, it was immediately agreed he should
have a pass to come down and be heard. One was accordingly sent him, and in a few days he came to town. He
took up his lodgings opposite the State House, and sent word
he was in town, and wished to know when he should wait
upon Council. He was immediately informed the Board
were ready to hear him. He soon appeared. He was a very
stout man, then in the prime of life, being about forty-five
years of age (he is now, 1804, a member of the Legislature
for Luzerne), and had the look of a soldier. He was accompanied by John Jenkins, another leading man among the
Connecticut settlers. He said he had come down to *answer*
any charges that could be made against the Connecticut
settlers, and expected he could convince the Board they had
been treated with injustice and cruelty. As Dr. Franklin
was not present, I told him he had requested a pass to come
and inform the Board of their reasons for being dissatisfied
with the treatment they had received from the Pennsylvanians; that we would now hear him, and, if they had any
real complaints, endeavor to redress them. He said he
expected first to hear the complaints against them; however,
he was ready to state theirs. He took up the business from
the Decree of Trenton, and gave a particular account of
every material transaction that happened in the settlement
from that time. He said Colonel Moore and his troops had
behaved exceedingly ill to the Connecticut claimants, but
General Armstrong* had behaved much worse, that finding

* Gen. Armstrong, as Secretary, was present during the time Franklin
was speaking. It was with some difficulty I could prevent him from inter-
rupting him. He told me afterward there was some truth in what he had

he could do nothing with the militia he had with him, he offered the settlers, that if they would deliver up their arms, they should all be suffered to return to their homes, and not be molested in any way whatever, and should have a fair and candid hearing, and if they had any real cause of complaint, they should be redressed; that being extremely anxious to return home, and live quiet and peaceable with their families, they agreed, and did surrender their arms. Immediately after they had delivered up their arms they were ordered into an old barn where there was no floor, and, although it was covered with mud and filth, they were obliged to lie down in it, and the sentinels had orders to fire on any one that attempted to raise his head. Some of those confined in this manner were old men, one of them upwards of seventy years of age. A number of them were afterwards marched to Easton gaol. He related many other circumstances of ill treatment they had received. Council informed him they would take the matter into consideration, and desired him and Jenkins to retire. Franklin, finding little encouragement, soon left the city. He was afterwards a very active man against the Pennsylvania landholders.

In this year there were two men executed in Franklin County, and although there were never any that deserved the gallows more than these men, there were petitions signed by most of the people in the county for a pardon. One of them was an old man, Josiah Ramage. He had been married to the woman he murdered seven and thirty years. Upon some dispute with her, he beat her in a shocking manner, hove

said, but he had mentioned several things that were false. Armstrong wrote the anonymous letter addressed to the officers and soldiers at the conclusion of the war. He showed me others that he had written, which were not published. Armstrong has very superior talents, but they are almost useless, he is so extremely indolent. Smilie, speaking in the House of Representatives of his expedition into Luzerne, compared him to Verres. The next morning, when I went to the State House, I found Armstrong walking before the door of the room in which the Representatives sat. Inquiring what he was doing there, he told me he was waiting to see Smilie. I persuaded him away, and afterwards had the affair made up. He by no means deserved a comparison with Verres.—AUTHOR'S NOTE.

14

her on the floor, and while she lay there senseless, he got
upon a table, and jumped upon her breast, which put a period
to her life. The other, John Hanna, was a young man who
had been from Ireland six months. He was beating a boy
about thirteen years of age, when the father of the boy came
up, took him away, and gave Hanna a kick. Hanna went
to the place where he had been working, got an iron bar
with which he had been at work, and while the father of the
boy was standing at his own door, he came behind him
and struck him on the head with the bar, which instantly
killed him. Soon after their condemnation, it was debated
at the Board whether a warrant should issue for their execution. Dr. Franklin not being in Council, the question was
put by me. There were then eight members present; of
these, Gen. Muhlenberg and Mr. George Ross, of Lancaster,
would never vote for the execution of any criminal. Two
other members joined them, so that it remained with me to
say whether they should be executed or not. Thinking it
would be an act of injustice to let such wretches loose upon
society, I should have voted without hesitation for their execution, but a motion for postponement was made and carried.
A warrant soon after issued for their execution. An
acquaintance of mine told me some time afterwards, that he
had them buried in his orchard; that before this he had his
orchard frequently robbed, but no robbery was committed
after he had these sentinels.

It is an easy matter to get a petition signed for a pardon,
or an office. Many people do not like to refuse, and will put
their names to a petition, although they know it is improper.
A sheriff of my acquaintance, who was frequently called on
to sign a recommendation to the Governor, by people who
had served him at his election, and whom he could not refuse,
waited on the Governor, and told him the circumstance, begging he would pay no regard to any recommendation he
should sign; that if he wished to promote the interest of any
of those he recommended, he would write a personal application. I called once on a friend of mine, who signed a petition
to Council in favor of a person of bad character, who wanted

to be a notary public, and asked him how he could put his
name to a petition in favor of such a rascal. Laughing, he
declared he had signed it in such a manner that he thought
no person could have supposed it to be him who had signed it.

At this time there was an application from my old friend
and schoolmate, Mr. Mathias Aspden, who had gone off with
the British, for a pardon. It gave me great pleasure to have
an opportunity of serving this worthy man. I sent him a
pardon, January 19, 1786, and he soon came to Philadelphia.
After he had been here a short time, he called on a gentleman of the law to know if, by the treaty of peace, he was
secure from arrest. The gentleman not knowing, and Mr.
Aspden not telling him, that he had a pardon from the Executive Council, told him that he did not think he was. As
soon as he got this opinion, without seeing any of his friends,
he immediately set off for New York, and embarked on
board a packet, then ready to sail for England, where he now
is, 1804. As he had ever been my friend, I was much concerned at his unfortunate situation. Just after the peace, he
had written me an affectionate letter, inquiring how the war
had left me, and offering his services, and sent me a coffee-
pot to keep in remembrance of him. He lives very retired
in London.

I had at this time an opportunity of serving another of my
old friends, Mr. P. Bond. Mrs. Bond, his mother, applied
to me to present a petition to Council, to obtain a pardon for
her son. Some intimate friends of the family were then in
Council, but they did not choose to interfere, as it was then
thought unpopular. As that was never a consideration with
me when my friends wanted my services, I presented the
petition, and the pardon was immediately granted and sent to
him. Soon after Mr. Bond came out as British Consul.

At the election in October, 1786, the Republican party being strengthened, fresh opposition to my being elected Vice-
President was encouraged by most of them, and much pains
and caballing exerted to carry their point. But a few of the
most independent, considering it as a most unwarrantable
attack, and the Constitutional party, although I had remained

as unconnected with the one as the other, generously giving their suffrages in my support, the design failed. The Republicans had agreed upon Gen. Muhlenberg as their candidate, expecting, as he was descended from a German family, he would have the votes of all the Germans in the House. In this, however, they were mistaken. I believe there was not a German in either Council or House of Representatives that did not vote for me. The evening before the election, the Constitutionalists had a meeting, and agreed to have their tickets printed, and a sprig of laurel on them. By this means I found that several of the Republican party, who declared they had voted for me, could not have done so. One member from Berks County was particularly anxious that I should believe he voted for me, and called on me to assure me that he had. As I appeared to doubt it, and told him it was of no consequence whether he had or not, he asked me if I did not suppose he had. I told him there were but few of the Republicans who did vote for me, and my opinion was that he had not. And this was the opinion in Berks, for he never was again elected. He never was popular in the county, and obtained a seat in the Legislature by betting with some of the most active men that busy themselves at election that he would not be in the Assembly. Having a dispute with the same person when I was put up in the county for Councillor, he declared to my brother James that he was as much my friend as any man in the county, and would do anything in his power to serve me. I desired my brother never to mention it to any other person, for if it was known that C—— was my friend, it would injure me with the good people of Berks.

One of the principal complaints against me by the Republican party was procuring the appointment of Mr. Tench Coxe as one of the commercial commissioners, and much was said against his political conduct, but he was chosen by the merchants of the city one of their committee, as he was known to be well qualified for this business. The fact was he had offended the directors of the Bank of North America (then the only bank on the continent), and they and their friends made a great clamor against him.*

The 17th of March, 1787, I dined at the City Tavern with the "Friendly Sons of St. Patrick." Returning home in the evening, I stepped into a hole and sprained my ankle so badly that for several days I could not go out of the house, and when I did, was obliged to use crutches. A Good Friday, in coming from Council, I was stopped on the State House steps by some person who had business at the Board of Property, where I was then going. Turning from him, in a hurry to be gone, I put my crutch on the edge of the step, when it slipped off, and I fell with great violence. My right leg was drawn up so that the first part that struck the pavement was my knee, the pan of which was split, and the leg much injured. I was carried immediately over to Napal's, a small tavern opposite the State House, and surgeons sent for. My own opinion was, that it would be necessary to amputate my leg. I was therefore very anxious to get home. I had Dr. Franklin's sedan chair brought, and was placed in it before any surgeon came. This was the most uneasy way I could have been carried home, for I was obliged to let my leg hang down, by which means, during the whole of the way (which was upwards of a mile, as I then lived in the Northern Liberties) I suffered the most excruciating pain. I should have suffered much less had I been carried by persons used to a sedan chair, but the men who attended Dr. Franklin not being present, my friends were obliged to get some invalid soldiers who then did duty at the State House. Their lameness made these poor fellows give me more pain than they

* Mr. Tench Coxe, the great-grandson of Dr. Daniel Coxe, of London (the proprietor of the Government of West Jersey), was the first and ablest politico-economical writer of this country. He was a member of the Annapolis Federal Convention, which led to the formation of our present Constitution, a member of the Continental Congress, and Assistant Secretary of the Treasury under Alexander Hamilton. The prodigious expansion of the cotton culture in this country is more due to the early and persistent exertions of Mr. Coxe than to those of any other man in America. See Simpson's Eminent Philadelphians.

otherwise would have done. I should have been carried home on a sofa, or in a cot. I sent one of my friends home to prepare Mrs. Biddle for my reception. Drs. Kuhn, Jones, and Hutchinson soon attended. The latter was the family physician, and to his skill and care I impute my recovery without the loss of my leg. My small clothes were cut off, and I was informed by the surgeons that I must keep my leg perfectly still, otherwise I should never have the use of it, as the least motion would prevent the pan from knitting. Although I had enough to make me feel uneasy at my situation, having a large family dependent on my exertions, yet as I always considered it a duty to submit with fortitude to everything unavoidable, I sustained the accident without repining, and never suffered myself to be depressed by it.

The day after the accident I wrote a letter to Council resigning my office of Vice-President, and sent it to one of the members. He would not deliver it, but called upon me and begged I would not think of resigning, as the members would with pleasure call on me when anything particular was to be done. If he had not mentioned this I should have resigned. It would have been extremely disagreeable to me to have held any appointment the duties of which I could not perform.

About a week after the accident, one of my seafaring acquaintances called on me a good deal intoxicated. I lay down stairs and it happened there was no person in the room when he entered. He came staggering up to the bedside, telling me he was very sorry for me, but, says he, "Messmate, you must not mind it; and as your leg must be cut off sooner or later, why let them chop it off at once." I was under great apprehension he would have fallen on my leg. As I could not stir, and had nothing within my reach to keep him off, I was thrown into a profuse sweat. Fortunately a servant soon came in and took him out. I should not have regarded what this man said about *chopping off my leg*, but I supposed he had heard the surgeons mention that it would be necessary. The next day when Dr. Jones attended, I requested he would candidly inform me whether he thought there would be a necessity of amputating my leg. He told me nothing of that kind was to be apprehended. Dr. Hutchinson coming in soon after, I put the same question to him and received the same answer. This greatly relieved me, for as my leg was uncommonly swelled, I thought it probable I should lose it. I then inquired of the doctors what would be the quickest method to bring a perspiration on one in my situation. After they had mentioned what they thought would be the soonest, I informed them of the visit from Mr. ——, his behavior, and the effect it had on me. They laughed, and acknowledged that was a way they had never thought of.

As Dr. Franklin was unwell the Executive Council attended at my house, and, as I could write, the business of the Council went on as usual. I lay for three weeks without moving my leg from the position it was placed in, and nothing but the declaration of the doctors, that it was absolutely necessary I should be moved, and their rousing me by inquiring if I was afraid to move, induced me to consent to it. A bed and bedstead were put at the end of the one I was in, and they shoved me gently from one bed to the other. Although it gave me little or no pain, the being stirred after lying so long in one position was extremely disagreeable. When I was so far recovered as to sit up, and it was ascertained I should have the use of my leg, among others I had the honor of a visit from Mr. Gardoqui, the Spanish Chargé d'Affaires, who told me, "If your constitution was not a very good one, and, let me add, your disposition also, you would never have recovered the use of your leg." I believe he was right so far as regarded my constitution, whatever he may have been as to my disposition. The evening of the day the accident happened they gave me laudanum, which was the first I had ever taken. Instead of composing it made me very restless. I refused to take any afterwards.

The nineteenth of May, this year, an application was made by Mr. Otto, Chargé d'Affaires for France, for delivering up de Brassines, charged with malversation in his office. He was delivered up to be sent to France.

It was the 31st of May before I left my house to attend Council, nor should then have done it, but that there was some business to come before the Board relating to a ship belonging to Messrs. Thomas & John Clifford and Mr. Richard Wells, seized for smuggling, and Dr. Franklin wished me to be present. It was said by the owners that the goods smuggled were the property of the officers of the ship, and taken on shore entirely unknown to them. This was probably the case: she was, however, condemned and sold. The comptroller, Nicholson, and the collector, Dr. Phile, gave offence to many of the citizens by putting on board the ship a guard of Invalids, instead of employing the civil officers. These old soldiers, being accustomed to an implicit obedience to their officers, and being told they must not let any one come on board, threatened to drive their bayonets into the captain and owners if they attempted to come on board. It was in vain their telling them they only wanted to go into the cabin where one of them could go with them.* The guard was removed by Council. It was at the request of Dr. Franklin that I attended, and he was in Council himself. I went in a carriage into which they were obliged to lift me, and to walk the horses. I had in the carriage with me Captain William Craig, brother to my late unfortunate friend, Charles Craig. He was a very stout young man, and could carry me with ease in his arms. Poor William soon after fell a sacrifice to his intemperance. He was the person who sat up with me the first night after I had broken my knee. When we were in the carriage, he told me that I started in the night in such a manner, and talked so wildly, that he was very much afraid I should not live to see daylight. Poor fellow! I have lived to see him buried. I imputed my starting and talking to the laudanum they had

* About this time some prisoners attempted to make their escape, and these invalids were sent for to suppress them, which they soon did with their bayonets. When they returned, they swore that if the disturbance had been among the debtors they would not have used their bayonets. I believe few of these honest fellows knew, and none of them cared, whether they were debtors or criminals, until after they returned.—AUTHOR'S NOTE.

given to *compose* me. After this day I generally attended Council, being in a few days so well as to go with crutches, which I continued to use for a considerable time. Returning the latter end of June from the Board on my crutches, I met Dr. Jones, who had not seen me for some time. He expressed his surprise at my still being on crutches, and declared he would take them from me in the street, if he could do it. He told me to use myself a little while without them, and I should find there was no occasion for them. At first leaving them off I was like a child learning to walk, catching at anything near me. I was soon able to go with a stick: my knee gave me no pain, but was weak, as it still is, and ever must be to the end of the chapter. No person could tell, six months after the accident, by my walking, that I had ever received any injury.

This year, 1787, the Convention for forming a Federal Constitution met in Philadelphia; I was acquainted with most of the members. Some of the best informed told me, they did not believe a single member was *perfectly* satisfied with the Constitution, but they believed it was the best they could ever agree upon, and that it was infinitely better to have such a one than to break up without fixing on some form of government, which I believe at one time it was expected they would have done. For my own part I have no doubt it is the best in the world, and as perfect as any human form of government can be. We had in the Convention many of the best and wisest men in this or any other country.

There were some disturbances this year in the Legislature about calling a Convention for the ratification of the Federal Constitution. A motion was made for that purpose the 28th of September. After some debate the further consideration was postponed until the next day. The following day nineteen members opposed to the measure staid from the House, by which means a quorum could not be made. The reason they gave for staying away, was that the business did not come regularly before them. The Sergeant at Arms was sent for them. When he returned he informed the Speaker and other members present, that he had seen the absent mem-

bers at the house of Alexander Boyd, that he informed them
he was directed by the Speaker and other members to request
their attendance.   Mr. Robert Whitehill, one of the leading
members, replied that there was no house, that they had not
made up their minds, and therefore would not attend.   The
day after (the 29th) those members not attending, the Sergeant at Arms and clerk were sent after them.   They saw
most of the members, but they refused to attend.   It is mentioned in the Journals of the House that Mr. McCalmont and
Mr. Miley appeared, by which means a quorum was made.
The fact is, some gentlemen went to Boyd's, where most of
the absent members lodged, and there found McCalmont and
Miley, and finding they could not persuade them, forced
them to the House, by which means they had a quorum, and
the resolution calling a Convention was adopted.*   Upon
a memorial being presented to Council from the members

---

* This well-known incident occasioned a serio-comic debate in the Assembly.

"The Speaker left the chair, and in a few minutes Mr. James McCalmont and Mr James Miley *entered the House.*   The Speaker resumed the
chair, and the roll was called.   .   .   .

"Mr. McCalmont informed the House that he had been forcibly brought
into the Assembly room contrary to his wishes, this morning, by a number
of the citizens whom he did not know, and that, therefore, he begged he
might be dismissed the House."

After some discussion :—

"Mr. McCalmont : 'I desire that the rules may be read, and I will agree
to stand by the rules of the House.'

"The rules were read accordingly, and it appeared that every member
who did not answer on calling the roll, should pay two shillings and sixpence,
or, if there was not a quorum without him, five shillings.

"Mr. McCalmont then rose from his place, and, putting his hand in his
pocket, took out some loose silver, and said, 'Well, sir, here is your five
shillings ; so let me go.' "

This proffer being refused, the discussion was resumed.   After a time :

"Mr. McCalmont now rose and *made towards the door.*   Mr. Fitzsimmons addressed him, but so as not to be heard—and the gallery called
out *stop him,* there being a number of citizens *at the door he went toward.*"

The two unwilling legislators being thus forced to remain, the Assembly
was able to order a Convention to consider the proposed Federal Constitution, and immediately adjourned *sine die.*   See Lloyd's Reports.

who had been dragged before the House, complaining of the conduct of those who had forced them there, and requesting they should be prosecuted, an order was given to the Attorney General to issue writs against them. Some of the gentlemen ordered to be prosecuted were my intimate friends, and they expected that I would not vote for this measure, but would oppose it. Although it was a very disagreeable business to me, I conceived it to be my duty, and therefore voted for it. I dined in company with one of them the day the resolution passed Council: he was displeased at first, but was soon satisfied it was right. Some of my friends who knew how I should vote, wished me to stay from the Board that day, but I despised this way of getting off doing what, although disagreeable, it was my duty to do.

The dragging McCalmont and Miley to the House, and some gross insults offered in the November following to the members at Boyd's, who were most of them those who had left the Legislature in September, was one principal reason of the removal of the seat of government from Philadelphia (although it happened long after), many of the country members declaring they could not speak their sentiments, or give their votes freely without risking their being insulted. From this time until they effected their purpose, they were continually attempting to remove from the city. Unfortunately, many of the principal people in the city looked upon and treated the Western members with great contempt. It was therefore natural for them to resent such treatment; they considered the inhabitants of the city as their enemies, who only wanted an opportunity to injure them, and were determined to do it without regarding the consequences to the State or themselves. A little more attention being paid to them by the citizens of Philadelphia would, I believe, have prevented their removing the seat of government, which was attended with a great expense to the State, and of no advantage whatever either to the members of the Legislature or any others, except to the tavern-keepers and those who kept boarding-houses in Lancaster; indeed, I believe to most of the members it was a disadvantage, for during the winter in the city, they could transact business for themselves and their neighbors, which they could not, by any means, do as well in Lancaster. The Western members were certainly to blame to let their resentment get the better of their judgment. I believe now, 1804, with a little management they could be brought back to the city, and if they were, it would be long before they would again leave it.

CHAPTER IV.

THE disturbances at Wyoming still continuing, and complaints being continually made to Council by the Pennsylvania landholders, who had occasion to go into the county, the Board thought it would be necessary to send some militia from Berks and Northampton counties. They therefore sent for Capt. Craig,* the county lieutenant of Northampton, to consult with him as to the number of militia necessary to be sent on the expedition. When Craig came to town, he gave it as his opinion that if John Franklin was taken, the other insurgents would soon be quiet, for that he was the man who occasioned all the disturbances. After mentioning our intention of sending out the militia, he said he would rather have a few old Continental officers than all the militia of Berks and Northampton, for it was only necessary to take Franklin, and if Council would allow him to take eight or ten of his friends, he would bring Franklin to Philadelphia, or never return. Council agreeing to let him have his own way, he chose seven officers who had served with him, three of whom I knew, Stevenson, Brady, and Erb, and more determined fellows never went upon any desperate enterprise. They were going to take from the midst of his friends a very stout, active man, as fearless as any of themselves. Although Craig and his companions were anxious to go, it was against my inclination they went, as I thought it highly probable they would all be sacrificed. Franklin has told me since that it

---

* John Craig, a very mild, worthy man, cousin of Col. Craig, and, like him, an intelligent, active, gallant officer. He served all the war in Moylan's Regiment of Horse.—AUTHOR'S NOTE.

was owing to the chapter of accidents that they were not. They went to Wilkes-Barre under pretence of purchasing land from the Connecticut claimants, for whom they pretended a great regard. Watching their opportunity when Franklin was alone in a tavern they attacked him. He called out that the Pennemites* were murdering him, but he was not heard. They got him down, and with great difficulty tied his hands behind his back, and gagged him. They had prepared themselves with a rope and gag before they took hold of him. He fought with great desperation, and there was not one of them that did not feel the weight of his arm. He hurt Stevenson so much that he would have shot him through the head if Craig had not prevented him. They got him at last on horseback, tied his feet under the horse's belly, and set off before his friends could assemble and arm themselves. They rode thirty-eight miles before they halted; they were closely pursued, and if they had halted sooner it is probable they would have been overtaken and killed, for they were all well armed and would not have surrendered. Craig appeared before Council about ten days after he set off; he sent the doorkeeper in for me, and informed me when I went to him, that he had brought Franklin to town. Council ordered him to gaol, and, as it was apprehended he would endeavor to make his escape, he was ordered in irons. Craig and his companions had three hundred pounds given them. They were entitled to much more; however, with that sum they were perfectly satisfied.

The bringing away Franklin did not settle the disturbances. The commissioners sent there by Council agreeable to an " Act for ascertaining and confirming to certain persons, called Connecticut claimants, the lands by them claimed within the county of Luzerne, and for other purposes therein mentioned," which act was much *in their favor* and against the Pennsylvania claimants, by whom it was complained of very much, were obliged to leave the county. Council recommended it

* Those who held under Pennsylvania were called Pennemites.— AUTHOR'S NOTE.

in their message to the Legislature to raise a number of men to be stationed in the county, which in their opinion was the only way to keep these turbulent people quiet. The passing this act, called the Quieting Act, was very improper, as it encouraged these people in their opposition. After it had been passed, the repealing of it gave them just cause of complaint. When a public act is passed, if the repealing is injurious to any individuals, it should not be done without their consent. Instead of repealing the act, the Legislature should have paid the Pennsylvania claimants for their land, and this in the end, I believe, would have been the cheapest way of settling this business. The public, no more than an individual, should ever break a contract because it is injurious to keep it.

About this time a society was formed in the city for Political Inquiries, of which Dr. Franklin was chosen President. I was elected a member. We had one gentleman in the party, who, by his writings and incessant talking, disturbed us very much. He often reminded me of a story Dr. Franklin used to tell of two French bishops, who were incessant talkers. They happened to meet at a friend's, when one of them began a story. He spoke for a long time, the other eagerly watching an opportunity to speak, when one of the company told him he had better walk away with him, for he would not be able to slip in a word. Yes, I will, answered the impatient bishop, "for he will soon be obliged to spit, and then it will be my turn." If our member had not been a very worthy man I should have told him the story. The society was not well attended, and never met after the death of Dr. Franklin.

A resolution of Council passed this summer, that eight days after the election of President and Vice-President there should be an election for Secretary to Council. There had been none from the time General Armstrong was first elected. The resolution was brought forward and adopted by those opposed to him. It was, however, very proper that those who sat at the Board should have a choice in their Secretary. Armstrong, supposing he would not be chosen, intimated to me that he had some thoughts of resigning; that as soon as he had made up his mind about it he would inform me.

This he soon after did, when I applied to my friends in Council for the appointment. One man at the Board had a relative whom he wished to be the Secretary, and he made all the interest he could for him. When the election came on,* Dr. Franklin, although at that time very much troubled with the stone, went to Council, and there voted, and used his interest for me. I should have been elected even had he not attended. His doing so was a strong mark of his friendship; to his family and friends he always expressed a great regard for me, and I never had any reason to doubt him. Calling on him a few days after my appointment, to see if he had any commands, he told me that the evening before he had received an anonymous letter recommending in very strong terms a friend of ours for an office just vacant, that although the hand was disguised he was pretty certain the person recommended had written the letter himself, and begged me to stay until he came, which he expected would be in a few minutes. Accordingly, soon after Mr. R—— came in. When seated, and we had talked of the news of the day, etc., the Doctor took the letter from his pocket, and read it to himself. He then handed it to me, and inquired if I knew the handwriting. I gave a glance at the person with us when the Doctor began to read, and saw that he was greatly confused; but when the Doctor handed me the letter, he turned very pale, and was so much agitated that I was afraid he would have fallen from his chair. As soon as he recovered himself a little, he pretended to recollect some business that required his immediate attendance, and very abruptly left us. After he was gone the Doctor laughed very heartily, in which I could not help joining, although I pitied the man very much. He did not for a long time after this call on the Doctor, and when he did never mentioned anything about the office which he was by no means qualified to fill. From the letter one would suppose he was qualified and deserved any office in the government. I should not have suspected

* October 23d, 1787.

him to have written the letter, but from his conduct there could be no doubt that he did.

In October, this year, my time having expired as a member of the Executive Council,* I was elected a member of the Legislature for Berks County. My good old friend Colonel Lutz was very busy at the election, threatening what he would do if he saw a ticket that had not my name on it. Henry Wertz was also busy there, as he had been when I was elected into the Supreme Executive Council. It was he who declared on that occasion that he had "often fought mid me," when we had not a gun on board at the time he sailed with me. The member for the county, who it was supposed voted against me as Vice-President, could not get a vote. I resigned from the Legislature without taking my seat, being well assured that I should be elected Secretary to Council, and I could not hold that office and be a member of the Legislature.

The 4th of July, 1788, was celebrated in a manner highly gratifying to all the inhabitants of the city. There was a grand Federal procession in which all classes of citizens joined. In front there were twelve axemen, dressed in white frocks; second, the First City Troop; third, the Cap of Liberty, carried by John Nixon, Esquire; fourth, four pieces of artillery, with the company of artillery men; fifth, Thomas Fitzsimmons, Esquire, carrying a white flag emblematical of the French alliance; sixth, Light Infantry; seventh, George

---

* In Council.

Philadelphia, Tuesday, October 9th, 1787.

On motion,

    Resolved, That the thanks of this Board be presented to the Honorable Charles Biddle, Esquire, our late worthy Vice-President, for the integrity, diligence, and ability with which he has discharged the various duties of that important office.

Extract from the Minutes.

James Trimble,
for John Armstrong, Sec'y.

Honorable Charles Biddle, Esquire,
    Late Vice-President of the
        Supreme Executive Council of Pennsylvania.

Clymer, Esquire, with a flag emblematical of the definitive treaty of peace; eighth, Colonel Shee, carrying a flag with the words, "Washington the Friend of his Country," in silver letters; ninth, the Second City Troop; tenth, Richard Bache, as a herald proclaiming a "New Era;" eleventh, General Muhlenberg carrying a blue flag with "Seventeenth of September, 1787," in silver letters; twelfth, a band of excellent music; thirteenth, the Constitution, the judges* in their robes seated in a car; fourteenth, Light Infantry; fifteenth, ten gentlemen, representing those States that had ratified the Constitution; sixteenth, Col. William William in armor; seventeenth, Light Horse, from Montgomery; eighteenth, representatives of foreign States in a car with their flags; nineteenth, judge, register, and marshal of the admiralty; twentieth, wardens of the port; twenty-first, officers of the customs; twenty-second, Peter Baynton as a citizen, and J. Melcher as an Indian chief, expressing their brotherly love; twenty-third, troop of dragoons, from Berks County; twenty-fourth, Federal edifice drawn by ten white horses, followed by about five hundred architects and house-carpenters; twenty-fifth, Cincinnati and militia officers; twenty-sixth, infantry; twenty-seventh, agricultural society; twenty-eighth, farmers with two ploughs; thirtieth, infantry; thirty-first, Marine Society; thirty-second, Federal ship, formerly the barge of the Serapis, fitted up remarkably well and rigged as a ship, commanded by Captain Green (my passenger from the bay of Honduras) well manned, had all her sails set, and was worked as if at sea. Nothing in the procession gave so much delight to the spectators as this ship. Canvass was nailed round her to conceal the wheels and machinery. Then followed the pilots of the port with their boat, boatbuilders, sailmakers, shipjoiners, ropemakers, shipchandlers, merchants and traders, light infantry, other trades and professions, their places determined

---

* The car was so very high that I did not think the Judges altogether safe. They had to go up a ladder to get into it. I thought they cut a very awkward figure going up the ladder. It reminded many of the spectators, as well as myself, of seeing men go up a ladder who never came down.

by lot. Cordwainers, coachpainters, cabinet and chairmakers, brickmakers, house, ship, and sign painters, porters, clock and watchmakers, weavers, bricklayers, tailors, instrument makers, turners, windsor chairmakers and spinning wheel-makers, carvers and gilders, coopers, planemakers, whip and canemakers; forty-eighth, blacksmiths, whitesmiths, and nailers, coachmakers; fiftieth, potters; fifty-first, hatters: fifty-second, wheelwrights; fifty-third, tinplate workers: fifty-fourth, skinmen, breechesmakers, and glovers: fifty-fifth, tallow chandlers; fifty-sixth, victuallers; fifty-seventh, printers, bookbinders, and stationers; fifty-eighth, saddlers: fifty-ninth, stonecutters; sixtieth, bread and biscuit bakers: sixty-first, gunsmiths; sixty-second, coppersmiths; sixty-third, goldsmiths, silversmiths, and jewellers; sixty-fourth, distillers, tobacconists; sixty-sixth, brass founders; sixty-seventh, stocking manufacturers, tanners and curriers, uphol-sterers, sugar refiners: seventy-first, brewers; seventy-second, perukemakers and barber surgeons; seventy-third, engravers: seventy-fourth, plasterers; seventy-fifth, brushmakers; sev-enty-sixth, staymakers; seventy-seventh, Light Infantry: seventy-eighth, civil and military officers of Congress; sev-enty-ninth, Supreme Executive Council; eightieth, justices of the Court of Common Pleas, and the magistrates; eighty-first, sheriff and coroner; eighty-second, board of wardens, city treasury clerks, constables, etc., a band of music, watch-men, street commissioners; eighty-fourth, gentlemen of the bar; eighty-fifth, clergy; eighty-sixth, physicians; eighty-seventh, students of the University; eighty-eighth, County Troop, brought up the rear.

After going through the city, they proceeded to Bush Hill, where there was an excellent cold collation provided. Judge Wilson delivered an oration, but owing to some mistake, the cannon began firing just as he began to speak, so that no one could understand anything he said. It was, however, after-wards printed and much admired. The scene from Bush Hill was truly magnificent. I never saw on any occasion so much satisfaction expressed on every countenance as there was on this day. No accident happened, and the utmost harmony prevailed during the whole day, which was a remarkably fine one. All the professions and trades carried emblematical flags, and many of the tradesmen were at work while the procession was proceeding on. The whole business of the day is fully described by Judge Hopkinson, chairman of the committee of arrangements, who was well calculated for such an undertaking.

In July, 1788, Colonel Eleazer Oswald was brought before the Supreme Court for a contempt of court in publishing a piece in his paper against Andrew Brown at a time a suit was pending in court between him and Brown. Upon his refusing to answer interrogatories he was sentenced to one month's imprisonment, and a fine of ten pounds. The fine was remitted by Council, but he suffered the imprisonment. When the Legislature met he applied to them to impeach the judges, and had there been a majority of Constitutionalists in the House, they certainly would have been impeached, for it ever has, and always will be, the case that the party in power will bend a little to one of their own party, and Oswald at that time was considered a Constitutionalist, although some time before he had been violent against them. In his memorial to the House he mentions that, "Judge Thorpe, in Edward the Third's time, was hanged for suffering the Court of Justice to be perverted: in Richard the Second's time eleven of the Judges were condemned to death, and, although only two were executed, all the others were forever banished as unworthy to enjoy the benefit of that law which they had so perfidiously and basely betrayed, and as an example to future judges, and forever to make their ears to tingle." I have no doubt but that Oswald would have been very glad to have seen our judges hanged, especially the Chief Justice* for whom he entertained an implacable hatred. I was in court when he received his sentence, which he heard with great composure. A number of people followed him, who as soon as they got out of court gave three cheers, and did the same when he went into gaol, looking on him as unjustly

* Chief Justice McKean.

sentenced. The resolutions offered by the parties then in the House will show their opinions on this business. October 3, 1788, the following resolution was offered by Mr. Clymer, and seconded by Mr. Peters.

" *Resolved*, That this House having in a committee of the whole, gone into a full examination of the charges exhibited by Eleazer Oswald, of arbitrary and oppressive proceedings in the Justices of the Supreme Court, against the said E. Oswald, are of opinion that the charges are unsupported by the testimony adduced, and consequently, that there is no just cause for impeaching the said Justices," which was carried in the affirmative.

It was then moved by Mr. Findley and seconded by Mr. Kennedy, to postpone the above, in order to introduce the following, viz:—

" WHEREAS, the Constitution of this Commonwealth has expressly secured to every citizen the right of trial by jury in criminal prosecutions ; therefore usages, however ancient, or from whatever quarter they may have been introduced, cannot supersede this positive right.

" Although the Courts of Justice, for their own defence and the protection of the course of justice, must necessarily possess the power of compelling obedience to their authority, as well as peace, order, and decency in their presence, yet this is no more than that right of repelling force by force, necessary for the existence and usefulness of the Courts of Justice, which is analogous to that right of self-defence which every man naturally enjoys ; yet, nevertheless, such freedom of writing or speaking, as is only calculated to disparage the persons of the Judges, or to influence the causes depending before the courts, and not read or uttered in the presence of the said courts, although punishable by indictment, ought not to be turned into contempt, by construction or implication, at the discretion of the Judges; therefore

" *Resolved*, That the proceedings of the Supreme Court against Colonel E. Oswald, in punishing by fine and imprisonment at their discretion, for a constructive or implied contempt, not committed in the presence of the Court, nor

against any officer or order thereof, but for writing and publishing improperly or indecently, respecting a cause depending before the Supreme Court, and respecting some of the
Judges of the said Court, was an unconstitutional exercise of
judicial power, and sets an alarming precedent of the most
dangerous consequence to the citizens of this Commonwealth.

"AND WHEREAS, Though the Constitution of the Commonwealth declares the printing presses be open for the examination of every department of government, yet the Legislature
hath hitherto neglected to define the nature of contempts, or
direct the nature or extent of their punishment, consequently
the Justices have been left to act under the influence of
arbitrary and illegal usages; therefore

"*Resolved*, That it be specially recommended to the ensuing
General Assembly to define the nature and extent of contempt, and direct their punishments."

This was lost, and the first resolution carried, which ended
the business with the Legislature. Many gentlemen of the
bar think the Legislature could not pass an act to "define
the nature and extent of contempt," but I am of a different
opinion. If the court have a right to confine a man a month
for a contempt of court, they may for any length of time.
The party who were so much in favor of the Chief Justice at
this time, a few years afterwards, when he was elected Governor, would have gone any length to have punished him, as
would the others to have supported him.*

Oswald was much pitied, especially by all the old Whigs,
on account of his former services. He had been a colonel in
the Continental army, and distinguished himself for his
bravery on several occasions, for which he had the thanks of
General Washington. When the war broke out in France,
he went there and served in their artillery. He was in the
battle of Jemappes and some other engagements. He, however, soon got tired of this service, and returned home. The
French had not at that time the discipline he thought neces-

---

* An act for defining and limiting the power of judges in commitments
for contempt of court is now (1883) pending in the British Parliament.

sary. He told me that the soldiers, to show how much liberty they enjoyed, or how little they cared for their officers, when ordered "to the right face," would face to the left. This was in the beginning of their Revolution. I suppose they learned to behave better afterwards, for certainly no troops fought better than they did.

There was at this time in the city of Philadelphia a society that called themselves the "Adopted Sons of Pennsylvania," among whom were some valuable "adopted sons." Oswald was much opposed to this society, and thinking such a society unnecessary and improper, he every day ridiculed them in his paper. One of the members whom he had personally insulted (Mr. Matthew Carey, a worthy man) challenged him. Oswald was always ready upon these occasions; he accepted the challenge, and they fought in Jersey. Mr. Carey was shot through the thigh, and was a long time before he recovered. Oswald would have had to fight some others of the society, if Captain Rice and some of his old brother officers had not declared he should not, that the next member of the society that wanted to fight should take one of them, and after some contention they agreed to let Rice, who was Oswald's most particular friend, be the first that offered. Rice was much such a man as Oswald. The society was soon after broken up.

The people of Luzerne, not contented with driving from the county the commissioners sent by the Executive Council, obliged Col. Pickering, the prothonotary of the county, to leave it. They treated him with great indignity. It was supposed when he was appointed, that as he was a native of New England and a man of great respectability, he would be able to keep those people quiet, and this he supposed himself he could do; but they regarded no person that opposed their designs. A Capt. William Ross, a young man of the county, distinguished himself in favor of government. He was wounded in apprehending some of the insurgents. Upon a representation of his good conduct to the Legislature, they gave him five hundred dollars, and Council made him a present of a sword.

In the month of September this year, Levi and Abraham Doan, two young men of Bucks County, were taken prisoners, and brought before the Supreme Court, then sitting in Philadelphia. Being outlawed, it was only necessary to identify them, to sentence them to death. As they were well known in Bucks County this was done, and they received their sentence. The case of these young men was exceedingly hard. When very young, their fathers were very ill-treated by some violent committee-men in the county, on account of their attachment to the British Government. The father of Abraham Doan had his plantation confiscated and sold, and these lads were threatened, if they did not voluntarily enter into the American army, they should be pressed. In consequence of this they went off and joined the British. It was said they afterwards committed depredations in the neighborhood of where they were born, and it is probably true. If the treatment of their parents did not justify them, it certainly was some excuse for their conduct. At the conclusion of the peace they returned to the county, as they said, to see their friends and relations; but one of them, it was generally thought, came back on account of a very handsome girl he was fond of before he went to the British, and his cousin would not leave him. They were concealed a considerable time by their friends; it at length, however, became known that they were in the county, when several who were, or conceived themselves injured by them, endeavored to have them apprehended; but as they were very stout, active, resolute men, and went always well armed, those who were in pursuit of them, were afraid openly to attack them. Probably there hardly lived a more active man than the younger, Abraham. If he was seen by persons on horseback in pursuit of him, and he on foot, he would run like a deer, and no fence could stop him a moment. He went over any fence without putting a hand on it. They were both tall, handsome men. A considerable time after their return into the State, they were taken by surprise in Chester County, by some young men who were out hunting, who from their appearance in the woods armed, and from their endeavors to conceal themselves, suspected them of having some bad intentions, and insisted on their going before a magistrate. They made no resistance, hoping as they were not known, that they would be immediately dismissed; in this, however, they were greatly mistaken. They were carried before Col. Hannum, who committed them to gaol. Had they not attempted to conceal themselves, they would not have been apprehended, for they told a very plausible story of their being New Jerseymen on the way to the westward to take up land.* After they were condemned, and a time was fixed for their execution, the father of Abraham, several female relations and friends, and some influential gentlemen, waited on Council to solicit a pardon for them, or if that could not be obtained, a reprieve. The latter was readily granted.

Hearing much of these men, and wishing to communicate intelligence which I knew would give great pleasure to these unfortunate men and their friends, I went to gaol to inform them that Council had granted a reprieve for one month. I wished also to prepare them for the worst that might happen. When I went into the room they were surrounded by their relations and friends, among whom were several females, two of them very handsome girls that had lived with them in the woods. It was to no purpose I told them that the prisoners were only reprieved for a month, and that it was probable they would not be pardoned. When they found they were reprieved, they gave way to the most extravagant joy;

* Had they applied to Thomas Ross, Esq., a gentleman of the Bar, who then lived at Chester (and was present when they were brought before Col. Hannum), within a day or two of their commitment, he would have had them liberated; but owing to some mistake they did not apply in time, and they were detained until, some people coming to Chester from Bucks County, they were known. As there was no reward offered for apprehending them, the people who took them were no ways anxious about their being kept in prison. Mr. Ross, who was their counsel when they were brought before the Court, has since told me that he lamented they had not applied in time to him, for he knew the family had been hardly used. He was born near where these young men were, and knew them well before they went off, but did not recollect them when they were brought before Col. Hannum.— AUTHOR'S NOTE

they all concluded that through the intercession of friends, they should be pardoned. This, I told them, they must not expect, although I had very little doubt myself but what a pardon would be granted. I always thought it wrong to grant a reprieve for any length of time, without granting a pardon; it is like putting a man to death in cold blood. Before the month expired the Legislature met, when they petitioned for a pardon, and if that could not be obtained, for a trial by jury. The Legislature were inclined to pass a bill in their favor, and appointed a committee consisting of Mr. Lewis, Mr. Fitzsimmons, and Mr. Rittenhouse, to confer with the Supreme Executive Council on the subject of their petition. This, I believe, was what proved fatal to these young men. Several of the members of Council thought the Legislature had no business to interfere, as the power of pardoning, by the Constitution, was given to Council. They refused to pardon, or to extend the time fixed for their execution. It was in vain the members of the Legislature and the minority in Council urged the peculiar situation of these unfortunate men; the majority were jealous of the interference of the Legislature, and it was carried by a very small majority that they should suffer. Going to Council the day after the conference, I met them going in a cart to the gallows, followed by their relations and friends. It was a very affecting sight. They died with great firmness.

After the election in October, 1788, there was a majority in Council of Republicans, and they were determined on making a change in some of the officers of Government. Among others, they intended to take the office of Prothonotary of the Court of Common Pleas from J. B. Smith, Esq. The candidates proposed by the party were James Wilson, Esq., and my brother James.* When Mr. Smith found he should be

---

* During the time I was Vice-President, Judge Bryan's time expired (the Judges being then elected for seven years), and my brother James was proposed to be elected in his room. Several of my Republican friends spoke to me, to endeavor to get him elected; and although he was as dear to me as it was possible for one brother to be to another, for he had been more than a father to me, I could not think of using any interest I had

displaced, he sent for me; he told me, he would for many
reasons prefer my brother being appointed to the office to
Mr. Wilson, and he had some thoughts of resigning, and asked
my opinion. I told him it was a subject he had better consult some of his other friends upon, as my brother was supposed to be a candidate I was not a proper person to consult.
This he said he would do, and desired me to call on him at
eight o'clock in the evening. At that hour I called, when
his son told me his father had just stepped out, that probably
he would soon return, and invited me in; I went, expecting
he would return in a short time. The night was cold, and
there was a good fire, by which I sat down, and taking up a
book read until the watchman cried "past eleven o'clock,"
when finding Mr. Smith did not make his appearance I went
home. The next day meeting Dr. Hutchinson he laughed
very heartily, and told me he had never been in such a disagreeable situation as he had been the evening before, that
Mr. Smith had requested another friend and himself to call
on him to consult about his resigning, that they were with
him at the time I knocked at the door, that not having finished their consultation, they did not wish to see me, and
just before I entered the parlor they opened a door that led
to the cellar, on the front step of which they stood during the
whole of the time of my being in the house. Hutchinson said
he was half crazy, having a particular engagement that evening at a relation of Mrs. Hutchinson's, who was to wait for
him. They would have come out of their hiding place, but
that they expected every minute I would go. I told him it
was fortunate for them that their situation was not known
to me, or they should have cooled themselves much longer.
It was ridiculous for them to go there, for if I had found
them together, Mr. Smith could have told me they had not
yet finished their business, and I should have gone off and
left them. After the consultation Mr. Smith concluded to
resign, which he did the next day, and my brother was elected.

against Mr. Bryan, with whom no fault could be found, and whose friends
had always interested themselves to serve me.—AUTHOR'S NOTE.

Mr. Smith is a worthy man, and nothing but the violence of party would have occasioned his being attacked. I sent off a servant express for my brother, who knew nothing of my intention to propose him as a candidate until the servant arrived at Reading, which was late at night. The next evening he came to town and took possession of his office, which he was well qualified to fill, having had it before the Revolution. As it was his wish to have this office, nothing could give me more pleasure than procuring it for him. Every one who knew this excellent man loved and esteemed him.*

There was a petition this year to the Legislature from William Moore, Esq. (before the Revolution an eminent merchant, afterwards Vice-President of the Supreme Executive Council), stating that Continental money was paid him when much depreciated for goods imported before the war, that he had offered in payment certificates in which he had invested the Continental money he received for the goods, but the British agents had refused to take them. The agents acted very properly in refusing to take the certificates. It was

---

* James Biddle, eldest brother of Charles Biddle, was born February 18, 1731, and studied law with John Ross, then considered at the head of the Philadelphia Bar, whose executor he afterwards became. He practised in Berks, Lancaster, and Northampton counties, residing in Reading until about 1760, when he removed to Philadelphia, on being appointed Deputy Prothonotary. Later he was made Deputy Judge in Admiralty, under the Royal Government, Mr. Jared Ingersoll being the Judge. In December, 1776, he removed to Reading, and continued the practice of the law until 1788, when he was made Prothonotary of the Court of Common Pleas of Philadelphia. In 1791 he was appointed President Judge of the First Judicial District of Pennsylvania, which office he retained until his death, in 1797. He was buried in the grounds of Christ Church, of which church he was a vestryman in 1776, and present at a vestry meeting on 4th July, of that year, when it was resolved to "omit those petitions in the Liturgy wherein the King of Great Britain is prayed for."

John Dickinson writes, July 7, 1797:—

"I sincerely sympathize with you all on the death of thy excellent brother. I had known him for upwards of forty years, and to know him as I did was to love him. I have always greatly esteemed your family; and their welfare will always give pleasure to thy truly affectionate friend,

JOHN DICKINSON."

certainly a great hardship upon Mr. Moore and others in similar situations, but it would have been very unjust to oblige the British merchants to take less than was actually due them. In cases of this kind, the Government should have made up any loss the merchant sustained. Many persons took advantage of the Tender Acts, as they were called, by paying off their bonds and mortgages when the money was good for little or nothing. There were, however, a great many who would not do this, but paid their debts honestly in specie. In Virginia, I have been informed, the Tender Act was much worse than in any other State, for there, it was said, owing to the great quantity of State money they made, it was much worse than the Continental money; so much so, that with a Continental dollar you could purchase forty State dollars, and thus with one Continental dollar pay a specie debt of forty dollars, and as sixty Continental dollars could be had for a silver dollar, you could pay a debt of two thousand four hundred dollars with one Spanish dollar. What a temptation to a thief! I heard of a great many people losing by the Continental money, but knew of but few. General Neville, who served with me in Council, sold the estate he lived on, in 1775, for twelve thousand pounds Virginia currency, which was paid by agreement in Continental money. At that time it had not depreciated. He went soon after to join the army, when he locked the money up carefully in his desk, and never touched it until the war was ended, when it was good for nothing. I never lost anything but once by the Continental money, and then I did not blame the gentleman who paid me, Mr. John Stanley, of Newbern. He purchased a quantity of rum upon a long credit, to be paid in whatever money should then be a legal tender. We used to laugh about our bargain, he telling me he considered the rum as a present, and I, that he would have to pay me in specie. When the time he was to pay came round, I called on him for the money, upon which he sent a bell-man round the town, sold a hogshead of rum at vendue, and paid me with less than one-half of what it sold for. At this some of my friends found fault with him, but I never did, for it was a fair bargain between us. Had I given him another year's credit, he would have had to pay me in specie, which I am sure he would have done without hesitation.

Some who were knowing enough to invest their Continental money in certificates, made their fortunes by it. For my own part, I never could see why those certificates should be redeemed any more than the Continental bills. Congress had pledged themselves as much for the redemption of the one as of the other. A considerable sum in certificates was sent from Charleston, belonging to the estate of my brother Nicholas, which my brother James (who knew as little about money matters as any man in the world, and none cared less about money) gave to a *knowing friend* for Continental bills. For some time after the commencement of the war I did not expect our paper would depreciate much, but when I saw it sent from Philadelphia by wagon loads I expected it would soon be of little value. We had in Pennsylvania, State Island* money, so-called because the island was to be sold to redeem it. This, however, soon depreciated to eight for one specie dollar. At this time Mr. William Bingham was in Reading; speaking to him of this money, he advised me to buy up some of it, but I expected it would go as the Continental money did, and therefore did not do it. I believe Mr. Bingham purchased a large amount of it. Soon after you could not get a dollar of it for a specie dollar, for it carried interest, and there was not enough of it issued to pay for the island, which was sold in lots, and purchasers were obliged to pay in their bills or in specie, so that the holders received principal and interest.

In February, 1789, going one evening to my brother's to see some friends from Reading, the pavement being slippery I was walking in the middle of the street, when, stepping to

---

* "In 1780 the State of Pennsylvania emitted £100,000 for support of the army, and to provide a fund for their redemption the Executive was empowered to sell certain properties in the city of Philadelphia as well as Province Island, in the township of Kingsessing."—Philips, Paper Currency of the American Colonies. Province Island was at the mouth of the Schuylkill, along the western shore.

one side to avoid a sleigh that was driving furiously along.
I fell, and again injured my knee so much that I could not
get up, nor get out of the way of the horses, who had nearly
released me from all my pain, for they passed close to my
head. As the sleigh did not stop, I supposed the people in
it did not see me. Some persons on the pavement soon came
to my assistance, and carried me to my brother's house, near
which the accident happened. Not a minute before, a sleigh
went by with an acquaintance of mine (Mr. Matthew Irvin)
in it, who wanted me very much to get in with him, but
being near my brother's I would not detain him. When
Dr. Hutchinson came and examined my knee, he said it was
very much injured, and that it would be a considerable time
before I could leave the house. Fortunately for me, in this
as well as every other misfortune that befell me, my spirits
were not much affected. When an accident happens to a
man it is well for him to console himself by thinking it
might have been worse. William Melvin, a sailor who was
with me several voyages, was engaged to go to the West
Indies. Shortly before the ship sailed he fell from the main
yard and broke his leg, which prevented his going in her.
The ship was supposed to be lost in a hurricane, as she was
never heard of after she sailed. Will often told me how
fortunate, it was he broke his leg. If a person can bring
himself to think thus, it will greatly tend to alleviate misfortunes to which we are all liable. I could on this occasion
have consoled myself by thinking I might have had my
scull fractured by the horses in the sleigh. A piece called
" Resignation to Providence," I believe written by Goldsmith,
has given me much relief when I have lost a relation or
friend, or met with any misfortune.

It was some weeks before Dr. Hutchinson would permit
me to be removed. The manner in which I was carried
home was a way proposed by myself. Late at night my
friends put me in a cot, and eight of them carried me home
on their shoulders. It was some time before I could walk
with crutches. Although the second fall occasioned me a
long confinement, I believe it was of service to me by placing

the knee better than it was before; for all my friends observed that I walked much better after than before the last accident.

At this time much was said for and against our State Constitution. We then had a Legislature consisting of a single branch. There is no doubt but such a Legislature will sometimes pass improper acts, but at the same time it must be admitted they will at times be prevented by a second House from passing what is necessary and proper. For my own part, I thought at the time, as the Council of Censors was soon to meet, there was no necessity for calling a Convention; however, it was a matter I was no ways anxious about. In the debate on this subject a resolution was offered to the effect that the Convention should publish their amendments and alterations for the consideration of the people, and adjourn at least four months previous to a confirmation. The yeas and nays being called, there was but one nay, and that was a friend of mine, William Lewis, Esquire, and he entered his protest. In it he says that although it was his wish that the Convention should adjourn for the purposes mentioned in the resolution, the Legislature had no right to interfere.

On May 9, 1789, my mother died of a fever, in the eighty-first year of her age. She retained her senses to the last, and was perfectly resigned, as I believe those who live to her age generally are. All her misfortunes, and she had her share, she bore with uncommon fortitude, never repining. I believe a more cheerful, better woman never lived. She had ten children, five of whom died before her. Although the death of a parent at her time of life is seldom much to be regretted, I was sensibly affected at her loss; for whenever I met with anything that made me uneasy, her conversation always consoled me. It has given me much pleasure since her death to think she never made a request I did not comply with. I was always happy to carry her any agreeable intelligence, or to do anything to please her. It must always give pleasure to a child, after the death of a parent, to reflect that he has been a comfort to her; and nothing, I should suppose, would

give a person more pain than knowing they had not done
their duty to a parent, even if that parent had not behaved
as it ought to have done. About four years before the
death of my mother, in coming down a dark pair of stairs,
she stepped on something lying on the stairs, fell, and broke
her thigh. I was apprehensive she never would have got
well, but she soon perfectly recovered. At the time of the
accident, nor afterwards, did she ever complain. When General Washington passed through the city on his way to New
York, after he was first chosen President of the United
States, as he was to pass my door, I brought her from my
brother's to my house to see him. Every person in the city
was anxious to see this great and good man. The road and
streets were crowded and so dusty there was no telling the
color of his clothes. It must have been a most fatiguing day
to him. My mother appeared to enjoy the procession as much
as any of those with her. Among her papers I found the
following: "In the year 1756 I lost my dear husband, and
was left without any fortune, with six children to provide
for, the youngest not five years old. I was enabled through
the mercy of God to keep them together with me, and give
them schooling. When my eldest son, James,* and my
fourth son, Edward, were, by their industry and care, enabled
to assist me, and their brothers and sisters, they performed it
with a cheerfulness which showed the goodness of their
hearts, and made their mother, in the language of Scripture,
sing for joy. When my third son, John, had it in his power,
he performed his duty with the same goodness. My fifth
son, Charles, followed the example of his brothers, and at his
expense I am now supported. My sixth son, Nicholas, has
done all for me in his power, and more than I could expect.
My seventh son, Thomas, studied with Dr. Thomas Bond,
took a degree at the college, went to Georgetown, South Carolina, and there settled, and is getting into good practice.
So that, although I have had many difficulties, I am a happy

* My second brother died an infant.

16

mother, and my soul is rejoicing in the Almighty, who has blessed me in my children,—1775."

She has added on the same: "In the year 1761 I lost my honored father, Nicholas Scull. In the year 1765 I lost my daughter, Abigail. In the year 1776 I left Philadelphia for fear of the British army. In the year 1777 my son John was an exile in New York. In the year 1778 my son Nicholas was lost in the Randolph. In the year 1779 my son Edward died at Baltimore. And now, O my Heavenly Father! I submit with resignation to thy holy will, and beseech thee in thy mercy to grant the affliction which thou hast permitted to fall on me may purify my soul and prepare me for that day and hour which is swiftly approaching."*

Hearing this summer that Mrs. Catherine Lux, wife of George Lux, a daughter of my brother Edward, was in bad health at Baltimore, and thinking it probable her native air would be of service to her, I went down and brought her up to my house. For some time I flattered myself she was getting well, and frequently told her what really was my opinion, that she was not so bad as she supposed herself. She used to smile, but made no reply. After she had been with us a few weeks, she sent for me early one morning. When I went into her room, she took up a bowl that was near her and desired me to look in it. I found it was nearly filled with clear blood. She very calmly said, " This has just come from my stomach, and I sent for you, my dear uncle, to let you see you are mistaken in your opinion about my health." Seeing

---

* The following appeared in the *Pennsylvania Gazette*, May 20, 1789:—
"On Saturday, the 9th inst., departed this life after a short illness, in the 80th year of her age, Mrs. Mary Biddle, of this city. The following Monday her remains were carried from her son's house, James Biddle, Esquire, in Chestnut Street, to Whitemarsh Township, attended by her friends and relatives, and there interred in the family burying ground.

"She was affectionate—ardently affectionate—liberal and benevolent in her sentiments, cheerful and gay in her disposition and temper, sociable and agreeable in her conversation and company, averse to dissimulation of every species; added to all, she possessed the advantage of a clear and intelligent understanding, and was favored with an uninterrupted enjoyment of health, till she reached a period of life in which years are truly venerable."

me extremely affected, she begged me not to be uneasy about her, that she was perfectly easy herself, that death had no terrors for her, that all her prospects of happiness in this world were gone, and that she looked forward with pleasure for the hour she was to be united to her father, mother, sister, child, and her other relations and friends who had already left this world. Finding I was speechless with grief, she took my hand, which she pressed to her bosom, and said everything she could think of to console me. It was a long time before I was composed enough to leave this dear, unfortunate girl, who a short time before was one of the liveliest and most entertaining of her sex. Her husband was at this time at my house. Sometimes I pitied him, at other times his conduct was such that it was with difficulty I could keep my hands off him. She departed this life about a month after the bleeding I have mentioned, in the twenty-sixth year of her age, retaining her composure and her senses to the last moment of her life. A few days before the death of Mrs. Lux I lost a beloved little daughter, about fifteen months old.

The 17th of April, 1790, Dr. Benjamin Franklin departed this life, aged eighty-four years and three months. For the last five years of his life I was very often with him, having been two years Vice-President when he was President of Council. The last year he was President I was Secretary, and from that time until he died very intimate in the family. The Doctor was certainly a man of great abilities, but I believe not a great political character. He at times made inquiries of me respecting the Constitution of Pennsylvania, that convinced me he had little knowledge of it whatever he might once have had. He was agreeable and entertaining to the day of his death, always cheerful, and had some amusing anecdote to relate. When he brought forward any thing in Council that he wanted carried, he always began by relating some anecdote applicable to the business.

It was not long before he left Europe I believe that he felt the stone. When he was troubled with it in Council he often mentioned to me that those who lived out the days of life must expect to suffer, that most of his present friends were the sons or grandsons of his former companions, that my grandfather, Nicholas Scull, Surveyor-General of Pennsylvania, was one of his most intimate friends. He was justly beloved and esteemed by all who knew him; notwithstanding his age his death was sincerely regretted by me. When it was mentioned in Council, the members of the Board, out of respect to his character, agreed to carry his corpse to the grave. This was mentioned to the family, who were much pleased with the offer. A difference, however, between two of the members of the Board prevented it. The Doctor often mentioned it as his opinion that we were the happiest people in the world. He used to say the reason why we had not so many old people as in Europe in proportion to our numbers, was that sixty or seventy years back there were but few born in the country. He thought no people in the world lived to a greater age than the Americans, or enjoyed better health.

In October, 1790, came on the election for Governor, the first under the new State Constitution. General St. Clair was the Republican candidate, and General Mifflin, the Constitutionalist, for although General Mifflin, a short time before, had been considered a staunch Republican, he had by some means given offence. Indeed it is a very difficult matter for any one in a public situation to act in such a manner as to please *all* his party, but it must, however, be acknowledged that General Mifflin was not *remarkable* for his prudence. At the head of the Republican party were Robert Morris, Frederick A. Muhlenberg, Col. Miles, and some other gentlemen, who published an address to the Republican electors, recommending General St. Clair. Great exertions were made by both parties. The Republicans were unfortunate in their choosing General St. Clair, who although a worthy man, was but little known in the State. Indeed I do not believe any man they could have set up would have carried the election against Mifflin, who had all the Constitutionalists in his favor, and a good many personal friends among the Republicans, yet if they had set up Miles or Muhlenberg they would have had a much better chance of succeeding. The Repub-

licans, since called the Federal party, have always been the
most wealthy, and generally the most respectable of our in
habitants, but they never make those exertions that are made
by the opposite party, especially on the election ground, the
most important place for exertions to be made. Having a
strong personal attachment for General Mifflin, I did everything in my power before the day of election, by writing to
my friends in the different counties, to promote his interest,
and on the day of election I was upon the ground from the
time the poll opened until it was closed. He was chosen by
a very large majority.

As the powers of the Supreme Executive Council expired
with the old Constitution my office of course became extinct;
however, from the warm friendship that General Mifflin had
ever expressed for me (having frequently declared there was
no man in the world he loved and esteemed half so much)
I had not the least doubt he would offer me the office of
Secretary to the Commonwealth, an office that many of the
members who formed the Constitution thought unnecessary.
And I believe there would not have been such an office in
the Constitution if it had not been for some of my friends
in the Convention. It was thought by many that it would
be better to give the Governor a Private Secretary. This
was my own opinion, and what I recommended, but those
spoken to by me knew I would not accept the office of
Private Secretary, and wished me in office. Some thought
it of little consequence whether there was a Secretary to the
Commonwealth or Private Secretary, but my friends and
myself were mistaken in General Mifflin. He wished to
appoint A. J. Dallas, Esquire, a gentleman of the Bar, to
whom he was attached, and from whom he perhaps expected
services that I could or would not perform. I do not
mean by this any reflection on Mr. Dallas, for I never knew
anything improper in his conduct in any way whatever. I
blamed the Governor because he had not been candid, and
spoken to me on the subject. This he told me some time
afterwards he wished to do, but was afraid from the warmth
of my temper that I should say something to affront him,

and that he would make any sacrifices rather than have a difference with me. He at last sent three or four gentlemen of the Legislature, our mutual friends, to speak to me. The moment they spoke to me on the business they came about I told them if the Governor thought my consent necessary to the appointment of a Secretary, as they appeared to think, he was at liberty to do as he pleased, that I cared nothing about the office, and despised him; and made use of some other harsh expressions. However, I was softened, and my resentment subdued a good deal, when they told me he was very unwell and wished to see me. I did not call on him, but a few days afterwards he came to see me. He was much affected, and said he was under obligations to me he never could forget, and that there was nothing he would not do to serve me. After this visit we parted on better terms than we were before. His mind appeared to be relieved. This difference with General Mifflin occasioned me at the time a good deal of uneasiness. It was, however, fortunate for me that it happened, for he was at that time frequently embarrassed for money, of which he was extravagant and thoughtless. On these occasions he always applied to me. When this coolness happened I insisted on a settlement, and the balance due being paid me. It is probable, had we remained on good terms, that we should never have had a settlement, certainly I should not have been paid. As I now kept myself at a distance from him he could not ask me for the loan of any money, or indeed to render him any services. At this time my intention was to give up all thought of any office, and take a voyage to sea. From the number of friends I had amongst the inhabitants I knew it would be easy for me to get the command of a good ship, and the consignment of her cargo. This I certainly should have done in the spring of 1791, although it was extremely disagreeable to Mrs. Biddle and the rest of my family, if it had not been for the death of Judge Bryan, of the Supreme Court, who died suddenly the beginning of this year. The day after his death the Governor sent to request me to call on him, and when I went, to. my great surprise, he told me he had appointed Edward Shippen, Esquire, who was Chief Justice of the Court of Common Pleas, in the room of Judge Bryan. As the Governor had declared to all my friends and written me that he would give me the first vacant place that should happen, I expected he would have appointed my brother James to the office held by Judge Bryan, and given me the Prothonotary's office.* I told him rather bluntly what my expectation was, and left the house immediately. He came to the door and called me back; he was very much agitated, and I was convinced he was sorry he had been so precipitate. He said his wish was that my brother James should be Judge of the Court of Common Pleas, and I should have the office of Prothonotary. I told him he must know the office Mr. Shippen held was worth very little, and my brother should not, with my consent, accept it. With this I left him, neither of us well pleased. Indeed I felt much dissatisfied with him, and now would have preferred going to sea to any office he could give me. Soon after we had parted the Governor called on my brother, and this best of men agreed to the arrangement he wished to make. I insisted, however, upon my brother receiving the emoluments of the Prothonotary's office until a further provision was made for the office he was to have, which was soon after done. The office of Prothonotary was not much with the heavy tax on it. My friends in the Legislature had the tax taken off; it amounted to between four and five hundred pounds per annum. The Governor told me some time after sending me the commission that he would have appointed my brother one of the Judges of the Supreme Court, but he thought it would be of advantage to me for him to preside in the

---

* In a letter before me, dated January 17, 1791, among other things he says: "I shall be solicitous to evince my zeal for your honor and interest; and as it cannot be long before I shall have it in my power to serve the public, and gratify myself, by inviting you to some station at least as respectable and beneficial as the office of Secretary, I fondly trust that the present explanation will effectually prevent any interruption of the harmony that has hitherto distinguished our intimacy, or any diminution of our reciprocal esteem and the good opinion which we have entertained of each other."

Common Pleas. Indeed if it had not been for my brother
I never would have undertaken to do the duties of an office
I was so totally unacquainted with. With his assistance I
soon acquired a knowledge of the business. The Governor
sent with the commission the following letter :—

My Dear Sir : It gives me sincere pleasure to enclose a
commission, appointing you to succeed your brother, as Prothonotary of the Court of Common Pleas of Philadelphia
County.

I am, with sincere regard,
Your friend,
THOS. MIFFLIN.

Philada., 1st Feb'y, 1791.
CHARLES BIDDLE, ESQ.

Although after this we visited each other, and the Governor never had any large party without inviting me, and did
everything in his power to keep up our former intimacy, I
did not feel that attachment to him I before had. I believe
when a man *knows* he has not been treated well, nothing
done afterwards will effect a perfect reconciliation. Some
years afterwards when General Mifflin got into difficulties,
I made every exertion in my power to serve him, and did
serve him essentially.

Mrs. Potts, an intimate friend of Mrs. Biddle, being advised by her physician to go to the seashore with a sick
child, and Mrs. Biddle wishing to take our children there, I
went to take care of them. We left the city in June, 1792,
in a small shallop, commanded by a drunken fellow who had
no person with him belonging to the shallop but his son, a
lad about sixteen years of age. The first night we anchored
near Marcus Hook. The night was so dark that a brig
bound up passed so near that we could have jumped on
board of her. As the heat below had obliged Mrs. Potts and
Mrs. Biddle to be on deck, they saw the danger they had
been in, and were very much terrified. Had the brig ran foul of
us, it is highly probable we should have foundered. Instead
of anchoring in the channel, we should have gone close in
shore. This I mentioned to the skipper when he came to,

but he said there was no danger, and I did not apprehend there was much. Owing to head winds, calms, and a drunken skipper, we were three days before we reached Cape May. At this time the accommodations at the Cape were bad. The shore is good to bathe, some think better than Long Branch. I, however, do not think so. The surf at the Branch is higher, but I never heard of any accident there. As to the sharks that are seen there, they are very different from those in the West Indies. I believe no more danger is to be apprehended from them than from a sturgeon.

We had been but a few days at the Cape when the revenue cutter anchored off there. Mr. Dulaney, the collector of the customs, Mr. John Nesbit, and General Robinson were on board. As my business required my being in town, I accepted a pressing invitation given me by these gentlemen to go up with them, and to return in a carriage for Mrs. Biddle and the children. In going up the bay, upon the appearance of a squall, I told Captain Montgomery, who commanded the cutter, that he had better shorten sail, for I was sure it would blow very heavy. However, he did not apprehend any danger, and thought it unnecessary to take in any of his sails. As it approached I was convinced it would blow hard, and advised him, as he was not well, to go below and leave the command to me. As soon as he was in the cabin, I took in all sail as fast as possible, intending to come to anchor, but before we could let go the anchors, the squall took us, and without any sail set we had nearly overset. In order to bring her up, we let go both anchors, and as the cables were not clinched to the mast, owing to the ignorance of the crew, they had nearly run out end for end. This tornado did a great deal of mischief at the wharves in Philadelphia and elsewhere. The gentlemen on board mentioned afterwards that it was happy for them they had persuaded me to come up with them.

Shortly after, I sat off for Cape May in a carriage. I took with me my son William, then about eleven years of age. At three o'clock in the afternoon of the day we left town, we came to a fork in the road where I was at a loss which way to take. However, as there was no house near, and the day excessively hot, it would not do to wait. I took the one that appeared to be the most frequented. We had not gone far before we came across a tree that had been blown down across the road. To get the carriage over this tree myself and servant worked very hard for half an hour. About a mile from this place we came to a house. The people here told us the road we were going led to a mill; that at the forks we should have taken the other road. This was grievous news to us, who, as well as the horses, were almost dead with fatigue. However, there was no remedy, we were obliged to again encounter the tree, and what was worse, found it would be impossible to get to the stage we intended to lodge at. We were therefore forced to stop at a miserable log house, where they were obliged to have a smoke at each door to prevent their being tormented with the mosquitos. The poor people furnished us with a bed upstairs, which I believe was the only one they had. The heat of the weather, and the smoke that was made in the room to keep out the mosquitos rendered it a shocking place. In the middle of the night I was awakened by William. I jumped out of bed and found he was almost suffocated. Taking him in my arms to a window, the fresh air soon revived him. Finding it in vain to try to sleep we both dressed ourselves and went below, where we remained the rest of the night. No person unacquainted with these insects can form an idea what a torment they are to people *not used to them* and not provided with means to keep them off. They are worse on this road than at any place I ever was at. Probably it may be better when the country is cleared of wood. The next night we got within a few miles of Hughes, the house where the family staid, and early the morning after reached there. Finding Mrs. Biddle anxious to be at home, and a pilot boat. going up two days after, I took one of the boys with me in her, and Mrs. Biddle and the family set off at the same time in the carriage. Having a fair wind, we were soon up. Mrs. Biddle suffered as much coming up in the carriage as we did going down. They missed the road, and if it had not been for a man accidentally meeting them, they would have had to remain all night in the woods.

In April, 1793, we had an account of Mr. Genet, the French Republican Minister, at Charleston. His motive for landing at Charleston and travelling by land thence to Philadelphia, must have been to find out whether the Americans were inclined to join the French in the war in which they were then engaged, and to endeavor to make them believe that the Republic of France was fighting for the liberties of mankind against the despots of Europe. He was very cordially received at Charleston, and at every place he stopped at on the road. At Philadelphia, a town meeting was called to congratulate him on his arrival amongst us. Curiosity took me to the State House, without knowing who had called the meeting, or what the intentions were of those who had called it. As soon as I got there, Dr. Hutchinson, Mr. Sergeant, and others, who had proposed the meeting, requested me to take the chair. I would have declined it, but that some of my friends were anxious that I should not do so, thinking, as they afterwards told me, that by being in the chair I should prevent some violent measures being adopted; and it is probable my being in the chair was in this respect of some service. It was agreed to present an address to Mr. Genet; and David Rittenhouse, J. D. Sergeant, Esq., Dr. Hutchinson, A. J. Dallas, Peter S. Duponceau, Esq., and myself were appointed to draft one. The meeting then adjourned until the next afternoon. In the morning the Committee met at my house, each having an address drawn up, from which we made out one. In the afternoon there were so many met at the State House, that we were obliged to adjourn to the yard, where, as chairman, I read the address. Like all addresses brought forward in this manner, it was highly approved, and a committee consisting of about fifty, besides those who drafted the address, appointed to deliver it to the Minister, who had taken up his quarters at the City Tavern in Second Street. We proceeded from the State House on our way there, attended by a great concourse of people. As we were going, Hutchinson, who was fat enough to act the character of Falstaff without stuffing, sent several messages to me, to beg I would not go so fast; however, thinking such exercise of service to him, every time he sent to me, I mended my pace, so that he was almost exhausted when he got into the house. Mr. Genet spoke tolerably good English. He was in high spirits, and gave us a most cordial reception. He told us how much gratified he was, and how pleasing it would be to the citizens of France to hear what a friendly reception he had met with from their brethren of America, and that he would answer our address the next day. When we were coming away the people assembled in the streets gave three cheers, and dispersed without doing any mischief, although some were much inclined to have a frolic.

Shortly after this, there was formed in the city a Democratic Society,* of which David Rittenhouse, Esq., was chosen President, and myself one of the Vice-Presidents. As I had never attended the meetings of those who proposed forming such a society, and as, when it was mentioned to me by Dr. Hutchinson who was one of the principal promoters of it, I told him my opinion was that it would do more harm than good, I was much surprised at finding my name among the list of officers, which I did not know until it was published in the newspapers; nor then until some of my friends, the morning it was published, told me they were sorry to see my name as an officer of such a society. Others thought I could be of service by moderating some of the most violent of the party who were inclined to do anything that would involve us in a war with Great Britain. Mr. Rittenhouse, I believe, never attended any meetings. Both our names were set down by Dr. Hutchinson, who wished us to belong to the society. As most of my friends were Federalists, and some of them violent ones, I was sorry the Doctor had proposed me as a member. However, as I knew he did not do it with any intention of giving me pain, I freely forgave him.

The first of June a dinner was given to Mr. Genet at Oeller's Hotel. It was attended by men of all parties, for at

---

* This was the first Democratic Society formed in the United States.

that time many who detested the proceedings of the French, did not wish to see them subdued, not knowing what would be the consequence to this country. At this entertainment I was appointed President, and Doctor Hutchinson Vice-President. On one side of me was Governor Mifflin, on the other Mr. Genet. Many toasts were given expressive of our love for our *sister Republic*. The *bonnet rouge* was passed from head to head round the table, and many patriotic songs, made to celebrate the day, were sung, some of them truly ridiculous; they served, however, to increase our mirth. The Marseilles Hymn was sung by Mr. Genet, and we had several other French songs. The day ended without any disturbance.*

I was much pleased soon after this, at hearing the Marseilles Hymn sung on board the frigate Ambuscade. Her yards were manned, and every person on board joined with the utmost enthusiasm. I believe there never was a more animating song composed. An American lady (Mrs. Montgomery, sister to the wife of Governor McKean) was at Bordeaux when some troops marched from there singing this hymn. She told me she could hardly refrain from taking a musket and joining them. Mr. Genet is a handsome, agreeable man, but, like most of his countrymen, of a hasty disposition. He frequently wrote and said what he afterwards severely repented. Being invited to dine the 4th of July with the Society of Cincinnati, he returned a very polite answer, but mentioned he could not sit down at table with the Count de Noailles. As the Count was a member of the society, such an objection gave great offence to many of the members, who were determined if Mr. Genet remained in the country he should never again be invited. A few years before he would have thought it a great honor to be at a table with the Count, such an honor as he never had an idea of. I suppose as Ambassador from the French Republic, he thought it an *official duty* to make the objection.

* This banquet created a great sensation throughout the country. An account of it is given in Westcott's valuable history of Philadelphia. See, also, Hilldreth, vol. iv. Mr. Peter S. Duponceau wrote a French Ode for the occasion, which was sung by the company.

In July I went to Long Branch, and lodged at Col. Green's with a number of my Federal friends, who upon my first arriving at the shore, congratulated me on my having the *honor* of being elected Vice-President of the Democratic Society; however, finding it was a subject I did not like, they soon dropped it. I left the shore before daylight on the day the action took place between the Ambuscade and Boston. Had I known of the Ambuscade's going out to attack the Boston, I should certainly have waited to have seen the action, which with glasses could be plainly seen from the shore. The contest was unequal, the French frigate being much superior to the British. The gallant commander of the Boston, Captain Courtney, fell in the action. The Ambuscade received so much damage that it was a long time before she could be repaired; so that if it had not been for the loss of Courtney the action was favorable to the British, for this French frigate had done much injury to their trade, and would have done much more but for this battle.

A few days after I returned from the seashore, Mrs. Jones and Judge Jones (most valuable friends who lived in Montgomery County) with Mrs. Biddle and myself, went to the Yellow Springs.* Returning from there we first heard there was a fever in Philadelphia, that occasioned great alarm among the inhabitants. Among other deaths, that of Mr. Peter Aston was mentioned. He was an old acquaintance of mine, whom I had sworn as a juryman the day before we left

---

* Once before I was at those springs. A friend of the family had received an express from there, informing him his wife lay at the point of death. He applied to my mother to let me go with him, as he was going in his chair, and was obliged to set off in the night, and could not see well enough to drive. As I was not more than thirteen years of age, my mother was not inclined to let me go; however, I was eager for the journey, and got her consent. Our friend was a remarkably cheerful man, and sang most of the night. When we arrived his wife was much better, at which he expressed great pleasure, and appealed to me how much he had suffered on our way upon account of his wife's indisposition. My real opinion was that he would have been much better pleased to hear that she had moved off. He should have given me my lesson before he made the appeal, for from my answer the good lady thought he had not suffered much.—AUTHOR'S NOTE.

town, when he was very hearty and cheerful. After the jury had delivered their verdict he came to me, and begged I would not so often put him on the jury list; little thinking, poor fellow, how soon he should leave us. Upon hearing of the fever I left Mrs. Biddle under the care of Mr. and Mrs. Jones, and set out for town, being very uneasy about the family. On my way I met a number of people moving out, all of whom gave a melancholy account of the ravages of the disorder. I had promised Mrs. Biddle to send the children out to her, and to be out soon myself, but such was her uneasiness that the next morning after my coming to town, although it rained excessively hard, she came home. My office being in my house, and people coming to it from the infected parts of the city, made it dangerous to the family, whom I was determined to send immediately out. Mr. Wm. Lardner, who had the year before married a sister of Mrs. Biddle, having a pleasant seat on the Delaware, and giving us a pressing invitation, we sent the children there, Mrs. Biddle declaring she would not leave the city without me. It was in vain I pointed out the necessity of my staying, she was deaf to everything. Although almost afraid to let him come into my house, I sent for Dr. Hutchinson, to advise with him about removing. Before Mrs. Biddle he just mentioned that there was a dangerous fever in town, and that we had best leave it, but when I went to the door with him, he told me he had never seen anything so alarming, and desired me to get Mrs. Biddle out of town immediately, and to go myself as soon as I could. He said, that as a physician he thought it his duty to remain, and let the disorder be ever so bad he would not leave town. I walked a little way down the street with him. At parting he gave me his hand, and said it was doubtful whether he should see me again. I laughed at him, little expecting this would be the last time we should ever meet. It was some days before I could arrange matters so as to leave the city, before which this worthy man was taken with the disorder, and died in a few days. He was a very able physician, and one of the best of men. A student of his, who staid with him, said he went to all the poor people, who sent for him. Visiting one of them, who was a poor old woman, he caught the infection. This student was with him, and said when the Doctor opened the door of the sick woman's room, there was such a stench came from it, that he ran out of the house. The Doctor went in, opened the windows, and sat some time in the room. That night he was taken with the fever which proved fatal to him. His death increased the alarm very much, and occasioned many to leave the city. He had a great deal of practice, and was esteemed and respected by men of all parties that knew him.*

It is not easy to describe the consternation of the inhabitants at this time; the streets were almost deserted. I have stood at my door at noon, and looking up and down the street for some time, could not see one person in it. Being myself used to see people in fever in the West Indies, particularly at Port au Prince, I did not feel that uneasiness many of my friends did. I thought then, and still think, that a person who had been long in the West Indies was not as liable to take the fever as those who had never been there, and therefore should not have thought of leaving the city but for my family. John Vannost, Esq., a gentleman of the Bar, who had lived with me from the time I was first appointed to the office of Prothonotary, agreed to stay in the house, which I committed to his care, and went to Mr. Lardner's, who did everything in his power to make our situation agreeable. A faithful black boy, born in the family, stayed with Mr. Vannost. The boy should have left town with me, but he preferred remaining, and it was the general opinion at that time that the blacks did not take the fever. This boy

---

* Dr. James Hutchinson was born in Bucks County in 1752, and served during the Revolution as Surgeon in the Continental Army, and Surgeon-General of Pennsylvania. He was one of the first trustees of the University of Pennsylvania, and Professor of Chemistry in that Institution up to the time of his death. He took a warm interest in the politics of the State, and was an active member of the then rising Democratic party. Eminent as a practitioner, he fell a victim to his noble efforts in behalf of the humbler class of his fellow citizens in September, 1793. His first wife, who died without issue, was Lydia Biddle, first cousin of Charles Biddle, and sister of Col. Clement Biddle.

used to meet me three times a week about a mile from town.
I would have ridden into town, but this could not be done
without giving great uneasiness to my own family as well as
Mr. Lardner's, and it would have been very ungenerous to do
anything that would give pain to a family who behaved so
kindly.

Dr. Hutchinson died the sixth or seventh of September.
A few days after, when it was thought almost certain death
for any person to go to Bush Hill (the place where all those
with the yellow fever were carried), Captain Stephen Girard
and Mr. Peter Helm offered their services to attend there.
Captain Girard was a Frenchman, married and settled in
Philadelphia many years; Peter Helm, a native of the city.
Both of them I knew well. With Girard I had long been a
manager of the Marine Society, and Mr. Helm lived in my
neighborhood. Their services should ever be remembered
with gratitude by the inhabitants of Philadelphia. Mr. Helm
told me after the fever was over that when he went out to
Bush Hill he never expected to return. The generous and
benevolent Girard was at the time, and I believe has been
ever since, of opinion that the fever was not contagious. He
therefore did not apprehend so much personal danger as Mr.
Helm. Too much praise cannot be given them. There were
many others who behaved with great firmness and benevolence. Some who were thought to be afraid of nothing were
much terrified at this disorder; among others an old friend of
mine, Commodore Barry, an officer of distinguished bravery,
retired to his country seat, and would suffer no person from
the city to come near his house. Captain Sharp, a member
of the Cincinnati, who had served in the artillery all the
Revolutionary War, was a man of undoubted courage. In
the beginning of the fever, his wife complained one night of
being unwell. Concluding she had the fever, he immediately
jumped out of bed, and shut himself up in another room.
He was frightened into a fever, and died in a day or two.
His wife was soon well. Mr. J. A. Lewis, whom I have
formerly mentioned, a very honest, faithful clerk of mine, was
a Hessian who came to America with General Knyphausen,

17

and was in all the principal actions fought during the war.
At the peace he stayed in America, married a worthy woman,
by whom at this time he had several children. Mr. Vannost
having informed me that Lewis was very much terrified at
staying in town, I told him if he wished to leave town, as
there was very little business in the office, he was at liberty
to go whenever he pleased, and I advised him to go, telling
him his wages should go on the same as if he stayed.
Willing, however, to make something at night by writing,
he said he was very much obliged to me, but he would remain in town. However, a few days after I had spoken to
him he wrote me a note informing me that in going home
the evening before he had seen twelve *corpuses* going to be
buried, which had terrified him so much that he had hired a
carriage and was just going into the country. No man, I
believe, in battle would behave with more courage than Lewis.
There were many other instances of men of great bravery
who were as much or more terrified than those I have mentioned, and some who were generally thought to be so timid
that they would have fled as soon as there was any danger,
stayed in town and distinguished themselves by their courage
and benevolence. Melancholy instances have been mentioned
of people deserting their relations and friends, and no doubt
some, driven by fear, left those whom they ought never to
have left. I, however, knew of no instance where it was
done, and believe it was seldom the case.

Some very sorrowful, and some ludicrous scenes happened
during the fever. A friend of mine, who had moved into
the country early in the disorder, being much afraid of
taking the fever, was very cautious of any person coming
out of the city. Riding one day in his chair, he overtook
a gentleman walking towards town, and invited him to ride
with him, which the gentleman accepted. My friend, finding him a very agreeable, intelligent man, when he got near
his own house, pressed the stranger very much to go in, and
dine with him. He excused himself, saying he had just
been out to see a sick friend. This alarmed my acquaintance.
"And where were you going in such a hurry?" "To Bush

Hill." "The devil you were! I hope you have not been there lately?" "Oh yes! I am Dr. Devoze, one of the physicians who attend the hospital." A highwayman with a pistol pointed at him would not have frightened him half as much. He soon got rid of the Doctor, and never afterwards invited a stranger to ride with him.

It was generally supposed, and it was my opinion, that the fever was brought to Philadelphia by the unfortunate people who were obliged to leave Hispaniola.* Very few of those people, or the black people, took the fever.

What added greatly to the distress of those unhappy persons who took the fever was the difference of opinion among our most eminent physicians respecting the proper treatment of it. What one recommended another would condemn, so that all confidence in them was lost. I believe that in general too much medicine was given. I was reminded at this time of an anecdote I had often heard Dr. Franklin tell respecting a malignant fever that was in Barbadoes, which swept off great numbers of the inhabitants. At last they were out of medicine, and it was expected they would all die. It happened, however, otherwise; for after the medicine was gone every person that had the disease recovered. I believe bleeding, keeping the body open, and the patient cool and clean, was the best method of curing the disease. I had determined, if taken with the disorder, to take very little or no medicine. The great quantity, if the patient recovered from the fever, ruined the constitution.

On the return day of the court, in September, my brother, Judge Biddle, went into the city to open and adjourn the

---

* Mr. Henry Sickel and myself were appointed to collect money in the ward we lived in for those distressed people, which disgusted me against raising money in this way. One gentleman, Mr. Samuel Blodget, gave us a check for two hundred dollars. One of his neighbors, a much richer man, with a good deal of persuasion, gave us four. To avoid giving offence we went into every house. Many people gave us cheerfully, more than they could afford. To some of them I would much rather have given than have taken anything. Others, who were rich, would give nothing.— AUTHOR'S NOTE.

court. I intended to have gone with him, but he requested me not to go, and, as Mr. Vannost was there, and little, if any, business to be done, I remained out of town. Before he went he made his will, which, without mentioning at the time what it was, he left with me. At court there were only five gentlemen of the Bar: Jonathan D. Sergeant, Jacob Bankson, J. R. Howell, John Todd, and Charles Neatly. Mr. Sergeant was a man of large fortune and great worth; he staid in town from motives of benevolence. Messrs. Howell and Todd were worthy men. I believe they remained in the city in expectation of being employed in writing wills. For this purpose they went to any persons that sent for them. They died shortly after the meeting of the court, and I believe took the fever from persons whose wills they drew. Mr. Todd told my brother when the court adjourned they had best leave the Court House as soon as possible, as the committee appointed for conveying persons with the fever to Bush Hill sat there.

I believe, that giving an emetic early in the disorder, moderate bleeding, keeping the body open, and the patient cool and clean, with good nursing, was the means of saving many who had the fever. The great quantity of mercury that was given by some of the physicians, if they recovered the patient from the fever, ruined the constitution. Although four thousand died of this fever, there were not a great many of the old inhabitants. They were mostly foreigners. Having lived long in the city, and being Prothonotary, occasioned my knowing most of the citizens. There were not more than eighty whom I knew, and many of these were natives of Europe. During the whole time of the fever, the markets were well supplied, and I believe none of the country people took the fever, except a very few who imprudently went to see their sick friends or, from curiosity, to improper places. I mention imprudently going to see their sick friends, because they could render them no assistance.

In November, the fever was so far abated that the citizens flocked to town as fast as they had before left it. People who had little or no acquaintance with each other before they left the city, appeared rejoiced at seeing each other. The loss was soon forgotten in the joy of getting back to the city.

In the year 1794, the excise had occasioned so much disturbance in the Western country, that it was thought necessary to send commissioners there to endeavor to bring the people to a sense of their duty. They had driven off Major Lenox, the Federal Marshal, who had been up serving processes against the delinquent distillers, and burned the house of General Neville, who was inspector of the district. At the attack on it, Major McFarlane, who commanded the insurgents, was killed. After this they declared they would oppose any force brought against them. Governor Mifflin spoke to me about going as one of the commissioners on the part of the State; however, I knew there were others better acquainted with the people of the Western country, and who would probably have more influence than I should. Chief Justice McKean and General Irvine were the two who went on the part of the State; Mr. Bradford, Attorney-General of the United States, James Ross, one of the Senators of the United States, for Pennsylvania, and Jasper Yeates, one of the Judges of the Supreme Court of Pennsylvania, went on the part of the Federal Government. I wrote a letter to the printer at Pittsburg, informing him that I had ever been a friend and advocate for the people of the Western country, but that the opposition they had given to the laws of their country had been such that every man who valued the peace and happiness of the country must lend his aid to bring them to justice. After his return, Mr. Bradford told me that Mr. Scull had shown him the letter, that he had it published, and that it had a good effect. If a longer time had been given the commissioners, I have no doubt but that the people would have submitted peaceably. However, as they did not submit within the time limited, it was thought necessary to send an armed force into the country. The two principal promoters of the disturbances were David Bradford, a lawyer, a native of Maryland, and John Marshall, who had been sheriff of Washington County, and formerly in the Legislature. They were anxious for the repeal of the Excise Law (as I be-

lieve a majority of the State was) and encouraged the people
to oppose it, but had no intention of carrying matters to such
lengths as they had gone. But you cannot say to such people as they had to deal with, a hardy, warlike race, thus far
you may go, but no further. It was not in their power to
govern those who acted under them. After several meetings
were had about this business, it is probable if Marshall or
Bradford had advised moderate measures they would instantly have lost their influence, been insulted and abused,
and perhaps shot. It unfortunately happened that in general, men of prudence and influence avoided these meetings,
and left the most violent to do as they pleased. Smilie, Findley, and Gallatin* were much blamed. I do not, however,
believe they deserved any censure, but on the contrary, that
they did everything in their power to prevent the people from
acts of violence. It is possible that their being suspected of
fomenting the disturbances, made them more anxious to put
a stop to them than they otherwise would have been.

Much complaint was made by the prisoners of the treatment they received from General White, who commanded
the party that brought them to Philadelphia. They said,
when they were first arrested, he had them confined in a
damp cellar, tied back to back, and kept there from Thursday night until Sunday morning with hardly any victuals
or drink. Certainly, none of them deserved such treatment,
and some of them were brave fellows who had served
with reputation during the Revolution, and were afterwards
proved to be innocent of the crimes laid to their charge.
When they reached the ferry at Schuylkill they were ordered
to put a piece of paper in their hats, with which they were
paraded down Market Street. It was pretended that this
was done to distinguish them from their guards, but their
dress was sufficient to make them known, without this dis-

* I was well acquainted with these gentlemen. The two former I have
mentioned before as members of the Supreme Executive Council. Mr.
Gallatin is allowed by his enemies to be a man of superior talents. They
were all of the same political party.—AUTHOR'S NOTE.

graceful badge. I believe no complaint was made by the prisoners of any officer but General White.

Hugh H. Brackenridge, in order to justify himself from charges made against him, published "Incidents of the Insurrection in the Western Parts of Pennsylvania." It appears from Mr. Brackenridge's own account that he acted a double part, which he thought his situation at that time not only justified but rendered meritorious. There is no doubt but that personal motives, more than public justice, actuated some of his enemies. In one part of his book he says, "At Parkinson's Ferry I fell in with Benjamin Parkinson carrying down a board, with an intention to fix it upon one of the liberty poles. I read the inscription; it was:—

" ' Equal taxation, and no excise.
No asylum for traitors and cowards.'

"Thought I, there are two of us, then, that ought to be away; for you are a coward, and I am a traitor, for I do not mean to go to war; and if you do, you will not fight." In another part he mentions his being consulted by one Fergus Ferguson, collier, who was taken up as an insurgent. "I was of opinion that as his employment and residence were subterraneous, he could plead the not belonging to the surface of the earth; or, if in strictness this would not bar the jurisdiction of the court, it would at least have weight with the Executive, to direct the Attorney-General to enter a nolle prosequi, inasmuch as he had been under ground through the summer, and had not heard of the insurrection until it was over." Mr. Brackenridge is now, 1805, one of the Judges of the Supreme Court of Pennsylvania.

Major Lenox, the Marshal, who went up to serve the writs, is a native of North Britain, a very worthy, good fellow. He was a captain in the American service, and was taken prisoner at Fort Washington.

About the middle of April, 1796, in riding out to dine, I felt in the upper part of my back something like a small boil. In the evening it gave me some pain; however, I went to bed without saying anything about it, expecting it would soon be well. In the night the pain increased and made me very restless, and it was painful all the next day, but not so much so as to prevent my going to court and attending to other business. Being much fatigued when I went to bed, I slept soundly until near daylight, when I was awakened with a most excruciating pain which made me jump out of bed and order a light. Mrs. Biddle looked at the supposed boil, and thought if it was opened with a lancet, that it would immediately relieve me. I sent for Mr. Wolf, who dressed me, and who was a good bleeder, and ordered the servant to tell him to bring a lancet. He came just at daylight, when going to the window I pulled off my shirt and desired that he would immediately open the boil. He told me it had a very strange appearance, that it looked purple and green, and that he did not think it was in a proper state to be opened. He begged me to send for the doctor—he went himself—and Dr. Wistar, understanding from Mr. Wolf that he had left me in great pain, came immediately. Upon looking at the supposed boil he told me it must not be opened, that it would confine me some time, and directed a poultice of bread and milk to be immediately made, and applied to it. He gave me some drops in which I believe there was laudanum. The next day he told me it was an anthrax, and must be cut out. I lay with my back poulticed for near three weeks before it was supposed to be fit to cut. Previous to this he advised calling in Dr. Kuhn, who attended every day with Dr. Wistar. After this Dr. Wistar told me that he should not have occasion to use the knife again. He was, however, mistaken, for in a few days he and Dr. Kuhn having examined my back, informed me that it would facilitate the cure if I was again cut, and Dr. Wistar was proceeding to say something about a person who had fallen a sacrifice to his obstinacy, when Dr. Kuhn stopped him. Dr. Wistar said he would perform the operation that day, or put it off some days. I told him if he thought it necessary I would prefer his doing it immediately. He went home, brought his students with him and his instruments, and began. This was the longest in performing and most severe of any of the operations he had performed.

The sweat ran down my hollow cheeks, and my shirt was as wet as if it had been in the river. I did not, however, utter a complaint. The Doctor was pleased to say that he never saw any one bear cutting so well. Soon after this I began to mend, and in a few days was well enough to ride out. The second or third time of my going out I had the curiosity to go into a neighbor's and get weighed. My long confinement had reduced me from one hundred and eighty to one hundred and thirty-four pounds weight. A sore mouth, such as young children have, I had after the anthrax was cut out, and for which the doctors gave me a great deal of vitriol. To this I imputed the loss of several of my teeth, which loosened and came out without any pain. Standing one day at the door waiting for the carriage, to go riding, being so weak that I was obliged to be supported by a servant, Captain Welsh, an old acquaintance, came up to me and exclaimed, " My God! is this Captain Biddle?" I shook him by the hand, and told him it was the remains of Captain Biddle, whom he formerly knew in the Bay of Honduras. " And is it possible," he again exclaimed, " that such a beautiful young man as you then were should be so much altered." His exclamation about my *beauty*, wreck as I was, made me laugh. There must have been a great alteration from the time my honest friend had seen me in the Bay; then I was florid, young, strong, and active, with an excellent set of teeth. He now saw me pale and weak, with the loss of some of my fore-teeth, and reduced to a skeleton. Notwithstanding my wretched appearance, my spirits were good, nor were they depressed during my confinement, which probably occasioned my recovery. A few days after my first leaving the house, an intimate friend called to see me. When I informed him of my being better and expecting soon to leave the room, he expressed much satisfaction, saying he had understood from the doctors, one or the other of whom he saw every day, that they had very little hopes of my recovery. Such persons should never be permitted to come into a sick-room without being cautioned as to what they may say. They depress the spirits, by which means they may injure a sick person materially. At one time I was of opinion myself that my disorder would prove fatal to me, in consequence of which I made my will, wrote a letter to Governor Mifflin requesting, should I not survive my complaint, that he would appoint some friend to my office who would collect the fees that would be due my family, and made every other preparation in my power for my departure. Although very few people had more to make life desirable than myself, being in good circumstances, happy in my family and friends, yet knowing the uncertainty of life, I prepared to suffer with fortitude a removal from this world, which, however, I never found so bad as many people have represented it. In fact, I believe very few have had less reason to complain of the world than myself, having my full share of the pleasures and comforts of life. During my confinement Dr. Wistar would frequently agree to let me have meat or butter, but Dr. Kuhn would never consent to any indulgence whatever. After riding out for some time my brother James purchased a fine green turtle for me which I had ever been very fond of, but when it was mentioned to Dr. Kuhn he requested me not to taste it. I was very weak for a long time, and in the fall had some apprehensions of being confined again. It, however, went off, and I have felt nothing of it up to this present year, 1805.

There being some bank troubles about this time, it was said that Governor Mifflin had overdrawn on the bank for a considerable amount. He was so much affected by the report that he took to his bed, and sent to request me to call on him. Having some particular business to attend to, I did not wait on him that day. The next morning he sent Col. Febiger, the Treasurer, who told me the Governor was very anxious to see me. When I went he was much affected, saying he was afraid I had left him, and would not call to see him. I soon eased his mind. What occasioned the report was that his relation, John Mifflin, who was Cashier, and on whom he entirely depended to keep his bank account, had let some notes lent the Governor by Chief Justice McKean and the Surveyor-General, Brodhead, lie over when they should and would have been renewed had these gentle-

men been applied to. In money matters few men were more
careless than Governor Mifflin. If he had what he wanted
for to-day, he thought not of to-morrow. If he had a sum
by him that he knew he would be called upon for the next
day, he could not refuse it to any of his friends who called
to borrow. By this unfortunate weakness he was continually
kept in want.

In the year 1797 I met with an irreparable loss in the
death of my brother James. He went from town the
thirteenth of June to hold a court at Norristown, and
returned home in the evening. I called at night to see him.
His daughter told me he was well, but complained of being
very much fatigued, and had gone to bed. In the night he
was taken extremely ill, and in two days we lost him. A
better man I believe never lived. To me he had ever been
the most affectionate brother. No father could have taken
more care of me than he did. Hardly anything could have
been so severe a blow to me as this loss. He was remarkably cheerful and good-tempered. I hardly ever remember
seeing him out of temper. He was careless of his health,
and in money affairs very few men more so. I believe no
man ever lived more beloved than my brother James. Two
years before his death he went to Long Branch with an old
schoolmate, Mr. Tench Francis. The day after they got
down they stripped to go into bathe. Just as they were
going in Mr. Francis stopped my brother, and said to him,
"James, are you sick?" "No." "Do you think bathing
will make you feel better?" "It cannot, for I never was
better in my life." "As that is the case," says Mr. Francis,
"let us put on our clothes, for I am of your opinion, that,
being perfectly well, we cannot be better by bathing."
Accordingly they dressed themselves, and did not go into
the sea all the time they were at the shore.

The loss of my brother having confined me a good deal to
the house, I thought it would be of service to take a journey,
and being advised by a friend who had been at Ballstown
Springs, and who intended going there again, to take a
jaunt there, I left town the first of August, taking my son

William with me. We got to Paulus Hook that evening, and intended to stay there all night, but finding the mosquitos very troublesome we crossed over to New York, where we arrived before ten o'clock. I do not think riding this distance in one day that a person feels more, perhaps not so much, fatigue as going forty or fifty miles in the same time; at any rate it is so with me. We were some days in New York before we could get a passage to Albany. During our stay at New York we passed our time very agreeably among the hospitable inhabitants, to several of whom I had letters of introduction. I intended before we left the city to have called upon Mr. William Seton, a very respectable merchant, who, I had some reason to think, was the same Mr. Seton who behaved so friendly to me when at St. Lucar in the year 1763, but the continual engagements I was under made me conclude to postpone my visit to him until my return from Ballstown.

We embarked on board one of the Albany sloops, and were tolerably well accommodated. I do not think this the best way to go from New York to Albany. The most agreeable, and often the most expeditious way, I believe is to go to Poughkeepsie by water, and then to take the land stage. We arrived at Albany two days after a great fire that destroyed a considerable part of the town. We were received and entertained very hospitably by the gentlemen to whom we had letters, particularly by Judge Taylor, who did everything in his power to make the place agreeable. There is nothing remarkable in Albany except it is the great number of stages. You can be accommodated with one here for almost any part of the continent. After remaining a few days here we went to Ballstown, distant from hence about thirty-seven miles, and a tolerably good road. Ballstown is surrounded by hills. I do not think it is an agreeable place, at least it was not so during the time of my being there. The houses were too much crowded for an invalid to receive much benefit. This may be remedied by building more houses, but you cannot bring the springs from the low ground, and there is no pleasant place to ride or walk to.

We one day made up a party to spend a day at Saratoga Springs. At the tavern there we had a most execrable dinner; the victuals were bad, and the cooking worse. An old acquaintance of mine, Col. Willet, of New York, who was one of the party, during the time we were dining kept praising the dinner, declaring he had never seen such a one before (this we all believed to be true), and said we ought to come often there to dinner. The landlord, who thought him serious, said he should be always glad to see him, and very gravely assured him that he should have as good a dinner whenever he came, provided he would give him notice of his coming. From what was mentioned to me while at Ballstown, I believe the waters are very good in some disorders, particularly in the gravel. A very respectable gentleman, James Reed, of Philadelphia, whose veracity could not be doubted, told me that before he came to the Springs he was so much afflicted with the gravel that his life was a burthen to him; that by drinking the waters, which he did in great quantities, he was perfectly cured. It was eight years before I saw him there that he first visited the Springs, and he had no return of his complaint. He came this season to accompany a friend.

The most agreeable place to spend some days in the summer that I know is Long Branch. There you have good living, a fine country to ride or walk in, a number of vessels constantly in sight, and generally good society. I have heard Major Lenox, who has been at most of the watering places in England, say there is none in that country so pleasant as Long Branch. If Major Lenox had any partiality, it would be in favor of England.

After being a week at Ballstown, we heard that the yellow fever had broken out in Philadelphia. As soon as it was confirmed to me by a letter from Mrs. Biddle, I set off immediately in the stage for Albany, where I arrived in the evening, and set off the next day for New York. Had it not been for the fever in Philadelphia, I should have stopped a day or two with my old friend, Gen. Armstrong, who lived a small distance from the road, but the reports of the fever being very bad, induced me to go on without stopping. The road over the Highlands was at this time very bad. Near Tarrytown we were shown the tree under which the militia guard were playing cards when the unfortunate Major André was passing. If he had not been off his guard at the time, or had he pushed on when they challenged him, it is probable he would have escaped, an event few Americans would have lamented, although the conduct of Paulding, Williams, and Van Wert, who apprehended him, was highly meritorious, and they well deserved the reward given them. For my own part, I sincerely wished he had escaped.

It was late in the night when we reached New York. The next morning I waited on Col. Burr, and requested he would go with me to Mr. Seton's. When we called, one of his sons told us that he had been taken very ill the day before, that the doctor who attended him was afraid it was something of a paralytic stroke. I now regretted exceedingly my not calling on him on my way to Albany. I left a note with Mr. McCormick for Mr. Seton, requesting to know if he was the same gentleman whom I had known at Mr. David Ferrier's, at St. Lucar. Mr. McCormick, who was soon after in Philadelphia, informed me that Mr. Seton was the same person I supposed him to be, that he remembered me perfectly well, and lamented very much his not seeing me, and was very angry that they did not bring me into his room. He told Mr. McCormick that he had such a strong impression of the little fellow (as he called me) that he was sure he would immediately know me. In this I suppose he would have been mistaken, for thirty-four years will make *some alteration* in most men, and as I was a boy when Mr. Seton knew me, it is not probable he would have remembered me.

Having staid in town the morning to see Mr. Seton, in the afternoon I crossed the river and set off in the stage for Philadelphia. At this time there was no difficulty in getting a passage there. Most of the inhabitants who could do so, were leaving the city, and very few going in. The dismal accounts we heard on the road made me very impatient to get there. We stopped at Mr. Lardner's, about ten miles from the city, and there I found Mrs. Biddle and some of the children, all well. I intended to ride into the city myself the next day, but Mrs. Biddle, when she found she could not persuade me to stay out, would go in with me. Just before we got to the door, two boys were going along the street, and one by accident pushed the other against the horses, which knocked him over, and I believe hurt him much. His companion helped him up, and was leading him down the street, when I got out of the carriage and was following them in order to bring him into the house, but Mr. Lewis, my clerk, ran after me and begged me to return, for a few doors below a person had just died of the fever. The city at this time presented a most melancholy appearance. We only staid to take out some articles of clothing of which we were in want, and to give directions to Mr. Lewis and a servant, who preferred remaining in town to leaving it (for I would not at this time even request a servant to stay). We crossed the bridge at Schuylkill, and went that evening to my friend, Judge Jones's, who, as well as Mr. Lardner, had sent his carriage down as soon as he heard of the fever being in town, to bring the family out to his house. Mr. Jones had before done that, when many people in the country were afraid to see any person from the city, and Mr. Lardner would have done the same. Such friends are invaluable. My clerk, Mr. Lewis, declared he was not the least afraid of staying in town. The black girl, however, told us he was very much alarmed, and she expected he would not stay long. It appeared that she was right, for a few days afterwards he begged me to get him a place in Germantown, which I immediately did. There was very little doing at the office, and it was contrary to my inclination that he staid in town. I had informed him that go when he would, his salary should be continued.

We passed our time between Mr. Jones's and Mr. Lardner's until the latter end of October, when the fever abating we moved into town. If it had not been for what we felt for the sufferings of those in the city we should have had an agreeable time of it, for it was remarkably healthy in the vicinity of the city, and the weather very fine. Those from the city, who could afford it, and the people in the country generally, subscribed liberally for the distressed persons in the city. We had some little alarm after we moved into town, one of our neighbors having died the day after we got in. The cold weather, however, soon set in, and our fears were over.

In 1798 the yellow fever again visited us, and all my family except Mrs. Biddle, who would not leave the town without me, staid at my friend Jones's. Soon after, when the fever got to be very bad, I was obliged to go with her to Mr. Jones's. What hurried us from town was a woman who came into the office for a deed. As she looked pale and sickly, I desired her to sit down, inquired if she would take anything, and what part of the town she lived in, and if she was unwell. She replied no, she was only fatigued, that her husband was at the hospital, and she had been attending him. "And what is the matter with your husband?" "Why, the doctors say he has the yellow fever." Although alarmed myself, I could not refrain from laughing at two men who happened to be in the office on business, and who ran out as fast as they could, not waiting to get their papers. When they were gone I told the woman it was of no consequence to her to have the deed at present, that after being at the hospital she should not be running about town, and to go immediately and take care of her husband, and see that he wanted for nothing that she could do to restore him to health. She appeared sensible that she was wrong in leaving him, and went off. When she was gone my honest clerk, Lewis, exclaimed, "There, Mr. Biddle, now I will be bound she has given it to us. We have got it." I felt uncomfortable, but told him not to be afraid; as we neither of us had touched her, there was no danger of her giving us any disorder. If there was danger we escaped it.

The fourth of August this year there was an attempt made to rob the Bank of Pennsylvania, but the villains were frightened before they had done any mischief. After this the two porters belonging to the bank were armed, and ordered to sleep in the bank. The last of August Nath'l

Potter, one of the porters, died of the yellow fever. At this time no person in whom confidence could be placed would sleep there, so that Thomas Cunningham, the other porter, remained alone in the bank. The second of September, early in the morning, Mr. Annesley, the runner, went to the bank about some business, when to his great surprise he found the back door and the cash vault open. He called Cunningham, who either was, or pretended to be, asleep. When he came down he expressed as much surprise as Annesley, declaring he had never heard the least noise. The runner went to Mr. Smith, the cashier, who lived a short distance from town, and informed him of the discovery he had made. Mr. Smith sent for the president, who immediately came to town. Upon their going to the bank they found that the locks must have been opened by false keys, as the wards were not the least injured. The money taken in gold and notes amounted to something more than one hundred and sixty thousand dollars. Everything was done by the officers of the bank and the directors that was possible to discover the villains who committed the robbery. Several persons were taken up in the city on suspicion, among others Patrick Lyon, a smith, who had been employed about the locks. Lyon had gone off a short time before the robbery to Cape Henlopen. When he heard that he was suspected of being concerned in the robbery he came up to town and delivered himself up, notwithstanding which many of the directors believed that no other person could have picked the locks but Lyon, who is certainly very remarkable for his skill in the business. However, his coming to town made me suppose him innocent. He was for a long time confined in gaol.

After some time one Isaac Davis, a house carpenter, who had been employed doing some jobs about the bank, was observed to alter his mode of living. He left off work, pretending he had made a great deal of money by an adventure he made to some of the West India Islands. He next set up his carriage and lodged a considerable sum in the Bank of Pennsylvania. It was also found he had deposited money in

18

the Banks of the United States and North America. When this was ascertained by the cashier little doubt was entertained of Davis being the robber. The cashier, without exciting any suspicion in Davis, got him to his house; the president was there. By threats and promises of a pardon he acknowledged his guilt, and declared that no person was concerned with him but Thomas Cunningham, the porter, who was taken ill with the fever and died in a few days. Davis delivered up all that he said he had, which, upon counting, was found to be something more than one hundred thousand dollars. They then took Davis before Robert Wharton, the Mayor, when he made a further confession. He said that the day Cunningham was taken ill, he sent for him and delivered him the remainder of the money in his possession. The president and cashier then went to Davis's house where they obtained what he had, which together with what was before received, amounted to within three thousand dollars of what had been stolen. His horses and carriage were also taken. Davis appears to have remembered the old saying, "honor among thieves," for he expressed much more unwillingness to give up what he called Cunningham's share than his own part of the booty.

At first no suspicion whatever was entertained of Davis or Cunningham, and if Davis had behaved with prudence his villainy might have remained a secret forever.

Davis and Cunningham were both born in Chester County. Cunningham was recommended by a number of respectable people to the directors of the bank, and probably if he had never been in it, would have supported the character of an honest man. It is my opinion, as well as that of others, that a young man from the country is not so proper to be employed in a bank, as they are more strongly tempted to commit a robbery than those who have been in the habit of seeing much money. Judge Peters says all the great and strange people we have in Pennsylvania are from Chester County. He kept a list of all he knew; at the head of it was Governor McKean; the next was Mrs. Ginnes, a very celebrated young woman that was with our army most of the war, and who behaved well in her care and attention to our sick and wounded officers. She had a trial in our court a few years since, and while there a person was speaking. She inquired of a man near her who he was. She was answered, "One of the gentlemen of the Bar." "Oh, no!" says she, "that cannot be, for I know all the *gentlemen* of the Bar."

Purchasers of property being often plagued about old judgments that were in my office for which there was no limitation as to the time of their being a lien upon land, I applied this year, 1798, to the Legislature, and procured an act declaring that no judgment should be a lien upon land for more than five years, unless revived by scire facias. This act was the occasion of my losing a great many costs, for many people never paid until there was a search, and judgments found against them. However, I considered the law of great public benefit, and therefore did not regard any loss that would accrue to me from it, and, as public officers or their sureties (or if dead their heirs or executors) were liable to a suit at any length of time, I had it inserted in the act that the suit should be brought within seven years from the time in which the cause of action should have happened. I knew the heirs of a security upon an administrator's bond paid a great number of years after he had been dead, when had he or the person for whom he had been surety been living, it is probable they could have satisfied the parties that brought the suit that there was no cause of action.

I was determined this year, 1799, to purchase a place within a short distance of town, that if we were obliged on account of yellow fever to leave it, we should not have occasion to trouble our friends. Ten acres of land with a small house being for sale in February, by the sheriff, situated in Islington Lane,* which is a little more than three miles from town, I purchased it.

The infamous and menacing conduct of the French at

---

* Islington Lane still retains its name, running from Ridge Avenue, near Twenty-sixth Street, past Glenwood Cemetery and Odd Fellows' Cemetery to the Lamb Tavern Road. What was once "three miles from town" is now twelve miles inside of the northeastern limit of the city.

this time to our Ambassador had aroused the resentment of our country against them. Before this time their horrid cruelty to many of their own best citizens, particularly to a number of excellent females, had occasioned a general disgust to them. It was suggested that it would be well for those excused by age from militia duty to associate to co-operate with the militia. This was mentioned to me by an old friend of mine, who appeared very anxious that something should be done by the old citizens. He was one who had been in Mr. Wilson's house when it was attacked, and said he was afraid from the number of foreigners that something of the kind would again happen. Approving of the idea, I did everything in my power to promote it. We had several large meetings at Dunwoody's tavern, and I was very much pleased to see such a number of hardy, jovial veterans as we mustered, many of whom, and some were upwards of seventy, were fit for almost any military duty, and would have fought as well as any men in the world had they been called into action. We had the following articles of association drawn up, and unanimously agreed to.

"To preserve our country from insult, outrage, and dishonor, to preserve her from a foreign yoke, and to maintain our freedom and independence, the Congress and Executive of the United States are adopting the most vigorous and energetic measures, the Governor of our State has issued a proclamation for enrolling, organizing, and equipping the great body of the militia, our sons have already associated in arms; at so awful a crisis, We, the subscribers, citizens of the United States, and inhabitants of the city and liberties of Philadelphia, above the age prescribed by law for the performance of militia duty, holding ourselves indispensably obliged to contribute to the public safety to the utmost of our ability, do agree,

"First, That we will, as early as possible, provide ourselves each with a good musket, bayonet, cartridge box, and twenty-four charges of powder and ball, and keep the same in good order at our respective houses, or such other place as may be hereafter agreed upon.

"Second, That when any company have associated together in sufficient number we will proceed to chose one suitable person as captain, one lieutenant, and one second lieutenant, by ballot or otherwise, as shall be agreed upon; and such other officers as may be found expedient.

"Third, That when the companies are completed the officers shall apply to the Executive for such commissions as it may be deemed proper to grant them, and make a tender of this association for the defence of the city and liberties, and support of the civil authority.

"Fourth. That if the militia and volunteers of the city and liberties of Philadelphia be drafted or ordered to actual service at a distance from home, we will make diligent inquiry, in our respective wards or townships, into the state of their families, and administer to their comfort and relief in the best manner in our power."

Mr. Richard North and myself went about in the ward we lived in, North Ward. It was requested that I would sign it first, which I did. Those in the ward that signed were,

CHARLES BIDDLE,
JOHN CAPP,
JACOB MILLER,
JOHN FRETWELL,
WILLIAM BELL,
MICH'L GUNKLE,
JOHN SPOONER,
JOHN EVARHART, Sr.,
JACOB ECKFELDT,
JOHN PEROT,
GERVAS HALL,
MARTIN SUMMERS,
MICHAEL ALBRIGHT,
CHRISTIAN KOUCH,
JOHN LITTLE,
CHARLES SOUDER, Sr.,

PETER CROSS,
JOSEPH DONNALDSON,
DAVID SICKEL,
TY. MATLACK,
JOHN KEBLER,
CHRISTOPHER BYERLY,
RICHARD RUNDLE,
JOHN STEINMETZ,
BENJ. SEVERN,
JOSEPH HORSFALL,
JOHN A. LEWIS,

The Rev. Doctor Smith signed in this way: WM. SMITH, D.D., wishes to associate with his old friends in any character, lay, clerical, or mixed, as they may think he can be useful.

We talked of forming a troop. If we had we should most of us have been like the old City Troop, very few of whom after the war could mount without going to a fence or horseblock. The fever breaking out soon after prevented our getting organized. At the last meeting advertised at Dunwoody's the fever was so bad in town that no one attended but myself. My old friend, who first spoke to me on the business, reminded me of what I had heard in the beginning of our Revolution of a New England colonel. The colonel was met going from his regiment when it was engaged. The person that met him inquired where he was going. He said he had " set them at it, and, as the Major understood fighting better than he did, he thought it best to come away." So my old friend set us at the business, and then left us, for he never attended after the first meeting. Mr. Levi Hollingsworth, a very public spirited merchant, was on this occasion extremely active, as he always was when anything that he thought would be of service to his country was to be done.

It was in the month of February this year that my friend Commodore Truxtun captured the French frigate Insurgent. When it is considered that he had not an officer on board but young lads, who, as well as most of the crew, had never seen a gun fired in anger before, this must be considered as a very gallant action. His manœuvering so as to lose but few men showed his skill as well as courage. After the capture he wrote me an account of it, and informed me that he had appointed Mr. Henry Bainbridge, who married his eldest daughter, agent for himself and crew. As I considered Mr. Bainbridge a very good young man, this appointment gave me pleasure; it was not long, however, after this before Mr. Bainbridge called upon me to inform me of his being very much embarrassed, and that he found he could not meet his engagements. I advised him to immediately stop payment, which is what every man should do when he finds himself in such a situation. He told me afterwards, that some months before he had found this must happen, in consequence of which he had called upon a respectable merchant on whom Commodore Truxtun had given him a credit,

to consult what he had best do, and that he had advised him
to go on as long as he could, perhaps something would turn
up. This advice he unfortunately pursued until he called on
me, when he had very little left, having lost a great deal on
notes he sold. Although I considered Mr. Bainbridge as a
good young man, I knew he was not prudent, and therefore
thought it a duty in me as the friend of Commodore Truxtun
to inform him of Mr. Bainbridge's situation. I therefore
wrote immediately to the Commodore, who was by this time
arrived at Norfolk. The letter I showed to Mr. Bainbridge.
The Commodore wrote me by return of the post to beg I
would take upon myself the agency. Although I did not
wish to have anything to do with it, my friendship for the
Commodore would not permit me to refuse it.

Commodore Truxtun set up Mr. Bainbridge in the grocery
business, and put into his hands ten thousand dollars, besides
giving him a credit for near three thousand dollars more.
It would have been better for both had he only given him
one thousand dollars. Mr. Bainbridge is sober and industrious, but having so much money in his hands, he entered
into foolish speculations that he would not have thought of
had his funds been more limited. Putting too much money
into the hands of young men frequently occasions their ruin.

On settlement, for the prize money, I found that nineteen
out of twenty had sold their shares for a mere trifle, some for
not more than ten dollars; the shares for the Insurgent
amounted to one hundred and six dollars and eighty cents
each. This perhaps could in some measure be remedied, if
the agent was not allowed to pay the crew on power of attorney, without some proof of the seamen not being defrauded.

During the fever while at my place in the country, a man
came there who said his name was Wm. Williamson, that
he had been a marine on board the Constellation, that in
coming from Georgetown, Maryland, where he lived, he
had lost his prize ticket and did not know what to do, that
he was in great distress, not having a farthing, and begged
me to let him have his prize money. I asked him respecting
the officers of the ship, all of whose names he knew, and men-

tioned several circumstances relating to the capture. I asked him whom he knew in Maryland or Virginia. He said General Washington knew him very well, and he could get any security to return the money I gave him. Having not the least doubt from the plausible manner in which he spoke that what he told me was true, I gave him what money was in the house, and after he had his dinner he went off, saying he would go back to Maryland. A few days after, happening to be in town, he called again, just after one of the officers of the Constellation went out. At this time he over-acted his part. He said he came to town to see a friend and was taken sick, and then had a fever. I told him if that was the case to go immediately away, and come when the fever was over. He wanted to get something, but I obliged him to go away. Had he not said he was sick, he would have got more money. A few days after a man called with a power of attorney, from a woman who had taken out letters of administration on the estate of Williamson. I mentioned to this man the circumstance of Williamson being at my house. He appeared surprised, said he would write to the woman who had sent him the letters of administration. Shortly after, to my great surprise, another man came and said he was the Williamson who had been in the Constellation, but had lost his ticket. I told him of the man who had been with me and received part of the money, and of the letters of administration. He knew very well the woman who took out the letters of administration. He said it was reported he was dead, and he supposed she believed it. The man he could give no account of, but thought it was some fellow who had heard him complain of the loss of his ticket. This man looked like an honest country lad. He said he was a blacksmith by trade, and as the fever was nearly over he would get work in town, that he did not want anything until he brought some of the officers who knew him. He accordingly went to work, informing me where he could be found. Soon after one of the officers being in town, I sent for the blacksmith, who was the true Williamson, and he had found his ticket, which on his producing I paid him his prize money. The fellow that came to my house I could never find. It is probable he left the State.

My house in Islington Lane being too small, I had to build an addition to it. The building went on slowly until the beginning of August, when we had a report of the yellow fever being in town. This induced us to hurry the carpenters. It was, however, the last day of the month before we could any how be accommodated, and then it was very badly, for we had but one room below to sit in, one above, and a garret for the family to sleep in; no outside doors hung, and the wind coming in from all quarters. However, being all in good health and spirits, we made out tolerably well, and as we had ten or a dozen carpenters at work, we were every day getting better. When we first moved out, my neighbor, Mr. Moylan, very politely offered me an empty house of his near ours; we, however, concluded it was better to stay where we were. While we were in this situation, I heard some person at the gate inquiring for me; it was my old friend, Commodore Truxtun, who was on his way to visit General Washington, who had written to him, requesting he would pay him a visit. He had left the stage at Frankford, and hired a carriage to call on me. As it rained very hard, I could not think of his leaving me that day, and we prepared a berth for him in our room below. He staid with us three or four days, when I took him as far on his way as General Robinson's, on Naaman's Creek, from whence he went in the stage as far as Mount Vernon. Shortly before this, Commodore Truxtun thinking himself injured by the President ranking Commodore Talbot above him, had resigned his commission in the navy. By the appointments General Washington made, Talbot ranked higher than Truxtun, but there were only three frigates fitted out, which were commanded by Barry, Nicholson, and Truxtun, and their commissions were numbered one, two, three, and Talbot not going into the service for a long time afterwards, Truxtun thought Talbot should not rank above him; and I believe he was right. Had it been determined by a board of officers, neither could have complained. President Adams, I believe, seldom con-

sulted any one; he determined the rank against Truxtun,
who immediately sent in his commission. I am sure Mr.
Adams did what he thought was right, for he knew Truxtun
well, and had a great regard for him.

Knowing it would be a loss to the navy for Truxtun to
leave it, I went with General Wilkinson up to Trenton to
speak to Mr. Stoddert, the Secretary of the Navy, about getting him again into the service. Mr. Stoddert made some
difficulty on account of the other captains, who he thought
would resign. I told him it was not probable they would,
that although most of them were very brave men, as a naval
officer none of them were equal to Truxtun. Wilkinson and
myself after some time persuaded the Secretary to send Truxtun his commission, and it was understood that Talbot and
he were not to be on the same station.

At this time our Ministers or Commissioners, Messrs.
Ellsworth and Davis, were here preparing to embark for
France. Mr. Hamilton, and some others, were at Trenton,
who, with Messrs. Pickering and Wolcot, were endeavoring
to prevent their being sent.* However, the President
thought it right they should go, and nothing could move him
to change his opinion. For my own part, I thought then,
and still think, it was the best thing we could do. It was
certainly our business to be at peace with France if it could
be done without submitting to improper terms. Taking this
method, could not, in Mr. Adams, proceed from want of
spirit, for none possessed more firmness than he did. Besides,
he had promised he would send ministers out when it was
assured they would be well received, and those assurances
were given.

This fall Chief Justice McKean was elected Governor in
the room of Governor Mifflin. I wrote to him for a renewal
of my commission as Prothonotary. I believe it was some
time before he made up his mind on the subject, for my commission did not come down until long after the other officers

---

* This refers to the well-known intrigue to rule the administration of
President Adams by the disaffected faction in the Federal party.

in the city had received theirs. I knew he was very much provoked at some severe pieces written against him by my nephew, Mr. Marks John Biddle. However, Governor McKean and myself had always been upon good terms, and I had a high esteem for him, believing him to be a very honest man, although a very violent one who had no command of his temper, but spoke whatever he thought upon all occasions. General Craig and Mr. Graydon, for whom I had formerly procured the office of Prothonotary, dined with me soon after the election. Mr. Graydon had shortly before married the daughter of Charles Pettit, whose son, Mr. Andrew Pettit, was married to the daughter of Governor McKean. On account of this alliance, and Graydon's merit and talents, it was thought he would have a great deal of influence with the Governor, which Craig begged he would use for a friend of his, whom he wished kept in office; but, to the surprise of most people, Graydon was one of the first removed from office. This led me to believe there was some truth in the report about town, that before the election there was an agreement between the Governor and some who had agreed to support him, what officers should be removed. After the removal of Graydon, and considering the violent pieces of my nephew, Mr. Marks John Biddle, and the knowledge the Governor had of my intimacy with Mr. Ross, his rival candidate for the office of Governor, it would not have surprised me if some person had been appointed to the office held by me.

My friend Governor Mifflin was obliged to leave town soon after the election in consequence of a process taken out against him by one of his relatives. He sent to inform me of his situation, and to request me to come out to see him. He was then at his place at the Falls of Schuylkill. I immediately went, and found him in bed. At seeing me he was very much affected, and I was not a little so myself seeing him so different from what he was a short time before surrounded by his friends or rather his acquaintances, and in high spirits, as he was elected a member of the Legislature, who were to meet soon at Lancaster. I thought it best he should go there, and advised him to it. " But what, my dear friend, shall I do when the sessions are over?" "That must be thought of afterwards, when we meet at Lancaster, which will be shortly." He went there the next day. Shortly after he had gone to Lancaster, Mr. Anthony Morris (formerly Speaker of the Senate) called on me. He told me he was very sorry to hear I had blamed him on account of the writ taken out against the Governor, that he had nothing to do with it. I told him he was misinformed, that I had spoken very freely of those who took out the writ, as it could answer no good purpose, but never supposed he had anything to do with it. This was the last time I ever saw Governor Mifflin. He died during the session. His situation preyed upon his spirits and rendered his life a burthen to him. General Mifflin was below the middle size, and very well formed; his countenance open, cheerful, and agreeable. Coming to see me one day he put a young lady and her mother from the country, who happened to be in the house, to the blush. After looking attentively at the girl, he said to her, "any one could tell you to be a Biddle." Had he known the mother was present he would not on any account have said it, but he really supposed the girl to be my daughter, and thought there was a strong family likeness. He was a kind, benevolent man.

On the 14th of December, 1799, died General Washington. The loss of this great and good man was most deeply lamented. Grief was pictured in every countenance when we had a certain account of his death. I had seen him during the war at my brother Edward's, and in camp. When he was in the Convention I dined several times in company with him, and had the honor of his company to dine with me. When he was elected President of the United States, he lived during the whole of the time that he was in Philadelphia nearly opposite to me. At that time I saw him almost daily. I frequently attended his levees to introduce some friend or acquaintance, and called sometimes with Governor Mifflin. The General always behaved politely to the Governor, but it appeared to me that he had not forgotten the Governor's opposition to him during the Revolutionary war. He was a most elegant figure of a man, with so much dignity of manners, that no person whatever could take any improper liberties with him. I have heard Mr. Robert Morris, who was as intimate with him as any man in America, say that he was the only man in whose presence he felt any awe. You would seldom see a frown or a smile on his countenance, his air was serious and reflecting, yet I have seen him in the theatre laugh heartily. Dr. Forrest, who laughs a great deal, desired me, one night at the theatre, to look at General Washington. "See how he laughs, by the Lord he must be a gentleman." The General was in the next box, and I believe heard him.* He was much more cheerful when he was retiring from the office of President than I had ever seen him before. Commodore Barry, Major Jackson, and myself were appointed a committee of the Society of the Cincinnati to wait upon him with a copy of an address, and to know when it would be convenient to him for the society to wait upon him. He received us with great good humor, and laughing, told us that he had heard Governor Morris (I believe of New Jersey) say that when he knew gentlemen were going to call on him with an address, he sent to beg they would bring an answer. If this were done to him, he observed that it would

---

* Anecdotes of Washington, however homely or trivial, are sure to be interesting. Perhaps this may excuse the record here of what has no other connection with the text. Within the memory of the present writer, an aged Philadelphia mechanic being asked if he remembered General Washington replied, "General Washington! oh yes, I remember General Washington well; I once see General Washington kick a fellow down stairs." He proceeded to relate that he and a fellow journeyman were once sent to the President's house to do a job of painting or glazing. Arriving early, they were admitted by a servant-maid who led the way up stairs. Whilst ascending the stairs his companion attempted some liberties with the girl, who gave a loud shriek as they reached the second story. Immediately the General sallied forth from the front room, half dressed and half shaved, and demanded the cause of the disturbance. Hearing the girl's story, he rushed at the man in a rage and started him down stairs with a violent kick from behind; at the same time he cried out, "I will have no woman insulted in my house," and called for Colonel Lear to put the rascal out the front door.

The language of the narrator was more graphic, if less decorous, than in the above repetition.

save him a great deal of trouble. He was in Philadelphia a
short time before he died, and I thought he never looked
better than he did at that time. He enjoyed remarkable
health, hardly ever having been confined by sickness. The
loss of no man was ever more severely felt by his countrymen
than General Washington. He was called the American
Fabius, but Fabius was not equal to George Washington.
He suffered Tarentum to be pillaged when it was traitorously
delivered to him, and his opposition and jealousy of Scipio
rendered the Roman unequal to the American hero.

The visit of Commodore Truxtun in the fall was a very
unfortunate one to my family. Two of my sons, James[*] and
Edward, hearing so much about the navy, took an inclination
to enter the service, and although I would not recommend it
to them it was not disagreeable to me, for if they found it
disagreeable to remain in the navy they would be qualifying
themselves to command ships in the merchant service. As
to Edward I did not wish him to follow the sea. Although
but little more than sixteen years of age he was one of the
best mathematicians in the country. I thought a short cruise
would be of service to him. I applied to Mr. Stoddert, then
Secretary of the Navy, and on the 14th day of February, 1800,
he sent them both warrants as midshipmen. As they were
to join the frigate President, then fitting out at New York
for Commodore Truxtun, it was not until July following that
they were wanted on board the ship. The 5th of July, 1800,
I set off with them for New York. It now gives me the
most painful sensations to think of this journey, which was
the most disagreeable I ever made. A thousand melancholy
reflections filled my mind, and a hundred times I secretly
wished some accident would happen to put a stop to it. We,
however, reached New York without any accident the 7th of
July. My mind at this time was so uneasy that it would
have given me pleasure to have heard the ship was burned or
sunk. The day we arrived was excessively hot, and the
place we lodged at was a tavern near the water-side, and was

* Afterwards Commodore James Biddle, U. S. Navy. See note E.

dirty and disagreeable. Soon after our being at the tavern Colonel Burr called with a servant to take our baggage and insisted on our going to his house. This was a very agreeable change to us, and his accomplished daughter (since married to Mr. Alston) did everything as well as her father, to make the place agreeable. We had every day during my stay some gentlemen to dine, among others, General Hamilton. At this time he and Colonel Burr appeared to be on good terms. The General invited Mr. Burr and myself to dine with him, but my short stay prevented me. I remained with the boys three days, and then left them to the care of Col. Burr and Commodore Truxtun. Just before leaving New York I sent a note to Commodore Truxtun, of which the following is a copy :—

NEW YORK, July 9, 1800.

Dear Sir: James and Edward, whom I have left with you, have ever behaved in such a manner as to gain the love and esteem of all their relatives and friends. They have a good education, and you, I suppose, will make them good officers. They know the advantage of being with you, and are informed that nothing will gratify me so much as meeting your approbation, nothing give me more pain than their not doing it. The heart of their mother has been torn with anguish at parting with them, and I feel everything that a parent, who would sacrifice his life for their happiness, can feel. The distress of their mother has affected them both; however, this they will soon get over. I shall only add that your care of them will be the greatest favor you can possibly confer on me, and will ever be remembered as the highest mark of your friendship.

Yours sincerely,
CHARLES BIDDLE.

Commodore TRUXTUN.

Commodore Truxtun in his answer assured me in the strongest terms that he would do everything.

I left New York very early in the morning. Both the boys came with me to the wharf. It is impossible to describe what I felt at taking leave of them. My eyes were not removed from them, as they stood on the wharf, until out of sight, and theirs were fixed on the boat. I had engaged to visit them at Amboy, as soon as the ship dropped down to the watering place. Accordingly when Commodore Truxtun wrote me that the ship was there, I set off with Mrs. Biddle for Amboy, about the eighth of August. When near Commodore Truxtun's we saw them walking the piazza; their tender mother was ready to jump out of the carriage as soon as she had a sight of them. The next day we crossed Staten Island to the watering place, a distance of about eighteen miles, and went on board the frigate. We found everything in excellent order, and their mother was more reconciled to their going than she was before she saw how well they were accommodated. Tom,* a faithful black who had been born and brought up in the family, agreed to enter on board the frigate and go with them. As we knew he would be a faithful servant, his going was a great consolation to their mother and myself. We arrived on Wednesday and staid with them until the Monday following. The parting between Mrs. Biddle and the boys was an affecting scene; to me a very painful one. They did not leave Sandy Hook until the beginning of September. Shortly after they sailed, we had some severe gales of wind. These gales reminded me of what I had somewhere read:—

"The winds howl with peculiar horror to him whose offspring is on the waves; the beating tempest of a winter's evening is painfully alarming to that parent whose social hearth seems forsaken through the absence of one that is at sea."

At this time parties were very busy about the election of President and Vice-President; and as usual on these occasions much abuse was published against the candidates. Believing it of little consequence to the country, whether Mr. Adams or Mr. Jefferson was President, I gave myself no

* The same servant that staid in town at our house during the yellow fever of 1793.—AUTHOR'S NOTE.

trouble about the election. I was indifferent as to Colonel Burr being elected Vice-President, for it was my opinion that it would be better for him to remain at the Bar, where he was making a fortune, than to be Vice-President of the United States. This, I believe, he afterwards thought himself. From the great exertions made by the partisans of Mr. Jefferson and Mr. Burr, I had little doubt of their succeeding. A number of my friends were as anxious about this election as if everything they had in the world depended on it, when in fact it was of as little importance to them which of the candidates succeeded, as it was to an inhabitant of Africa.

Mr. Jefferson and Mr. Burr having an equal number of votes, the Federal party thinking of two evils they would choose the least, did everything in their power to have Mr. Burr President. Some people blamed Mr. James Bayard, of Delaware, for not behaving with that firmness he ought to have done. Mr. Bayard is a respectable man, and no doubt did what he thought right. It was said Mr. Burr intrigued to get appointed President. If he did, he managed badly, for he should have gone to Washington, where he certainly could, if he wished it, have been elected. It was owing to the chapter of accidents that he had not more votes from the electors than Mr. Jefferson. Colonel F. Nichols, who informed me he was spoken to by some members of the Legislature to be one of the Federal electors for Pennsylvania, was by accident prevented from being at Lancaster, by which means another person was chosen in his room. Colonel Nichols has told me often since, that knowing the Federal party could not carry their man, he was determined to give a vote for Colonel Burr, under whom he had served, and for whom he had a great esteem. He lamented that he did not ride up and get his friend Coleman to give a vote for Colonel Burr.

Mr. Coleman, who was one of the electors, has frequently told me he intended to vote for Colonel Burr, and was with difficulty persuaded from it, and Colonel Robinson, of Delaware, who was an excellent officer of the Pennsylvania line, informed me that when he was spoken to to be one of the electors, (which he had always been) he informed his friends he should

19

vote for Burr, who was one of the officers of the Revolution. One of the electors who came in as they were voting told Mr. Coleman that he intended to vote for Colonel Burr, and wished to speak to him, but had not an opportunity. Coleman was sorry he did not, as he would have advised him to vote for Burr.

In October, while in court, Mr. Kitchen, keeper of the City Tavern, called me out, and informed me that he had just received an account of Commodore Truxtun's safe arrival in the West Indies. On account of the violent gales we had for some days after he sailed, this intelligence gave me great pleasure, and knowing how pleasing it would be to their mother, I immediately went to our place to inform her. A few days afterwards we had letters from James and Edward, who were pleased with their ship and commander; and Commodore Truxtun wrote me he was much pleased with their conduct since they had been with him, and that he had no doubt of their being an honor to their country. They wrote afterwards by several opportunities.

In December I received a letter from Edward, giving an account of St. Kitts, and mentioning how much he was pleased with his situation and with his commander, and that he and James were very hearty. A day or two after, as I was dressing to go out, one of my clerks came from the office, and told me a gentleman wanted to speak to me. When I went into the office it surprised me to find it was Mr. Thomas Biddle, a cousin of mine, who wanted me. I was laughing at him for being so ceremonious, when I was stopped by perceiving that something extraordinary was the matter with him. He inquired in a faltering voice if I had heard anything from the President. Surprised at the question, I said I had not expected to hear from him, having no business with him. During this time it never entered my head that he alluded to the frigate President, but had supposed it to be Mr. Adams. He then put a letter into my hands. It was from Mr. Blake, one of the midshipmen belonging to the frigate, to Mr. Tilghman, giving an account of the death of Edward! Of Edward! so dear to his friends. Of Edward!

so beloved by his parents and family. An affectionate parent, who has unexpectedly an account of the loss of a most excellent son whose life was infinitely dearer to him than his own, may form some idea of what I felt on this occasion. None but such can know the inexpressible anguish this fatal letter gave me. I cannot at this time think of it without being greatly, very greatly affected. I put the letter in my pocket, and went up stairs with an intention of sending for some of Mrs. Biddle's female friends to break the dreadful intelligence to her, but my clerk, Lewis, coming into the parlor to speak to me, and seeing Mrs. Biddle reading, had no doubt but it was the letter that contained the melancholy news. He said, with a countenance expressive of great concern, how very sorry he was for the loss of—. He had proceeded thus far when she looked wildly at him, and exclaimed, "What loss? What do you mean?" Perceiving she was not acquainted with what had happened, and frightened at the terror he had occasioned, he would not utter a word. Finding he was gone without answering her, she immediately thought of James and Edward, and screamed, "Oh, Mr. Biddle! Mr. Biddle! What is the matter? What is the matter?" I ran immediately down stairs; she was now frantic with terror. I carried her up stairs, and did everything in my power in vain to soothe her. I sent for some of her female friends in town, and expresses to her sister Mrs. Lardner, and her very dear friend, Mrs. Jones. It was a long time before we could get her any way composed; her screams even now seem to strike my ear, and never shall I forget this melancholy scene. Her friends came round her, and at last, being quite exhausted, she was put to bed. Mrs. Jones set off for town as soon as she received the note I sent her. Never shall I forget the looks of this amiable woman when she entered the house. It was a long time before she could utter more than, "Oh, Mr. Biddle! What a loss we have sustained!" Being a lady of great fortitude I got her soon composed enough to see her unfortunate friend. No person could console her so well as Mrs. Jones, who was a native of North Carolina, and intimate with Mrs. Biddle from her infancy. Mrs. Jones was very fond of all our children, particularly Edward, who had the year before, when she was unwell, attended her to the seashore, and she felt the affection of a parent for him. She staid with us a week, and during this time Mr. Thompson, chaplain to the frigate President, who brought the fatal letter, arrived in Philadelphia. Although extremely anxious, I dreaded to see him, for I was under great apprehension for James, who had not written by Thompson, nor had Commodore Truxtun. He afterwards told me that he felt too much distressed to write. Mr. Thompson relieved us about James, who was on shore when he left the ship, which he had done suddenly and unexpectedly. He assured me that James, although greatly distressed, was in good health. He informed me that he did not apprehend Edward to be in the least danger until the morning he died, nor should he then, but when he went to his cot, he found Tom, who lay under it, in tears. Tom told Thompson softly that he was much afraid his master Edward was very ill. Thompson went up and finding Edward awake, inquired how he was. He answered that he was better. He then said, "Edward, do you know me?" The dear youth appeared irritated, and replied, "Know you, Thompson? To be sure I do. Why do you ask such a question?" These were the last words he ever spoke. In half an hour after this a person came to the mess to inform them that he was no more. What must have been the feeling of my dear James at this time? I should have felt my loss much more if it had not been for the situation of Mrs. Biddle, which obliged me to make exertions that nothing else would have done.

One of the officers of the frigate wrote to his friend a letter, which was published in Relf's paper, giving an account of our dear Edward's loss. He writes:—

"From Brown's paper of Dec. 30th, 1800. Extract of a letter from a gentleman on board the frigate President, to Mr. Peter Delamar, Professor of Mathematics in the Philadelphia Academy, dated St. Pierre, Nov. 20th, 1800.

"On the 14th inst., to windward of Descada, at 8 o'clock,

we had the misfortune of losing your friend and pupil, Mr. Edward Biddle, midshipman, aged sixteen years, who died of a fever after a few days' illness, universally lamented. To form an estimate of the merit of this accomplished youth, would be, with a good disposition to unite all those rare qualities of the head and heart, which, when properly blended and matured, constitute the philosopher and the hero. Nature, which had so highly gifted his mind, had been equally profuse in forming his person, which was at once elegant and interesting, his stature near six feet, and his limbs finely proportioned. In a word, he was one of those figures from which we might draw a Hercules or an Adonis.

> " ' As into air the purer spirits flow
> And sep'rate from their kindred dregs below,
> So flew his soul to its congenial place.'

" To the foregoing extract it may be added that Mr. Biddle's education was liberal and finished ; but he principally excelled in an extensive knowledge of the mathematics, for which his penetrating genius and solid judgment seemed particularly fitted."

So great was his acquaintance with this abstruse and difficult science, that at the age of fifteen, when he quitted school there was not a teacher in this city who could yield the least assistance, and perhaps he was the only person of that age, the celebrated Clarant excepted, who ever made himself complete master of Sir Isaac Newton's Principia without the help of a tutor. Read, oh youth! and emulate.

Our friend Mrs. Jones came to town in February to spend a few days with us. I was much shocked at seeing her so much altered. I believe her grief for the loss of Edward, and the melancholy that she saw preying upon the spirits of her friend, brought back a complaint in her stomach which it was thought had been entirely removed. Soon after her return home she was confined to her bed, from whence she never rose. She lingered until the first of April, when this best of women departed this world. To lose such a friend, and such a son as Edward, in a few months was almost too much for Mrs. Biddle, and it affected me greatly.

My friend Judge Jones intending to go to the Warm Springs in Virginia, and being anxious I should accompany him, we set off from his house, about twelve miles from Philadelphia, on a Sunday, the latter end of July, and the next Sunday, in the evening, arrived at the Warm Springs, a distance of near three hundred and forty miles, part of it a very rough road. We travelled in a light Jersey wagon that I purchased for the purpose, and we had a pair of very stout horses belonging to Mr. Jones. Perhaps two better horses could not be found in any country, and I believe we could not have travelled the distance in the same time in any other carriage than one of these Jersey wagons. Two of the days that we were on the road it rained very hard. We went through Lancaster, York, Hagerstown, Martinsburg, Winchester, and Staunton. The road from Winchester to Staunton is good, and the country is excellent. The accommodation on the road is generally good. The tavern at Martinsburg was one of the best I ever was in, indeed there are few gentlemen's houses in which one could be better entertained. I understood that the landlord, Mr. Gather, had been a man of fortune, but that some unfortunate affair had occasioned his keeping tavern. He had the manners and appearance of a gentleman. When we reached the Springs we fortunately had some of the Philadelphia papers, printed the day before we set off; otherwise, some of the good people at the Springs would have thought we were *mistaken* as to the time when we left Philadelphia.

The Warm Spring is most delightful to swim in. It is a large body of water, perfectly clear, and just warm enough to be agreeable. I never was in so charming a bath. It is pallisaded round; you enter by a small door into a room where you undress. The entertainment, when we were there, was very bad, for which reason we staid there but one day, when we went to the Hot Springs, which are five miles from the Warm Springs. Here there was a very good tavern. This Hot Spring is very extraordinary. My friend went in every day, expecting it would be of service to his gouty complaints, and he told me that it was. We met here with Colonel Washington who behaved so gallantly in South Carolina. I remember it was a saying during the Revolution, when speaking of Colonels Lee and Washington, that Lee would never attack the British but when he had an advantage, that Washington would whenever he had an opportunity. They were both excellent officers.

Colonel Washington was going to Philadelphia. He advised me to go to the Sweet Springs, saying that it was very pleasant there, and it was worth taking the ride if it were only to see Major Jack Willis, one of the biggest men in the world. Having nothing to do at the Hot Springs, I went there, about forty miles further up the country, over a rough and hilly road. One mile on this side the Sweet Springs are the Red Springs, the waters of which are much the same as the Sweet Springs. It is a pleasant, healthy country, and if it were not for the number of gamblers who always frequent this place it would be very agreeable. I think this place and the country round it preferable to Ballstown Springs. If the water be not, the ride to either must be of service to almost any invalid.

I saw here the celebrated Major Willis. He was by very far the largest man I had ever seen. It was mentioned by some who knew him when an officer in the army, that he was then a slender, genteel man. The year before I saw him, he had been on board a British man-of-war in Hampton Roads, and he astonished all the crew. As they were not permitted to go on the quarter-deck, they manned the tops, shrouds, and yards to get a sight of him. He was very active for one of his size.

After staying two weeks at the Sweet Springs, I returned to the Hot Springs, and with much pleasure found my friend Jones ready to return to Philadelphia. Having no gout nor any other disorder, I did not go into the Hot Springs, but, one evening, sat over it, and washed my feet. The water is warmer than you could wish for that purpose; in a few minutes my shirt was almost as wet with my perspiration as if I had gone into it.

We left the Hot Springs on a Wednesday, and the next Wednesday dined at Mr. Jones's. Notwithstanding we drove

near fifty miles the last day to dinner, the horses came home
so fresh that when near Mr. Jones's there was hardly any
keeping them in. I never saw so good a pair. In the afternoon I got one of Mr. Jones's horses and rode home.

Wishing to leave the house in which I had long lived, in
Market Street, which brought to the recollection of the
family our dear, lost Edward, I rented a house in Chestnut
Street, and the owner dying soon after, I purchased it.* It is
of advantage to most people to leave a house after they have
lost a relation or friend very dear to them.

One evening in May, 1802, a letter was thrown into the
entry of my house, directed to me under the signature of
" Charles Belmont." It was written in capital letters, so that
it was not easy to find out the author. The writer begins by
saying: " You are rich, I am at present poor. You must
deposit in the post-office three hundred dollars directed to
me. It shall be returned in three months with honor. If
you neglect doing it, your son Nicholas, or one of your daughters, shall be stabbed. This you may depend upon shall
surely be done, if what I have requested is not complied with ;
and what then will be your reflections when your son or
daughter is brought home dead?" He said a great deal more
to induce me to do what he requested. From some parts of
the letter I was convinced that, whoever the author was, he
had frequently been in company with me. Unfortunately I
was out when the letter was thrown into the house, and Mrs.
Biddle received it. Upon my return home I found her
greatly agitated, and with difficulty could compose her. If
it had not been on her account, I should not have felt the
least uneasiness whatever, being convinced that a person intending to murder would never mention it. The next day,
agreeably to his directions, I put a letter in the post-office,
not, however, with bank notes, but with some pieces of news-

---

* This house stood on the present site of No. 431, the office of the Pennsylvania Company for Insurances on Lives and Granting Annuities. The
old number was 159. Charles Biddle's house in Market Street, from which
he removed, was No. 243. The President resided at No. 190 Market Street.

paper; and desired Colonel Patton, the postmaster, to inform
his clerks that they should be handsomely rewarded if they
would apprehend the person who called for the letter. After
waiting two weeks, and no person calling for it, I mentioned
the circumstances to several of my friends and acquaintances.
A few days after I received another letter from the same
Belmont, saying I must certainly take him for a fool to suppose he would so soon have called for the letter, that he knew
the directions given to Patton's clerks, that if I had waited
a month without saying anything he should have called and
been taken, and his being taken would have made more noise
in Philadelphia than anything that ever happened in it before.
I strongly suspected an unfortunate foreigner to be the author
of these letters, and never afterwards met him without
endeavoring to discover something to justify my suspicions.
I let him know it would give me pleasure to render him any
services in my power. He expressed himself as very grateful, but always declared he wanted for nothing. I sometimes
thought he supposed himself suspected as the author of the
letters, for he knew of them. If the gentleman had requested
a loan of the sum mentioned, or more, I would have lent it to
him, even if I had been certain it would never have been
returned, for he was much to be pitied, having been driven
from his country where he had lived in affluence. He was
at this time much altered from what he had been; from being
cheerful and easy, he was dull and melancholy. He soon
after left America, and not long after left the world. Sometime afterwards, mentioning the affair to one of my neighbors,
he told me he had received such a letter, and being alarmed
for his family had sent the money as directed.

We had in December of this year a very curious trial in
the Court of Common Pleas, between Dr. Glenn and Captain
James King. Captain King was riding in a chair with his
daughter and another young girl, when between Germantown
and Frankford by carelessness he overset the chair. The
girls were very little hurt, but it was thought King's legs
were both broken. He was carried into a house near by, and
surgeons were immediately sent for. The first that came

was Dr. Glenn, who being a young man, would do nothing more than make preparation for amputation, until some more experienced surgeon came. Dr. Shippen soon afterwards made his appearance. He immediately declared it would be necessary to amputate both legs. King swore they should take off but one. Dr. Shippen, who is a very eminent surgeon, tried to persuade him of the necessity of taking both off; telling him it was probable that his life depended on it; but King was obstinate and declared, let the consequence be what it would, they should take off but one. They then took off his right leg, and set the left as well as they could, and Glenn living near attended him constantly. King's pleas for not paying Glenn's bill were, that it was in the first place exorbitant, and that he came merely to get an insight into his business. He wrote his attorney that "Shippen and Glenn were ignorant of their business, that they made a mistake by taking off his left leg, that was not broken, instead of his right that was broken in two places. To prove this he had the bones of the leg and foot that were taken off ready to be seen by any person that chose to examine them." His letter was not allowed to be read. As Dr. Glenn was proved to be a regular bred surgeon, a man of very good character, to have constantly attended King during his confinement, and his bill to be reasonable, the jury gave a verdict in his favor without going out of court. Dr. Wistar, who was also called on (King said if he had been so fortunate as to have had Dr. Wistar at first he would not have lost the leg Shippen took off), told me that although the right leg was not broken, the flesh was torn in such a manner that it was absolutely necessary to take it off. King, in his letter, which Mr. Hallowell showed me, gave a humorous account of his doctors; he wrote as he spoke, like an old sailor.

This year, December, 1802, I purchased the house the family now reside in. I took the house of Mr. John Field, merchant, who had married Miss Williams, daughter of Mr. Daniel Williams, who built it. I gave to Mr. Field eleven hundred dollars for two years. There was some expectation at the time the house was leased to me, that it would be sold to pay a debt of Mr. Williams. I therefore made Mr. Field give me security that he would keep me in peaceable possession of the house for the term he had leased it, which as he did not, I recovered five hundred dollars of his surety. When he found the house would be sold, he called to beg I would not interfere with his wife. However, before the sale she died, which released me from my promise, and I purchased it for nine thousand one hundred dollars. It would have been struck off to me for seven thousand five hundred dollars, at which price it stood a considerable time, but a friend of mine came in and ran it up to the price I gave. He declared he did not know he was bidding against me. This was not probable, as I stood near the sheriff and bid loud. However, the house was cheap at the price it sold for, and it was not my wish to get it for less. I had made up my mind to go much higher for it.

My son James sailed this year up the Mediterranean with Commodore Murray. They cruised off Tripoli for some time, and had nearly captured a number of their gunboats, having got within gunshot of the rear, and were getting fast up with them, when the pilot declared, if they did not haul off immediately, they would lose the ship. They fired at some troops drawn up on the beach, and set them scampering. James and some of the other young officers blamed Commodore Murray for not standing in longer, but Murray was certainly right. In his situation it would have been wrong to run any risk of losing his ship. Soon after James returned, he was ordered on board the frigate Philadelphia, commanded by Captain Bainbridge. They sailed from Philadelphia in July, 1803. The last of October following, she chased one of the Tripolitan cruisers close in shore, and in hauling off, when they supposed themselves entirely out of danger, they struck upon a reef of rocks. Although Captain Bainbridge is a valuable officer, it appears from the deposition of Lieutenant Porter that they first endeavored to force her over the shoal, which was certainly wrong. I do suppose if a small anchor had been carried out (they had no boat to carry out one of their bowers) with two cubbs bent to it, and they had hove upon them as they lightened her forward, it is probable she would have been got off. It is not, however, easy to say what could have been done by a person not on board. When Captain Bainbridge found the ship was inevitably lost, he sent Lieutenant Porter and James in the barge to inform the Turks that they had surrendered. Just as James was going into the boat he put into his boots four half eagles. When they were boarded by the galleys they stripped him of his coat, waistcoat, etc., but left his boots, by which he saved his money. They were taken immediately on shore in the barge, and upon landing they were surrounded by a mob that he expected would have massacred them before they reached the palace. The loss of this ship to such an enemy gave great uneasiness to those related or connected with the prisoners. To my family it was a severe blow; we had, however, the day after we heard of the capture, a letter from one of the young officers, giving an account of their being all well and that they were well treated. When we first had an account of the loss of the ship (which was four months after the accident happened, by a vessel that arrived at Liverpool from Malta, and published an account of it in one of the English papers), I intended to fit out a fast-sailing vessel, taking in a cargo for Leghorn or Malta, and after landing it, to go off Tripoli in order to assist in procuring the liberation of the prisoners, at any rate to get James liberated; and this I should certainly have done but for a letter I received from Mr. Jefferson in answer to one written him by Captain Gamble, J. Douglass, Esq., and myself, each of whom had a son among the prisoners.

It was a matter of regret to me afterwards, that I had not gone on this expedition, as it is probable I should have persuaded Commodore Preble to have concluded a peace with the Bey; for he has since told me, it was his opinion that peace should be made, and he would have done it if Captain Chauncey had arrived a few hours later than he did. And he would have done it after his arrival, if Chauncey had not told him it was expected in America he would be able to make peace and get the prisoners without paying anything.

In this he was certainly mistaken, nothing of the kind was expected, it could have been made on very honorable terms, and if it had been done at that time, it would have left a strong impression in favor of the Americans; they would have said, if those people with so small a force can bring the Bey of Tripoli to such terms, what cannot they do with a fleet of frigates? At any rate, it is probable had I gone I should have prevailed on the Commodore against sending in the fireship, or whatever she was called, commanded by Somers, whom I had known from the time of his being a small boy. It has always appeared to me that those gallant and valuable young officers, Somers, Wadsworth, and Israel, were foolishly sacrificed. This vessel, if sent in at all, should never have gone without being convoyed by the galleys, or some way have been contrived to have got them off. As they went it was almost going to certain destruction. I have been told, and have no doubt of the fact, that she was in no way fitted for such an enterprise.

CHAPTER V.

THE 12th of July, 1804, while we were at breakfast, my neighbor, Mr. William Bell, called and told me it was reported about town that General Hamilton had the day before killed Colonel Burr in a duel. Persecuted as I knew Colonel Burr had been, I felt distressed. Soon after another gentleman came and said the report was that Burr had killed Hamilton. This proved to be the fact. Judge Peters, an intimate friend of Hamilton's, was talking of him and Burr when Mr. Bell came in. He was mentioning that Hamilton had said to him some short time before, that they were not as bad as we were in their political disputes; that in New York, although they differed in politics, they never carried party matters so far as to let it interfere with their social parties, and mentioned himself and Colonel Burr, who always behaved with courtesy to each other. It is impossible to conceive the noise that this duel made in New York; there was as much or more lamentation as when General Washington died. What occasioned much more noise than otherwise would have been made, were the violent pieces for some time before published against Colonel Burr in the American Citizen. The editor of this paper, who had done everything in his power to set Burr and Hamilton to fighting, affected the most violent grief at the death of Hamilton.

Having an acquaintance and some business with Mr. Pendleton, the second of General Hamilton, I wrote to him the day after we heard of the duel to know if everything was fair and proper on the part of Colonel Burr. He answered me by the return of the post, and his letter I now have, that the only thing the seconds differed about was, which fired first. Certainly it was of no consequence which first fired. It was said Burr had practised for some days before the duel in firing at a mark; but this was not true, he had no occasion to practise, for perhaps there was hardly ever a man could fire so true, and no man possessed more coolness or courage. Judge Burke, who was his second when he fought Church, told me that there was not the least alteration in his behavior on the ground from what there would have been had they met on friendly terms. He said that when he loaded Colonel Burr's pistols, by mistake he put a wad with the ball, and was hammering to get it down, when Burr called to him, and told him not to mind it, if he missed him then he would hit him the next shot. However, after the first fire Mr. Church made an apology. I think General Hamilton would have done so had he fortunately been missed.*

It will be perceived by the correspondence between General Hamilton and Colonel Burr that there was an evasion in General Hamilton's first letter of what he at last virtually confessed. General Hamilton was certainly a man of very superior talents to most men, and I sincerely lamented his death, but as an old military man Colonel Burr could not have acted otherwise than he did. I never knew Colonel Burr speak ill of any man, and he had a right to expect a different treatment from what he experienced. Commodore Truxtun dined in company with Hamilton and Burr the week before the duel; he has since told me he had not the most distant idea of there being any difference between them.

When I found what a disturbance there was in New York about this unhappy affair, I wrote to Colonel Burr, and requested he would come and stay with me. He came in two or three days. Here there was a great clamor about the duel, and several of my friends were angry at me for having him at my house; and some people, it was said, came from New York with an intention of taking him. In consequence of

---

* This duel took place Sept. 2, 1799, and is described in Parton's Life of Burr, p. 240.

this report (my family being at my house in the country where I used to go every evening) I staid with him several nights. He would not have been easily taken.

I received a letter, of which the following is a copy, from Mr. Van Ness, the second of Colonel Burr:—

Dear Sir: I shall answer without hesitation the interrogatories you have put to me, as I conceive it my duty to communicate with freedom the circumstances that attended the interview between Colonel Burr and General Hamilton. After the necessary preparations had been made, which you will find detailed in the printed statement of the seconds, the parties took their places; General Hamilton raised his pistol as if to try it, and again lowering it, said, "I beg pardon for delaying you, but the direction of the light sometimes renders glasses necessary." He then drew forth his spectacles and put them on. The gentleman whose duty it was to give the word, then asked the parties whether they were prepared, which being answered in the affirmative, the word "present" was then given, on which both parties presented. The pistol of General Hamilton was first discharged, and Colonel Burr fired immediately after. On this point I have the misfortune to differ from the friend of General Hamilton, and without doubting the sincerity of his opinion, I can safely declare that I was never more firmly convinced of any fact that came under my observation. On the discharge of General Hamilton's pistol, I observed a slight motion in the person of Colonel Burr, which gave me the idea that he was struck. On this point I conversed with Colonel Burr, when we returned, who ascribed the motion of his body to a small stone under his foot, and added, the smoke of General Hamilton's pistol for a moment obscured his sight.

When General Hamilton fell, Colonel Burr advanced towards him, but I immediately urged the importance of his repairing to the barge. He complied with my request, and in a few minutes I followed him. When I arrived at the boat Colonel Burr was just stepping from it. He said to me, "I must go and speak to him," I replied it would be obviously improper, as General Hamilton was surrounded by the surgeons and bargemen, by whom he ought not to be seen, but that if he would remain I would go and see the General, which I did, and on my return to the boat ordered the bargemen to proceed immediately to the city, which was done.

Thus, sir, I have related to you such circumstances respecting the late unfortunate interview between Colonel Burr and General Hamilton, as have not hitherto been published. It is but justice to add that Colonel Burr so far from exhibiting any degree of levity on the occasion to which I have alluded, or expressing any satisfaction at the result of the meeting, his whole conduct while I was with him was expressive of regret and concern.

Yours, etc. etc.
W. P. VAN NESS.*

Had General Hamilton in his answer to the first note sent by Colonel Burr mentioned what he afterwards did, viz., that he did not intend any reflection on the private character of Colonel Burr, everything would have been settled, but he himself threw down the gauntlet. Colonel Burr told me a short time before the duel, when he was in Philadelphia on his way to New York from Washington, that he was determined to call out the first man of any respectability concerned in the infamous publications concerning him. He had no idea then of having to call on General Hamilton.

Burr was much blamed for challenging Hamilton. If in this he acted as a sinner, Hamilton did not act as a saint in accepting it. General Hamilton in giving an account of Major André, very justly observes, "That a man of real merit is never seen in so favorable a light as through the medium of adversity. The clouds that surround him are so many shades that set off his good qualities. Misfortune cuts down little vanities that in prosperous times serve as so many spots in his virtues, and gives a tone of humanity that makes his worth more amiable. His spectators who enjoy a happier lot, are less prone to detract from it through envy; and are much disposed by compassion to give the credit he deserves,

* See note F.

20

and perhaps even to magnify it." This was the case as to General Hamilton.

In July, 1804, my friend General Armstrong was appointed Ambassador to France. Wishing to get my son Nicholas with him, as his secretary, I spoke to him and he agreed to take him. Nicholas left us the last of July.*

The following letter was sent open to me to be forwarded to Governor Bloomfield. General Smith and Giles were afterwards among the most violent of Colonel Burr's enemies.

WASHINGTON, Nov. 24, 1804.

Sir: We whose names are written at the end of this letter, Senators of the United States, have seen with much sensibility and concern a prosecution instituted, and as far as we are informed, still continued in one of the Courts of New Jersey, upon a charge of murder against the Vice-President of the United States and President of the Senate. Our feelings have been still further excited by information that attempts are now making to demand the person of the President of the Senate to answer the alleged offence, as a fugitive from justice. We understand the real offence charged to have been committed by him, is causing the death of the late General Hamilton in a duel, every circumstance attending which was marked with all the etiquette and fairness usually observed amongst gentlemen upon similar occasions.

Whilst we wish to avoid every expression which might give any sanction or approbation whatever to the custom of duelling, or call in question the policy of the laws of New Jersey which makes no discrimination between a death thus produced, and that by a common murder with premeditated malice and without the survivor exposing his own life to an equal hazard, yet we cannot help observing that there exists a great difference in the two cases in the opinion and usages of most civilized nations, of the people of the United States, and particularly of that part of the United States where the offence in the present instance is said to have been committed. In support of this we beg leave to call your Excellency's at-

* See note G.

tention to two cases of a similar nature which have occurred
in the same county within a few years past, and others bearing near resemblance to these might also be cited. The first,
the case of Mr. Livingston and Mr. Jones; the other, the
case of Mr. Eaker and the younger Mr. Hamilton. We are
informed that no judicial proceedings were had in either of
these cases, and that shortly after the unfortunate fate of Mr.
Jones, Mr. Livingston was promoted to one of the highest
judicial offices in the State of New York, in which we believe he continues with advantage to his country and honor
to himself; and we believe Mr. Eaker also shortly after the
untimely fate of young Mr. Hamilton, received some judicial
appointment. These cases demonstrate not only that the
same rules of judicial proceedings have not been applied to
different persons in similar situations. But the general
understanding of society discriminates widely between this
offence and the case of a common murder; so much so, that in
the cases referred to, instead of the survivor receiving the
reprobation attached by society to common murderers, the
offences have been deemed no obstacle to judicial preferment.
Nor can we help remarking in the present case, that although
we are advised that the laws of New Jersey make no difference between the offences of principal and second in the event
of a death by a duel, and although the seconds are as well
and generally known as the surviving principal, yet as far as
we are informed no judicial proceedings have been had
against either of them. Whilst, therefore, we are willing to
rely implicitly upon the ultimate justice of the Courts of
New Jersey, we are constrained to express our regret that the
same rule should be so unequally applied to different individuals in similar circumstances, and particularly that this
inequality should be directed against the President of the
Senate whilst engaged in the discharge of official duties ; nor
can we avoid intimating the unpleasant embarrassment of the
Senate if the attempt meditated of demanding his person
whilst thus engaged should be prosecuted.

Under such circumstances it would, in our judgment, be
conducive to the public interests, and particularly gratifying

to our feelings that the prosecution should be discontinued, thereby to facilitate the public business by relieving the President of the Senate from the peculiar embarrassments of his present situation, and the Senate from the distressing imputation thrown on it, by holding up its President to the world as a common murderer. Avoiding the expression of any opinion in every other respect whatever, it is but justice to the President of the Senate to add, that in that character he has at all times, as far as our observations have extended, acted with dignity, ability, and impartiality, and has thus been instrumental in promoting the public business. In this delicate state of things we confide in your Excellency's firmness and patriotism to take this subject into consideration, and to adopt such measures therein as may be consistent with right, and the laws and usages of New Jersey.

Be pleased, sir, to accept assurances of our high consideration, etc. etc.

(Signed)   THOS. SUMTER,
ROBERT WRIGHT,
WM. B. GILES,
WM. LOCKE,
STEPHEN R. BRADLY,
GEO. LOGAN,
T. WORTHINGTON,
S'L SMITH,
JAMES JACKSON,
JOS. ANDERSON,
JOHN SMITH.

To His Excellency, Gov. BLOOMFIELD.

Governor Bloomfield was the intimate friend of Colonel Burr, and had been from the time they were boys. He frequently expressed to myself and others the utmost esteem and regard for Burr; but he would not issue a nolle prosequi, saying he did not think the Constitution of New Jersey gave him the power of doing it. But I believe the real cause was the fear of injuring his popularity; and the same reason induced him to oppose the friends of Colonel Burr from applying to the Legislature for a law in his favor. The Governor is a worthy man, but he is too much influenced by his wish to keep well with all parties. This is hardly possible to do; almost every man who attempts it is called a trimmer, and often loses his consequence with all parties.

Hamilton and Burr were about the same age; both small, well-made men. They were considered in the army as very valuable officers, and had they been of the same political party would have been very good friends. If General Hamilton had not opposed Colonel Burr I have very little doubt but he would have been elected Governor of New York, and if he had it would have been a fortunate circumstance for the country, as well as themselves and their families.

In this unfortunate affair Mr. Rufus King was blamed, I think deservedly, for not endeavoring to prevent this fatal duel. He is the moderate, judicious friend General Hamilton alludes to in the paper inclosed in his will.

Mr. Van Ness told me that the morning of the duel, when he went to Colonel Burr, he found him in a very sound sleep. He was obliged to hurry on his clothes to be ready at the time appointed for the meeting.

In April, 1803, I lost a worthy old friend, Dr. Enoch Edwards. He was as entertaining a man as I ever knew, and although seldom well, was always in good spirits and cheerful. He, as well as his brother, Major Evan Edwards, served during our Revolutionary war with great reputation. He was the thinnest man I ever knew, had a spitting of blood for upwards of thirty years, was cadaverous, and had a very bad cough. He used to tell a great many stories about himself. He said that he had the advantage of all his friends, they all changed, but he never could look worse. He said he went on business to a farmer in Montgomery County. The man was not at home, the wife asked his name. He told her he was Dr. Edwards. "Dr. Edwards!" says the woman, "why my husband said you were the thinnest and ugliest man he had ever seen. I don't think you are so very ugly." The husband coming up soon after, the Doctor laughing, told him what his wife had said; at which he was

much confused. He went to England in 1793. Part of his
business was to sell some land for Mr. Nicholson, who told him
he should be careful not to let the people who wanted to purchase the land know he was born on it. Some years before
he died, walking down Market Street, he received an accidental stroke in the breast from a porter, who was hauling a
cask out of a cellar. The stroke would have done no injury
to a person in health, but it almost killed the Doctor. He
went home that evening, and in the night was taken very ill,
and early in the morning sent for me. I immediately went
up to his farm, which was in Byberry, about thirteen miles
from town. He informed me that he was very ill and desirous of making his will, which he did. In the night, Mrs.
Edwards was sitting on one side of the bed, and myself on
the other, expecting from the pain he was in that he would
hardly live out the night, when rousing himself up and smil-
ing, "Now," says he, "I have been thinking for some time,
that if Mrs. Biddle goes off" (she was then every day expecting to be confined) "and I should go, as probably will be the
case, you two would be married in six months." He, however, lived many years afterwards, making a voyage to
England, and after that to France, whence, at Paris, he wrote
me that he had a severe fit of sickness. From what was told
him by his French acquaintance, a person would suppose that
all Paris was alarmed and inconsolable about him. He spoke
highly of their politeness and attention to him. It appears
incredible that these people should be guilty of crimes disgraceful to human nature. It has often been mentioned that
Mr. Monroe encouraged Thomas Paine to write the infamous
letter he sent to General Washington. The Doctor often told
me that Monroe sent him to Paris and did everything in his
power to prevent his sending or publishing the letter. Paine
told him that anything Mr. Monroe wrote, it was of no consequence whether it was suppressed or not, but what he wrote
was for posterity. Paine as a writer was certainly eminent,
but in every other respect he was and is truly contemptible.
He took great care during our Revolutionary war to keep
out of danger. In 1793 the Doctor and several of my friends

who were displeased with Governor Mifflin, wanted me very much to let them run me for the office of Governor in opposition to him; but independent of its being a very troublesome office, I had a sincere friendship for Mifflin.

Being anxious to get Commodore Truxtun again in the navy, I wrote a letter in 1805, to Mr. Dallas, the intimate friend of Mr. Secretary Smith, saying that I was very certain the Commodore had no intention whatever of resigning his commission when he resigned the command of the Mediterranean squadron, and that I understood the Secretary, after the appointment of Morris, said he hoped Commodore Truxtun would not resign. Mr. Dallas inclosed my letter to the Secretary, which brought on a correspondence between Truxtun and the Secretary. The Secretary wanted some proof that he had no intention of resigning, and the Commodore applied to Captain Dale and myself. I mentioned what he had written me at the time; and Dale, what he had said to him.*

The Secretary gave Truxtun reason to suppose he wished him in the navy again, and that it was very probable he would soon be called into service. If he wished him in service, he took a very improper method to obtain it, for he wrote to all the captains in the navy to give their opinions

* Copies of the letters between Commodore Dale and myself.

PHILADELPHIA, Sept. 7, 1805.

Dear Sir:—When you arrived at Norfolk from the Mediterranean did you understand from Commodore Truxtun that, when he gave up the command of the squadron to Morris, he had resigned his commission in the navy, or have you at any time since heard him say he had resigned?

Your most obedient servant,

Commodore DALE.   C. B.

Answer.

PHILADELPHIA, Sep. 7.

Dear Sir:—In answer to your inquiries of me, respecting what I heard when I arrived at Norfolk from the Mediterranean about Commodore Truxtun's resigning, I can with confidence say that I did not understand so at that time; and from that time to the present I have heard Commodore Truxtun say he did not resign his commission.

I am yours respectfully,

C. BIDDLE, Esq.   RICHARD DALE.

whether Commodore Truxtun ought to be again in the navy
and hold the rank he had before he left the Chesapeake.
This, as was to be expected, ended in their all, except Commodore Murray, being against his holding the rank he formerly had.   Truxtun thought the calling upon the captains in
the navy in this way, a very improper mode of proceeding,
and I believe few would think otherwise.   Truxtun wrote to
the Secretary that he had acted like a base hypocrite, that he
was a coward and scoundrel.   I suppose the Secretary thought
it would be foolish in him to fight every officer that conceived himself injured.   '

In September, 1805, to the infinite joy of the family, James
returned from Tripoli.*   He was in perfect health, for his
usage was much better than we could expect from such an
enemy.   He was but a short time home before he was ordered
to take charge of Gunboat No. 1, then lying at Charleston.
If it had not been perfectly agreeable to him he should not
have gone, but should have resigned.   As he was, however,
anxious to go, I would not oppose it.   He was appointed
lieutenant, and had rank from May, 1804.

The latter end of January, 1806, I went with my friend
John Dunlap to Lancaster.   The business that carried me
there was that my commission as Prothonotary had not been
renewed, although all the other officers of the government in
the city had received theirs, and I knew not whether Governor McKean intended to renew mine.   I was received by
the Governor with great kindness, and he ordered my commission to be made out and given to me immediately, it
having been neglected by mistake.   During the time we were
there Mr. Dunlap and myself gave a dinner to the Governor,
the Speakers of both Houses, and some of the members.
This dinner reminded me afterwards of what I had heard of
a Dutch merchant who had a turtle sent him as a present.
He said he hoped no person would send him another, for he gave
a dinner to a large party which cost him a considerable sum,

---

* The officers and crew of the Philadelphia were held prisoners at Tripoli
from October, 1803, until June, 1805.

and he had disobliged many of his friends by not inviting them. Some of our acquaintances in both Houses were displeased at not being of the party, and this with their hatred of the Governor* I believe was the occasion of a law being passed soon after, that the Prothonotaries of the County courts should annually pay into the treasury all the fees they received exceeding fifteen hundred dollars. As this would make my office of no value, I returned to Lancaster, and procured an alteration in the law; but it was not such a one as it should have been. The law is obviously unjust, for in some of the county offices it had no effect at all. The true way of making it bear equally was to have laid a tax upon writs. I have reason to believe that this dinner was the occasion of this law. At this time I cared very little about the office, in fact I only wanted it put into the hands of some person who would collect and pay the fees due me.

During this summer Mr. Burr was frequently in Philadelphia, and my family being in the country, he was often with me. The latter part of it he spent chiefly at Morrisville.† His daughter, Mrs. Alston from Georgetown, was there with her son. General Moreau lived there, and he and Colonel Burr, I understood, were often together; as military men this was natural. From this place Colonel Burr wrote to me that he had some business of importance to communicate to me, and that he would soon be in town. A few days afterwards he called, and after conversing on different subjects, he told me that a number of gentlemen of the first respectability in every part of the Union wished him to form a settlement on the Mississippi of military men; that the Spaniards he knew were ripe for a revolt, and it would make the fortunes of all those concerned in revolutionizing that country. I told him that such a plan, if carried into effect, would probably involve us in a war with Spain, and I would

---

* The Governor at this time spoke with the utmost contempt of the majority of the Legislature, calling them geese, ignoramuses, clodhoppers, rascals, and scoundrels. They certainly were not very enlightened men, nor was the Governor the mildest of men.—AUTHOR'S NOTE.

† Opposite to Trenton.

therefore have nothing to do with it. He said whether we invaded the country or not, we should have a war with Spain. I mentioned Miranda's expedition as one that should have never been countenanced by any person in this country. He said Miranda was a fool, totally unqualified for such an expedition. Finding I would not listen to his plans, and that no arguments he could use would have any weight with me, he expressed great regret. After a silence for some time, he said he never was more at a loss than he was to know whether he should communicate this business to Commodore Truxtun. I told him, of that he was the best judge, and then left him. He afterwards went to see the Commodore and opened himself much more fully to him than he had to me. I was sorry afterwards, on his account, that I had not let him proceed, and heard the whole of his plan. It is probable an immediate stop would have been put to it, which would have been fortunate for him. He told me he would not do anything that could injure his country. I believed then he thought so, and at this time, 1813, have not changed my opinion. He would have collected a number of military men round him near the lines, formed a barrier between us and the Spaniards which would have prevented their ever disturbing us. From the intimacy between Colonel Burr and myself, many people believed me perfectly acquainted with his intentions, but I have related everything known by me respecting this (to Colonel Burr) unfortunate business. Colonel Burr soon after this went into the Western country.

In December, this year, a servant boy named Virgil, born in the family in North Carolina, had been out late for several nights. One night, after the family were in bed, he opened the cellar-door and went to a dance, and did not return until after daylight. Being determined to put a stop to such practices, the next evening I took him in the garret, and locked him up, telling him that in the morning he should have a new cowskin worn out on his back. In the morning, to my very great surprise, I found he had contrived to get the room door opened, and had moved off. I immediately sent off to New York, and had advertisements put up on the road, offering a reward of forty dollars and a pardon if he would return, but could hear nothing of him. On the first of January, about twelve o'clock at night, I took two constables with me, and we searched every house in the lower part of the city and in Southwark that we could hear of there being any dance at. We disturbed some parties of whites, blacks, and mulattoes all dancing together, but could hear nothing of Virgil. He was a very handsome black, and a most excellent servant until he got into bad company, which kept him out at night. Had I punished him in the evening instead of locking him up he never would have thought of running away. Soon after he left us Mr. Bennet, who keeps a tavern at Long Branch, and who knew him well, saw him in New York. He told Mr. Bennet that he was there with me. As we never heard of him since, it is probable he went to sea, and was lost.

In the month of February, this year, 1807, I received a letter from the unfortunate Colonel Burr, informing me that notwithstanding the grand jury had acquitted him he was apprehended, and was on his way to Washington under a guard. He requested me to inform his friends of his situation; that he could write nothing but what was to be seen by the officer who commanded the escort.* I sent a copy of

---

* *Copy of Col. Burr's Letter.*

"FORT STODDERT, 22d Feby, 1809.

"*D'r Sir :*—I was arrested a few days since by a party of the United States troops near this place and am now moving towards the city of Washington under military escort. This proceeding is the more extraordinary as the grand jury summoned for the purpose, before the Supreme Court in Adams County (Natchez), the day before my departure from that place, acquitted me in the completest manner of all unlawful practices *or designs*. The report of this grand jury also censured the conduct of government in some particulars concerning me, and for this reason I am told that the printers have not thought it discreet to publish that report entire. The pretence of my having forfeited a recognizance, though sanctioned by the proclamation of Governor Williams, is utterly false. The details of the prosecutions against me cannot now be given—they are beyond all example and in defiance of

his letter to Colonel John Swartwout, who, as well as his
brother, I knew were his warm friends, and who would do
everything in their power to serve him. One of the brothers,
Mr. Samuel Swartwout, a brave, generous young man, was
with him at Richmond, and challenged General Wilkinson
after the trial. I also sent a copy of the letter to Mr. Van
Ness, his second in the unfortunate duel with Colonel Hamilton. During the trial Colonel Burr was very anxious for
my being at Richmond. He said that although I could not
be a witness, my being with him would be of importance to
him; but, as my own opinion was different, I concluded not
to go. For a great number of years no three men were more
intimate friends than Wilkinson, Burr, and Truxtun. At
this time Truxtun would not speak to Wilkinson, and was not
upon good terms with Burr. Wilkinson and Burr were
bitter enemies. I was intimate with them all, and nothing
in this unpleasant business interrupted the harmony that had
always subsisted between us. They all wrote to me from
Richmond. Truxtun abused Wilkinson as having acted the
part of a base hypocrite; and Wilkinson wrote of him in
such a manner that they would have fought had they seen
each other's letters. Truxtun told me that Wilkinson, in his
dispatches (cipher letter) from New Orleans, had mentioned
him and myself as being concerned with Burr. He was
much disappointed when I told him if it was so it gave me
no concern whatever. I, however, wrote to Wilkinson to
know if it was true. He declared upon his honor that it
was a most infamous falsehood, and wished to know who had
informed me. I wrote him that this was not necessary, as
his denying it satisfied me it was not true. At the time of

all law. Please to communicate this to my friends in New York. What
I write must be inspected by the officer of the guard.''

The following is an extract from the finding of the grand jury :—

" The grand jury of the Mississippi Territory, on a due investigation of
the evidence brought before them, are of opinion that Aaron Burr has not
been guilty of any crime or misdemeanor against the laws of the United
States or of this Territory, *or given any just cause of alarm or inquietude
to the good people of the same.*''

Colonel Burr's being in the Western country my old friend Truxtun and myself had several conversations about the intended expedition. He would sometimes get offended at what passed between us, and would not come to my house for several weeks. Meeting him one morning he told me he had not closed his eyes all night. "What ailed you?" "Did you not see in the Aurora of yesterday the mention that 'a distinguished American commander was concerned with Burr'?" "Yes, I saw that in the Aurora, but why should that give any uneasiness? "Why, because the person alluded to must be me." "And are you concerned with Colonel Burr?" "You know I am not." "Then why uneasy at anything said in the papers about this 'distinguished commander'?" "Let me ask you, my friend, if you would not be hurt at such a publication?" "Not in the least. I should not have the vanity to suppose it was intended for me." He was highly offended at some part of what was said, and for a month did not speak to me.

After the trial of Colonel Burr, Wilkinson was in Baltimore, and for something H——* had done he challenged him. H—— (as Randolph had done before) refused to fight him, saying that he must acquit himself of the charges that were against him, before he would put himself upon a footing with him. Wilkinson told me, that as soon as he reached Baltimore he should challenge H——, that if he was to meet him in the street he did not believe he could command himself so much as to refrain from attacking him. When Truxtun heard of H—— refusing to fight Wilkinson, he called on me. "Well, you see H—— would not accept of Wilkinson's challenge." I told him a poltroon always found some excuse for not fighting. "Why, you do not think me a coward, and I would not accept a challenge from him." I told him my opinion was, that until a man was found guilty of a dishonorable action, and held a commission in the army, he was upon a footing with any gentleman. Something more passed upon this occasion, for which he again did not speak to me for several weeks.

* Possibly General Hampton.

Although Colonel Burr always spoke of giving freedom to the people of New Spain with enthusiasm, I have no doubt he would have given up his expedition if he could have procured any appointment that would have made him independent. My reason for thinking so is that on the resignation of Judge Shippen he requested me to speak to Governor McKean, and endeavor to get him appointed in his room. This, as Colonel Burr then stood, I thought would be improper, and told him so. However, I spoke to the Governor's son, Joseph B. McKean, who being of the same opinion as myself, the Governor was not spoken to on the subject.

Nor do I believe Wilkinson was ever concerned or knew what Colonel Burr intended until Mr. Swartwout informed him. I do know that some of Colonel Burr's friends in New York were very anxious to know how Wilkinson would receive him; but I thought then, and shall ever think, that from the long intimacy and friendship he always professed for Colonel Burr, that he should have informed him of the consequence of his proceeding upon his expedition. If he had done this Burr would have desisted, and it would all have died away. This I told Wilkinson when he came here, but he seemed to think it was necessary for him to act as he did. It was always a mystery to me how it happened that General Dayton was not tried, as well as Colonel Burr. It was generally believed that he was concerned in all his schemes, whatever they were. It was thought by many that Dayton would keep out of the way, but he was too much of a soldier for that. It is to be lamented that such men should be thought of being tried as traitors to their country. Burr was always of opinion that Bonaparte would give us some trouble in New Orleans, and wanted, long before this time, to take measures that would put it out of his power to do us any injury; but Mr. Jefferson either was afraid of Bonaparte, or had a better opinion of him than he deserved.*

The latter end of June we had an account of the attack of the Leopard upon the Chesapeake. Although many people blamed the Government for not delivering up the men claimed

* For some letters relating to this period see note F.

by Captain Douglass, every American felt indignant at the
manner in which the attack was made. In Philadelphia we
had, on the first of July, a town meeting. Matthew Lawler,
the Mayor, was in the chair. We entered into a resolution
to support the General Government in every measure they
should adopt to avenge the insult offered to our flag, and
pledged ourselves to make any sacrifices and encounter every
hazard. Several other resolutions were entered into. As the
inhabitants of Norfolk and its vicinity had behaved well, I
offered a resolution thanking them for their gallant and manly
conduct. This was unanimously agreed to. We then
appointed a committee consisting of Mr. Lawler, Charles
Biddle, Paul Cox, David Lenox, Thomas Forrest, Richard
Dale, Walter Franklin, George Clymer, Michael Lieb, Thomas
Leiper, Francis Gurney, James Engle, Joseph Hopkinson,
George Bartram, Edward Tilghman, M. Bright—nine Democrats and seven Federalists. The afternoon of the day we
were appointed, a number of people collected on board an
English brig called the Fox, lying at Pine Street wharf. It
was reported that she was loaded with provisions and water
for the fleet in the Chesapeake. Upon hearing of it I went
immediately down to the wharf, and found there was a great
number of people on board very busy in unbending her sails
and unrigging her. Some other gentlemen of the Committee
coming on the wharf, we sent and procured a company of
militia, commanded by Captain Wharton, to come down.
He soon restored order on board the brig. On the wharf the
people seemed very much disposed for a riot. One of the
crew of the Fox hearing a person damning the British for a
set of cowardly rascals, for attacking the Chesapeake in the
manner they had done, swore they were cowardly rascals that
called them so; that he was an Englishman, and he would
fight any damned Yankee in the country. He was pulling
off his jacket to prepare for battle, and several fellows were
gathering round to seize him, when I went up to him, and
with some difficulty got him out of the crowd and persuaded
him to go to his lodging. He was a short, well-built young
man, whose name I was afterwards sorry I did not ask him.

Nelson could not have behaved with more intrepidity than this brave fellow, who was perfectly sober.

Returning from the theatre the night after the town-meeting, with two ladies, when near Mr. Bond's (the British Consul) house, there were two large stones thrown from across the street at it. They struck the door and rebounded very near us. I immediately crossed the street, when the fellows ran away. After seeing the ladies home, I went to Mr. Bond's and staid with him until it was late. Mr. Bond did not apprehend any danger, but he felt very indignant at the insult offered to him; and the family were much alarmed. Although Mr. Bond had gone from Philadelphia with the British (at the time of the Revolution), he deserved no insult from the inhabitants, for while in England and in Philadelphia he took every opportunity of serving his countrymen. When my son James went out with Commodore Bainbridge, he gave him letters to some of the British officers in the fleet up the Mediterranean, and to Sir Alexander Ball, Governor of Malta. This gallant officer behaved with great kindness to James, and after his capture by the Tripolitans, sent him porter, cheese, and other articles he wanted. I wrote to thank Governor Ball and pay him for what he so generously supplied James with, and nothing would have gratified me more than an opportunity of convincing him how much I considered myself obliged to him.*

* Letter from Sir Alexander Ball.

MALTA, 25th June, 1805.

Sir :—I beg leave to offer you my sincere congratulations on your son's release from Tripolitan slavery, and particularly on his having obtained it by a peace the most honorable for the United States. I am glad to find his health has not suffered by his exile, and with respect to his mind, it is proble he will he will be a better and happier man by the adversity he has experienced.

I did not answer your letter acquainting me with your wish to purchase your son's redemption, because I saw the necessity of abstaining from an act that might raise the demands of the Bashaw and hurt the American cause. I was persuaded from your character that on this I should be anticipating your patriotic spirit, more especially as I foresaw and predicted that

One of the ladies returning from the theatre with me when stones were thrown at Mr. Bond's house, was Mrs. Ashley, an English lady, who was very much alarmed, for I believe that she thought the stones were intended for her. Late that night a set of vagabonds went before Mr. Ashley's door and played the Rogue's March. Mr. Ashley, a very respectable English merchant, thought they were complimenting him, and was going down to order them wine, when one of the servants told him the tune they were playing.

In September this year, the ship Argo, from New Orleans, bound to Philadelphia, struck a rock upon the Bahama Bank, and bilged. The crew and passengers took to their boats. The small boat was driven into the Gulf Stream, where they fell in with the ship Comet, Captain Dixey, on board of which was the Hon. Daniel Clarke,* the owner, who being informed of the disaster, determined to cruise for the crew of the long boat, which they did for four days, when they were discovered on the Great Isaac Rock and taken on board the Comet. Mr. Clarke had property in the Comet to the amount of one hundred thousand dollars, which was jeopardized by his deviation. Mr. Wharton, who was on board the Argo when she was wrecked, having mentioned the generous and humane conduct of Mr. Clarke in a company where Mr. Henry Pratt, some others, and myself were spending the evening, we thought a public dinner ought to be given him, and Mr. Pratt agreed to call upon me in the morning, which he did. When we were near the house at which Mr. Clarke lodged, Pratt stopped. "Biddle," said he, "we are going to invite Mr. Clarke to a dinner in the name of the citizens of Philadelphia, are we not?" "Yes." "And how do you know whether we can get subscribers." "That, I do not

a persevering blockade *only* would soon terminate the war to the honor of the United States. I beg you to command my services when they can be useful. I have the honor to be, with much esteem,

Your most faithful and obedient servant,

CHAS. BIDDLE, Esq.   ALEX. J. BALL.

* The Mr. Clarke who was afterwards so prominent in the controversy growing out of Burr's expedition.

21

know, but if we cannot get subscribers, we can get a company, and you are rich and can pay for the dinner. If you
do not choose that. I will pay one-half, for he deserves and
must have a public dinner." We agreed to make up any
deficiency, and went on to Mr. Clarke's lodging. He told us
he had done nothing but what any other man would have
done; that, however, he could not refuse the honor done
him, and would dine with us on any day we should agree
upon. We appointed the 30th of October, when we gave
him a splendid dinner. We had Messrs. Jefferson and Bray
from the theatre, and some others of the company that sang
remarkably well. Most of the toasts were made by Major
Jackson, who was often called upon on these occasions. The
first was made by my son William :—

"Our distinguished guest; the wreath of honor belongs to
him who saves his fellow men."

Mr. Clarke at this time had no difference with Wilkinson.
He complained that both Burr and Wilkinson gave him a
good deal of trouble about their affairs. A few days after
the dinner given him, he went to Washington to attend
Congress, of which he was a member. He had been there
but a short time before he joined Randolph in everything he
did to ruin Wilkinson. Mr. Clarke was friendly to Burr,
and perhaps Wilkinson's conduct to that most unfortunate of
men had some influence on Mr. Clarke. A transaction that
Wilkinson would have been much gratified to hear, and
which would probably have been of great service to him,
came to my knowledge at this time, but as it was communicated in confidence I could not mention it. Wilkinson
wrote me respecting his dispute with Clarke, and wanted to
know if I could give him any information of what passed
between Burr and him in Philadelphia. What I did know
could not be communicated; I therefore did not answer him.

Colonel Burr at this time kept himself concealed in a French
boarding house. When I used to call of an evening to see
him, he was generally alone with little light in his room.
He was very pale and dejected; how different from what he
had been a short time before when few persons in the city

were not gratified at seeing him at their tables, where he was always one of the most lively and entertaining of the company. It would not have surprised me on going there to have found he had ended his sufferings with a pistol. If ever man could be justified in committing such an act it was Colonel Burr. To have found he had could hardly have given me more pain than I have sometimes felt on seeing him in this melancholy situation. Going one night to see him with a friend from New York, we mistook the house, and as it was not customary to knock, we went upstairs and opened the door that we supposed to be his, when to our surprise we found ourselves in the bed-chamber of some ladies. We effected a retreat without any ill consequences.

While in the city this time Mr. Burr was taken by the sheriff at the suit of Mr. Wilkins, of Pittsburgh. Mr. Burr declared that he owed Wilkins nothing, that he (Wilkins) had not complied with his contract. Late at night he was brought to my house, and the sheriff waited a considerable time with him and Mr. Pollock for me to come home. Mr. Pollock is a highly respectable gentleman, intimate in my family, a relation and friend of Colonel Burr, and a man of large fortune. It was very distressing to all my family to know that these gentlemen were in my office with the sheriff's officer. Colonel Burr was perfectly composed; at this time scarcely anything could disturb him. At length one of my neighbors was sent for, Mr. Hollowell, a gentleman of the Bar, who came immediately and pledged himself to be answerable for Mr. Burr's appearance in the morning. In the morning Mr. Pollock was accepted as the bail. Owing to some mistake of the plaintiff's attorney Mr. Pollock was discharged from the bail. Having suffered severely by being bail, I had made up my mind never to be security for any person whatever, but in this case I could not have seen Mr. Burr carried from my house to gaol. I would lend any money I had cheerfully, but not endorse a note, or run any risk of involving myself or family.

Early in the year 1808, I was consulted by my friend

Judge Jones about his son Richard's leaving the navy.* He
was at this time only a midshipman, commanding a gunboat
at New York. As there was no prospect of a war, and he
was about getting married, I advised him to leave the service.
Our administration was unfriendly to a navy, and, in fact, to
commerce.

Having had much plague as executor to the estate of Mrs.
Brodhead (before she married General Brodhead, the widow
of Samuel Mifflin, Esq.) I did not intend ever acting again,
but within a few years past three of my old friends died
leaving me their executors, Dr. Enoch Edwards, whom I
formerly mentioned, General Jacob Morgan, and Joseph
Donaldson, Esq., a respectable merchant. General Morgan
was a friend of mine from my first going to sea. At one
time he rendered me a very important service, by calling on
me, and preventing my doing what I should ever after have
regretted. He was Major to Dickinson's regiment, to whom
the Quaker Light Infantry was attached. The General had
been an officer in the Provincial service. He was a brave,
active, intelligent officer, in whom the regiment had the utmost
confidence. He was with us when the regiment was at
Elizabethtown Point, and at the water side when we embarked
on the expedition I have mentioned. One of the men who
was to have gone with us was, or pretended to be, taken
suddenly so ill just before we embarked that he could not go
with us. Major Morgan would have gone in his room, but
we all thought he was of too much importance in camp to
leave it, and there were enough privates glad to go. The
sick person is now, 1813, living and hearty. He had much
better have insisted upon going, even if he had died in the
boat, for whether he was really sick or not, he was suspected
of being shy, and treated with some degree of contempt. As

* Young Mr. Jones had been a prisoner at Tripoli with James Biddle,
afterwards Commodore Biddle, son of Charles Biddle. There were with
them several other Philadelphians—James Renshaw, Benj. Franklin Reed,
and Bernard Henry. The last named was father of the present Mr. Morton
P. Henry of the Philadelphia Bar.

executor to the estate of General Morgan I had but little trouble.

I used frequently early in the morning this summer to take two or three of the boys with me in a chair near the Upper Ferry on the Schuylkill to learn them to swim. One morning after bathing and dressing myself I walked on, leaving the children, when they were dressed, to follow me in the chair. It was but little after sunrise. In crossing the common I saw three shabby looking fellows coming towards me. After consulting together, one, who was lame, walked to a fence at some distance; the other two who had bludgeons in their hands came directly towards me. I looked anxiously round the common to see if there was any person to call on, but none was to be seen but these vagabonds. I had in my hand a cane that had the appearance of a sword cane. As they drew near I stopped, and holding the cane in a position as if going to draw they very civilly inquired the time of day. Telling them I had no watch they passed me, when the fellow at the fence halloed out, " You damned cowardly rascals! you are afraid of one man." They then walked up to him. By this time, although I did not quicken my pace, supposing if I had done so they would think me afraid and chase me, I was much pleased at reaching Market Street. If I had then met any person to have joined me I would have pursued them, and if we could not have caught them all we would have got the lame fellow. I went after them when the boys overtook me with the chair, but they were not to be found. Nothing prevented my being robbed and perhaps murdered, but my having a cane which they supposed was a sword cane.

This year Mr. McKean's time expired as Governor of the State. Many of my friends thought I would obtain more votes than any other Federal candidate, and therefore wished me to be set up. For my own part I had no wish to be Governor of the State had it been in my power; it would have obliged me to live out of the city a great part of the year, which I did not wish. Mr. James Ross, of Pittsburgh, was fixed upon. He had been the candidate opposed to Governor McKean. As usual with men set up for public office they had many stories to tell against Mr. Ross, that he was a land-jobber, a miser, and what was against him with some people, he was a lawyer. The Democrats, for what reason no one could tell, took up Simon Snyder; they had many among them better qualified. The only reason I ever heard assigned for his being taken up was, that he was a German, and that they wanted a German Governor (the descendants from all other countries born in America call themselves Americans, and why these people should call themselves Germans I never could learn). The Germans are a very useful, good class of citizens, but I remember when a boy, when the Germans were much more numerous in the city than they now are it was a great disgrace to a boy to have it said a Dutch boy beat you, even if he was much older and stouter. It is to be hoped the distinction will be dropped, and every man born in the country will be proud of calling himself an American. Mr. Snyder was elected, and such a Governor no State could produce. I do not believe him a bad man, although much has been said against him; but he has nothing to recommend him to that station. Since his election to this time, now 1813, he has never been in the city.

When the Legislature met, Mr. Dorsey of the Senate wrote to beg I would come up to Lancaster, and speak to the Governor about renewing my commission. He said the Governor spoke of me in the most favorable terms. I informed him it would be inconvenient and, in my opinion, useless, to see Mr. Snyder. He then wished me to send up one of my sons, but as this was equally disagreeable, it was declined. The Governor in appointing a person in my room as Prothonotary, gave as a reason that there ought to be frequent changes in a Republican government, that although no fault whatever could be found with me, I had held the office for many years. Long before this, I wished to resign the office, but as there were fees due to me to a large amount, I wished to have a successor who would collect them for me, and not keep them himself. The tax on the office had made it of little value. The first notice I had of my removal, was seeing a notice in the Democratic Press, that Frederick Wolbert

was appointed Prothonotary for the county of Philadelphia.
The next day Mr. Wolbert called upon me. He declared he
never made any application for the office, how much he respected and esteemed me, and that he would agree to any
arrangement I pleased to make. As he was a man who I
thought would take some pains to collect my fees, his appointment was not disagreeable to me; but no man that is in
embarrassed circumstances should be appointed to an office
where he is to receive public money. Mr. Wolbert was soon
obliged to resign, or was dismissed for not settling his
accounts. The last ten months that I was in office, I
paid in over three thousand dollars, as will be seen by the
treasury accounts.

It was early in this year that Mr. Sloan, of Jersey, made a
motion for a removal of the seat of government from Washington to Philadelphia, and it had nearly carried. I was
always of opinion that Trenton would have been a much
better place than either Washington or Philadelphia. It is
situated between Philadelphia and New York, in a fine,
pleasant, healthy country. Washington, notwithstanding all
that can be said in favor of it, I believe would never have
been thought of for the seat of government, but for the good
and great man it is called after. Madame Pechon, wife of
Mr. Pechon, Chargé d'Affaires of France, told me that when
she first went to Washington, it was late in the night, the
roads excessively bad, and very dark before they got there.
Some time before they reached the tavern, she called to the
coachman, "How long before you get to Washington?"
"Why, madame," says the fellow, "you have been in Washington this hour." She had not seen a house.

In the beginning of December of this year, in walking
from the Coffee House, the conversation turned upon the
advantage it would be to the country, if we could get an
office established for the insurance of lives, granting annuities, reversions, etc. We met the next day and agreed to
call a meeting of some of our friends and acquaintances,
which we did that evening. Messrs. Paul Beck, Edward
Burd, S. Meeker, W. Gaw, A. Denman, M. Levy, David

Lewis, Robert Waln, E. Kane, Henry Pratt, William Poyntell, and myself agreed to be managers. We opened a subscription a few days afterwards for a capital of half a million of dollars. As the citizens had confidence in the managers, it was filled immediately, and a much larger sum could have been obtained. Such a number came forward to subscribe that we were obliged to limit the number of shares each person should have. It was with difficulty we could keep the crowd off. We sent two gentlemen up to Lancaster to get an act of incorporation. The Legislature would have passed the act we wanted, but another company being formed, the members of the Legislature supposed it would be very profitable, and postponed the bill until the next session. As we only wanted to see such a company formed, and as the others applied, we gave ourselves no further concern about the bill. One of the gentlemen who went up said that during the debate on the bill, one of the German members spoke against it. "Mr. Speaker, I am against dis bill, and I will tell you for what. If you bass dis bill, old McKean* will get his life insured, and so we shall never get rid of him." This was not to be got over. At the next session the bill of the other company was lost by a small majority. The session afterwards, they obtained an act but with many alterations made by persons totally unacquainted with the business.

In May, 1810, Mrs. Spaight, the widow of Governor Spaight, who came from North Carolina the summer of 1809, sent for me to consult with me about her children, two sons and a daughter. When I waited upon her she complained of a cold and a slight pain in her breast; she spoke cheerfully, and I did not suppose her by any means dangerously ill. After some conversation about the children, I left her. Two days after, the person she lodged with sent me word she was dead. She was a most amiable woman, and a few years before her death one of the most lovely of her sex; but from the time of the death of the Governor until her own she was very seldom out of her room, and she kept her

---

* Then Governor of the State.

children constantly with her, never letting them go outside of the door. Had she lived a few years longer, she would have destroyed their constitutions. When they were left to my care, I had them taken out every day when the weather would permit it, and sent a few miles from the city in a healthy part of the country, and they are now fine, hearty children. Their father, Governor Spaight, was killed in a duel by John Stanley, Esq., since that time a member of Congress. The Governor, as well as myself, were intimate with the father of Mr. Stanley, and had often been at the house together when the son was a child. The duel was occasioned by some good-natured friends carrying tales from one to the other. The duel would have terminated without injury to either party, but for a scoundrel that was second to the Governor. They fought on the Common, near Newbern, and great numbers of the inhabitants were looking on. Some of them would have interfered, but this rascal of a second swore he would shoot any man who attempted to do so. They fired five shots before Mr. Stanley's took effect. The Governor some years before this fatal duel had been extremely ill, so much so that he was reduced to a skeleton, and as helpless as a child of a month old. The first physicians on the continent were consulted, but they could do nothing for him, and gave him up as incurable. Some person recommended him to apply to Mrs. Bran, a woman well known at that time in the city, as is her daughter Patty now (1813). Mrs. Bran made a perfect cure of him, and for some years before his death he was as hearty a man as any in the world. He was broken out in sores all over his face, all his limbs and body, so that from being a handsome, he was a most miserable object. I believe it was with malt tea she made the cure.

A short time before the election this year a committee of the City Conference called on me to know if I would consent to be run as State Senator. They were pleased to say they could carry me, and that they did not know any other Federalist they could get elected. I told them there were other gentlemen who would command as many, and perhaps more votes than myself, and, if elected, it would be disagreeable to me to spend the winter at Lancaster; I must, therefore, request they would place some other person on the ticket. Going soon afterwards a journey in the country, I was surprised upon my return to find my name on the ticket to be run as Senator. Mrs. Biddle advised my sending to the Committee to request they would put some other person on the ticket in my room, but, as I had no expectation whatever of being elected, I declined it. To my surprise the ticket was carried by some hundreds. My son Nicholas was at the same time elected a member of the House of Representatives. Mr. B—— and some of my Democratic acquaintances said it was they who occasioned my being elected. I thought that its being known that I was opposed to the Mechanics and Commercial banks, then applying for charters, would have prevented my election. Enos Clark, an honest Irish tenant of mine, called on me the morning of the election in much distress. He said just as he was putting in his ticket, one of his friends called to him to come down; that he put in the ticket and came to him, when he said: "Clark, do you know what you have been doing?" "Yes, to be sure, I have been putting in the ticket that D. S—— gave me, and he, you know, is one of us." "Damn you; do you know you have been voting against your landlord, who has been so kind, and so good to your family?" "I hope it is not so, Mr. Biddle, for I would not do that for all the world." I comforted this good fellow by assuring him that on this occasion I did not want his vote.

At the opening of the session I went to Lancaster with Mr. Barclay, of the Senate, and Messrs. Morgan and McEuen, of the House of Representatives. We agreed to lodge at Slough's,* who we knew kept an excellent house, and we

---

* When Judge Jones and myself were going to the Virginia Springs, just before we reached Lancaster we overtook Mr. Edward Badger, a young lawyer of Philadelphia. He was talking to a countryman. When he joined us at the tavern he told us he had a curious conversation with the farmer, who inquired where he intended to put up in Lancaster. Badger told him he did not know, he was a stranger. Well, says the farmer, come with me to Adam Weaver's, he keeps a very good house. Badger told him he heard Mr.

could not possibly have been better accommodated than at this house. Mr. Slough had been a captain in the army under General St. Clair, and was shot through the body at the time the General was defeated by the Indians. Notwithstanding this he was remarkably strong and active, and very attentive to his guests.

The most important business that was before the Legislature this session was the application of the Trustees of the Bank of the United States for a charter. This they did after Congress had refused to renew their charter. Although I had some doubt whether giving them a charter would not be a disadvantage to the Bank of Pennsylvania, of which I was, and had been ever since it was first instituted, a director, I thought it would be of advantage to the State, and, therefore, voted, and used what interest I had for it. My son in the House of Representatives made a speech in favor of it that was much admired. But there was a majority of both Houses who were informed that the shares were held by foreigners, and who thought the shares should be held by our own citizens. The refusing to grant the charter I considered as a loss to the State of the sum the trustees would have given, which was six hundred thousand dollars. Mr. Girard bought the banking house, which he has opened on his own account. Our Government acted a shameful part in selling out the shares belonging to the United States at an advance of forty-five per cent. shortly before the charter expired, and then refusing to renew it.

One evening during this session, Mr. Barclay, Senator from the county of Philadelphia, sent over to Slough's to request I would come to the House immediately, as the question was about being taken on a bill he was very anxious should pass. I went over with the doorkeeper, and took with me Mr. Brady, a member of the Senate, who happened to be at

Slough kept a very good house. "Oh yes, be sure, Slough he keeps a good house, but that won't do for you and me, for none but gentlemen go there." Badger had on a short jacket, which he declared he would never ride in again.—AUTHOR'S NOTE.

Slough's. When we went into the Senate I offered a new section to the bill, which Mr. Barclay opposing, Brady and myself voted against his bill. Had he not sent for us he would have carried his bill.

At the end of this session I intended to resign my seat, but some of my friends, having business in the Legislature, begged me to serve the next session, but it was with much reluctance that I consented. My son Nicholas being engaged to be married, refused standing a candidate for the House of Representatives. In October he was happily married.* Charles had married a few years before equally to my satisfaction.†

At the anniversary meeting of the Cincinnati this year, 1811, I offered the following resolution, which was unanimously adopted:—

Resolved, That a committee of this society be appointed to prepare a plan for raising by subscription such a sum of money as they shall deem sufficient for erecting a monument to the memory of the late Father of his Country, General George Washington. That the plan, when prepared, shall be submitted to the standing committee, and when approved by them, shall be carried into effect. That —— —— be a committee for the above purpose.

The blank was afterwards filled up with the names of Major Lenox, Judge Peters, Major Jackson, Mr. Biddle, and Mr. Binney.

The committee agreed to the following address and plan:—

To the People of Pennsylvania.
    Friends, Countrymen, and Fellow-citizens.

Under a deep and heartfelt impression of its propriety, and as the most grateful subject that could engage their attention, the preceding resolution was unanimously adopted by the Pennsylvania State Society of the Cincinnati. As a portion of the surviving military associates of the immortal

---

* To Miss Jane M. Craig, daughter of Mr. John Craig.
† To Miss Ann H. Stokes, daughter of Mr. James Stokes.

Washington, they believed they should render an acceptable service to their fellow-citizens by becoming the organs of their wish to consecrate the memory of the patriot, hero, and statesman, who was not only the boast and delight of our nation, but an object of veneration to all mankind.

As the committee appointed to carry the resolution of the society into effect, it is our pleasing duty at this time to address you, and as no argument could be adduced to increase the influence which expands every American heart with gratitude, love, and reverence for the great Father of our Country, we beg leave to submit to your consideration the annexed plan for erecting a monument to perpetuate the remembrance of his glorious achievements, and to transmit to posterity the grateful expression of a people's love.

(Signed)   DAVID LENOX,
RICHARD PETERS,
WILLIAM JACKSON,
CHARLES BIDDLE,
HORACE BINNEY.

Plan.

First. In order to make the proposed monument a peculiar testimony of the veneration in which our immortal patriot is held by the citizens of the Commonwealth, it is the intention of the Cincinnati not to solicit contributions from persons who do not reside in Pennsylvania, but to make application to citizens of this State as particularly as possible, and to give to every one an opportunity within his own county of offering his donation to persons acting under the appointment of the society; with this view books will be sent to two or more persons in each organized county in the State with a request that they will receive subscriptions for the object. Similar books will be committed with a like request to several of the citizens of Philadelphia, and after the books are closed, which will be on the fifth of July, 1812, they will be deposited among the archives of the society, as a perpetual memorial of such of the citizens of this State as had virtue to honor the illustrious character of General Washington, and gratitude to consecrate a portion of their means to this lasting commemoration of his services.

Second. Subscribers under twenty dollars will pay their subscriptions at the time they are made; for, or above that sum, they may pay it when it is made, or when they shall afterwards be called upon for that purpose.

Third. All moneys received will be forwarded or handed over to Charles Biddle, Esq., Treasurer of the Cincinnati of Pennsylvania, and by him be deposited in one of the banks of the city of Philadelphia, subject only to the draft of a majority of the committee.

Fourth. As soon as the books are closed and the amount of subscriptions ascertained, the committee will proceed with the utmost promptitude to carry the resolution into effect. The splendor of the monument must depend essentially upon the extent of the subscriptions. But the committee have no doubt that neither the affection nor the pride of Pennsylvania will be satisfied with any memorial which shall not be worthy, in some small degree, of the hero it is to commemorate.

When the books were ready Majors Lenox and Jackson, and myself went to every ward in the city, and engaged eight gentlemen in each ward to go round their wards and obtain subscriptions. We also procured twenty-four gentlemen in Southwark, and as many in the Northern Liberties for the collection in their districts, and we forwarded books to the several counties in the State. In order to prevent it being considered a party affair we chose gentlemen of each party to collect subscriptions. To forward the business my son Nicholas delivered an oration, which was much admired.*

At the commencement of the session I attended the Legislature at Lancaster. The trustees of the Bank of the United States again endeavored to procure a charter from the State, but in vain; the real or pretended fear of British influence prevented anything being done. Had the charter been granted, it would have been of great advantage in improving the State,

---

* The monument is at this time (1883) being cast in Germany, and is to be placed in Fairmount Park.

and it would have prevented the Legislature from chartering such a number of banks as they have since done.

Some violent resolutions were brought forward by Mr. Gemmil in the Senate, and adopted by both Houses of the Legislature. The Federalists wanted to have France, who in my opinion behaved much worse than the British, included in the resolutions, but they could not. I believe these resolutions occasioned the war, as our Senators at Washington would not have voted for it but for them. Mr. Gemmil, who introduced them into the Senate, was a clergyman from Chester County, a man of talents and highly respectable, but a most bitter enemy to the British Government. I believe he imbibed these prejudices from some renegade Englishmen, who spoke of their administration as the most corrupt upon earth. I always found those wretches more violent against their country than any American.

At the end of the session when I returned to the city, it was the general opinion we should not have a war. I, however, thought otherwise, for it was pretty certain if we did not, that the present administration would be turned out. Mr. Madison, I believe, did not wish for war, but he wanted firmness to oppose such men as Giles, Williams, Clay, and a few others, who supposed they could soon bring Great Britain to their own terms. Mr. Porter, a member of Congress from the neighborhood of Canada, declared we had nothing to do but send a few men there and erect a standard, and the whole country would join us. The probability of a war induced my son Thomas to solicit me to permit him to join the army. This I reluctantly consented to, and he obtained a captain's commission in Colonel Pike's regiment. Colonel Izard soon after wishing him in his regiment, and Thomas consenting, he was transferred from the infantry to the artillery. As soon as war was declared my son John told me he must go in the army. I was much more averse to his going than to his brother Thomas, as his temper was too warm, and I knew he frequently took offence when none was intended. He appeared, however, so unhappy that I was obliged to consent, and his brother Nicholas writing to Mr. Monroe, he had a commission sent him of second lieutenant in the Third Regiment of Artillery, commanded by Colonel McComb. James not being attached to any ship, went to New York to offer his services as a volunteer with Commodore Rodgers. He, however, notwithstanding his utmost exertions, and no person could have made more, did not arrive in New York until Rodgers had got to Sandy Hook. He hired a boat but could not get on board.

In the unprepared state of our country I was much opposed to the war, and I was of opinion that although we had cause of complaint against Great Britain we had much more against France.

As parties ran high I expected we should have some disturbances, and therefore wished to see the citizens above the age of forty-five associated in order to preserve the peace of the city. I had spoken to some gentlemen on this subject, when I observed in one of the Democratic papers a meeting called at Oellers's tavern, next door to me. As the notice was general for all those above the age prescribed for military duty, I went there. The room was full; all of them were our warmest Democrats. Among them were Messrs. Matlack, Barker, Mayor of the city, Leiper, Patterson, Smily, Brown, etc. As I was well acquainted with these citizens they all expressed themselves glad to see me. Soon after my entrance it was proposed having the meeting organized. I was unanimously called to the chair, and George A. Baker, Esq., appointed Secretary. As soon as I mentioned that we were ready for business, and requested whoever had given the notice to come forward with his plan for an association, immediately a little, dark-looking foreigner came forward, and, with much ceremony, handed me a paper which he begged should be read. It began :—

"Whereas, our beloved country being involved in a war with the most cruel enemy upon earth, and, whereas, we have a great many traitors among us, Therefore Resolved." Here followed a number of violent resolutions against what he called the friends of Great Britain. It provoked me to hear a fellow lately come among us talk of our " beloved country."

After reading them myself I put them in my pocket, telling him, with a look of contempt, that it was not the intention of the meeting to enter into such resolutions, but for the purpose of associating to preserve the peace of the city, or defending it in case of attack. He appeared much mortified, but retired without saying anything. If I had not been at the meeting it is probable these resolutions would have been carried unanimously. This man's name was Puglia; I believe he belonged to the Board of Health. After some time it was observed that a meeting to form an association was to be held at the Indian King in a few days, and we adjourned to meet there. Before this meeting took place I prepared some resolutions which I knew could, by my speaking to a few of the members, be easily carried. We met at the Indian King on the first of July; there were present a great many respectable citizens of both parties, and there were some that did no credit to the party they belonged to; amongst these was Mr. Puglia. At this meeting I was called to the chair, which as soon as I had taken Mr. Huston, a stout man, whom Puglia had offended at Oellers's, came up to me, and asked me if I would allow him to kick Puglia out of the room. It was with some difficulty I could persuade him to let him alone, that he was not worth his notice. We passed the following resolutions unanimously:—

Resolved, That in the present interesting situation of our country it is the duty of every man to contribute by all the means in his power to promote the public welfare; that an association of the citizens of Philadelphia, the Northern Liberties, and Southwark, above the age prescribed by law for the performance of militia duty, to aid the civil authority in the preservation of domestic order and tranquillity, and for the defence of the City and Liberties in the absence of the younger citizens, would be highly expedient.

Resolved, That the members of this meeting hereby agree to form an association for said purpose, and that the following persons be a committee to prepare a plan for organizing this Association, viz., Charles Biddle, Chairman; for the City, John Miller, Alex. Cook, George A. Baker, John Barker,

22

Wm. Wray, Paul Beck, B. McMahon, R. Patterson, Wm. Smiley, Conrad Hance, Levi Hollingsworth, J. E. Smith, Captain Wm. Jones, and John Douglass. We also appointed seven from the Northern Liberties, and as many from Southwark. We passed other resolutions that when the Committee were ready to report they should call a meeting at the State House. After several meetings we agreed upon a plan, and met at the State House to carry it into effect; but before we held this meeting there were several violent publications by the Society of American Republicans reprobating the war, and abusing the administration. This gave great offence to some of the Democrats, and we were not by any means as sociable as before. One of the Democrats proposed we should call ourselves "The Friends of Government;" one of the Federalists that we should be called "Supporters of the Law." For my own part I thought it of little consequence. We at last broke up without doing anything.

One evening in August hearing there was a mob in Dock Street going to tar and feather an Englishman for saying something against the Americans, I went there with Mr. Keppele, the Mayor. We found a great concourse of people, most of whom were for punishing the poor devil, particularly a man of the name of Alcorn, who said the fellow was an Orangeman. I inquired of the man what he had said or done. He declared that he had said nothing; that the man who occasioned his being taken up was a ladies' shoemaker, and that they had a dispute as to which was the best workman. Finding he was in liquor, we thought it best to lodge him in gaol and bind over Alcorn to keep the peace. The binding over this man, it is probable, put an end to any further disturbance during the summer. We had in the city at this time a number of vagabonds who would have been pleased to see the same proceedings here that had disgraced Baltimore the year before.

Expecting there would be some disturbance at the election, I advised Mr. Keppele, the Mayor, to hire a few men to assist the constables in keeping the peace. This he did. On the day of the election Alcorn marched up at the head of a pack of shoemakers. The Mayor met him, and there had like to have been a serious scuffle. Alcorn and his gang passed on, and after voting dispersed. In the evening seeing a number of people going into the Court House, where I knew Mr. Keppele then was, and apprehending some disturbance, I went over. When within the door, seeing Captain Sprogel and a few others who could be depended on, I desired they would prevent any more from entering; this with great difficulty they did. About nine o'clock the crowd about the door had increased very much, and they were very clamorous. One man whose name was Reynolds, who from his size was called Big Ben, was let into the room where the Mayor, Mr. Wharton, and a few others of us were assembled. He told us that he was as desirous to have the election conducted in a peaceable manner as any man in the city, that if the Mayor and Mr. Wharton would go home he would pledge himself that the people at the door should disperse, and no injury be done; but if they did not go home he believed both their houses would be pulled down, and then addressing me, he said, " And the people are very much displeased with you, Mr. Biddle, for they think the Mayor is directed altogether by you." I told him that as to what the people, as he called the mob at the door, thought, it was a matter of perfect indifference to me; and inquired if the people at the door, without Mr. Keppele and Mr. Wharton going home, could not be dispersed. He said he believed not. " And what do you intend to do?" " To stand by the people." " What, whether they are right or wrong?" He answered, yes. I then gave it as my opinion that it would be both dangerous and disgraceful for the Mayor to go home, or any of those with him, and requested Reynolds to retire, which he immediately did. I now thought of poor Lingan murdered at Baltimore.* Mr. Wharton told me afterwards that he was also thinking of the massacre at Baltimore, and he thought it probable if the villains at the door broke

---

* In the political riots in Baltimore, in 1812, General Lingan was killed, and General Lee, Light Horse Harry Lee of the Revolution, was crippled for life.

in, we should be treated as bad as those in gaol were at that place. At this time Captain Morrel came to me and said, " Mr. Biddle, only give the word, and Captain Ross, Cadwalader, and some others of the Light Horse are ready, and will be here in a few minutes and disperse these fellows. I was much pleased to hear this, but wishing to prevent the effusion of blood, and believing we could keep the door from being forced, I thought it best for them to remain ready to act. I was sorry afterwards we had not directed the horse to gallop to the door, and halt before it, to see the rascals run. We all went quietly home about eleven o'clock. The Democrats carried the election by a large majority, which I believe was in a great measure owing to the Federalists leaving the ground at an early hour, and this has frequently occasioned the loss of the election.

The President of the United States this year appointed me one of the Commissioners for signing the Treasury Notes. When Mr. Smith, the Cashier of the Bank of Pennsylvania, mentioned this to me, I told him there must be some mistake. He, however, answered me that it was so. This was a business I did not want to have anything to do with ; however, having three sons in the service, I thought the refusing to sign the notes would appear as if I was unfriendly to the administration. This induced me to sign them. Before signing them, I did not suppose I could have written my name so often in a day. Some days I signed fourteen hundred ; and one day eighteen hundred.

At the time I was preparing to set off for the Legislature I was informed that there was a memorial sent to the Speaker of the Senate, requesting that an inquiry should be made whether my signing these notes did not vacate my seat as a Senator. Upon conversing with some of my friends on this subject, I found they differed in opinion. Mr. Ingersoll, the Attorney-General, when I first spoke to him, laughed at it ; but he afterwards thought it was such an appointment as did vacate the seat. His altering his opinion it was thought by some gentlemen was owing to his conversing with his son Charles about it. As Charles was a Democrat, perhaps he was consulted before the memorial was signed. I do not mean any reflection on Mr. Ingersoll, who is a worthy and highly respectable man. I waited in the city until the Legislature adjourned for the holidays. An influential member told a friend of mine that it was not worth while for me to go up, for he knew there was a large majority in the Senate who considered signing the notes as vacating the seat, and who would vote accordingly; and that he was very sorry it was so. Notwithstanding this, the wishes of my family, and my not caring how the Senate should vote, I considered it my duty to go up to prevent this being brought into a precedent. I therefore sat off one of the coldest days we had in January. When we reached Downingtown a gentleman from Harrisburg handed me a letter from Mr. Lane, the Speaker of the Senate, informing me that the Committee had reported the seat vacated. Notwithstanding this I was determined to proceed. When the sleigh was about a mile from Downingtown, Mr. Morgan, a friend of mine, going to put on his gloves, found he had left them at the tavern. I laughed at him, and observed he must be a very thoughtless fellow to leave his gloves such an extra cold day. As my ears at this time felt very cold I went to put my great coat round them, when I found it was also left at the tavern. Upon my arrival at Harrisburg I went immediately to the Senate and soon found my seat would not be considered as vacated, a large majority coming round me and expressing their satisfaction at my appearance amongst them. The report of the Committee was taken up a few days after my being in the Senate. On this occasion Mr. Gemmil made a speech that affected the audience very much. After expressing his opinion very fully upon my right to retain the seat, he spoke of my family, mentioned my three sons then in the service, of Edward whom I had lost with Commodore Truxtun, of my brother lost in the Randolph, and something flattering of me. Mr. Beale, who was in the chair, was a considerable time before he could speak. After some time Mr. Weaver answered Mr. Gemmil. He declared there was no member of the Senate had a higher opinion or greater esteem and respect than he had for Mr. Biddle, but that he was sworn to support the Constitution, and he believed the appointment given to me by the President vacated my seat. The question was then taken and decided against the report. When the Speaker resumed the chair the yeas and nays were called for on adopting the report of the Committee of the Whole, and were as follows: Yeas, Messrs. Baird, Barclay, Beale, Brady, Burnside, Erwin, Gemmil, Graham, Gross, Hamilton, Laird, Lowrie, Newbold, Roe, Rehm, Ralston, Watson, Wilson, Lane, Speaker—twenty, The Nays were Messrs. Bender, Gilliland, McFarland, Shoemaker, Smith, Stroman, Weaver, Worrel—eight. So it was determined that the seat was not vacated. The eight who voted against the vote of the Committee all came up to me after the question was taken and expressed their satisfaction at the report being adopted, and except one I believe they really were so.

I lodged this session at Harrisburg with my old friend, Captain Graydon, a gentleman who has published his memoirs, in which he has mentioned an affair that happened at the commencement of our Revolutionary war: we went out to fire at a mark, and my ball striking a child at a great distance. He also mentions the assistance I gave him in getting him appointed Prothonotary for Dauphin County.

This session the Legislature voted a sword to my son James, for his gallant conduct on board the Wasp when she captured the Frolic.

Towards the close of the session, I was anxious to have some provision made for the defence of the Delaware, and for this purpose read a bill in the Senate granting —— dollars for the defence of the bay and river Delaware. The blank for a small sum would have been readily filled, but when I moved to fill the blank with a hundred thousand dollars, most of the members thought it too high and voted against it. They would have given ten thousand dollars, but I thought it was not worth while to take so small a sum, and therefore had the bill postponed.

Soon after my return to the city, the Secretary of the Navy wrote to my son James to know if he would take command

of the flotilla fitting out for the defence of the Delaware.
James accepted the command with pleasure. This made me
more anxious than I was before to have a sufficient force to
meet any attack the British should make. A few who were
as desirous as myself to have something done, had two or
three meetings without being able to effect anything. After
the brutal conduct of the British at Havre de Grace, about
twenty of us met at the Coffee House and subscribed one
hundred dollars each. At this meeting it was the opinion
of Mr. Daniel W. Coxe and some others, that if I would take
the chair we could have committees appointed in each ward
and the Districts, and we could have a sufficient sum collected
to build what barges we should want, and some galleys that
would answer our purposes much better than Mr. Jefferson's
gun boats, which were not by any means equal to those we
had during the Revolutionary war. I took the chair, and
Mr. John Sergeant acted as secretary. At this meeting,
which was held the 6th of May, 1813, the following gentlemen were appointed a committee to assist the officers of government in building barges, and manning the flotilla, viz:
Charles Biddle, Henry Pratt, Daniel W. Coxe, Henry Hawkins, Charles McCallister, Robert Waln, Chandler Price, James
Josiah, Richard Dale, David Lenox, William McFadden,
John Connolly, Thomas W. Francis, Manuel Eyre, and Daniel Smith. Major Lenox and Mr. Smith never met the committee. We had committees appointed in each ward and
district, and had a handsome sum collected, but we found
that many of our richest citizens gave little or nothing. We
therefore presented a memorial to our City Councils, and
with some difficulty got them to agree to give us thirty
thousand dollars, upon which we determined to return the
money we had collected from our generous fellow citizens,
many of whom had paid more than they could afford. We
built six large barges, much superior to any the British had,
and a schooner. We procured some seamen from New York.
The barges and schooner went down the river about the middle of June. As these would protect the inhabitants near
the shore from the British barges, they had now no pretence

for supplying them with anything; before we could give them this protection, we had no right to complain of their connection with the enemy. After the barges got down, we heard no more of the British burning our craft coming up with wood and lumber.

About this time the Secretary of War, Armstrong, wrote General Bloomfield. that if the city would advance sixteen or twenty thousand dollars, he would build a fort at the Pea Patch. I had some time before mentioned to General Bloomfield the importance of having a strong fort at this place, believing it would forever prevent the British from making an attack upon Philadelphia, and would be a protection to New Castle and Wilmington. The Secretary mentioned further, that if we would get a cession of the soil and jurisdiction, he would return the money advanced. I thought this of so much importance, that I agreed to go with General Bloomfield to Dover, where the Legislature was in session. To them we applied, and with the assistance of Mr. George Read, we got a law passed giving the United States the soil and jurisdiction. The expectation of a peace prevented anything further being done. The Committee got the Secretary of the Navy to take the barges, schooner, etc., on account of the United States, so that the city was at very little expense and had the shallops coming up from the bay effectually protected from the enemy.

The Legislature meeting the first Tuesday in December, I sat off on Monday the 6th, and arrived there the next day. In crossing the Swatara we were very near being overset in the middle of the creek, and if we had, some of us must have perished, as it was very cold, the creek high, and the stage full, with the curtains all fastened down. We soon, however, tore the curtains loose. Expecting we should have to swim I stripped my clothes off. A boat coming to our assistance we got safely on shore. At this time they were building a bridge which was so far finished that we passed over it on our return to the city at Christmas.

At this session we passed a law for establishing a number of banks, which the members from most of the counties were anxious to have. I thought that in some of the counties banks would be useful, and would have voted for them; but this bill I thought would be injurious, and therefore voted against it. By an agreement among the members they carried it by a large majority. "Do you vote for the bank in my county, and I will vote for yours;" and this, although they must have known the bill would be against the interest of the State, by lessening the value of their stock in the other banks they had so much of their money invested in. The Governor, with great firmness, did everything in his power to prevent the bill from passing, but he could not do it. He returned the bill to the House of Representatives, where it originated, with his reasons for not signing it, but they had a majority of more than two-thirds, and soon passed it. In the Senate it had nearly been lost. Mr. Gemmil was sick in Harrisburg, and we tried to get him out, but he was too unwell to leave his room. His vote would have destroyed the bill.

Upon my arrival at Harrisburg after the holidays, I found my old acquaintance General St. Clair. He had applied to several members of the Senate from the Western counties, in one of which he resided, to present a petition praying for an alteration in a law passed in his favor. But the General was unpopular in those counties ever since his defeat by the Indians, and he could get none of the members to present his petition. When this was told to me I called on him, received his petition, and presented it, and upon my application to the Committee, got them to report a bill in his favor. Some of his friends and myself had a good deal of difficulty in getting the bill passed the House of Representatives. It was, however, done, and the General went home in high spirits. He had served his country faithfully in the field, and as Speaker of the House of Representatives of the United States, but was now so much reduced as to live in a miserable hut on the Allegheny, where, it is said, he sold whisky and entertained foot travellers with lodging. He was now upwards of eighty years of age.

James O'Hara, an old Revolutionary soldier who had been

applying in vain to Congress for a pension, begged me to try if he could not be put on the State pension list, but as he belonged to Hazen's regiment there was some doubt about his being entitled to anything from the State of Pennsylvania. I presented his petition and had it referred to a committee who reported a bill in his favor. Upon reading the bill a second time, I mentioned that I had known O'Hara for a great number of years, that he was a quiet orderly man, and was old and infirm. Mr. Barclay, who sat near me, said in a low voice, "O'Hara lives near me in the Northern Liberties. He is a noisy vagabond." Mr. Watson, a member from Lancaster, got up immediately, and observed, "There must be some mistake about this O'Hara. The gentleman from the city says he is a quiet, orderly man. The gentleman from the county, who lives in the Northern Liberties near one James O'Hara, says he is a noisy, worthless vagabond. They cannot mean the same man. We had better postpone the bill generally." While Mr. Watson was speaking, General Baird, who was anxious that O'Hara should get the pension, came round to me, and begged me to have the bill postponed for the present, until we could speak to Watson. I told him to make himself easy, as Watson should soon be satisfied. When he sat down I told the House that Mr. Barclay and myself did mean the same person; that O'Hara differed from us in politics; that I never heard him noisy except when ringing his bell, which was often the case, as he was crier to the constable's vendue; or at the time of an election, when he made a good deal of noise by huzzaing for Jefferson, or Madison, or Snyder, or some of the party. When he saw me he would change his note, and huzza for General Washington; but at all other times he was a quiet, orderly man. Mr. Barclay saying he seldom saw him but at the time of elections, and that he could not doubt anything I said about him, the bill passed immediately.

At the end of the session I returned with much pleasure to the city, being determined never to suffer my name to be put up as a candidate for any office that could occasion my going to Harrisburg; not that I had any complaint to make of the place, for it is a handsome village, and will, I have no doubt, in time be an important place. But it was very disagreeable for me to leave my family for so long a time as it was necessary for me to be from home. During the four years I served in the Senate in Lancaster and Harrisburg, I never was absent at any meeting of the Senate when I was at the seat of government, which was nearly all the time the House sat. If they met two or three times in the twenty-four hours, I always attended, which I do not believe any other but myself did.

It was about the last of March when I returned home. My son Thomas was then about marching for Canada with a very fine company, and John was soon afterwards ordered to join his regiment on Long Island.

The latter end of June Mrs. Biddle, our two daughters, and myself set off for New London. We lodged the first night at Bristol, the second at Brunswick, and arrived the next day by twelve o'clock at New York. I had heard much said in favor of the steamboat plying between New York and Paulus Hook, but I did not expect to find it such an excellent mode of conveyance across the river as we found it to be. Having several times crossed in the ferry-boats I was sensible of the great advantage of the steamboat. It is much better than a bridge, for you are as safe, and you enjoy a fine prospect while crossing.

During our stay we lodged in Broad Street at the house of Mrs. Wilkinson, an amiable lady, whose situation in the early part of her life had given her reason to believe she should never be under the necessity of keeping a boarding-house.

I was acquainted with some of the most respectable people in New York, and had letters of introduction to Governor Tompkins, Mr. Clinton, the Mayor, and many others; but the first person I inquired for, and went to see, was my unfortunate friend, Colonel Burr. He lived in a small house in Wall Street. He was much affected at seeing me, and I was not a little so at seeing him. How different was his situation when I was at New York in 1800! He was then surrounded by a number of persons who called themselves his friends, and who were with him to concert measures for procuring his election as Vice-President, and was on good terms with General Hamilton and most of the leading Federalists. I know no man whose prospects at that time were more flattering than those of Colonel Burr. I had been informed that he was very much altered, that he appeared much older than he was, and his spirits broken by his misfortunes. The scenes he had gone through were enough to break down any man. He, however, did not appear to me or my family much altered. He called several times at my lodgings to see me, and was at times as cheerful as usual, but the loss of his amiable daughter, Mrs. Alston, and his grandson had weaned him from the world, and it was a matter of perfect indifference to him when he left it. I was sorry to find that some of his old friends did not visit him. Men that are unfortunate are often neglected.

We left New York on Saturday, the 2d of July. We were informed that if we attempted to travel the next day we should be fined and stopped at the first town we came to. Being determined to travel we rode on to Fairfield, breakfasted, and proceeded. When within four miles of New Haven a man on horseback rode up to the carriage, and, in a loud voice, demanded the occasion of our travelling on that day. Mrs. Biddle being unwell, and having her great coat on, I told him we had a sick lady in the carriage. He bowed, said travelling on that day was contrary to law, and rode off without saying anything more. We proceeded to New Haven without any further interruption, and stopped at Ogden's, one of the best houses of entertainment on the continent. The next day being the 4th of July we were awakened by the firing of cannon. Our landlord, who was much opposed to the war, did not like this rejoicing. After breakfast we proceeded on our journey; we stopped at Guilford, and intended to dine there, but we found the tavern full of people, and nothing to be had without waiting a considerable time. An oration was to be delivered by a Mr. Tod at twelve o'clock, which we had some thoughts of staying to hear, but

were apprehensive of being detained too long. The militia
made a handsome appearance, but their music was more
adapted to a country tavern than to a company of soldiers.
It consisted of fiddles and some wind instruments. The tune
they marched to must have been excellent, for it set us all a
laughing. The citizens, who marched in the rear of the
militia, were well clothed and very orderly. We proceeded
that evening to Pratt's at Saybury. This is a good house,
but not equal to Ogden's.

In the morning we crossed the ferry, which was such a one
as I had never seen before. The flat our carriage was put in
was towed across the river by a sail-boat lashed alongside of
her. We had a fair wind, and, as it blew fresh, we soon
crossed. In a calm or head wind it must be a very tedious
matter. Three miles from New London we met James and
his purser in a gig.* James got into the carriage, and Mr.
Zantzinger and myself drove off in the gig to bespeak dinner.
After having dined we went in the Hornet's gig up the river.
Being late we passed the U. S. Ships Macedonian and Hornet
without going on board, and landed about half a mile from Nor-
wich, at a most delightful place that James had taken for us.
After remaining a week at this place, during which time we
frequently went on board the Hornet, which was well manned

---

* The Hornet, Captain Biddle, with the Macedonian and United States,
all under command of Commodore Decatur, were at this time blockaded
by a large British force. The officers were, of course, greatly chagrined
that they were prevented from seeking fresh laurels on the ocean, but that
they managed to keep up their spirits may appear from the following incident. Alderman Binns, of Philadelphia, was deputed to present to Captains
Decatur and Biddle the swords which had been voted by the Legislature of
Pennsylvania. Decatur, not being a ready writer, was quite uneasy as to
the set reply which he ought to make, and showed to Biddle the result of his
cogitations, asking his opinion of it. The speech was approved, perhaps
with amendments. When the time came for the formal presentation, the
junior officer of the two, according to rule, was to make the first reply to
Binns's oration. To Decatur's dismay, Biddle responded by repeating,
word for word, the speech which had been submitted for his criticism, and
which a quick memory had enabled him to retain. The joke gave no offence,
and all went off in great good humor.

and in excellent order, we proceeded by Hartford for New York. While at New York I went with General Williams[*] to visit Castle Williams and the other fortifications in the harbor. In viewing the castle I unfortunately mentioned that in my opinion the embrasures were not of sufficient width. My good friend Williams took up so much time to convince me of my mistake that we were detained until the middle of an excessively hot day.

A day or two after this I received a letter informing me of the death of my much lamented friend and relation, Colonel Clement Biddle, one of the best of men.[†] General Washington, with whom he corresponded until the General died, always expressed the highest esteem and regard for him. We set off a day or two afterwards, and reached Philadelphia in two days, being just three weeks on our journey.

At this time the enemy were in the Chesapeake, robbing and plundering the defenceless inhabitants. In August they destroyed Washington. Had an able officer commanded there this would not have happened. General Winder, who commanded, was much esteemed, but he had very little experience, and had too many to advise with, and unfortunately an opinion prevailed that the British would never attempt to make an attack upon Washington. Mr. Secretary Jones has been much blamed for burning the vessels in the navy yards. He expected the British would burn them, to prevent which he had them burned himself; in doing this he was certainly wrong. He was accused of cowardice, but I have reason to believe him to be a brave man. It is much easier to find out after an affair of this kind has happened what should have been done than before.

The burning of the capitol roused the people everywhere. In Philadelphia a meeting of the city and adjoining districts, agreeably to public notice, convened the 26th of August in the State House yard. There was a very large and respectable meeting. Thomas McKean was appointed President, and Joseph Reed, Secretary. Messrs. J. Ingersoll, C. Biddle,

* General Jonathan Williams.   † See note H.

J. Sergeant, John Goodman, Robt. McMullen, T. Leiper, and John Barker were appointed to consider what measures were necessary for protection and defence. They reported the following resolutions, which were unanimously adopted:—

Resolved, That Charles Biddle, Thomas Leiper, Thomas Cadwalader, James Steele, George Latimer, John Barker, Henry Hawkins, Liberty Brown, Charles Ross, Manuel Eyre, John Connolly, Condy Raguet, William McFaden, John Sergeant, John Geyer, and Joseph Reed, for the city of Philadelphia; and Jon. Williams, John Goodman, Dan. Groves, John Barclay, John Naglee, Thomas Snyder, I. W. Norris, Michael Leib, Jacob Huff, and James Whitehead, for the Northern Liberties; and James Josiah, R. McMullen, Jos. Thompson, E. Ferguson, Jas. Ronaldson, P. Minken, R. Palmer, P. Peltz, for Southwark, etc., be a committee for organizing the citizens of Philadelphia and the districts for defence, with power to appoint committees under them; to correspond with the governments of the Union and the State; to receive the offers of service from our fellow-citizens in other parts of the State and Union; to make arrangements for supplies of arms, ammunition, and provisions, places of rendezvous, and signal of alarm; and to do all such matters as may be necessary for the purpose of defence.

Resolved, That the committee be authorized to make such applications as they may deem necessary for the purpose of procuring an adequate disbursement of the funds provided by the Commonwealth for military purposes.

Resolved, That the committee be authorized to call upon the City Councils, and upon the corporations in the Northern and Southern Districts in the name of the citizens, to make such appropriations as may be necessary for the purposes aforesaid.

Resolved, That the committee be authorized and requested to make provision for the families of such of the drafted militia and volunteers, as during their absence in service may be in want of assistance.

(Signed)   THOMAS McKEAN;
Chairman.

JOS. REED, *Sec'y.*

The next day twenty-seven of the committee met, and chose me as their chairman, and J. Goodman, secretary. Two of the committee, Messrs. Barclay and Norris, never attended, and several of them but seldom. The city and districts put into our hands four hundred and twenty-five thousand dollars, and many of the citizens subscribed handsomely for the relief of the volunteers and militia, but many of our richest citizens gave nothing. We appointed different committees, and did everything that we possibly could to put the city in a state of defence. All the best young men in the city and districts turned out cheerfully, and were provided in the best manner we could. Our Governor for the first time since his election visited the city, but his presence was of no service. The day of the election he was grossly insulted. This I was very sorry for, believing him to be an inoffensive man.

The account of the death of General Ross* was received in the city with much satisfaction. It is to be lamented that such a man should have fallen in such a cause. It is said that two lads had straggled from the camp, and seeing some British officers standing under a tree, they concealed themselves among some bushes, and advanced towards them. When getting near, one of them observed to the other, "That man," pointing to General Ross, "is a general." "Why do you think so?" "Because all the officers, as they come up, salute him; and I will have a crack at him." He fired and killed him.

November 10, 1815. Walking with Mrs. Biddle this afternoon, we were stopped by a man I did not recollect to have ever seen before. After looking very earnestly, he very civilly inquired if my name was Biddle. Having answered him, "Captain Biddle, I presume." "Yes." "My name, sir, is Gilbert, I am a potter." It struck me immediately he was the son of the man Captain Graydon or myself had hit when practising with our pistols in 1776; or that perhaps, he was the person. I told him if he had anything to say to

---

* In the attack on Baltimore.

me, to call at my house. He made a low bow, and said he would.

The year I moved to Philadelphia from Reading, I became a member of a club that once a week dined, and spent the evening at each other's houses. The club consisted of twenty. The following gentlemen were natives of Ireland: Stephen, John, and Jasper Moylan, brothers; John and Alexander Nesbit, General Walter Stewart, Commodore John Barry, James Collins, George Campbell, Sharpe Dulany, Matthew Mease, and afterwards Michael Morgan O'Brien. They were all of them very respectable, and most of them rich. They have all of them long since retired from this (I hope) to a better world. The rest of the club were Americans, three of whom with myself are still here, July, 1816. Our Irish members generally remained longer at the table and drank more than the others, except one American; this was Major Moore, who was in the service all the war, and was an excellent officer. He would drink and eat, I believe, more than any two of the club; and this, it is probable, was the occasion of his soon following our Irish friends. The Irish are generally generous and brave. You will seldom find among them a miser or a coward; but they are thoughtless and extravagant. Most of the friendly, good fellows I have mentioned left their families in distressed circumstances.

The 8th of August I set off with Mrs. Biddle and my daughters for Schooley's Mountain. When we reached Mitchell's Bridge, which is thirty-five miles from the city, three laborers he had employed building a house broke off from work and set off on foot for Philadelphia to see the unfortunate R. Smith, condemned for the murder of Captain Carson, executed. After being a few days at Schooley's Mountain we went to Sussex Court House, and from thence to Easton. We intended to have gone from Easton to see my friend General Craig, but upon inquiry, I found he was in Easton. I requested a gentleman who was going there, to look for him, and to tell him a person at the tavern wanted to see him, and told him not to mention my name. The General was very much surprised at seeing me. He held me

23

in his arms for some minutes, and it was some time after before he could speak. He was so much agitated that I was sorry I had surprised him. He reminded me that it was just seventeen years since he left my house in the city, from which time we had not seen each other. This brave and generous man, who never could be provoked to strike a man he had a regard for, could not now, although seventy-four years of age, keep his hands off a fellow who he thought behaved like a rascal, and he was then attending the court for committing an assault upon a fellow who lived in his neighborhood.* There are few men at this time he could not beat, there are none from whom he would suffer an insult. Generals Craig and Wilkinson I was intimate with before the Revolution, as also Captain A. Graydon, who was a captain in the service when Fort Washington was taken, with Commodore Truxtun and Colonel Burr during the Revolution. All these are at this time, September, 1816, hale, hearty men; they have all been unfortunate. The sufferings of General Wilkinson and Colonel Burr are well known.

A few weeks before the general election this year I thought it would be of great service to my friend Truxtun, if he could do so, to reside upon his farm in Jersey in the summer, and in the winter in the city, and to be Deputy Sheriff. Having very little to do, and his estate not being productive, I thought he wanted some employment, and this office would employ him, and he could make more by it than would maintain his family. At this time the Deputy Sheriff, Elliot, who was a very good officer, had been agreed upon by the Federal conferees to be run as Sheriff. When I mentioned Truxtun they all agreed he deserved the office, but that he was a Jerseyman, and could not be commissioned if he had

---

* General Thomas Craig, a Revolutionary officer of great merit, entered the service as captain in 1776, and was in the Canada campaign. He was afterwards colonel of the Third Pennsylvania Regiment, and was present at the battles of Brandywine, Germantown, and Monmouth, and at Valley Forge. After the war, in 1783, he was lieutenant of Northampton County. In the next year he was Associate Judge in Montgomery County, but shortly returned to Northampton and died in 1832, aged 92 years.

a majority of votes, that it was too late to think of him, and that by running him we should get in a Democrat for a Sheriff. My opinion being otherwise I went with him all over the county, and, some other of his friends and myself using our exertions, we got him elected by a very large majority. Owing to the sureties being obliged to give a judgment bond we had much difficulty in procuring persons who would join in his bond. I offered Mr. Conrad Wile five hundred dollars to sign it, but although he wished to serve me he was afraid it would injure him in his business. We, however, afterwards obtained sureties without paying anything, twelve men of large property engaging the sureties should suffer no loss. Thinking Truxtun would have some difficulty at Harrisburg, I went there with him. Our ride to Harrisburg was a very disagreeable one; we left the city in the rain about 8 o'clock in the morning, and at seven the next morning were at Harrisburg, having stopped only about two hours in the night at Elizabethtown. At Middletown the landlord told us we would probably be overset, but that it would only be in the mud. When we arrived at Harrisburg we found there was a memorial against the election. In it they said they could prove Truxtun was a citizen of Jersey, etc. We, however, procured the commission. If Truxtun had not been run we should have had a Democrat for our Sheriff.

In October, 1817, I was foreman of the grand jury for the District Court of the United States. Among other presentments there was one against Jacques Tardy for murder. It appeared that this man, who was called Dr. Tardy, took passage in a schooner at Boston bound to Philadelphia, commanded by Captain Norton, who related that Tardy was on the wharf every day while the schooner was loading. He had with him a servant man, and requested a passage for a poor fellow, who he said, had been shipwrecked, and wanted to get to his friends in Philadelphia. The morning after they sailed Captain Norton observed something white on the sugar. Upon inquiring of the steward what it could be, he said he did not know what it was, but believed it was flour.

Norton, although he had no suspicion of its being poison, threw it overboard. The next morning after breakfast the crew and a German passenger were taken with a violent vomiting. Norton inquired of the doctor what could be the matter with them. He told him they were poisoned, but he would soon cure them. He gave to each a teaspoonful of sweet oil. Norton not finding himself relieved, spoke to the doctor who told him he must take some laudanum. Norton told him laudanum had always a bad effect upon him, and he and the crew refused to take any. The German had taken some before Norton refused to take it. About twelve o'clock Tardy came to Norton and told him the German was dead and he should be buried immediately. Norton told him they must keep him until the next morning. The doctor said if his body was kept it would infect all the crew. He then with his servant and the sailor passenger hove the remains of the poor German overboard. The captain and crew remained sick for some days, but they recovered and arrived safe. The doctor told Norton that the German, just before he died, told him that for his care and attention he should have everything he had on board. Upon this Norton let him take everything he had out of the vessel. A few days after this the doctor met a young man named Jones, whom he had formerly known in South Carolina. Upon inquiring of Jones what he was doing, he told him he had a wife and two children, was out of employment, and did not know what to do. Tardy told him he would do something for him, and desired him to call upon him the next day. When he called the doctor took him into a private room, and after telling him he must be secret as to what he was going to communicate, he told him he had taken his passage with Captain Harrison for Charleston, that when they should be at sea he intended to poison the captain and crew and take the vessel to some of the West India islands, sell the cargo and divide the proceeds; that he understood navigation well, and could take the vessel into any port. He said he had been used ill by the Americans, and would be revenged. Jones was shocked at what this man proposed. He agreed to go to Captain Harrison and engage his passage. He went to Captain Harrison and inquired if a Dr. Tardy had engaged a passage for himself and servant. Harrison replied that he had, and also wanted a passage for another person. Jones then related what had passed between the doctor and himself. They then went before the Mayor, and made oath to what they knew respecting the doctor; upon which a bill was found against him for the murder of the German. Before this he was tried for a misdemeanor in attempting to poison Captain Norton and his crew, and sentenced to hard labor for seven years. There was not a man upon the grand or traverse jury, but what believed Tardy murdered the German. The charge of Judge Washington saved him. The grand jury, among others, put the following questions: Did Tardy understand navigation? He answered that he did, he had been an old privateersman. Did he know you had a valuable cargo on board? He did, for he was on the wharf every day while the vessel was loading. Nothing of this was mentioned before the traverse jury. Judge Washington in his charge said, " What object could this man have in destroying the crew? He knew nothing of navigation; nor does it appear that he knew of her having a valuable cargo on board." What the Judge said about his not understanding navigation saved this wretch from the gallows.

January 1st, 1818. I feel perfectly well, but my sight is not as good as it has been. I can, however, write as well as ever. I never have used spectacles.

May the 12th. I went to the Court of Oyer and Terminer to get an old friend from serving on the grand jury. Upon my representation the Court excused him. I remained in court until the grand jury was called, when finding me Judge Rush called upon me and requested I would serve. Having no excuse, I served, and was appointed foreman.

June 1st. I feel perfectly well, but I know this is frequently the case with men at my time of life, just before leaving the world; and this is infinitely better than a lingering illness.

I was elected to the Cincinnati in 1789. In 1785, when

Dr. Franklin was elected President of the State of Pennsylvania, and I was elected Vice-President, we had a procession of all the members of the Legislature, public officers, etc., that went from the State House in Chestnut Street to the Market House in Second Street, where the Doctor was proclaimed President, and myself Vice-President. There was assembled an immense concourse of people in order to see the Doctor, and among others who were in the street was Baron Steuben. The Baron was to us a very valuable officer in disciplining our army. He was about fifty-five years of age, five feet five inches high, and stout made. He was in the crowd to see the procession, and pulled off his hat to the Doctor as he passed. Dr. Franklin hurt himself in taking off his hat, and remarked to me that it was very wrong to pull off your hat to any gentleman in a procession. Mr. Wolf, who was in the family of Steuben, speaks very highly of him as an officer, but thought him an unprincipled man. The Doctor was very glad when the procession was over, but made no complaints at the march we had.

In walking to the bank two or three months since with my friend Mr. Haga,* he observed to me, " You have such an iron constitution that no weather whatever seems to affect you." I believe few men ever regarded the weather less than I did, and unless it rained or snowed, however cold, I never wore a great coat, and would not then had I not thought it improper in a person of my age to be seen without one. Mr. Haga and myself were elected directors of the Bank of Pennsylvania in the year 1793. He was frequently confined with the gout.

May 10, 1819. I have now no complaint whatever, except a weakness in one of my eyes. I, however, can write now without spectacles.

I spent five weeks this summer at Schooley's Mountain. This I believe to be a very healthy spot, and if there was a good

---

* Mr. Godfrey Haga, who resided in the house known as the "Gothic Mansion," Chestnut Street above Twelfth.

house, or houses, it would be a pleasant place. Mr. Heath, the proprietor, is a worthy man, but he has not capital enough to put it in good order.

On Monday the 26th of October this year, I went to Bordentown to see the improvements made by Joseph Bonaparte, the late King of Spain. The place he resides at I frequently visited in the year 1777. Mr. J. Douglass, a friend of mine, then lived there. The place was much improved, but in my opinion it could have been made much better for less than one-half the $150,000, which Mr. Hopkinson informed me it cost the Count Survilliers, the title he has now taken. The Count is a very affable, unassuming man. I understand he does not expect any particular attention paid to him, but he is pleased when it is tendered.

Charles Biddle died April 4, 1821, at his residence No. 310 Chestnut Street (now 1108), to which he had removed in the year 1818. He was buried in Christ Church burying ground, Fifth and Arch streets, in his own family vault. His three sons, William Shepard, James, and Charles, and his daughter, Mrs. Ann Hopkinson, are also buried there. His son Nicholas lies with his wife's family in St. Peter's Churchyard. Edward was buried at sea, John at Detroit, Major Thomas Biddle at St. Louis, and Richard at Pittsburgh. His daughter, Mrs. Mary Biddle, was interred at Laurel Hill Cemetery.

NOTES.

NOTE A. (Page 1.)

WILLIAM BIDDLE, one of the early Proprietors of West Jersey, having served, it is believed, as an officer in the Parliamentary Army during the civil war, whilst still a young man had joined the Society of Friends. Shortly after the Restoration in 1660, the Quakers were subjected to violent persecution under pretence that they were aiding and abetting the schemes of the "Fifth Monarchy" men. In the "Abstract of Sufferings of Quakers, London, 1738," vol. iii. p. 269, is a "List of Persons Imprisoned by Mayor Brown," 337 in number. William Biddle is upon this list, which was of date 1660-61.

In Best's Sufferings of Quakers, vol. i. p. 366, under the year 1660, we find "In the months called December, January, and February he sent thither [to Newgate] Two Hundred and Eighty persons whose names are distinguished in the Index hereto annexed." Amongst those so "distinguished" are William Biddle, Thomas Biddle, and Esther Biddle.*

It seems probable, therefore, that he was born about A. D. 1630, or a few years prior thereto. From the minutes of Friends' meeting in Bishopsgate Street, London, it appears that he married Sarah Kemp, 12th month, 1665 (February, 1666), and that the names and dates of births of their children were as follows:—

Elizabeth, born 4th mo. 25, 1668, died in childhood.

William, born 10th mo. 4, 1669.

John, born 10th mo. 27, 1670, died in childhood.

Joseph, born 12th mo. 6, 1672, died in childhood.

Sarah, born 10th mo. 2, 1678.

At page 24 of a very rare pamphlet,† a copy of which is in the Library of

---

* Esther or Hester Biddle was one of the most zealous of the early Friends, both as writer and preacher. Quite a number of her Tracts are to be found in the Bodleian Library—"Something in Short unto the Sons and Daughters of Men as I was Moved by the Lord;" ",Wo to the Town of Cambridge;" "The Trumpet of the Lord Sounded forthe unto these Three Nations, etc." Dixon, in his "Life of Penn," says : "Hester Biddle forced her way into the presence of the grand monarch of Versailles, and commanded him in the name of God to sheathe his destroying Sword." His reference is, "Gerard Croese, 468."

† "An Abstract or Abbreviation of Some Few of the Many (Later and Former) Testimonys from the Inhabitants of New Jersey and other Eminent Persons who

Mrs. Brown Carter, Providence, Rhode Island, is given " An Abstract of a Letter from Daniel Wills to William Biddle (then living in Bishopsgate St., London) who, with his wife and family, is this present 5th month, 1681, with several servants, gone for New Jersey." This letter, dated 6th of 11th month, 1679–80 (February 6, 1680), somewhat abbreviated, and with some changes in phraseology, is copied into Smith's History of New Jersey, p. 115, with a note appended, giving the time of removal as "the summer of 1681."

In the "Records of Friends' Meeting at Burlington," begun in 1678, the name of William Biddle appears as a witness of the marriage of Thomas Barton and Ann Bourton, "the 8th day of the 4th month, 1681" (June 8, 1681).

This would indicate a removal at an earlier date than that given above.

In Hotten's List of Emigrants to America, p. 446, is found : " Barbados, Anno, 1680," "List of inhabitants in and about the Town of St. Michael's, Barbadoes," in which is the entry of " Wm. Biddle and Wife, Two Children, 1 Hired servant, 3 Slaves."

It is possible, but not probable, that this is the same person who came in the next year to New Jersey, since many of the early settlers of the Middle Colonies came hither, as we know, after a brief sojourn at some of the West India Islands.* In Philadelphia there was a Barbadoes Company before 1700, and the Barbadoes House stood at the N. W. corner of Second and Chestnut streets.

In a tract, printed at Philadelphia in 1699, by the pugnacious Governor Jennings.† "Truth Rescued, etc.," he says in reference to Billing, with whom he was now at daggers drawn (if we may so speak of quarrelsome Friends) :—

"It was his intent suddainly to come and settle the affair to thæt hearts content of all concerned ; and to back all this, a Ship was then newly arrived in which were Passengers, *William Biddle, Elias Farr, and Benjamin Scott*, with divers others, but these I mention as of most note, and intimate with Billing, who declared," etc.

The context, however, does not fix the exact date, nor has it been found possible to ascertain it with greater precision. Smith, in his History of New Jersey (p. 109) includes William Biddle in a list of persons " who arrived at Burlington about this time [1678], and a few years afterwards."

---

have wrote particularly concerning That Place." London, Printed by Thomas Milborn in the year 1681.

* In 1681, "Many families [in Barbadoes] unable to endure the rigor of his [Governor Dutlin's] administration abandoned the country and sought elsewhere an asylum from the persecution which they suffered at home."—Poyer's History, p. 116.

† Reprinted in fac-simile in 1881 by Mr. Brinton Coxe, himself a descendant of Dr. Daniel Coxe, of London, Governor of West New Jersey in 1687, and at that time the largest proprietor.

It has been mentioned above, that William Biddle, before coming to America, was residing in London. The family, however, which is identical with that of Biddulph, was originally seated in Staffordshire, whence different branches spread into Warwickshire and Gloucestershire. From the latter county came the famous Socinian divine, John Biddle, usually called "the father of English Unitarianism."

Recent researches of Mr. John Biddle-Cope, now resident in England, lead to the belief that William Biddle was himself born in Staffordshire, and removed to London, at the same time with several others of the Biddulph family, to engage in trade. Some authorities as to the *name* of Biddle will be found at the end of this note.

He was accompanied to America by his two surviving children, William and Sarah, eleven and two years of age respectively. More than five years prior to his embarkation William Biddle had, undoubtedly, along with many other Friends, seriously considered this important step, and in contemplation of it had made three purchases of proprietary interests in the province of West Jersey. His total purchases of those interests were as follows:—

1. January 23, 1676. From William Penn, Gawen Lawrie, Nicholas Lucas, and Edward Byllinge—one-half share.

2. April 1, 1677. From Thomas Hutchinson and Joseph Helmsley—one-fourth share.

3. October 29, 1678. From Nicholas Bill—one-sixth share.

4. August 8, 1684. From Joseph Helmsley—one-fourth share.

5. August 21, 1684. From Samuel Clay—one-sixth share.

6. May 20, 1686. From Thomas Hutchinson—one-fourth share.

7. November 10, 1691. From executors of Anna Salters, widow, deceased, less first dividend—one-sixth share.

By these purchases William Biddle became entitled to 42,916⅔ acres of the province. The deeds for the above purchases, and a transcript of his land account, are in the possession of his descendants.

As one of the proprietors his name is affixed to "The Concessions and Agreements of the Proprietors, Freeholders, and Inhabitants," etc. (See Appendix, "Smith's History, N. J.," page 521 and 539.)

Shortly after his arrival in West Jersey he selected a spot for his residence on the bank of the Delaware, at what is now known as Kinkora, about midway between Burlington and Bordentown, where he took up 500 acres on the mainland, and 278 acres, the area of an adjacent island, which still bears the name of Biddle's Island. To this homestead, or as he styled it "Plantation," he gave the name of "Mount Hope." It may not be amiss to state that his much esteemed friend William Penn, under erroneous impressions as to riparian rights, laid claim to a part of this island. He writes to Logan: "Tho' the channel goes between that [the island] and Pennsbury, yet it always belonged to the Indians of our tribe that lived at Sepassin, now Pennsbury. Move in it as most prudent or advisable."—Penn and Logan Correspondence, vi. p. 294.

Their respective claims were submitted to the adjudication of a committee, duly appointed according to the "discipline" or rules for the government of the Society of Friends, and by that committee the title of the island was declared to be vested in Biddle.

That he was esteemed by his fellow citizens a man of honorable principles and sound judgment may be inferred from his repeated appointment to public offices requiring such qualifications. He became a member of the Governor's Council, of the General Assembly of the Province, of the Board of Commissioners for Laying out Land, and of the Council of the Proprietors of West Jersey. These appointments were as follows:—

The Assembly of West Jersey, in the year 1682, elected him one of the ten members of the Council, one of the Justices of the Peace for Burlington County, and one of the ten Commissioners for Laying out Land (Smith's History, New Jersey, p. 152). Again, on the 15th day of the 3d mo., 1683, the Assembly re-elected him one of the Council, and one of the Commissioners for Laying out Lands. The duties of the members of Council are stated as follows:—

"The engagement and promise of the Council elected by the Assembly. We, underwritten, being elected and chosen by the general free assembly members of council, to advise and assist the governor in managing the affairs of the government, do solemnly promise, every one for himself, that we will give our diligent attendance from time to time, and him advise and assist to the best of our skill and knowledge, according to the laws, commissions, and constitution of this province; and do further promise not to reveal or disclose any secret of Council, or any business therein transacted, to the prejudice of the public" (Smith's History, New Jersey, pp. 164–165).

At a meeting of the proprietors of West Jersey, held the 14th day 12th mo., called February, 1687, it was decided to appoint eleven of their number "Commissioners and Trustees" to conduct the business of said proprietors. At this meeting he was appointed one of the Board, called the council of the proprietors who were to hold office until "the tenth day of the second month, A. D. 1688" (Smith's History, New Jersey, pp. 199–201). He was re-elected a member of this body for the ensuing year (Smith's History, pp. 203–204), and probably for many years thereafter, as in the years 1706 and 1707, he was president thereof (Smith's History, pp. 285–288). And, to end the list, we find that when the proprietors of East and West Jersey surrendered to Queen Anne their rights of governing these provinces, and Lord Cornbury, having been appointed Governor of New Jersey, convened the General Assembly at Perth Amboy, on the 10th of November, 1703, William Biddle was elected one of the ten representatives of the western division in this Assembly (Smith's History, New Jersey, p. 276).

That he was equally respected as a member of the religious society of Friends would appear from the fact that for "a considerable time" one of their meetings for worship, on the first day of the week (Sunday), was held at his residence, where also " Burlington Quarterly Meeting was held from

1682 to 1711" (Smith's Manuscript History of Pennsylvania," chapter 20, in Library of Historical Society of Pennsylvania; Hazard's Register, vol. vii. pp. 101, 102).*

Sarah, wife of William Biddle, died on the 27th day of 2d mo., 1709, O. S., in the 75th year of her age, and he departed this life in the early part of the year 1712, N. S., at a very advanced age.

The following facts relative to his last will, which is on file in the office of the Secretary of State of New Jersey, at Trenton, are interesting. It was executed June 23, 1711, proved at Burlington, March 3, 1712, and approved and sealed by his excellency, Colonel Hunter, and the probate seal, the 24th March, 1711, O. S. (April 5, 1712, N. S.).

By it the following bequests were made:—

His plantation of Mount Hope, containing 500 acres, and the island, known as Biddle's Island, containing 278 acres, to his son William and Lydia the wife of his son, during their lives, and the life of the survivor, and then to their son William, his heirs and assigns forever.

To his cousin, Thomas Biddle, 500 acres of land.

To Thomas, Sarah, and Rachael Biddle, children of his said cousin, Thomas Biddle, each a small legacy in money.

To his aforesaid grandson, William Biddle, £75.

To each of his four granddaughters, Elizabeth, Sarah, Penelope, and Lydia Biddle, £37 10s.

To his grandson, Joseph Biddle, 500 acres of land and £37 10s.

To his grandson, John Biddle, 500 acres of land and £37 10s.

To each of his executors, Samuel Bunting and John Wills, £7 10s.

To William Plumstead, son of Clement Plumstead, of Philadelphia [by his second wife], £7 10s.

To his cousin, Dorothy Sherwin, 100 acres of land.

To William Satterthwait, 100 acres of land.

"And lastly, all the rest and residue of my estate, both real and personal, of what kind or quality soever and wheresoever, I give, devise, and bequeath unto my said son, William Biddle, and to his executors and assigns forever."

Of the five children of William and Sarah Biddle, it has been already stated, two only survived to accompany their parents, in the year 1681, from England to America, namely, William 2d, and Sarah. Of William 2d, but little is known by his descendants, now surviving. He married, about 1695, Lydia Wardell, of Shrewsbury, N. J., a member of the Society of Friends, a great-granddaughter of Thomas Wardell, and a granddaughter of Eliakim Wardell,† French Huguenots, who settled in New England, much earlier in

---

* Smith's History of New Jersey, being without an index, the following references are given to William Biddle and his son William : pp. 95, 109, 115, 152, 164, 165, 200, 203, 204, 276, 285, 286, 538, 554.

† For an impartial account of the persecution of Eliakim Wardell and his wife (née Perkins), see page 102 of a remarkably able work, recently published, enti-

the 17th century. The minutes and records of Shrewsbury Monthly Meeting, for some years prior and subsequent to her marriage, were for a long time mislaid, and consequently the precise date thereof has not been ascertained.

On the 2d day of November, 1703, William Biddle, Jr., John Wills, and John Reading were appointed by the Council of Proprietors of West Jersey, Commissioners to "go up to the Indians above the Falls, and particularly to Caponockous, in order to have the tract of land lately purchased of the Indians marked forth, and get them to sign a deed for the same," etc. (Smith's History, New Jersey, note, p. 95).

Having, on the death of his father, in the early part of the year 1712, inherited an ample fortune, he continued during the remainder of his life, at least thirty years, to reside at Mount Hope.

His landed property was largely increased after his father's death, his share of what was called the "Lotting Purchase" amounting to 12,905 acres. This was a large tract of land purchased from the Indians above the Falls of the Delaware, and *allotted* among such of the West Jersey proprietors as had contributed money to make the purchase.

Sarah, daughter of William and Sarah Biddle, was, on the 21st of October, 1695, O. S., married at the residence of her father, to William Righton, of Philadelphia, and as he was not a Friend the marriage ceremony was performed in the presence of three justices of the peace. Out of regard, probably to the feelings of her parents, the Friends did not "disown" her. Her husband having died very soon after their marriage, she returned from Philadelphia to Mount Hope, and resided with her parents, having no issue.

On 1st mo. (March) 14, 1703–4, O. S., she was again married, by Friends' ceremony, at the residence of her father, to Clement Plumstead, of Philadelphia, who, subsequently, in the years 1723, 1736, and 1741, held the office of Mayor of the city. The guests at the wedding were the first families in Philadelphia and New Jersey: Governors Samuel Jennings and William Penn, Jr., Robert Monposson, Francis Davenport, Joseph Kirkbride, James Sansom, John Wills, and Samuel Carpenter and William Hall, of Salem County. The only issue of this marriage was a son named William, who died when a few months old. On the 17th of the 6th mo., 1705, Sarah Plumstead died leaving no issue, and consequently all the descendants of William Biddle, first, and Sarah his wife, now surviving, are descendants of their son, William 2d.

William 2d, leaving no will, it is presumed that his estate was divided amongst his children under the intestate laws of the Province. He probably died about the year 1743, aged 73. He had by his wife Lydia seven

---

tled "The Quaker Invasion of Massachusetts," by Richard P. Hallowell, Boston, 1883.

"The first child born at this place [Shewsbury] was Elizabeth, daughter of Eliakim Wardell, afterwards wife of John Wills, in 1667."—Smith's MS. Hist. of Penna., chapter xx.

children, namely, William, Elizabeth, Sarah, Penelope (m. Whitehead), Joseph, and John; the last named being born in 1707.

Joseph Biddle, second son of William (2d) and Lydia, his wife, married (1st) Lydia Howard, and was the only one of the three brothers who remained in New Jersey. His children were Mary (m. Shinn), Arney, Joseph. By a second marriage, he left issue, William (died young) and Sarah (m. 1st Monroe, and 2d Joseph Harker).

It is believed that no descendants of Joseph bearing the name of Biddle now remain in New Jersey, but that there are a number who are descended from Thomas Biddle, cousin of William (1st), and mentioned by the latter in his will.

From Arney Biddle, son of Joseph, there are many descendants of the name in Ohio and other northwestern States, and one, the Rev. Arney Biddle (Presbyterian), now resides at Cabin Hill, Delaware County, in the State of New York.

William Biddle, the eldest son, and John Biddle, the youngest son of William Biddle (2d) and his wife Lydia Wardell, both removed to Philadelphia between 1720 and 1730, and were the progenitors of the great number of the name in that city.*

William Biddle (3d) married Mary Scull, April 3, 1730, d. 1756, and had issue:—

James, b. Feb. 18, 1731.
Nicholas, b. 1733, died in infancy.
Lydia, b. 1734.
John, b. 1736.
Edward, b. 1738.
Charles, b. 1745.
Abigail, b. 1747, died young.
Mary b. 1749, died unmarried.
Nicholas, b. 1750.
Thomas, b. 1752.

I. JAMES, eldest son of William Biddle (3d) and Mary Scull, his wife (see page 236), born 1731, m., June 30, 1753, Frances Marks, and had issue: Thirteen children, of whom eight died under ten years of age; the others were—

---

* It is believed that still another Biddle came early to Philadelphia, whose descendants cannot now be traced. Some of the same name were in New England as early as 1639; "the name being sometimes spelled Biddell or Beadle."—See Savage's Dictionary.

At a much later period, about 1760, there came to Delaware three brothers, Mark, Luke, and John Biddle, whose elder brother Matthew remained in England. These were of the Gloucestershire branch of the family, still living near Wotton-under-Edge.

(1) Joseph, lost at sea, page 139.
(2) William, lost at sea, page 141.
(3) Marks John, b. 1765, d. 1849.
(4) Lydia, m. James Collins.
(5) Elizabeth, m. George Eckert.

Marks John Biddle commenced the practice of law in Berks County about 1788, and at once entered upon a large business which he retained until advanced in years. In 1817 he was in the State Senate, and was appointed by Governor Heister Prothonotary of Berks County. His life was marked by a lofty sense of professional and private honor, and he was up to its close in the enjoyment of the highest respect and affection of the people of Reading. He m. Jane Dundas (niece of Sir Ralph Dundas, Major-General in the British Army, and a cousin of Sir Ralph Abercrombie) in 1793, and had issue:—

1. James Dundas m. Frances Wood (1815), and d. 1822. Issue: Marks John and James Dundas. Marks John Biddle m. Isabella Hamilton, and *their* son, John C. Mercer Biddle, b. 1856, is, by right of descent, the legal representative of the William Biddle who first came to New Jersey.

2. Hannah D. m. Jonathan D. Good, and 2d Abraham Addams, and died 1859. Had issue by 1st marriage—John, Thomas.

3. Frances Dundas m. Joseph R. Priestley [grandson of the famous Dr. Priestley], and d. 1878. Had issue: Joseph (m. Hannah Taggart), Eliza (m. Thos. Lyons), Marks J. B. (m. Mary Taggart), Fanny (m. Henry Toulman), Jane (m. Conyers Button).

4. Lydia m. David F. Gordon, of Reading [Judge of Common Pleas, Berks County], and d. 1848. Had issue: James B., d. s. p., Elizabeth F., Jane Dundas (m. J. Brinton White), Clara.

5. Elizabeth Eckert m. Edward Anderson, and d. 1876. Issue: Alexander (m. Anise Hull), J. Lesley (m. Hester Agnes Carroll), Marks Biddle.

6. Jane, d. unm. 1849.

7. Ann, d. unm. 1882.

Lydia, daughter of James Biddle and Frances Marks, m. James Collins. Issue: Frances m. Saml. Wood. Issue: Marks John, d. young, and Lydia M. (m. 1st Pawling, 2d Osborne, and left issue), Jane B. m. Robt. Frazer (issue, Robert and Fanny B., m. Herbert Welsh).

Elizabeth, daughter of James Biddle and Frances Marks, m. Geo. Eckert. No issue.

II. LYDIA, daughter of William Biddle (3d), m., December 3, 1752, Captain William McFunn, who had been an officer of the British Navy, and held high office in Antigua. He d. in 1767 or 1768. Issue:—

(1) William Biddle McFunn, who changed his name to Wm. McFunn Biddle, m. (1797) Lydia Spencer, dau. of the Rev. Elihu Spencer. He d. in 1809. Mrs. Biddle removed to Carlisle in 1827, and d. in 1858, aged 92 years. Her children were:—

1. Lydia Spencer m. Samuel Baird, and had issue: William M., Samuel, Spencer F. [now at the head of the Smithsonian Institution], Rebecca P., Lydia Spencer, Mary D. [married Major Henry J. Biddle, who died July, 1862, of wounds received in the seven days' battle before Richmond], Thomas.

2. Valeria, dau. of Wm. M. Biddle, m. Charles B. Penrose [a descendant of John Biddle and Mary Owen], and had issue: William McFunn, Richard Alexander Fullerton [Professor in the Medical Department of the University of Pennsylvania], Sarah C. [married William S. Blight], Clement Biddle [Judge of Orphans' Court, Philadelphia], Lydia, Charles B.

3. William M., son of Wm. M. Biddle, m. Julia Montgomery, and had issue: Lydia Spencer, Thomas M., Edward M., Mary M., William McFunn, Julia M.

4. Mary E. D., dau. of Wm. M. Biddle and his wife Lydia Spencer, m. Major Blaney, U. S. Army, and had issue: Valeria Biddle, Catharine M., William Biddle, Lydia Spencer.

5. Edward Biddle, son of Wm. M. Biddle, m. Julia A. Watts, and had issue: David W., Lydia Spencer, Charles Penrose, Frederick W., Edward W., Wm. McFunn.

(2) Mary Biddle,* dau. of Captain Wm. McFunn and his wife Lydia Biddle, m. (1773) Collinson Read, and had issue:—

1. James, Major U. S. Army, d. s. p.
2. Thomas, unm.
3. Edward, unm.
4. Charles, purser, U. S. N., killed in mutiny, d. unm.
5. George, unm.
6. Susan, m. Thos. Collins, of Pittsburgh, 4 children.
7. Sarah, m. General William Gates, U. S. Army (d. 1865), 6 children.
8. William M., U. S. Army, 4 children.
9. Lydia, d. unm.
10. Maria, m. John Dennis, of New Brunswick, N. J., 5 children.

III. JOHN, second son (omitting from the enumeration an infant, dec'd) of William Biddle (3d), m. Mrs. Sophia Boone. He was Deputy Quarter Master in the Provincial Army in General Forbes's Campaign against Fort Du Quesne. At the time of the Revolution he held office as Collector of Excise of Berks County, and, though opposed to the measures of the government, was, like many prominent Whigs of the day, not in favor of separation from the mother country. In 1778 his property was confiscated, and he was banished to New York, whence he proceeded to Nova Scotia, where he remained until the time of his death. His family, after the war, returned

---

* For this information we are indebted to the " Provincial Councillors of Pennsylvania," recently published by Mr. Charles P. Keith, a work of immense research and remarkable accuracy.

24

to Pennsylvania, and resided at Reading and Greensburg. His children were:—

(1) Edward, m. at Mackinac, Mich. Issue: Sophia, John m. Ashman, Sarah m. Durfee.

(2) James, resided in Pittsburgh, m. McNichol. Issue: two children.

(3) Sophia m. Michl. P. Cassily, of Cincinnati, and had issue: Ann (m. Dr. V. Marshall, one dau., Sophia), Mary (m. Wm. A. Adams, four children), Henrietta (m. B. B. Whitman, ten children), Edward (m. —— Hunt, one child), Charles (m. —— Lee), William.

(4) Lydia m. Mr. DeFord. No issue.

(5) Sally m. Andrew Boggs. Issue: two children (one of whom, Biddle Boggs, still living).

(6) Mary, d. unm.

IV. EDWARD BIDDLE, third son of William Biddle (3d), see page 75, and Note C., m. (1761) Elizabeth, dau. of Rev. Mr. Ross, and had issue:—

(1) Catharine m. George Lux, of Baltimore, and had two children, both dying in infancy.

(2) Abigail m. Dr. Fall, of Md., d. s. p.

V. CHARLES BIDDLE, son of William Biddle (3d) and Mary Scull, Author of this Memoir, b. 1745, d. 1821, m. (1778) Hannah Shepard, and had issue:—

(1) William Shepard, b. 1781, d. 1835, m. Circe Deronceray; 2d Elizabeth B. Keating (née Hopkinson). No issue.

(2) James, b. 1783, Commodore U. S. Navy. See Note E; d. unm. 1848.

(3) Edward, Midshipman U. S. Navy, d. November 14, 1800, on board the frigate President, off the Island of Descada, West Indies.

(4) Nicholas, b. 1786, d. 1844. See Note D; m. Jane M., dau. of John Craig. Issue:—

1. Edward m. Jane J. Craig, née Sarmiento. Issue: Edith (m. Van Rensselaer), Frances, Agnes (m. Ward), Edward (m. Emily Drexel), Mildred.

2. Charles John, member of the bar, entered the U. S. Volunteer Army at the time of the Mexican War as Captain of Voltigeurs, breveted Major for gallantry at the storming of Chapultepec, City of Mexico. In 1861, Colonel of 42d Pennsylvania Regiment, until he took his seat as member of 37th Congress in December of that year. Died 1873. m. Emma Mather. Issue: Emma (m. Thos. E. Dixon), Charles, John Craig, Adèle, Dillon, Alexander Mercer, Catharine.

3. Craig, member of the bar, member of the Legislature of Pennsylvania, aid-de-camp of Gen. Patterson in his Campaign in the Shenandoah Valley, military aid to Governor Curtin, of Pennsylvania, 1861 and 1862, and now Judge of the Court of Common Pleas, Philadelphia; m. Mary C. Rockhill (d. 1852). Issue: Mary, d. in infancy.

4. Meta Craig m. James S. Biddle. Issue: Jane Craig, Nicholas (m. Eliza I. Butler), Meta Craig.

5. Adèle.

6. Jane.

(5) Charles Biddle, b. 1787, engaged in business in Philadelphia until 1826, admitted to the bar, Nashville, Tennessee, in 1827. In 1835, being a warm personal and political friend of General Jackson, was sent by him as commissioner to report upon routes for trade across Central America and the Isthmus of Panama. In 1836, at Bogotá, he obtained a concession of the right to navigate the Cruces River, and to construct a railroad or a macadamized road to Panama; also the exclusive right to steam navigation on the Magdalena River. Died 1836. m. Ann H. Stokes (1808). Issue:—

1. Sarah m. Major Jno. S. Lytle, U. S. Army. Issue: Eliza L. (m. Robert Campbell; children, Sally, Helen).

2. Charles, d. in infancy.

3. Mary m. Peter Vandervoort, of New York. Issue: Anna, Charles, Mary, Catharine, Theodore, Elizabeth, Meta, Gertrude.

4. Ann, m. Saml. Leonard. Issue: Catharine (m. Edw. S. Harlan), James $. (m. Catharine Pepper), Rosalie.

5. Catharine C.

6. James S., entered U. S. Navy, 1833; resigned 1856. m. Meta Craig Biddle (1846). Issue: Jane Craig, Nicholas (m. Eliza I. Butler), Meta Craig.

7. Hannah S.

8. Elizabeth N.

(6) Thomas, b. 1790, entered the army in 1812, served with distinction as Captain in Colonel Pike's Regiment on the Canada frontier. He was afterwards transferred to the artillery, and was twice wounded at the battle of Lundy's Lane, and again in the defence of Fort Erie, being breveted Major for the latter service. General Winfield Scott always referred to Captain Biddle's conduct in action under him with affectionate enthusiasm (see his Autobiography). In 1820 he accepted an appointment as Paymaster, and was stationed at St. Louis. In 1831 he fell in a duel with Mr. Spencer Pettis, member of Congress, in a quarrel arising out of a violent political contest. He m. Ann, dau. of John Mullanphy, and died without issue. See Simpson's Eminent Philadelphians.

(7) John, b. 1792, d. 1859, also entered the army in 1812 with his brother Thomas, and served in the same operations, being also promoted to major. Resigning after the war, he settled in Detroit, was a delegate in Congress in 1829–31, and President of the Convention which formed the first Constitution for the State of Michigan. m. Eliza Bradish. Issue:—

1. Thomas, d. s. p.

2. Margaretta m. General Andrew Porter, U. S. Army. Issue: Biddle Porter m. Elizabeth M. Rush.

3. William S. m. Susan Ogden. Issue: Susan, Eliza, John, Stratford, Margaret, Andrew, William, Annie.

4. James m. Margt. Terry. Issue: Louisa and Catharine.

5. Edward J. m. Frances Davidson. Issue: Beatrice, Nicholas, Constance, Violet, Guy.

(8) Richard, b. 1796, d 1847; an eminent member of the Pittsburgh Bar, member of Congress 1837–41, author of "Life of Sebastian Cabot." m. Ann Anderson, of Pittsburgh. Issue:—

1. Richard.

2. Grace m. Rev. Hall McIlvaine (issue: Annie, Grace, Edith).

(9) Mary, d. 1854, m. John G. Biddle (who d. 1826). Issue:—

1. Anne E. Biddle.

(10) Ann, b. 1800, m. Francis Hopkinson, and d. 1863. Issue:—

1. Hamilton, d. unm.

2. Thomas.

3. Charles, d. unm.

4. Ann m. Rev. Edw. A. Foggo, D D.

5. Emily m. Alden Scovell. of Camden, N. J. (issue: Emily, Florence, Alden C.).

VI. NICHOLAS, fifth son of William Biddle and Mary Scull, b. 1750, killed on board frigate Randolph, 1778, unmarried. See page 109 and Note D, also Simpson's Philadelphians.

VII. THOMAS, youngest son of Wm. Biddle and Mary Scull, b. 1752, became doctor of medicine, and died, February, 1775, at Georgetown. South Carolina, unmarried.

JOHN, the youngest son of William Biddle (2d)—refer back to pages 366–7 —was born in 1707, and March 3, 1736, m., by Friends' ceremony, Sarah Owen; among the witnesses were Nicholas and Abigail Scull, William (3d) and Mary Biddle, and Mrs. Penelope Whitehead (sister of the groom). Issue:—

1. Owen, b. 1738.

2. Clement, b. 1740.

3. Sarah. 4. Ann. 5. Lydia.

I. OWEN BIDDLE [see Note II] b. 1738, m. Sarah Parke, and had issue:—

(1) Jane.

(2) John m. Elizabeth Canby, and had issue: Samuel, Sarah, Margaret, Jacob (m. Hopkins, one dau.), James C. (m. Sally Drinker. Issue: Eliza'th m. Rev. Mr. Halsey, Henry D., Hetty D., Mary D.), Frances (m. Thos. C. Garrett. Issue: Eliz'th, Rebecca, Frances, Philip C., John B., Martha, Hetty B.), William (m. Eliz'th C. Garrett. Issue: John W., Samuel), Edward C., President of Westmoreland Coal Company (m. Hetty H. Foster.

Issue: Hetty F., William F.), Rebecca (m. Alfred Cope. Issue: James B.), John, President of Locust Mt. Coal Company (m. Mary B. Foster. Issue; Hetty B., John, d. young, Mary, Elizabeth).

(3) Rebecca m. Peter Thompson, 4 children.

(4) Sarah.

(5) Tacy B.

(6) Owen m. Eliz'th Rowan, 4 children.

(7) Thomas B.

(8) Robert B.

(9) Clement m. Mary Canby. Issue :—

Martha.

Robert m. Anna M. Miller. Issue: Charles M. (m. Hannah McIlvaine), Henry C. (m Anna McIlvaine), Hannah M. (m. J. C. W. Frishmuth), Elizabeth (m. Frishmuth), Martha C.

William Canby m. Rachel M. Miller Issue: Clement M. (m. Lydia Cooper), Frances Canby (m. Clement A. Griscom), Helen (m. George B. Thomas), Mary (m. Howard Wood), Hannah N. (m. Charles Williams).

Henry, d. young.

Clement m. 1st Susan T. Walton. Issue: William W. (m.,Mary Taggart), m. 2d Susan W. Cadwallader. Issue: Canby, d. young, Francis C. (m Sarah Pennock), Anne.

(10) Anne m. John Tatum.

II. CLEMENT BIDDLE,* son of John Biddle and Sarah Owen [See Note II], b. 1740, m. 1st Mary Richardson, 2d Rebecca Cornell. Issue, by second wife only :—

(1) Francis, d. in infancy.

(2) Thomas, b. 1776, d. 1857, the eminent banker, founder of the house of Thomas A. Biddle & Company, m. Christine Williams. Issue:—

1. Clement, d. unm.

2. Thomas Alexander m. Julia Cox. Issue: John, Henry W. m. Jesse Turner, Anna m. Andrew A. Blair, Alfred, Wm. Lyman, Francis, Julia m. Arthur Biddle.

3. Henry J., Adjutant-General *of Penna. Reserve, d. July, 1862, of wounds received in the seven days' battle before Richmond, m. Mary D. Baird (descendant of Wm. Biddle (3d) and Mary Scull), and had issue: Jonathan W., Lydia M. (m. Moncure Robinson, Jr.), Spencer F. B., Christine, Henry J.

4. Alexander, Lieutenant-Colonel of 121st Pennsylvania Regiment in war of 1861-5, and specially distinguished at Gettysburg, President of Board of City Trusts, m. Julia W. Rush. Issue: Alexander W. (m. McKennan), Henry R., Julia, James W., Louis A., Marianne, Lynford.

---

* A full statement of the descendants of Clement Biddle, prepared by Mr. Walter L. C. Biddle, has recently been printed in Bougher's Repository.

5. Jonathan Williams, d. 1856, m. Emily Meigs. Issue: Christine (m. Richard M. Cadwalader), Charles M., Williams, Mary, Thomas, Emily W.

(3) George Washington, d. 1812, at Macao, China.

(4) Mary, eldest daughter of Clement Biddle, m. General Thomas Cadwalader. Issue:—

1. John, Judge of U. S. District Court, d. 1879, m. 1st Mary Binney. Issue: Mary B. (m. Wm. Henry Rawle), Elizabeth B. (m. Geo. H. Hare), and m. 2d Henrietta M. McIlvaine, née Bancker. Issue: Sarah B., Frances, Thomas, Charles E., John (m. Mary Helen Fisher), Ann (m. Rev. H. J. Rowland), George.

2. George, Major-General in the Mexican War, and in the war of 1861-5, d. 1879, m. Frances Mease.

3. Thomas.

4. Henry, U. S. Navy, d. 1844.

5. William.

(5) Rebecca C., daughter of Clement Biddle, d. 1870, m. Dr. Nathaniel Chapman. Issue:—

1. Emily C., m. Jno. M. Gordon. Issue: Chapman, John M., Susan F., Emily, Rebecca C.

2. John Biddle, m. Mary Randolph, of Virginia. Issue: Gabriella m. the Marquis de Podestad Fornari, and Emily m. Prince Joseph Pignatelli DeAragon.

3. George W., Lieutenant U. S. Navy, d. 1853, m. Emily Markoe. Issue: Mary R. m. John B. Thayer, Elizabeth C. m. Wm. D. Winsor, Henry C. m. Hannah Megargee, Rebecca m. Jas. D. Winsor, George, d. in infancy.

(6) Clement Cornell Biddle, son of Clement Biddle, d. 1855; entered the navy 1799, resigned 1804, commanded Penn. Regt. Light Infantry (volunteers) in 1812-14, the principal founder and for many years President of Philadelphia Savings Fund Society, writer on political economy. m. Mary S. Barclay. Issue:—

1. John B., Professor of Materia Medica, Jefferson College, m. Caroline Phillips. Issue: Anna C. m. C. S. Phillips, Harriet m. DeGrasse Fox, William P., Lieutenant U. S. Marines, Clement, Surgeon U. S. Navy, Elizabeth R. m. Samuel M. Miller, M.D., Caroline.

2. George Washington, eminent member of the Bar of Philadelphia, m. Maria McMurtrie. Issue: George m. Mary H. Rodgers, of New York, Algernon Sydney m. Frances Robinson, Arthur m. Julia, dau. of Thomas A. Biddle.

3. Chapman, d. 1880, member of the Bar of Philadelphia, commanded the 121st Pennsylvania Regiment in the war of 1861-5, was present at the battle of Fredericksburg, and greatly distinguished on the first day of Gettysburg, where he commanded a brigade and was wounded. m. Mary L. Cochran, of New York. Issue: Mary C., Clement C., d. young, Walter L. C. m. Pauline Davis Carter.

(7) Ann, d. in infancy.

(8) Lydia II., d. young.

(9) Sarah T., d. young.

(10) Ann W., dau. of Clement Biddle, d. 1878, m. Thomas Dunlap. Issue: Sally, Juliana, Lydia, Mary, Rebecca, Nannie m. George M. Conarroe, Thomas m. Margaret A. Levis.

(11) John G., son of Clement Biddle, banker with his brother Thomas Biddle, d. 1826, m. Mary Biddle (dau. of Charles Biddle, writer of this work). Issue: Ann Eliza.

(12) James Cornell, son of Clement Biddle, d. 1838, a member of the Bar of Philadelphia, m. Sarah C. Keppele. Issue:—

1. Thomas, U. S. Minister to Ecuador, d. at Guyaquil, 1875, m. Sarah F. White. Issue: Caldwell K., Harrison W., Sarah, James C., Elizabeth C.

2. Caldwell K., d. 1862, m. Elizabeth Meade, née Ricketts.

3. Catharine K. m. William P. Tatham.

4. Rebecca, d. unm.

5. James C. m. Gertrude G. Meredith. Issue: Catharine M., Sarah C.

(13) Edward R., son of Clement Biddle, removed to New York. Married. Issue: Edward R., James (Major U. S. Army).

III. SARAH BIDDLE, dau. of John Biddle and Sarah Owen (refer to page 372), m. 1st James Penrose, 2d John Shaw, 3d Rudolph Tellier. By first marriage left issue:—

Clement Biddle Penrose m. Anna Howard Bingham.

IV. ANN, dau. of John Biddle and Sarah Owen (page 372) m. General James Wilkinson. U. S. Army. Issue: John, James, and J. B.

V. LYDIA, dau. of John Biddle and Sarah Owen (page 372), m. Dr. James Hutchinson, and died without issue.*

----

* The genealogical matter inserted in this note has been put together as probably of some interest to the members of the family, and with this view alone. It would have required much time and labor to have made it complete, but it is believed that what is here recorded is accurate, and will enable those who may be so disposed to pursue the subject. On the next page is a table brought down to the 3d or 4th in descent from William Biddle (1st).

William Biddle d. 1712.　Came to America 1681.　m. Sarah Kemp.

William Biddle d. 1743.
m. Lydia Wardell.

Sarah m. Righton.
" Plumpstead.
d. s. p.

William d. 1756,
m. Mary Scull.

Elizabeth.　　Sarah.

Joseph
m. 1st, Lydia
Howard.

Penelope
m. Whitehead.

John d. 1789,
m. Sarah Owen.

James　Lydia　John　Edward　Charles　Abigail.　Mary.　Nicholas Thomas
m. Marks.　m. McFunn.　m. Boone.　m. Ross.　m. Shepard.　　　　　　(U.S.N.).

Joseph,　(Wm. McF.)　Edward,　Catharine,　William S. m. Keating,
William,　Biddle　James,　Abigail.　James (U. S. N.),
Marks John　m. Spencer,　Sophia　　　Edward (U. S. N.),
m. Dundas　Mary　m. Casely,　　Nicholas m. Craig,
Lydia　m. Read.　Lydia,　　　Charles m. Stokes,
m. Collins,　　Sally,　　　Thomas m. Mulhanphy,
Elizabeth　　Mary.　　　John m. Bradish,
m. Eckert.　　　　　Richard m. Anderson,
　　　　　　　Mary m. Biddle,
　　　　　　　Ann m. Hopkinson.

Mary
m. Shinn.
Arney,
Joseph,
m. 2d wife,
William,
Sarah
m. Harker.

Owen　　Clement　　Sarah　　Ann　　Lydia
m. Parke.　m. Cornell.　m. Penrose,　m. Gen.　m. Hutch-
　　　　　" Shaw,　Wilkinson.　inson.
　　　　　" Tellier.

Jane,　　Francis,　　(Clement B.) John,
John　　Thomas　　James　J. B.
m. Canby,　m.Williams (Clement B. Penrose.)
Rebecca　George W.,
m. Thompson,　Mary m. Cadwalader,
Sarah,　　Rebecca C. m. Chapman,
Tacy R.　　Clement C. m. Barclay,
Owen　　Ann,
m. Rowan,　Lydia H.,
Thomas B.,　Sarah T.,
Robert R.,　Ann W. m. Dunlap,
Clement　John G. m. Biddle,
m. Canby,　James C. m. Keppele,
Anne　　Edward R.
m. Tatum.

It has been said above that the names Biddulph and Biddle are identical. Macaulay, in writing of William Penn, refers to a loose habit of spelling names as "characteristic of the age." In fact, even the monosyllabic surname of the founder of Pennsylvania is spelled by Pepys in three different ways: Pen, Penn, Penne.

A stronger illustration may be found in the Lives of the Lindsays, vol. ii. p. 412, where *eighty-eight* ways of spelling Lindsay are exhibited, all of them taken from documentary title papers of the same family in regular descent.

In Lower's Patronymica Brittanica, at pp. xxix. and xxx. the author gives a full account of the sources of English surnames and remarks: "The most valuable of these documents are the two folio volumes known as the "Rotuli Hundredorum" or Hundred Rolls of the date of 1273," etc. At page 26, he gives:—

"BIDDLE 1. A modification of Biddulph.

2. Ang-Sax, a beadle, messenger, herald or proclaimer. Biddle, without a prefix, is found in the Rotuli Hundredorum.

BIDDULPH.—A parish in Co. Stafford, very anciently possessed by the family who descended from Ricardus Forestarius, a great Domesday Tenant. —Erdeswick's Staffordshire."

In Keith Johnson's Royal Atlas, recent edition, the index gives the name "Biddle or Biddulph," referring to the town about eight miles from New Castle-under-Lyne. In Domesday Book, which was finished A. D. 1086, this town is entered as Bidolf. Freeman briefly describes Domesday Book as intended "to report who had held the land in the time of King Edward, and who held it then."—Norman Conquest.

In Shaw's History of Staffordshire, vol. i. p. 352, is the "Pedigree of Biddulph, of Elmhurst." It begins at "48 Edward 3d," and runs in direct descent to—

Simon Byddell, buried in 1579.

His son Simon Biddulph, died 1596.

His son Simon Biddle, died 1632.

His son Michael Biddulph, died 1657.

In the same pedigree occurs the spelling Bedulph.

The Michael Biddulph who died in 1657 is given, in the pedigree, ten sons. The names of four only are set forth, and Mr. Biddle-Cope is confident that the William Biddle who came to New Jersey was one of the "*Six other sons*" who are there mentioned.

In the Harleian MSS., No. 2643 Br. Mus., is an interesting account of the siege of Lichfield Close by the Roundheads, during which Lord Brooke was killed. We find there:—

"Lord Brooke . . . . had a great desire to march on foot to see what execution was made against the gates or wall. And out of Mr. Michael Biddle's (alias Biddulph's) house, a little below the Market house, his lordship came forth in a plush cassock," etc.

In Brewer's Description of Warwickshire, under Birdlingbury, p. 93, he says: "By this lady the estate was conveyed in 1687 to Symon Biddulph, Esq. The family of Biddulph were originally seated in Staffordshire, and took their names from the village of Biddulph in that county 'of which,' says Dr. Thomas, 'they have been lords since the conquest.'"

In Nightingale's Staffordshire, published in 1813, p. 1071, he says: "But these people of Biddulph, or as they call it Biddle, seem to be a totally different race," etc.

The colloquial usage is the same at the present day, as confirmed by the personal observation of Mr. Biddle-Cope; namely, that by the country people the two final letters of Biddulph are not sounded, and the word is commonly pronounced as if written Biddle.

It would be easy to extend this line of remark, but this may suffice.

NOTE B. (PAGE 1.)

Nicholas Scull, the Surveyor-General of Pennsylvania, was the eldest of the six sons of Nicholas Scull, who emigrated to America (it is supposed from the county of Cork, Ireland) from the port of Bristol, in England, in the ship Bristol Merchant, John Stephens, commander, landing at Chester on the 10th of ninth month, 1685. The first progenitor of the family in England was a Norman, Sir John Scull, who was one of the twelve knights mentioned in "Bernard Burke's Landed Gentry," etc., and in Theophilus Jones's "History of Brecknockshire," who accompanied the renowned warrior Bernard Newmarch into North Wales, and who, in course of time, conquered the country. The family spread into the adjoining counties of England; and at some early period—probably in the reign of Henry II.—some of them might have accompanied the Welsh Baron, the Earl of Pembroke (Strongbow), into Ireland, and have given the name to the large parish and town of Scull, in the southwestern part of the county of Cork. When William Penn, as a young man, visited his father's estates in that county, some of the members of the Scull family doubtless fell under his religious influence, and were induced to accompany Major Jasper Farmer to America. Major Farmer was of the same county, and came over in the same ship with the father of the subject of this notice.

Nicholas Scull was born near Philadelphia, in the year 1687, and, in all probability, was an apprentice of Thomas Holmes, the first acting Surveyor-General. He married Abigail Heap in 1708, who was a relation of his partner. He was a friend of Franklin, who mentions him in his "Autobiography" as a member of the "Junto," formerly called the "Leather-Apron Club." He says: "We also had as a member, Nicholas Scull—afterward the Surveyor-General—who loved books, and who sometimes made verses." There were thirty-eight members, but it was afterward increased to fifty.

Franklin proposed the formation of a library, and that each one should pay forty shillings, and subscribe ten shillings more annually for fifty years. At their debating club, the members of the "Junto" had previously brought their books to the room, and left them there as common stock. Robert Grace, one of the most active members, allowed them the use of a chamber in his house in Pewter-Platter Alley, for their meetings. The library was organized in 1731, and in 1739–'40, a room in the State House was appropriated for the reception of the books. In 1742 it was incorporated as "The Library Company of Philadelphia." The share of Nicholas Scull was numbered "thirty-two," and was dated March 29, 1732. It was forfeited in May, 1770, was renewed in March, 1857, and is now held by Mr. Edward Lawrence Scull. The late Thomas I. Wharton, Esq., in an interesting article on the early literature of Philadelphia, written in 1825, says:—

"In 1727, Franklin instituted a club of mutual improvement, which was named the 'Junto,' and which continued nearly forty years without its nature and objects being publicly known, though 'the chief measures of Philadelphia,' it is said, 'received their first form here.' The 'Junto' is described by its distinguished founder as 'the best school of philosophy, morality, and politics, that then existed in the province.' And it appears to have exerted a powerful influence on the fortunes of some of its members, and probably contributed in no small degree to foster that literary taste and philosophical spirit which have been the honorable distinction of this city. They met every Friday evening, and each member paid a penny a night, to recompense the landlord for fire and light. Economy was one of their characteristic virtues. Terrapin and whiskey were unknown to their frugal and temperate deliberations. A copy of the set of twenty-four rules and questions to be asked at each meeting, to draw the members out, formed in the time of Dr. Franklin, and probably written by him, is still in existence. They show in a very strong light the importance, while they display the machinery of the institution."

While still a very young man, Nicholas Scull was actively engaged in surveying the wild and uncultivated parts of the province of Pennsylvania, and thus acquired a knowledge of the Indian dialects, several of which he spoke with fluency. He was, in consequence, frequently called upon to act as one of the interpreters between the Indian chiefs (some of whom where his friends) and the agents of Penn, and he was present at many councils and treaty ratifications with the Delaware and Conestoga tribes. The earliest occasion recorded on which he acted as interpreter was at a council held in Philadelphia, April 18, 1728, when, after all business was transacted, it was "ordered that three matchcoats be given to James Letort (an Indian trader) and John Scull, to be by them delivered to Allummapus, Mr. Montour, and Manawkyhickon, etc."

In one of the publications of the Historical Society of Pennsylvania, it is stated that on the 22d of June, 1726, Governor Gordon arrived in the province with a commission from Springett Penn, the grandson and heir of

William Penn. Some trouble having arisen "by reason of some rude insults from a few strange Indians, who ranged among the inhabitants of the
province, and some anxiety existing among those who relied on the continu-
ance of the protection and friendship exhibited toward them during the life
of William Penn, Governor Gordon appointed a council to be held with them
at Conestoga, to which place he repaired in person." The council was held
at the Indian town above named on the 26th of May, 1728, and concluded
on the 27th. There were present four chiefs of the Conestoga tribe, three
of the Delaware Indians on the Brandywine, five of the Gawanese, and three
chiefs of the Shawanese tribes. Shakawtawlin, or Sam, interpreter from
the English into the Delaware; Captain Civility, from the Delaware into
the Shawanese and Mingoe (alias Conestogoe); Pomapeehtoe, from the
Delaware into the Gawanese language; and Nicholas Scull, John Scull (his
brother), and Peter Bizallion acted as assistant interpreters. Conciliatory
speeches were addressed to them by the Governor, and presents of strowd
matchcoats, duffells, blankets, shirts, gunpowder, lead flints, and knives,
were delivered. One of the Conestoga chiefs replied (which was rendered
into English by John Scull on the second day of the council); then belts of
wampum of eight rows, and wampum of four strings were presented to the
Governor as a pledge of amity, and after rum, bread, tobacco, and pipes,
were delivered to them, and particular presents of a strowd matchcoat and
a shirt to Captain Civility, and the same to Sam, and one shirt to Poma-
peektya, and the Governor taking each of the chiefs by the hand, the council terminated, and the Indians departed for their homes.

In the year 1730 Nicholas Scull, accompanied by his apprentice, John
Lukens, was sent by the Provincial Government into what is now Northampton County, around the Delaware Water Gap, to report upon the occupation
of certain lands by the Hollanders, who had tilled their soil unmolested, and
which extended for forty miles on both sides of the river. Here they had
dwelt in a little secluded Arcadia for nearly one hundred years, quite unknown to the outside world. The venerable Samuel Preston wrote in 1828,
concerning this very curious fact, as follows:—

"In 1787 the writer went on his first surveying tour into Northampton
County. He was deputy under John Lukens, Surveyor-General, and received from him, by way of instruction, the following narrative respecting
the settlement of Meenesink, on the Delaware River, above the Kittatinny,
or Blue Mountains; that the settlement was formed a long time before it
was known to the Government of Philadelphia; that when the Government
was informed of the said settlement, they passed a law in 1729, that any
such purchases of the Indians should be void, and the purchasers indicted
for *forcible entry and detainer*, according to the laws of England; that in
1730 they appointed an agent to go and investigate the facts; that the agent
so appointed was the famous surveyor, Nicholas Scull; and that he, John
Lukens, was then N. Scull's apprentice to carry the chain and learn surveying; that he accompanied N. Scull, as they both understood and could talk

Indian. They hired Indian guides and had a fatiguing journey, there being then no white inhabitants in the upper part of Bucks or Northampton County; they had a very great difficulty to lead their horses through the Water Gap to Meenesink Flats, which were all settled with Hollanders. With several they could only be understood in Indian. At the venerable Samuel Dupuis's they found great hospitality and plenty of the necessaries of life. John Lukens said the first thing that struck his admiration was a grove of apple trees, of size far beyond any near Philadelphia. And further, that as Nicholas Scull and himself examined the banks, they were fully of opinion that all these flats had at some former age been a deep lake, before the river broke through the mountain, and that the best interpretation they could make of Meenesink was, "the water is gone;" that Sam Dupuis told them that when the rivers were frozen he had a good road to Esopus from the mine-holes, on the mine road, some one hundred miles, and that he took his wheat and cider there for salt and necessaries, and did not appear to have any knowledge or idea where the river ran, where Philadelphia market was, or of their being in the government of Pennsylvania. They were of opinion that the first settlements of Hollanders in Meenesink were many years older than William Penn's charter; and, as Samuel Dupuis had treated them so well, they concluded to make a survey of his claim, in order to befriend him if necessary. When they began to survey the Indians gathered around. An old Indian laid his hand on Nicholas Scull's shoulder and said : " Put up iron string. Go home." That they then quit and returned.

Before the death of William Penn, a grant of land had been made to him by the Delaware Indians for a certain consideration. He was to have as much land as a man could walk over in a day or a day and a half. There are conflicting statements as to the time; but the latter is believed to be correct. Why the terms of the grant had never been carried out before has not, as far as known, been explained. However, in September, 1737, it was decided by the Governor and Council to claim the execution of the stipulations of the grant, and agents were appointed to carry it out. They accordingly proceeded to Bucks County, and the distance was walked over by James Yeates and Edward Marshall, who had been selected for the occasion by the Governor and Council. Nicholas Scull and the Surveyor General of Bucks County, Benjamin Eastburn, and others were present, besides the Indians. "Lady Jenks," as she was called, was also present. Thomas Penn, the Governor, was represented as a man of a cold and formal deportment.

"But, it would seem, however, he was sufficiently susceptible of softer and warmer emotions, he having, it was said, brought with him to this country, as an occasional companion, a person of much show and display called 'Lady Jenks,' who passed her time 'remote from the city,' in the then wilds of Bucks County; but her beauty, accomplishments, and expert horsemanship made her soon of notoriety enough to make every woman, old and young, in the country her chronicle. They say she rode with him at foxhuntings, and at the famous 'Indian walk,' in men's clothes (meaning, without doubt, their simple conceptions of the masculine appearance of her riding-habit array), garbed like a man in a petticoat."

This "great walk," as it was called, was from that time until after the Revolution a very sore subject with the Delaware Indians of that locality, and was for many years, in Bucks County, the occasion of much discussion and angry animadversion against the Provincial Government. Dr. John Watson, the father of the annalist, sided very warmly with the "poor Indians," for whom he was always a strenuous advocate. He alleges that they were cheated out of their lands by the Provincial Government, and wrote a circumstantial narrative, which was deposited in the library of the Philosophical Society of Philadelphia. It is entitled "A Narrative, by John Watson, of the Indian Walk, being a Purchase of Land made of the Indians in Pennsylvania," 1756. This, the writer regrets, he has never had the opportunity of perusing; but it appears that it is asserted in it that "the Government publicly advertised a fee of £5 for the greatest walker for one day, and procured Marshall, who ran over four times as much ground as the Indians expected." Dr. Watson argues and supposes that all the country northwest of Wrightstown meeting-house was taken from the Delawares without compensation. His son, in his "Annals," says:—

"Complaints were made about the year 1755, '56, by Tedenscung, at the head of the Delaware Indians, 'that they had been cheated in their lands, bought on one-and-a-half day's walk along the Neshamina and forks of the Delaware, back forty-seven miles (N. Scull says fifty-five statute miles) to the mountains; and I have seen the whole repelled in a long manuscript report to Governor Dennie by the Committee of Council, in which the history of all the Indian treaties is given, and wherein they declare that till that time (1757) the Penn Proprietaries had more than fulfilled all their obligations by treaties, etc., paying for some purchases, to different and subsequent nations, over and over again. The paper contained much reasoning and argument to justify the then Penns."

Incorporated in the above report or defence was the following, from Nicholas Scull, Surveyor-General—

"Who came into Council, and acquainted the Governor that in September, 1737, he was present at running the line of the Indian purchase of the lands in the forks of the Delaware, with respect to which the Proprietaries were, as he was informed, publicly charged with defrauding the Indians; that he had put down in writing what he had remembered about it, and requested that he might be examined thereto, which being done he signed the paper, and his affirmation was ordered to be entered as follows:—

"Nicholas Scull, of the city of Philadelphia, surveyor, on his solemn affirmation according to law, saith, that he was present when James Yeates and Edward Marshall, together with some Indians, walked one day and a half back in the woods, pursuant to a grant of land made by the Delaware Indians to the Hon. the late Proprietary, William Penn, deceased; that the said day-and-a-half's walk was begun at a place near Wrightstown, in the county of Bucks, some time in September, 1737, and continued from the place aforesaid to some distance beyond the Kittatinny mountains; that he believes the whole distance walked not to be more than fifty-five statute miles; that Benjamin Eastburn, Surveyor General, Timothy Smith, Sheriff of said county of Bucks, and he, this affirmant, attended at the said day-and-a-half's walk from the beginning until the same was ended; that he well remembers that particular care was taken not to exceed the time of one day and a half, or eighteen hours; that he, this affirmant, then thought, and still thinks the said walk to be fairly performed, and believes that the said walkers did not run or go out of a walk at any time, nor does he remember that those Indians who were present made any complaint of unfair practice; that Benjamin Eastburn and this affirmant, with some others, lodged the night after the said walk was completed at an Indian town called Poakopoh-kunk, where there were many of the Delawares, among whom he well remembers there was one called Captain Harrison, a noted man among the Indians; and this affirmant further saith, that he does not remember that the said Captain Harrison, or any other of the Indians, made any complaint, or showed the least uneasiness at anything that was done relating to the said day-and-a-half's walk; and he verily believes that if any complaint had been made, or uneasiness shown by the Indians concerning said walk, he must have heard and remembered it.

NICH'S SCULL.

Affirmed in Council, 25th January, 1757.

WM. DENNY."

Compared with the recent pedestrian feats of Weston and others fifty-five statute miles in one-day-and-a-half's walking, even through the woods, does not seem to be a very great achievement. But it is quite certain the Indians thought differently about the distance gone over, for the authority above quoted says:—

"The Indians always cherished a spirit of revenge against Marshall, and a party of warriors once came from their settlement at Wyoming to seek his life. He was from home, but his wife was made prisoner, and his children escaped by an Indian thoughtlessly throwing his matchcoat over a bee-hive, which caused the party to be so attacked and stung that they went off without the children. The mother, being pregnant, could not keep up with the party, and her bones and remains were found six months afterward on the Broad Mountain.

"In the Revolutionary war the Indian warriors again returned from west of the Ohio into Tinicum or Noxamixon Township, still aiming at Marshall's life, and he again escaped by being from home. They then went back through New Jersey. This they told themselves after the peace. When Edward Marshall, who performed the extraordinary Indian walk, became offended with his reward, he cursed Penn and his 'half-wife' to their faces."

Nicholas Scull was elected Sheriff of Philadelphia in the years 1744, '45, and '46. In the "Annals" it is mentioned that it is known that the first person who ever had the boldness to publish himself as a candidate for Sheriff, and to laud his own merits, occurred in the person of Mordecai Lloyd, in the year 1744, begging the good people for their votes by his publications in English and German. At the same time Nicholas Scull, an opposing candidate, resorted to the same measure, and apologized for "the new mode" as imposed upon him by the practice of others.

On the 10th of June, 1748, he succeeded William Parsons as Surveyor-General. On the 21st of October, 1758, a grand council was held with the Indians at Easton (where his two sons, Nicholas and Jasper, lived), where the members of the Pennsylvania Council received a message from Mr. Conrad Weiser, "that the chiefs of the United Nations were met in council with their nephews, the Delawares, at the house of Nicholas Scull, and that the Delawares had something to say to their uncles," etc., etc. This was the last time, probably, that he acted as interpreter.

In 1752 an English surveyor appeared in the province, and made some adverse criticisms upon the practice of his profession, which called forth the following letter from the Surveyor-General, Nicholas Scull, to R. Peters:

PHILADELPHIA, March 17, 1752.

Sir:—I have perused Mr. Jack's letter, and think his method of finding the meridian, the tangent line, and running the circumference of the circle to be good, as well as plain and easier to be conceived. His opinion also of the insufficiency of the needle in running of long lines is doubtless very just. But I must own myself at a loss to understand him when he says that there is nothing at all in the objection that a line run with stakes will be an arch of a great circle, and not a parallel of latitude, or east and west line. For my part, I must confess that I always understood an east and west line and a parallel of latitude to mean the same thing, and I conceive nothing more evident than that a great circle cannot be a parallel of latitude. If so, then a line run with stakes cannot be an east and west line. However, as I am convinced by Mr. Jack's letter that he is far superior to me in mathematical learning, I shall at present submit to his better judgment; but lest some people on this side the water should think him mistaken on this point, I think it my duty to advise the having it settled at home before the lines between the provinces are begun. I am your assured friend,

NICHOLAS SCULL.

To RICHARD PETERS, Esq.

N. B.—I forgot to observe above that we have no such instrument as Mr. Jack mentions.

There are still extant, in good preservation, a number of admirably executed maps of Philadelphia, and views of the river front of the city, of an early date, from the office of the Surveyor General, bearing his own imprint and that of Scull & Heap. He died in the year 1761-'62, in Philadelphia, and was buried in the old family ground near Scheetz's mill, at Whitemarsh. His tombstone was standing forty years ago, but has since disappeared. The headstone of his wife still remained two or three years ago. On it was the following inscription, written by him :—

> To the memory of ABIGAIL, the wife of Nicholas Scull,
>   who departed this life the 21st of May, 1753, aged
> sixty-five years.

> " The ashes of the tender wife lie here—
>   The tender mother and the friend sincere :
>   Her mind each female ornament possessed,
>   And virtue reigned triumphant in her breast."

Another interment was made in the ground, near the above, early in the present century, that was attended by an aged aunt of Mr. Samuel J. Christian's. It was of Lydia, the daughter of Mrs. Mary Scull Biddle, who married Captain McFunn, of the Royal Navy, and Governor of the Island of Antigua, whose only son—William Biddle McFunn—took the surname of Biddle, in conformity with the wish of his uncle Edward, who left him a large estate. He married Lydia Spencer. His grandfather—William Biddle—was the son of the William Biddle who emigrated in the time of William Penn from England to West Jersey. Mrs. Mary Biddle inherited from her father his poetic faculty—for she too " loved books, and sometimes made verses." Many of these have been preserved in the family, but I am not aware of any of them ever having appeared in print. The following impromptu, from her pen, was written July 20th, 1788, and was addressed to her niece, Sally Tellier, who was about to embark for England, on her way to Berne, Switzerland :—

> " While you to distant climes prepare to go,
>   I too must travel, but I travel slow.
>   Near eighty years since first I saw the light,
>   And now approaches near the expected night.
>   You different nations, various scenes, will meet ;
>   See rocks and precipices beneath your feet ;
>   Mountains whose summits seem to reach the skies,
>   With pastoral cottages beneath them rise ;
>   While I a foreign country must explore,
>   From whose lone banks and desolated shore
>   No traveller returns to tell us where
>   This country lies, or who inhabits there.
>   Ah, no ! My fancy paints its verdant plains,
>   Delightful groves, and clear, transparent streams ;
>   Its bowers of bliss—for Peace herself is there,
>   And from her presence flies that harpy, Care.
>   Love, faith, and joy divine the soul employ,
>   And raptures such as saints enthroned enjoy !

25

This is the country I have striven to gain—
Through life's long pilgrimage my constant aim.
Sweet, cheering Hope attends me on my way,
And leaves me not, I trust, on that important day.
May you, my dear relation, friendship meet,
And every good, in Berne's delightful seat.
Blest in a husband and an only son,
My prayers you'll have until my course is run.

"God bless you!
"From your affectionate aunt,
"MARY BIDDLE."

The old burial-ground of the "Scull family"—mentioned in a recent chapter of Wescott's "History of Philadelphia"—formed part of "Springfield Manor," an estate of four hundred acres that was purchased by Nicholas Scull in 1688, and laid out on December 24, 1692.

John Lukens was a native of Horsham, and succeeded to the Surveyor-Generalship on the death of Nicholas Scull, in December, 1768. John Biddle was also an apprentice with John Lukens under Nicholas Scull, and married, in 1736, Sarah Owen, daughter of Owen Owen. James, the youngest son of the Surveyor, married twice, and had five sons and three daughters. His oldest son, Peter, was born December, 1753, and was bred a lawyer, but entered the Continental army as major. He was aide-de-camp to General Washington at the battle of White Plains. He was an accomplished and gallant officer, and was one of three candidates for the office of Secretary of the Board of War. Washington indorsed his claims before a committee of Congress by saying: "Gentlemen, Major Scull is a young man, but an old officer." He was a friend and connection by marriage with Alexander Graydon, the author of "The Memoirs," etc., and is several times mentioned in that work. His commission as major of a regiment of foot commanded by Colonel John Patton is dated January 11th, 1777. He was also Secretary of the Board of War July 17th, 1779. His name is appended to the commission granted by Congress to Henry Savage, gentleman, to be second lieutenant in Colonel Crane's regiment of artillery. His health failing, he was ordered abroad by his physician, and sailed from Chester for France, October 20th, 1779, in the frigate Confederacy, but he died at sea, as certified to by Nathan Dorsey, surgeon of the ship, December 4th, 1779. The late Andrew Graydon, of Harrisburg, had in his possession in 1850 Major Scull's papers. There were letters referring to his illness, his will, an inventory of his books, clothing, etc., and some note-books. His will is dated November 23d, 1779. To his friend, Dr. Potts, he bequeathed the thanks of a dying man; to his friend, Alexander Graydon, his pocket-pistols; to Geo. Lux the sword given to him by his honored father-in-law, and his friend and protector, Edward Biddle; to Colonel Morgan Conner his greenhilted hanger; and to Colonel Patton, of Philadelphia, his silver buckles. His executors were his mother (his father's second wife), Susannah, and his friends James Biddle and Alexander Graydon.

A tragical occurrence is thus related in the *Gentleman's Magazine* :—

"Philadelphia.—On Wednesday, August 27th, 1760, Mr. Robert Scull, of this place, with some company, was playing at billiards, when Mr. Bruleman, lately an officer in the Royal American regiment, was present, who without the least provocation levelled a loaded gun he had with him, and shot Mr. Scull through the body as he was going to strike his ball; for which he was afterward tried, and on the 8th of October executed. Bruleman was by trade a silversmith, which business he left and went into the army, where he was an officer in the royal American Regiment, but was discharged on being detected in counterfeiting or uttering counterfeit money. He then returned to Philadelphia; and, growing insupportable to himself, and yet being unwilling to put an end to his own life, he determined upon the commission of some crime for which he might get hanged by the law. Having formed this design, he loaded his gun with a brace of balls and asked his landlord to go a-shooting with him—intending to murder him before he returned. But his landlord, not choosing to go, escaped the danger. He then went out and met Dr. Cadwalader, who spoke to him so politely that it quite turned him from his purpose against him. He then went to a public house, where he drank some liquor; and hearing people at play at billiards in a room above stairs, he went up to them, and was talkative, facetious, and seemingly good humored. After some time he called to the landlord, and desired him to hang up the gun. Mr. Scull, who was at play, having struck his antagonist's ball into one of the pockets, Bruleman said to him: 'Sir, you are a good marksman, and I will now show you a fine stroke.' He immediately levelled his piece and took aim at Mr. Scull (who imagined him in jest), and shot both the balls through his body. He then went up to Mr. Scull (who did not expire nor lose his senses till a considerable time after), and said to him: 'Sir, I had no malice or ill-will against you—for I never saw you before; but I was determined to kill somebody that I might be hanged, and you happened to be the man; and as you are a very likely young man, I am sorry for your misfortune.' Mr. Scull had time to send for his friends and to make his will. He forgave his murderer, and, if it could be done, desired that he might be pardoned."

Of this unfortunate affair, Charles Biddle has left the following account, which should have been inserted in its proper place. Robert Scull was his cousin.

Sitting one evening at my mother's door with Captain Robert Scull, a cousin of my mother's, one Bruleman went by. He was a genteel looking man. As he walked along he had a cane in his hand, which he kept throwing up, and catching as it fell. Mr. Scull inquired what strange fellow that was. I told him he was a jeweller, who lived with a Mr. Milne, a few doors from us; that he had been an officer in the army, but was dismissed the service on suspicion of being concerned with some coiners; that he appeared to be an inoffensive man, but was supposed, since his dismissal, to be a little deranged. Mr. Scull expressed himself a good deal concerned for him. A day or two after this, Bruleman went to the Schuylkill with a loaded gun with an intention to shoot himself in the woods, but he said he could not do it. He was then determined to shoot some person in order that he might be executed. The first he met after he had made up his mind was Dr. Cadwalader, who politely pulled off his hat to him. This saved the Doctor. Another person he met spoke to him in so kind a manner, that he could not shoot him. One other he saw in the woods, but he said there was no person that could be a witness against him. He then went into the billiard room at the Centre Tavern, pulled off his coat and hung it up. Captain Scull was then playing. In passing by where the coat was, he accidentally threw it down; and immediately after, making a good stroke, Bruleman took up his gun and presenting it at Captain Scull, saying at the same time, "Sir, you have made a good stroke, I will show you a better," and fired across the table. One of the balls went through his body and lodged in the door. He walked to the corner of the room, leaned upon his mace which broke, and he fell. When the gentlemen in the room went up to him, he said, "The villain has murdered me." In the confusion, Bruleman could have got off, but this he did not want. He requested one of the company to load his piece and shoot him. He was carried to gaol, and soon after tried and executed. He suffered with great fortitude, appearing anxious to leave the world, saying no man should remain in it who had lost his character. Captain Scull was in the prime of life, and had just acquired an independent fortune.

See also Watson's Annals, vol. i. p. 560.

NOTES. 389

Mr. Robert Scull was buried at the corner of Fifth and Arch streets. He left a son, John, a minor, who was sent to Carlisle to be educated—a faithful slave, Cæsar, attending him. John Biddle and John Lukens are named in Mr. Scull's will as his brothers-in-law.

Nicholas Scull, the Surveyor-General, had nine children, viz.; Mary (born August 2, 1709, died, 1790, in Philadelphia), married William Biddle, father of Charles Biddle; Nicholas, born October 26, 1711; Elizabeth, born April 2, 1714; Edward, born October 26, 1716; Jasper, born December 3, 1718; John, born January 28, 1721 died March 21, 1769; Abigail, born December 28, 1724; Ann Scull, born November 13, 1727; and James, born November 22, 1730.

Edward, John, Jasper, and James Scull, sons of Nicholas Scull (second), removed to Reading, Pennsylvania, where some of their descendants still reside. John Scull, a son of Jasper Scull, went to Pittsburgh in 1786, and established the *Pittsburgh Gazette*, which was the first newspaper published west of the Allegheny Mountains. This John Scull was the ancestor of the branch of the family settled in Westmoreland County of this State. Nicholas Scull, the oldest son of the Surveyor-General, according to the records of Christ Church, was married October 7, 1732, to Rebecca Thompson.

Descendants of James Scull (brother of Mrs. William Biddle) are living in Florida, and the Rev. William Dundas Scull, a clergyman of the Episcopal Church, recently died in Alabama or Florida.

The wife of the late Alderman Peter Christian, of this city (sister of the late William Biddle Scull), was a lineal descendant of Joseph Scull, sixth son of Nicholas Scull (first), her father being Benjamin Franklin Scull, a godson of Dr. Franklin. Two of her brothers settled in Arkansas (Pine Bluff) about 1800; and one brother, Joseph, went to Cuba about the same time, all leaving numerous descendants.

For the information contained in this note, we are indebted to Mr. G. D. Scull, now residing at Rugby Lodge, Oxford, England.

NOTE C. (PAGE 75.)

Edward Biddle, brother of Charles Biddle, was born in 1738, and at the age of sixteen entered the Provincial Army, the name of "Ensign Biddle" appearing under the head of "Provincial Officers—1754," in Pennsylvania Archives, 2d series, vol. 2, p. 557-8. He was again appointed in 1757 ensign in Colonel Burd's battalion of the Pennsylvania Regiment and promoted to lieutenant in 1759. February 24, 1760, he was commissioned a captain in Colonel Hugh Mercer's battalion. (Same vol., p. 607.)

He served in the campaign of General Forbes in 1758, and was present at the capture of Fort Du Quesne (now Pittsburgh) in November of that year. It is believed that he was also at the capture of Fort Niagara the following year by the celebrated Sir William Johnson.

He subsequently resigned from the army, receiving for his services a grant of five thousand acres of land, and, after the usual course of study, established himself as a lawyer in Reading, Berks County.

He represented that county in the Assembly of Pennsylvania from 1767 to 1775, and in October, 1774, was chosen Speaker, in place of Mr Galloway. "Mr. Biddle," says Gordon, "had long represented Berks County, and enjoyed the confidence of the House in an eminent degree, being placed upon the most important committees, and taking an active part in all current business."

A meeting of the freeholders of the county of Berks was held at Reading, July 2, 1774, to consider the Boston Port Bill, at which Edward Biddle presided. Resolutions of the most decided character were adopted and "the thanks of the assembly were unanimously voted to the chairman for the patriotic and spirited manner in which he pointed out the dangerous situation of all the American colonies, occasioned by the unconstitutional measures lately adopted by the British Parliament, expressing at the same time loyalty to our sovereign, and the most warm and tender regard for the liberties of America."

In July, 1774, he was elected, with seven others, to represent Pennsylvania in the first Continental Congress. That body met on the 5th of September. Mr. Biddle was present during the whole of the session and took a prominent position, being placed on important committees.

He was again elected a delegate to Congress in December, 1774, and in November, 1775. He was also a member of the Provincial Convention, held in Philadelphia, January 23 to 28, 1775.

It was about this time that he met with the accident mentioned in the text, which permanently disabled him from taking any further active share in public affairs. On the 15th of March, 1775, he resigned the Speakership on account of ill health, and was unable to attend the Congress of that year. We find him, however, chosen by the Assembly, June 30, 1775, together with his brother James, and his cousin, Owen Biddle,* a member of the Committee of Safety.

In 1778 he again became a member of the Assembly, and on the 20th of November was chosen, with six others, a delegate in Congress for the ensuing year. The next day, "Mr. Biddle, one of the gentlemen chosen yesterday to represent this State in Congress, informed the House that his state of health, as well as his private affairs, could not, consistent with a regard to either, permit him to accept the honor they had done him, and therefore desired that he might have leave to resign, which was accordingly granted."

------

* See note H.

On 5th February, 1779, he was appointed with three others upon a committee to bring in a "bill for the abolition of slavery within this State." In March, 1779, the House proceeded to elect three delegates to Congress in the room of Edward Biddle, Dr. Roberdeau, and William Clingan. His last appearance in public life was in the Assembly in March, 1779; and on the 5th of September of that year he died at Chatsworth, near Baltimore, the residence of his daughter, Mrs. Lux. In St. Paul's churchyard, Baltimore, upon a flat tombstone, is the following inscription:—

> Under this Stone
> are deposited the remains of
> Edward Biddle, Esq., Counsellor at
> Law,
> Some time Speaker of the House of Assembly of
> Pennsylvania,
> And Delegate in the first and second
> Congress.
> He departed this life Sept. 5, 1779,
> In the 41st year of his age.

General Wilkinson says in his Memoirs (vol. i. p. 330): "I took Reading in my route, and passed some days in that place, where I had several dear and respected friends, and among them Edward Biddle, Esq., a man whose public and private virtues commanded respect, and excited admiration from all persons; he was Speaker of the last Assembly of Pennsylvania under the Proprietary government, and in the dawn of the Revolution devoted himself to the cause of his country, and successfully opposed the overbearing influence of Joseph Galloway. Ardent, eloquent, and full of zeal, by his exertions during several days and nights of obstinate, warm, and animated discussion, in extreme sultry weather, he overheated himself, and brought on an inflammatory rheumatism and surfeit, which radically destroyed his health, and ultimately deprived society of one of its greatest ornaments, and his country of a statesman, a patriot, and a soldier: for he had served several campaigns in the war of 1756, and if his health had been spared would, no doubt, have occupied the second or third place in the Revolutionary armies."

The notice of him which appeared at his death, written by Mr. James Read, then a member of the Supreme Executive Council, has been inserted at page 127.

In his forced retirement near the close of his life, when distressed by the vexatious and conflicting proceedings of the different State authorities, he is thus mentioned by Graydon, p. 265:—

"Mr. Edward Biddle, then in a declining state of health, and no longer in Congress, apparently entertained sentiments not accordant with the measures pursuing; and, in the fervid style of elocution for which he was distinguished, he often exclaimed that he really knew not what to wish for. 'The subjugation of my country,' he would say, 'I deprecate as a grievous calamity, and yet sicken at the idea of thirteen unconnected, petty democracies; if we are to be independent, let us, in the name of God, at once have an empire, and place Washington at the head of it.'"

In 1761 Edward Biddle married Elizabeth Ross, daughter of the Rev. Mr. Ross, a clergyman of the Church of England, and brother of the distinguished George Ross. Two daughters were born of this marriage, Catharine, married to George Lux, of Baltimore, and Abigail, married to Dr. Falls, of Maryland. Neither of these left any descendants.

See Sketch of Edward Biddle, by Craig Biddle, in vol. i. of Pennsylvania Magazine of History; also Graydon's Memoirs.

The following extract from the Colonial Records, vol. iv., contains a letter written by Edward Biddle, then a youth of seventeen, in the year 1755, when there was an alarm occasioned by an Indian incursion about where the town of Womelsdorf now stands.

"A Letter from Mr. Edward Biddle at Reading to his Father in the City.

"*My dearest Father :*—I'm in so much horror and Confusion I scarce know what I am writing. The Drum is beating to Arms and Bells ringing & all the people under Arms. Within these two hours we have had different tho' too uncertain Accts all corroborating each other, and this moment is an Express arrived dispatch'd from Michael Reis' at Tulpehoccon, 18 miles above this Town, who left about 30 of their people engaged with about an equal number of Indians at the s'd Reis'. This night we expect an attack, truly alarming is our situation. The people exclaim against the Quakers, & some are scarce restrained from burning the Houses of those few who are in This Town. Oh my Country! My bleeding Country! I recommend myself to the divine God of Armies. Give my dutiful Love to my dearest Mother and my best love to brother Jemmy.

I am, Honored Sir, Your most affectionate & obedient Son,

E. BIDDLE.

Sunday, 1 o'clock. I have rather lessened than exaggerated our Melancholy Account.

Copied from the original.

JAMES BIDDLE."

NOTE D.   (Page 110.)

The first commission of Nicholas Biddle runs as follows:—

In Committee of Safety.

To NICHOLAS BIDDLE, Esquire.

We reposing especial trust and confidence in your Patriotism, Valour, conduct and Fidelity, Do by these Presents constitute and appoint you to be *Captain* of the Provincial Armed Boat, called the Franklin fitted out for the protection of the Province of Pennsylvania, and the Commerce of the River Delaware, against all hostile Enterprizes, and for the defence of American Liberty: you are therefore to take the said Boat into your charge, and carefully and diligently to discharge the duty of *Captain* by doing and performing all manner of things thereunto belonging. And we do strictly charge and require all Officers, Soldiers and Mariners under your command to be obedient to your orders, as *Captain*. And you are to observe and follow such orders and directions from time to time, as you shall receive from the Assembly or Provincial Convention, during their Sessions, or from this or a future Committee of Safety for this Province, or from your Superior Officer, according to the Rules and Discipline of War, pursuant to the trust reposed in you; this commission to continue in force until revoked by the Assembly or Provincial Convention, or by this or any succeeding Committee of Safety.

By order of the Committee.

B. FRANKLIN, *Presid't.*

Philadelphia, August, 1st 1775.
WM. GOVETT, *Sec'ty.*

Captain Blake, who commanded the Marines on board the Moultrie, thus describes the engagement in which the Randolph was blown up:—

Dear Sir:—Agreeable to your request I would endeavor to recollect and state what happened during the unfortunate cruise in which the Randolph was blown up. I was ordered with a detachment of the 2nd South Carolina Continental Regiment, to embark on board the General Moultrie, and sailed in company with the Randolph and the Briggs Notre Dame, Fair American and Polly, in the month of February, 1778. The object of this Armament was understood to be an attack on the Carysford frigate, Perseus twenty-gun ship, and Hinchenbrook brig of sixteen guns, who had for some time annoyed the trade of this place, and so completely blockaded it that very few vessels escaped them either bound in or out. Our little squadron was sometime detained in Rebellion Roads, by contrary winds, and the want of a full tide to carry the Randolph out; her draft of water being eighteen feet. The first chance that offered we proceeded to sea and were over the bar by eight o'clock in the morning, and after discharging the pilots stood to the eastward without seeing any enemy. The next day we retook a dismasted ship from New England, which had been taken by a small ship from St. Augustine, called the Lord George Germain, which having no cargo on board, after taking out the people with six light guns and a few stores we set her on fire. From this time nothing extraordinary happened till our arrival in the West Indies when we cruised to the eastward and nearly in the latitude of the Barbados and for several days had stopped and examined a number of French and Dutch vessels. The only English vessel that we saw, was a schooner from New York to Grenada, who mistook us for an English squadron, and never discovered the mistake till he spoke the Polly who took possession of her.

The day this capture was made I dined on board the Randolph, when, I recollect, Capt. Biddle expressed himself to this effect: "We have been cruising here for some time and have spoken a number of vessels who will no doubt give information, and I should not be surprised if my old ship should be sent after us, but as to anything that mounts her guns on one deck, I think myself a match for her." I don't recollect her name, but understood her to be a 50 or 60 gunship which he had formerly served on board of, and which was then supposed to be the only two-decker the British had in the West Indies. Two or perhaps three days after this, about 3 o'clock in the afternoon a signal was made from the Randolph for a sail to windward in consequence of which the squadron hauled on the wind, and stood for her. It was near 4 o'clock before she could be seen from our quarterdeck when I could plainly discover through a glass that she was a ship. About 6 o'clock I again looked at her through the glass, and if I had not before satisfied myself of her being a ship I should without hesitation have declared her to be a large sloop. At this time she had neared us so much that her topsails were out of water and her topgallant sails being handed and she coming down before the wind she had the appearance of a large sloop with only a square-sail set. About 7 o'clock the Randolph, being to windward, hove to; the Moultrie being then about 150 yards astern and rather to leeward also hove to, the Notre Dame rather astern and to leeward of us. I don't recollect the situation of the other brigs. About 8 o'clock the British ship fired a shot just ahead of us, and hailed asking what ship it was. The answer was, the Polly. "Where are you from?" Answer, from New York. She took no further notice of us, but immediately hauled her wind and hailed the Randolph. At this time, and not before, we discovered her to be a two-decker. One or two questions being asked and answers returned as she was ranging up alongside of the Randolph, and had got on her weather quarter, I heard Lieutenant Barnes very distinctly call out, "This is the Randolph," who immediately begun the action. The British ship's stern being then clear of the Randolph the Captain of the Moultrie gave orders to fire, and in consequence of it three broadsides were fired, the last of which I am satisfied must have gone into the Randolph as the enemy had shot so much ahead as to bring her between us. I then mentioned with some warmth to our Capt. that instead of assisting we were firing into the Randolph, in consequence of which we immediately made sail to get ahead and engage her on the bow, but before this could be effected the Randolph blew up. The Capt. then came to me and said, "Capt. Blake, the Randolph is blown up, what can we do?" I answered that it appeared to me, we ought now to consult our own safety by getting away as fast as we could. The man at the wheel called out, "It is impossible, Sir, to get off, the ship is now aboard of us," and asked the Capt. if we should pull down the colors, who answered, "Yes, you may do what you will." I told Capt. Sullivan it was of little consequence whether the colors were up or not. I requested him to encourage the people to make sail. He then went on the main deck for that purpose. Perceiving the man at the wheel very much alarmed, he having repeated to me that it was impossible to get away, and that the enemy was then yawing to get her broadside to bear which would rake us fore and aft, I mentioned to the Sailing Master that unless he removed him we should probably be taken in a few minutes, in consequence of which he kicked him from the wheel and took it himself for some little time.

I am extremely sorry that I have mislaid Davis's statement which you furnished me with as it may have brought something to my recollection which I have forgot, but believe I have mentioned every material occurrence, but not being a seaman it is possible I have not done it so correctly as I wish but am persuaded nothing of consequence has escaped me. I think Davis mentions that the Randolph spoke us and informed us that he knew the enemy's ship, which is untrue. I was not off the quarter deck from the time the signal was made until the unfortunate termination of the business, and declare unequivocally that we never during that time spoke to each other.

I am with regard, Dear Sir,

yours truly,

J. BLAKE.

Charleston, 7th Oct. 1804.

To THOMAS HALL, Esq.

The following verses by Freneau are typical of the style of eulogium then prevalent in England and America on occasion of military or naval battles.

ON THE DEATH OF CAPTAIN NICHOLAS BIDDLE,

COMMANDER OF THE RANDOLPH FRIGATE,

Blown up near Barbadoes—1778.

What distant thunders rend the skies,
What clouds of smoke in volumes rise,
    What means this dreadful roar!
Is from his base *Vesurius* thrown,
Is sky-topt *Atlas* tumbled down,
    Or *Etna's* self no more!

Shock after shock torments my ear ;
And lo ! two hostile ships appear,
  Red lightnings round them glow :
The *Yarmouth* boasts of sixty-four,
The *Randolph* thirty-two—no more—
  And will she fight this foe ?

The Randolph soon on Stygian streams
Shall coast along the land of dreams,
  The islands of the dead !
But fate, that parts them on the deep,
Shall save the Briton, still to weep
  His ancient honours fled.

Say, who commands that dismal blaze,
Where yonder starry streamer plays ;
  Does *Mars* with *Jove* engage ?
'Tis BIDDLE wings those angry fires,
BIDDLE, whose bosom *Jove* inspires
  With more than mortal rage.

Tremendous flash !—and hark, the ball
Drives through old Yarmouth, flames and all ;
  Her bravest sons expire ;
Did Mars himself approach so nigh,
Even Mars, without disgrace, might fly
  The Randolph's fiercer fire.

The Briton views his mangled crew,
" And shall we strike to *thirty-two*,
  (Said Hector, stain'd with gore)
" Shall Britain's flag to *these* descend ?
" Rise, and the glorious conflict end,
  " Britons, I ask no more !"

He spoke—they charg'd their cannon round,
Again the vaulted heavens resound,
  The Randolph bore it all,
Then fix'd her pointed cannons true—
Away the unwieldly vengeance flew ;
  Britain, thy warriors fall.

The Yarmouth saw, with dire dismay,
Her wounded hull, shrouds shot away,
  Her boldest heroes dead—
She saw amidst her floating slain
The conquering *Randolph* stem the main—
  She saw, she turn'd, and fled ! .

That hour, blest chief, had she been thine,
Dear *Biddle*, had the powers divine
  Been kind as thou wert brave ;
But fate, who doom'd thee to expire,
Prepar'd an arrow tipt with fire,
  And mark'd a wat'ry grave,

And in that hour when conquest came
Wing'd at his ship a pointed flame
　　That not even *he* could shun—
The conquest ceas'd, the Yarmouth fled,
The bursting Randolph ruin spread,
　　And lost what honour won.

NOTE E.　(Page 286.)

James Biddle, son of Charles Biddle, was born on the 18th of February, 1783. He had made considerable progress in his studies, and acquired a taste for literature, which he retained through life, when he left the University of Pennsylvania to enter the navy. He and his brother Edward sailed as midshipmen in the President, under Commodore Truxtun, in September, 1800, for the West Indies. Edward Biddle, a youth of great promise, died during the voyage. This event did not, however, abate the inclination for the sea of his brother James. On the reduction of the navy, in 1801, he was retained in the service. Early in 1802, he sailed in the Constellation, under Commodore Murray, for the Mediterranean, on a cruise against the Tripolitans. In 1803, he was transferred to the Philadelphia, Captain Bainbridge. On the 31st October of that year, the ship struck upon a rock, off the coast of Tripoli. After every effort to get her afloat had failed, and all resistance to the enemy's gunboats had proved unavailing, Captain Bainbridge surrendered his ship, and, with his officers and crew, was subjected to a close and rigorous confinement. The known barbarity of the Moors, in their treatment of Christian captives, excited much apprehension for the fate of the prisoners. The family of young Biddle proposed, through Sir Alexander Ball, the Governor of Malta, to effect his liberation by the payment of a ransom; but he positively refused to take advantage of an arrangement by which he alone would be benefited, and declared his resolution to share the lot of his comrades. Their release was at last obtained through negotiation, by the Government of the United States, after an imprisonment of twenty months. From this time he was constantly in active service; and at the commencement of the war with Great Britain, he sailed from Philadelphia, in the capacity of first lieutenant of the sloop-of-war Wasp, Captain Jacob Jones. On the 18th October, 1812, after receiving some damage from a heavy gale, the Wasp fell in with six British merchantmen, two of which mounted sixteen guns each, under convoy of the sloop-of-war Frolic, Captain Whyngates. Captain Jones immediately determined to attack them. The merchantmen sailed away, while the Frolic waited for the Wasp, which bore down upon her on the larboard side. The Wasp commenced the action at about sixty yards distance, maintaining the weather-gage. The English fired with more rapidity, the Americans with more precision and effect. Finally, Captain Jones ran his ship athwart the

enemy's bow. so that the Frolic's jib-boom came in between his main and
mizzen rigging, and two of his guns entered the bow-ports of the Frolic,
and swept the whole length of her deck. After one broadside delivered in
this position, the conquest was completed by boarding. Lieutenant Biddle
led the boarders; he and a seaman named Jack Lang were the first to gain
a footing upon the deck of the enemy. The conflict lasted just forty-three
minutes. In this action, there was almost a perfect equality of force, the
Frolic's armament slightly exceeding that of the Wasp. It is cited by Sir
Howard Douglass, in his treatise on gunnery—one of the highest British
authorities—as a remarkable instance of American superiority in that art;
an acknowledgment that is in strong contrast with the elaborate misrepresentations by which some English contemporary writers endeavored to
palliate the reverses of their navy. One of the most dishonest of the works
composed with that object, and dignified with the name of History, it is,
perhaps, worth mentioning, was written by William James, who for some
time exercised the calling of "veterinary surgeon" in the city of Philadelphia; but the mortality among his equine patients exposing him to imputa-
tions of malpractice, he returned to his native land, and devoted his skill to
the studied depreciation of the exploits of American commanders. There
is an exposure of some of his errors and misrepresentations in two articles,
from the pen of Fenimore Cooper, in the Democratic Review, vol. x., A. D.
1842; and the Edinburgh Review (vol. lxxi., A. D. 1840) condemns his
"bitter and persevering antipathy to our transatlantic relations. . . . .
Almost every original remark made upon them by the author bears traces
of the unworthy feeling we have mentioned."

Soon after the action between the Wasp and the Frolic, a British seventy-
four, the Poictiers, fell in with them, and Captain Jones was obliged to
surrender his ship, with her recent prize, and they were taken into Bermuda.
The officers, however, were soon liberated by exchange. Lieutenant Biddle
acquired great distinction by his conduct in this action. Among other honors
conferred on him by his fellow-citizens and public bodies, were a sword from
his native State, a medal from Congress, votes of thanks, etc. He was also
immediately promoted to the rank of master-commandant, and placed in
charge of a flotilla of gunboats, for the protection of the river Delaware, and
soon after transferred to the command of the Hornet sloop of war, which,
with the frigates United States and Macedonian, formed a squadron, under
Commodore Decatur. Soon after leaving New York, they were compelled,
by the presence of a superior British force, to put into the harbor of New
London, Connecticut, where they were closely blockaded. During this
period of inaction, what was considered as an overture from the British
officers, led to a negotiation for a "challenge fight." Commodore Decatur
sent Captain Biddle to Sir Thomas Hardy, the British commodore, to propose that the two American frigates should meet two of his ships of the same
class. It was found impossible, however, to obtain the assent of Sir Thomas
Hardy to this proposal. Captain Biddle did, however, succeed in adjusting

the terms for a meeting between his own sloop of war, the Hornet, and the sloop-of-war Loup Cervier. These terms, however, did not receive the unqualified approval of Commodore Decatur, because they admitted, for the Loup Cervier, the advantage of a picked crew from the other ships of the British squadron. Captain Biddle instantly forwarded another proposal, so varied as to obviate the objections of his superior officer; but, without returning any reply, the captain of the Loup Cervier put to sea, and did not come back again to that station. Such maritime duels are not, however, to be commended. The aim in public warfare should be to use advantages, not to neutralize them, by voluntary stipulations. There must be incident, too, to such encounters an unnecessary and desperate protraction, leading to a useless waste of life, which does not attend ordinary conflicts. That the usual obligations of duty are thought to be transcended, appears from the fact that Captain Biddle, before closing the negotiation on his own behalf, had deemed it proper to obtain the assent of his crew; avowing that he considered the national honor to be so peculiarly involved in the result of such a meeting, that in no possible extremity should his ship be surrendered. This determination is characteristic not only of the individual, but also of the transaction in which he was then engaged.

There being no prospect of an abandonment of the blockade, and an escape from it being deemed impracticable, it was ordered by the United States Government that the frigates should be hauled up the river and dismantled; the charge of them in this condition being assigned to Captain Biddle, in the Hornet. To one of his enterprising character, nothing could be more irksome than the sphere of inactivity to which he had now been confined for nearly seventeen months. He feelingly compared it to his long imprisonment in Tripoli; and urgently and constantly solicited permission to attempt a passage through the blockading squadron, expressing the most sanguine expectation of success. At length, the permission was yielded to his importunity. He instantly effected his purpose; passing out unperceived through the British squadron, on the night of the 18th November, 1814.

Being then ordered to join the East India squadron, he arrived the first at the place of rendezvous, the island of Tristan D'Acunha, on the 23d March, 1815. When about to cast anchor, a sail was descried to the southward. Captain Biddle immediately stood off from the land, placed himself upon the course of the other vessel, and waited for her. The stranger, a British ship of war, manoeuvred very cautiously, and reserved her fire till within musket-shot distance. The conflict was "short, sharp, and decisive." Again it was the fortune of Biddle to demonstrate the superiority of American gunnery. It was subsequently narrated, by the British first lieutenant, that his captain, Dickinson, after about fifteen minutes' firing, said to him. "This fellow hits us every time; we can't stand his fire; we must run him aboard." The attempt to board was, however, ineffectual. The Hornet's fire still told fearfully upon her antagonist, and one of the British officers called out that they surrendered. Captain Biddle ceased his firing, and, standing on the taffrail, asked, "Have you surrendered?" At this moment two of the English marines fired at him from about twelve yards' distance. A ball passed through his neck, and struck him down from the taffrail, but he refused to go below, and gave the order to wear the ship round for another broadside, when a general cry of surrender rose from the British ship, and she struck her colors. She was the Penguin, a ship of the Hornet's class, size, and metal; and she had been carefully fitted out to cruise for the Young Wasp, a vessel somewhat heavier than the Hornet. Only superior discipline and skill could account for the fact that, in an action of twenty-two minutes, the Penguin's mainmast was crippled, her foremast and bowsprit shot away, and her hull so riddled that it was not thought advisable to send her to the United States, and she was therefore scuttled. On the other hand, the Hornet's principal damage was in the rigging, and, in a few hours, she was again fit for service. The British historian, Sir Archibald Alison, thus mentions the engagement: "On the 23d of March, long after peace had been signed, the Hornet met the Penguin, and a furious conflict ensued, both commanders being ignorant of the termination of hostilities. Both vessels were of equal size and weight of metal, but the American had the advantage in the number and composition of her crew; and, after a desperate conflict, in the course of which the brave Captain Dickinson was slain in the very act of attempting to board, the British vessel surrendered, having lost a third of her crew, killed and wounded."[*]

It was a curious coincidence that, as after the capture of the Frolic, Biddle soon fell in with a British seventy-four, the Cornwallis, which immediately gave chase to the Hornet. The pursuit was continued for three days. Though Captain Biddle was still much debilitated by his wound, and his first lieutenant (Conner) had been disabled in the late action, every expedient that nautical skill could suggest was vigorously used to increase the Hornet's speed; finally the anchors, boats, shot, guns, and every other heavy article were thrown overboard. The gigantic pursuer several times got near enough to open fire, but did not succeed in overtaking the Hornet. Fenimore Cooper says, in his Naval History, "Captain Biddle gained nearly as much reputation for the steadiness and skill with which he saved his ship on this occasion as for the fine manner in which he had fought her a few weeks earlier. In the promptitude with which he had continued his cruise, after capturing a vessel of equal force, the nation traced the spirit of the elder officer of the same name and family, who had rendered himself so conspicuous in the Revolution."

Captain Biddle put into San Salvador on the 9th of June, 1815, and there heard that peace had been made with Great Britain.

On his return to the United States, he was promoted to the rank of Post

---

[*] Alison's History of Europe, chap. lxxvi.

Captain, and received the honors due to his gallantry from Congress, his native State, and his fellow-citizens.

After the termination of the war he was constantly employed in the ordinary routine of naval duty, which, though arduous and important, presents few details of interest to the general reader. He, at three different periods, held commands upon the coast of South America, and displayed great ability and conduct in the complex relations which then existed between the United States and Spain and her revolted colonies. One incident, which occurred at Valparaiso, excited at the time considerable attention. The government of the United States had not yet recognized the independence of Chili, and therefore the authorities omitted to notice the offer of Captain Biddle to exchange the usual salutes on his arrival at Valparaiso in the Ontario. The Chilian navy was under the command of Lord Cochrane, who had been dismissed from the British service after being convicted of fraud in a conspiracy to affect the public funds. Captain Biddle was about weighing anchor, to proceed on his voyage, when Lord Cochrane desired him to submit to a detention in port until after the sailing of a secret expedition. For reasons which he deemed sufficient, in view of the late omission to salute his flag, Captain Biddle declined to accede to this request. Immediately two ships of the Chilian navy slipped their cables, and took up a position to command the mouth of the harbor. By all on board of the Ontario it was understood as a menace. Biddle instantly cleared for action, and bore down upon the ships placed in his way. They suffered him to pass between them, and proceed to sea without molestation.

Among special services rendered by him, we may enumerate that, in 1817, he took possession of Oregon Territory; in 1826, he signed a commercial treaty with Turkey; from 1838 to 1842, he held the post of Governor of the Naval Asylum, at Philadelphia; in 1845, while in command of a squadron in the East Indies, he exchanged the ratifications of the first treaty with China, and acted as United States Commissioner to that country; he also touched at Japan, and made an earnest effort to conciliate, by kindness and forbearance, its singular and exclusive people. From Japan he sailed to California, and took command of the United States naval force in the Pacific Ocean, then engaged in prosecuting the war against Mexico. Immediately on his arrival at this station, his nice appreciation of belligerent rights was exhibited, by the revocation of a general blockade of the west coast of Mexico, which had been declared by his predecessor, and the substitution of a blockade of special ports, maintained by the presence of a competent force. It is in conformity with this practice that a European congress has since abolished "paper-blockades," and adopted the American principle upon this subject.

He reached home in the month of March, 1848, worn with the toils of long and faithful service, and, on the 1st of October following, died at Philadelphia, aged sixty-five years. He had never sought repose in ex-

26

emption from duty, and, with unremitting zeal, his whole life was devoted to his country.

Commodore Biddle was a well-read scholar, thoroughly conversant with general literature, international and military law, the practice of courts-martial, and the usages of the naval service. No man was more exemplary in all the private relations of life. He never married, and the affection of his warm and generous nature was bestowed upon a large circle of relatives and friends. His manners were marked by scrupulous refinement and delicacy. He was slight in person, and it was by the force of an indomitable spirit that he surmounted hardships and difficulties. His temperament was quick and impulsive, but controlled by a strong sense of justice, and a careful regard for the rights of others. Rigid in all the essentials of discipline, he had none of the exacting spirit that vents itself in minute and harassing attention to insignificant details. His character commanded the respect, and won the affection of his officers and his crew. Few men have more completely fulfilled the duties of their station in life; and he may be with truth cited as one of the best examples of the American naval officer.— *Simpson's Eminent Philadelphians.*

NOTE F. (PAGES 305 AND 318.)

In Davis's Life of Burr will be found a number of letters to and from Charles Biddle. In a letter to his son-in-law Joseph Alston, written the day before his duel with Hamilton, Burr says :—

"My very worthy friend, Charles Biddle of Philadelphia, has six or seven sons, three of them grown up. With different characters, and various degrees of intelligence, they will all be men of eminence and of influence. Call to see the father as you pass through Philadelphia, and receive the sons kindly."

The letters which are here given relating to the duel have never been in print. The first, upon another subject, will serve to show Burr's high sense of public duty.

With regard to the duel, Mr. Parton, the fairest of Burr's biographers, says : "Gates, De Witt Clinton, Randolph, Benton, Clay, Jackson, Decatur, Arnold, Walpole, Pitt, Wellington, Canning, Peel, Grattan, Fox, Sheridan, Jeffrey, Wilkes, D'Israeli, Lamartine, Thiers, and scores of less famous names are found in Mr. Sabine's list of duelists.[*] In all that curious catalogue there is not the name of one politician who received provocation so often repeated, so irritating, and so injurious as that which Aaron Burr had received from Alexander Hamilton."

---

[*] Sabine's Notes on Duels and Duelling.

In point of fact, there was among gentlemen at that day practically no aversion to duelling, nor was General Hamilton himself ever known to be opposed to the practice until he so declared in the few last days of his life. He had acted as second to Colonel Laurens in his duel with General Lee, and had earnestly invited a challenge from Mr. Monroe in 1797. In that dispute Burr acted as the friend of Monroe, who, doubtless with his concurrence, honorably declined being drawn into a duel. The outcry against Burr in New York on this occasion was owing almost wholly to political hostility. The Federalist hate of Burr was of course intensified by the result of the duel, whilst the rage of the Clintonian wing of the Democracy against the man who stood in no fear of their whole aristocratic array was perfectly frantic.

The effect of General Hamilton's death in bringing discredit upon this mode of settling disputes has been greatly exaggerated. Certainly, among military, and we speak with confidence in saying, especially among naval men, for at least thirty-five years after Burr's duel it would have been deemed an act of poltroonery to refuse a challenge, unless the challenger by some gross misconduct had clearly forfeited his right to be recognized as a man of honor.

As late as the year 1838 a fatal duel between two members of Congress was witnessed by half a dozen fellow members and at least one senator.

After Hamilton's death there was a curious difference of opinion between the two seconds, as to whether Hamilton had fired at his adversary; Mr. Pendleton, his friend, asserting that he had not. Mr. Van Ness and Colonel Burr were of the contrary opinion, and Burr's letter to Charles Biddle of July 18th, one week after the duel, is important evidence. Hamilton, strange to say, was under the impression—his mind probably affected already by physical pain—that he had *not fired at all*. Some foolish friends afterwards pretended to have discovered the *precise twig* of a tree high in air, which had been severed by Hamilton's ball. Great stress, also, has been laid upon his declaration before the duel that he did not intend to fire at Burr. But he had a perfect right to change his intention at the last moment, being under no pledge whatever to any one as to his course of conduct. This is what actually occurred in 1826, in the famous duel between Clay and Randolph, where the latter changed his mind on the ground and fired one shot at Mr. Clay.

After Burr's duel he came to Charles Biddle's house in Philadelphia, and was received and welcomed by one of the sons, then a youth, the rest of the family being out of town. It is believed that he remained there until he sailed for the South.

WASHINGTON, 15th Mar. 1802.

My Dear Sir: Your letter of the 13th. is rec'd this Evening. I left you a Case and desired you to put into it one of the Medals. Again I beg you to accept it. But what has become of all the Copper ones? I should like a great number of them—and the acct. not yet sent.

It must not be mentioned abroad but between you & me I suspect Truxtun will not go out with the Squadron. It is more probable that you may
see him in Phila. in the course of a fortnight: I will write to the officer
who may succeed to the command (say Morris) recommending James.

The letter of Murrray which you enclosed to me was immediately put
into the hands of the Sec'y—and I hope will have the effect desired. You
need never have the least hesitation about writing to me in favor of any one
in whom (begun the wrong side of the sheet, but can't copy) you take an
interest. We understand each other so well that your recommendations
can never embarrass me, because if the thing you desire should, for some reason unknown to you, be impracticable or inexpedient, I can frankly say so.
On the other hand I should be quite mortified if anything which you wished
should not be attended to merely because you had from motives of delicacy
refrained from writing to me. This must not be.

I have a long letter of four very closely written pages from Wilkinson.
Unfortunately for want of a document left at N. Y. I can't read one line of
it, nor even conjecture what it is about. It is dated in Feb. when I presume
he was well.

God bless you

A. BURR.

Ch. BIDDLE Esqr.

18 July, 1804.

My Dear Sir: Your letter of the 13th was particularly acceptable. It is
too well known that Gen'l H. had long indulged himself in illiberal freedoms
with my character. He had a peculiar talent of saying things improper &
offensive in such a manner as could not well be taken hold of. On two different occasions however, having reason to apprehend that he had gone so
far as to afford me a fair occasion for calling on him, he anticipated me by
coming forward voluntarily and making apologies and concessions. From
delicacy to him and from a sincere desire for peace, I have never mentioned
these circumstances always hoping that the generosity of my conduct would
have had some influence on his. In this I have been constantly deceived,
and it became impossible that I could consistently with self-respect again
forbear. With regard to the immediate cause of the late event, I refer you to
the Morning Chronicle of the 17th inst. though in this, many circumstances
not favorable to H. are suppressed. The following incidents will show what
reliance may be placed on those declarations of H. which assert that he did
not mean to injure me &c. &c. (contemptible disclosures, if true,). When the
parties had taken their places, having their pistols in their hands, cocked,
Mr. P. who was to give the word, asked the gentlemen if they were ready:
"Stop," said Gen'l H., "in certain states of the light one requires glasses."
He then levelled his pistol in different directions to try the light. After this,
he put on his spectacles and repeated the same experiment several times; he
kept on his spectacles and said he was ready. When the word "present"
was given, he took aim at his adversary & fired very promptly. The other

fired two or three seconds after him & the Gen'l instantly fell exclaiming " I am a dead man." Both he & Mr. P. while on the ground, appeared a good deal agitated and not to be in a state of mind suitable for observing with accuracy what passed. H. looked as if oppressed with the horrors of conscious guilt. It is the opinion of all considerate men here, that my only fault has been in bearing so much & so long.

You will remark that all our intemperate and unprincipled Jacobins who have been for years reviling H. as a disgrace to the country and a pest to society are now the most vehement in his praise, and you will readily perceive that their motive is, not respect to him, but malice to me.

The last hours of Genl. H. (I might include the day preceding the interview) appear to have been devoted to malevolence and hypocrisy. All men of honor must see with disgust the persecutions which are practised against me. Among other unusual steps, a Coroner's Jury has been called and will meet for the *fourth* time this evening. The object is to procure an inquest of murder, which will probably be effected, although the transaction took place in another State. Upon such an inquest a warrant may issue to apprehend me and if I should be taken, bail would probably be refused. The friends of Genl. H. and even his enemies, who are still more my enemies, are but too faithful executors of his malice.

Respectfully & affectionately Y'rs.

Cn. BIDDLE, Esqr. A. BURR.

18th July, 1804.

My Dear Sir: It is not yet determined how I shall dispose of myself for the residue of the Summer, perhaps I may visit your city on my way, God knows whither. In such case I may probably enough ask a room in your house in town for two or three days.

A late event has so demolished all my projects that the Chariot Hanse has made will be useless to me. You can judge what chance I should have in our Courts on a trial for my life, though there is nothing clearer to a dispassionate lawyer than that the Courts of this State have nothing to do with the death of Genl. H.

Your son Charles to whom I am indebted for a very civil letter about this same Carriage, must call on Hanse & know by what means he has charged more than 200 Dls. above the price agreed. " A chariot complete" I thought included every thing usual. He now charges separately for Lamps, Cover, &c. &c. Desire him to ask Mr. H. at what loss he will keep it. It is perhaps unlucky that I have paid him in advance (I think) 175 Dls. I hope he won't have the conscience to ask so much. I shall be within reach of the Post office in N. York long enough to receive your answer to this.

I had written a letter to Armstrong concerning Nicholas, but kept it, not knowing where to address him & expecting him daily in N. York.

Your most affec. friend & st.

A. B.

Do not let the enclosed letter go out of your hands.

Cn. BIDDLE, Esqr.

Commodore Truxtun to Charles Biddle.

EXTRACT.

PERTH AMBOY, 19th July, 1804.

Dear Sir: I lament the Death of Hamilton as much as I could the death of a brother of equal talents and worth to human society, but I must at the same time justify Burr, and will everywhere justify him on Hamilton's own confession, inclosed with his will and addressed to his executors. "It is not to be denied that my animadversions on the political principles, character, and views of Col. Burr have been extremely severe, and on different occasions, I in common with many others have made very unfavorable criticisms on particular instances of the private conduct of this gentleman." If the laws of honor in any case between man and man will justify the practice of duelling (and there are some cases in which I think a devout Bishop would almost countenance it*) surely the ground of Burr's correspondence with Hamilton must be admitted as one of those cases, and if men and soldiers once go to the field there ought to be no trifling, and this I should be gratified in having an opportunity of showing Robert Smith, (the apology for a Secretary of the Navy) but he shelters himself behind the embrasures of his office where he will lie skulking until he is pop'd into another skulking place still more secure—the *seat* of Judge Chase.

NEW YORK, 26th July, 1804.

Dear Sir: There is the devil to pay in this city about the late duel, and I am abused as being a friend of Col. Burr though I have ever been a sincere friend to the deceased. I never knew a business of this kind so treated in any part of the world, the inquest have not yet given in their verdict—they remain as before 9–3 as I understand from good authority, at least as I think good authority. I regret the event as much as any man can do of this unfortunate duel, but as it cannot now be helped, as Hamilton cannot be brought back—& as there is no doubt but the duel was a fair one according to the laws in such cases—why this abominable persecution? I detest and despise it. Mr. Prevost is of opinion that it would be extremely wrong for Col. Burr to venture in Jersey in the present state of things, and from what I hear otherwise I am clearly of the same opinion. Mr. P. thinks also that if he goes to Carolina for two or three months it will be the best thing that he can do, and by that time the public mind now much agitated will have subsided or become quieted in a great degree. Your mention of any correspondence between Col. Burr & myself and yourself can do neither him or us any good; it is best to be silent about it. Just do you & him write to me as

---

* The Commodore's views of the license allowable to the clergy were sometimes startling to his friends.

usual at Amboy where I shall be to-morrow—being here on the subject of employing in a speculation some money, for I am sick & tired of Idleness. Show this to Col. Burr.

Your friend,
THOMAS TRUXTUN.

CHARLES BIDDLE, Esqr.

Commodore Truxtun to Charles Biddle.

EXTRACT.

PERTH AMBOY, 11th Aug. 1804.

I cannot believe it is intended to give Burr any trouble, out of New York, but of Mr. Jefferson's political Myrmidons in that State he can form a much better opinion than I can, and of the object and intentions of the two families* under mourning for General Hamilton outwardly and rejoicing inwardly. God forgive me if I judge of any man wrongfully but the conduct of these men past and present when contrasted looks like bare faced hypocrisy and shows a duplicity which insults the common understanding of mankind.

ST. SIMONS, 1st Sept. 1804.

My Dear Sir: It is now just a week since our arrival. The passage from Newcastle to this Island was 13 days, but we were two days getting in. The Capt. was civil and obliging.

On Tuesday the 4th. inst. I go to St. Mary's and thence to St. Augustine if I can find a conveyance. Travelling in this region is done by water only. My further projects are, to return to this place before the 20th. then through Savannah and Augusta to Columbia, Camden and Statesburg, at which last place my daughter now is. I wish that you would immediately on receipt of this address a letter to me at Statesburg, South Carolina. Tell me what you may hear of the state of things in New York and enclose me a few Newspapers. I propose to leave Statesburg on my return homeward the first week in October; you will therefore have no time to spare for writing.

In this neighborhood I am overwhelmed with all sorts of attention and kindness. Presents are daily sent of things which it is supposed I may want, so that I live most luxuriously.

Your affectionate friend and serv't
A. BURR.

CHAS. BIDDLE.

The following letters refer to the period when Colonel Burr was tried and acquitted on charges of treason and of misdemeanor. In Wilkinson's letter we have italicized what seems important.

---

* Probably meant for the Livingstones and Clintons.

WASHINGTON, March 18th, '05.

My Dear Sir: I have just received your favour of the 13th, & hasten to answer it. Nicholas is perfectly correct in his observations, on the effect of Military standing in France, and I have every disposition to forward his views, but the absence of the President from the Seat of Government, & the extreme caution with which the Secretary of War proceeds in all things, may render their accomplishment impracticable. I will however make the attempt to-morrow & shall apprize you of the result the day after—if we proceed at all it must be in the *Corps du Genie*, which by the bye is held in first respectability in France & furnishes the richest uniform of our Service.

I thank you for your congratulations & shall be able to tell you more of *my Government 12 Months hence. In the mean time I can only say the Country is a healthy one, & that I shall be on the high road to Mexico.*

Our friend Burr leaves this for Philadelphia to-morrow, from whence he proceeds Westward & we may expect to find him in New Orleans in June. The President has thought proper to appoint Dr. Brown, on the sole recommendation of Mr. Burr, to the Secretaryship of the Territory of Louisiana.

Commodore Preble, with whom I am charmed, will leave this to-morrow & will carry you a Letter of Introduction. He is truly a Man formed to Command & should be at the Head of our Navy. You will find him modest yet collected, intelligent, correct & possessing manners the most agreeable. My Ann's health is improving, & I hope the season will confirm it. She and our Sons join me in affectionate regards to Mrs. B. thyself & Children.

Your Affectionate Friend & Servt.

JAS. WILKINSON.

CHAS. BIDDLE, Esq.

LEXINGTON, 27 Augt. '05.

My Dear Sir: Who would have thought that Naval Talents were in such estimation at 600 miles from salt water? The enclosed I took from the door of the hotel in Nashville (Tennessee). General Jackson who is the owner of this celebrated quadruped, is one of the most distinguished men in that State. He says that as the Commodore stands unrivalled at sea, so is the horse Truxtun on land, and that if he should ever be beaten, he will change his name.

I have been amusing myself here these eight days and think of going hence to see Wilkinson. This would be the business of a month & would keep me on this side the Mountains till after the middle of October. Of my very long and interesting tour you shall have an account when we meet. My health has been uniformly good, very good.

Most affec'y Y'rs.

A. BURR.

RICHMOND, 18th Ap. 1807.

Dear Sir: On the 13th inst. I received a letter from Commodore Truxtun dated 30th March, to which he desires an answer by return of mail. It has no postmark and I am totally ignorant of the channel through which it came.

The Commodore desires me to declare whether I wrote to Genl. W. that he (Truxtun) had gone on a Mission from me to Jamaica.

It is obvious that as well this letter as the reply which I might make to it are intended for publication, and to this, at a proper time, there could be no exception. It is admitted also that he has a right to make the enquiry and to expect an answer. But as the deposition of Genl. Wilkinson is very soon to be the subject of legal investigation, there would be a manifest impropriety in permitting any declarations or remarks to escape from me anterior to that examination, and such conduct might expose me to very serious inconvenience and injury in a matter which touches my honour. I have therefore to request that the Commodore will forbear to press his demand until the termination of the business now depending in this city, and I pledge myself to give him full satisfaction on the subject so soon as the trial shall be concluded. As this event cannot be more than five or six weeks distant, it is hoped that he will see the propriety of acquiescing in the delay.

It is with great hesitation that I ask you to communicate the preceding to Commodore Truxtun; but I presume that the peculiar circumstances in which I am placed will excuse the freedom. To have written even thus much directly to the Commodore, might, if made public, have defeated the views with which the delay is desired & have exposed me to the evils sought to be avoided, which will also apologize to him for this mode of communication.   Yours Affectionately,

                                        A. BURR.

CH. BIDDLE, Esqr.

Commodore Truxtun to Charles Biddle.

(EXTRACT.)

                                        RICHMOND, 30th May, 1807.

My Dear Sir: Richmond I am delighted with and from the Governour down, throughout the Society of " Worthies," of all polities, I have been at home and had welcome shown me in every house, most conspicuously. I dine every day at 1–2 past 4, rise at 8 from dinner and am at an evening party at 1–2 past 8, and in bed at 12—up at 6—go to Court at 10, adjourn at 3. This is very well you will say, but I wish the business that caused the unpleasant errand, was over and persecution at an end. Burr sticks to it, that he never wrote the cyphered letter,* or caused it to be written or mentioned my name, as it has been therein mentioned, but on the contrary, that I declined his overtures at once, which is the fact & tho' I have not yet seen him but in Court, he has done ample justice to me as I had early required, and confirmed the message you delivered me from him in Phila. of his innocence in not mentioning my name.

---

* What Col. Burr denied was the correctness of Wilkinson's version of the letter.

RICHMOND, 25th June, 1807.

Dear Sir: I have postponed writing to you for some time as I have nothing important to say, the newspapers having detailed everything here that I know relating to the trial of Col. Burr, who is now in close prison, in consequence of the Grand Jury having yesterday found and brought into Court a True Bill against him for Treason and another True Bill for a Misdemeanour, and also the like bills against Mr. Blennerhasset.

The witnesses on the part of the United States were 51 in number, mostly from the Westward and New Orleans, and it is said that there has been some hard swearing, but of this I give report only. No witness on the part of the accused has been yet examined and of course all opinion ought to be suspended until we see their evidence before the Court and petit Jury, and especially as I am told some of them are men of great respectability from the Ohio and its neighbourhood, who speak loudly against Gen. Wilkinson.

The Cyphered Letter was not lost as had been mentioned at Washington, but obtained from W. by the Grand Jury, and is a very different thing, it is said to his interpretation to the Government. It acknowledges receipt of a letter from Col. Burr with postmark of 13th. of May. You recollect that it was stated that the Cyphered Letter was written in July 1806. And I am told it says "Our affairs are going on better than I could wish" *or words to that effect,* and it states other matters in the plural number, but I trust the public will see that letter at full length in proper time, when all will be able to judge more correctly of its contents and the case.

The affair with the English and American National Ships off the Chesapeake, renders war inevitable or pusillanimity the order of the day.

Yours Sincerely,

THOMAS TRUXTUN.

To CHARLES BIDDLE, Esq.

(Turn over.)

What is on this side is of a private nature.

The letter containing my papers may or may not have been opened at the Post Office, but whether or not, my papers were all received and not detained, and hence you were premature in writing to Patton.

I have not spoken to Wilkinson. I cannot countenance such conduct as I have seen in his operations. But more of this hereafter. I will write you fully on this subject in proper time or when more at leisure.

T. T.

P. S. Let my family want for nothing in my absence and write me of them &c. &c. &c. I know not how long we will be detained here, there will be various presentments to-day, after which, the Grand Jury close their Session.

When you receive this, call on the Marquis and tell him that some witnesses have been produced, as I understand, which have slandered him, but what their evidence is, I know not—except that he had engaged to supply

Burr with arms and money, as it is reported out of doors. Now as I am of opinion that the Marquis had no sort of connection with Burr, but on the contrary watched him, I am obliged to say here I am persuaded it is all a lie.

The Jamaica story and my name is proved a lie by the answers of the Governor and Admiral from Jamaica to Wilkinson's letters. I demanded in a letter to the Grand Jury these answers, knowing it was an infamous invention, and it has turned out that W. had no data to go by but the cyphered letter, and a vessel he says arrived at New Orleans and mentioned it. What a tale! And I know nothing of such infamous proceedings, I do assure you.

T. T.

PHILADELPHIA, 11th July, 1807.

CHARLES BIDDLE, Esquire.

Dear Sir: The letter you have received from General Wilkinson complaining of my refusing to speak to him, and that he would have explained to my satisfaction his conduct, as respected me, had I given him opportunity, I am surprised was ever written. For how could W. attempt to explain to my satisfaction his abominable conduct as respected me.

Without my going into the designs of Col. Barr, in which he declared to me that Wilkinson was the projector, and told you he would never have thought of such designs but for the importunities of Wilkinson—and without even touching the subject of the cyphered letter which was decyphered by Wilkinson (by a key established between them since 1804, as W. acknowledged before the Grand Jury) and sent to the President of the United States with false and infamous allusions to me.

I say, Sir, without my going into the subject of Mr. Burr's designs and that letter and the circumstances connected with both, of which so much may be most grievously said by me, let me call to your attention a very offensive and additional fact. About five months after the foolish and ridiculous cyphered letter was written, which Col. Burr solemnly denies to you ever to have written—has denied also to General Lee—to me and to others, and that he never caused to be written: and when from the intercourse between New Orleans and Philada. it might on inquiry have been easily ascertained—that I was not only at that time in this city—but had not been out of the United States since the peace with France in 1801: I say, Sir, that notwithstanding these incontrovertible facts, General Wilkinson prematurely dispatched a vessel (see copy of my letter to the Richmond Grand Jury) from the former place at the nation's expense to Jamaica, warning the Governor, Sir Eyre Coote, and Admiral Dacres against giving me any aid, &c. &c. &c., in an expedition from thence to co-operate with Col. Barr (at least such was the purport of the dispatch).

These high and honorable officers were astonished, as they well might be, at such dispatches being directed to them, particularly from such a quarter, and replied to Wilkinson accordingly that they had never before heard of such expedition. Now, Sir, let me ask of you whether this undertaking in

General W—— to send an express of such a nature, of himself (and unauthorized by the Executive of the U. S.), to a foreign Government and Admiral on that occasion, was not only stretching his powers a great length but was premature. And as it respected me, and the exposure of my name to a distant Government and people, was it not cruel in the last degree—more especially as Wilkinson has known me in the character and walks of a man of honor for thirty years?

But I will not stop here; injury most poignantly felt forbids it.

After this act was done and could not be recalled, and after Wilkinson had discovered that I had not left the United States on any sort of mission or business whatever for years—and after he had received answers to his letters from Sir Eyre Coote and Admiral Dacres—was it not due to me, was it not due to a sense of justice and to common decency for him to have made some explanation and apology, *unasked by me*, for this extraordinary conduct? Was it not due from a man with whom I have long been in habits of apparent and sincere friendship, by his own expressions—and was it not due from a man who had so often before and since this transaction expressed such affection and esteem for me (and who once, as he told me himself, gave an entertainment at Natchez in honor of my conduct) to have written me then an explanatory letter? Ought I not to have expected it and looked for it from this statement of facts—ought I not to have expected that Wilkinson, the boasted patriot and friend, would have hastened to have told me from New Orleans, in the plain and honest language of friendship, that he rejoiced to find he had (as respected me) been most egregiously mistaken or deceived in prostrating my name? But no such thing—no sort of compunction for profaning Truxtun—but on the contrary a total silence and indifference until he meets me at a large dinner party at Richmond, and then advances under this load of aggression to me for the purpose of renewing social intercourse and affects to be hurt because it is refused. But away, Wilkinson! while I tell you, the door is forever shut between us, until you verify your good disposition toward me differently and convince me that you are pure and unspotted in your accusations against Burr. As respects the famous cyphered letter—there is assertion against assertion—Burr assured me, yourself and many others, that he was not the author of that letter—and Wilkinson says he is, as I am told. And as to the Jamaica project, Swartwout declares and swears most bitterly at and against Wilkinson, and that he never said to him a single syllable about me, or such project. And how could he, for I never saw Mr. Swartwout to my knowledge until I saw him at Richmond, and in the first moment I declined Mr. Burr's proposal to me, agreeable to my affidavit. But again, Dr. Bollman says that Wilkinson was the first man he ever heard make any mention of my going to Jamaica and that it was at New Orleans he so heard it. Thus you see how the account stands among them, and they may settle it in their own way; I have labored and done my part, and my duty to my honor and my family by an inquiry, and by addressing a letter to Col. Burr on the subject, and receiving his flat denial in the affair, and by hearing evidence and conversations detailed. *Nay I have gone farther*—I requested Mr. Stoddert to have from Dr. Bollman's own mouth, what I assert, which he did obtain, to satisfy me, in consequence of my calling on him (Bollman) at Richmond, to explain to me how this affair was.

As to Col. Burr—although he denied everything in which his name had been mentioned as concerned me, yet I had no intercourse with him at Richmond, until after I had given in my affidavit before the Grand Jury, and after the bills of indictment were found against him to be true bills. I then felt compassion for his degraded situation and recollecting his former standing in society, and as he had previously denied ever having mentioned me, as had been disgracefully stated, I called on him once at his desire and received from him a letter for you (on the subject of money matters I suppose) which I delivered you on my arrival from Richmond. I called at the same house twice, to see Mr. Martin, who had visited me at Major Gibbon's and thus I was thrice at the house Mr. Burr occupied at Richmond while I was in that city. Let the rancorous and miserable and inhuman wretches, that would insinuate otherwise, blush and be ashamed, for I disregard them in this world, more than the dirt under my feet—as they will answer for their misdeeds in the world to come.

I have been induced to write this letter to justify myself, as to keeping General Wilkinson aloof—and to convince you that I never saw an old friend with a new face without a just cause.

As to any dissatisfaction of Wilkinson, or anything he may say in consequence of my sense of his wrongs, I disregard it. The fact is, it is me that feels cause of complaint—and have great cause—not him. And while I do not desire to offend society by any improper conduct from reports that I pass Wilkinson without a just cause, I shall take some pains to prevent any sort of misrepresentation from any quarter in this affair—and this you may inform him, when you exhibit this letter for his perusal. I am the guardian of my own reputation, and will forever defend it at all hazards. And if I know my country and my country justly knows me, as I trust it does (notwithstanding a variety of evils I have experienced as well as Wilkinson's late conduct, which has had a tendency to do me infinite injury—but from my own vigilance and attention to do myself justice have defeated it), it is all I desire, with a few select and sincere friends, to pass my *unemployed* hours away.

I am not, my worthy friend Charles, anxious for very many associates—my injured estate and large family forbid it—I only desire those I select to be honorable and prove honorable in all situations in life—and I wish to know no man that is not a *real and true patriot* and who does not in sincerity love his country, next to his God, above all other things.

Having forever been unconnected with any sort of plot, I write as I feel, and carry the flag of defiance at the main against my ungrateful enemies.

I do not hesitate to say that I am not bloody minded, it is incompatible with a true soldier to be so—hence I have charity, some charity for Burr in his present situation, but as I have said to you before, I never can again hold Mr. Burr in the estimation I once did or ever make a companion of him—yet I am no savage or barbarian to let Burr feel my determination in his present state, and as to money he has no claim on me for any and I have none for him. As to security (if he is cleared by a traverse Jury) in the suits instituted against him at Richmond on his protested bills, I cannot be be one of them, or guarantee any persons there who would. My time of life and large family forbid my involving or hazarding for such an acquaintance as Mr. Burr has been; and recent conduct too puts it out of the question with me—but you can do as you please.

I find young Decatur—in his affidavit before the Grand Jury, detailing Mr. Burr's overtures to him—says that in December, 1805, Col. Burr told him that the Government were acquainted with his views and that General Wilkinson had offered his services, &c., and that Wilkinson knew more about the resources than he did. Now this differs from what Burr told me in some respects, for Mr. Burr declared to me that the Executive was not privy. But it seems that Decatur never gave the Government any information as to the overtures of Mr. Burr to him, untill subpœnaed as a witness—though before the Grand Jury oath was made by Wilkinson that he was to go to New Providence after a fleet and join me from Jamaica. What fabrications!

Yours,

THOMAS TRUXTUN.

At Burr's trial Commodore Truxtun testified, "I know nothing respecting any overt act or of any treasonable practice, design, or conversation of Colonel Burr."

Being asked by Burr, "Did I ever speak of dismembering the Union by separating the Western country or of seizing New Orleans?" He replied, "Never, and I have spoken it a thousand times." . . . . "I would have got out of my bed at 12 o'clock at night, if my services were wanted against England, France, or Spain, at any time."

The following extract from a letter written several years after the so-called conspiracy shows the later friendly relations of Truxtun and Burr.

Commodore Truxtun to Charles Biddle.

WOOD LAWN, August 22, 1812.

You say Colonel Burr has much business in New York and doing well. I am glad to hear it, and should rejoice to hear he had exposed that *incomparable* villain *Jefferson*, as I dare say he can do, and nothing should prevent it after his sufferings. I say incomparable with the exception of Madison and Bonaparte, and those of the Junta. . . . . If any friend is going to New York enclose this to Colonel Burr as a mark of my esteem, and having no opportunity to write him from here, or I would do so, though I have no subject for a letter.

NOTE G.   (PAGE 306.)

Nicholas Biddle was born on the 8th of January, 1786, at Philadelphia. At the age of thirteen, he had completed the course of study at the University of Pennsylvania; he then entered Princeton College, where he took his degree in his fifteenth year, dividing the first honor with a competitor of maturer years. He then studied the law in Philadelphia, for three years; but, being under the age for admission to the bar, he, in 1804, went to Europe, as Secretary to General Armstrong, the United States Minister to France. He was present at the coronation of the Emperor Napoleon, in Paris.

At this time, the purchase of Louisiana and the indemnification for injuries to American commerce were in progress, and young Biddle, at the age of eighteen, managed the details with the veterans of the French bureau, in whom his juvenile appearance and precocious ability excited much surprise. Leaving the legation, he travelled through the greater part of the Continent of Europe; to his classical attainments, he there added a thorough mastery of the modern languages, which he retained through life. Arriving in England, he became Secretary to Mr. Monroe, then minister at London. An anecdote is told of his delighting Monroe by the exhibition of a knowledge of the modern Greek, when, in the company of the English scholars at Cambridge, some philological question arose relating to the present dialect, with which they were unacquainted.

On his return to America in 1807, he engaged in the practice of the law, and devoted a portion of his time to literary pursuits. He became associated with Joseph Dennie in the editorship of the Portfolio in 1811, and wrote much for it at different times. His papers on the fine arts, biographical sketches, and critical essays were written with great force and elegance, and exhibit a discriminating taste. He also penned various literary trifles, and wrote occasional verses, with the taste of the scholar and humorist.

When Lewis and Clark had returned from their explorations, their journals and memoranda were placed in the hands of Mr. Biddle, who prepared from them, and the oral relation of Clark, the narrative of the expedition, and induced Mr. Jefferson to pen the preliminary memoir of Lewis. It was simply conducted through the press by Paul Allen, to whom the stipulated compensation was liberally transferred, when the political engagements of Mr. Biddle withdrew him from further attention to the work.

He was in the State Legislature in 1810, advocating a system of popular education with views in advance of his times. It was not until 1836 that the ideas broached by him were fully carried out by legislative enactment. When the question of the renewal of the charter of the old United States Bank was discussed in the session of 1811, he advocated the measure in a speech, which was widely circulated at the time, and gained the distinguished approval of Chief Justice Marshall.

During the war with England, he was elected to the State Senate, and gave a zealous and powerful support to the measures of the national administration for carrying on the contest. He and all of his brothers were now engaged in the service of the country—in the public councils, the navy, the army, and the militia; of whom Commodore James Biddle, Major Thomas Biddle, and Major John Biddle gained particular military reputation. The youngest of the brothers, Richard Biddle, during the war a volunteer at Camp Dupont, afterwards settled at Pittsburgh, and was for many years an acknowledged leader of the bar of that city. He also represented that district in Congress, with great ability. He found leisure for some important contributions to literature; his memoir of Sebastian Cabot has been justly characterized by an eminent critic as "one of the finest monuments of American research."

After the capture of Washington, when an invasion of Pennsylvania was expected, Nicholas Biddle, in the Senate, initiated the most vigorous measures for the defence of the State.

Towards the close of the war, he replied to the address of the Hartford Convention, by an elaborate report, which was adopted in the Pennsylvania Legislature; a state paper which attracted universal attention, and added greatly to the reputation of its author. In the successive elections of 1818 and 1820, he received a large vote for Congress as the nominee of the Democratic party, but was defeated by the Federal candidates.

In 1819 he became a Government Director of the Bank of the United States, on the nomination of President Monroe, who, about the same time, assigned to him, under a resolution of Congress, the work of collecting the laws and regulations of foreign countries relative to commerce, moneys, weights, and measures. These he arranged in an octavo volume, entitled "The Commercial Digest."

In 1823, on the retirement of Mr. Langdon Cheves, Mr. Biddle was elected to the presidency of the Bank, and to the conduct of its affairs he thenceforth devoted all his energies. For many years the institution was entirely disconnected from politics, and furnished to the whole country equal exchanges and a sound and uniform currency, everywhere receivable, and immediately convertible into specie. Beside the parent bank at Philadelphia, twenty-five of its branches were established throughout the Union, and its control was everywhere felt by the State banks. Whatever political objections may be urged against the existence of a national bank, the eminent financial services which it rendered under Mr. Biddle's administration cannot be denied, and that the loss of these services has not since been adequately supplied, seems to be amply proved by the subsequent history of the American banking system. The following view of the subject was taken by the Hon. Horace Binney, in a debate in the House of Representatives in the year 1834: "The Bank of the United States has performed her great offices to this people by the concurrence of two peculiarities which belong to her— her structure, and her employment in the collection of the public revenue.

No State banks, by any combination, can effect the required exchanges to any considerable extent. No Bank of the United States, without the aid of the public revenue, can effect them to the extent which the necessities of trade require. The structure of the Bank of the United States contributed to this operation in a way which every one may comprehend. The whole circulation of the United States is employed in effecting the exchange of the crop and the merchandise of the country. It is employed in transporting the crops to market, and merchandise to the places of its consumption.

"Now, a national bank, with branches spread over the whole Union, knows, from experience and her means of observation, where the amount of demand will rise and fall, and at what time these dealings will occur. She knows, beforehand, where she may with safety diminish her resources, and where she must enlarge them. Wherever her resources are placed for use, it is the same thing to the bank—her profit is the same everywhere; and this ability to give them the position which the trade of the country requires, is sustained by, and in a great degree dependent upon, her employment as the depository of the public revenue. In this character the bank receives the revenue, and holds it until the time of disbursement; and the knowledge which her accomplished President and the Board of Directors obtain through their relations to the Treasury, and by intimate acquaintance with the fiscal operations of the department, enables them to reconcile all the demands of the Treasury, with all the demands of trade; at the same time they preserve the whole currency of the country in that due proportion to demand which makes it, and which alone makes it sound and invariable. . . . . . . Sir, the project of the Secretary of the Treasury surprises me—it is the clearly avowed design to bring, a second time, upon this land the curse of an *unregulated, uncontrolled State bank paper currency.* . . . . I should regard that man as one of the greatest benefactors of his country, who would devise, for the use of this people, some control over the paper currency of the State banks, and relieve us from the perpetual recurrence of constitutional doubts and party contention to which the career of a Bank of the United States seems necessarily exposed. Control of some kind is essential—it is indispensable; there can be no property, or what is the same thing, no security or uniformity to its value, without it."

President Jackson, at the commencement of his term of office, declared his hostility to a renewal of the charter of the United States Bank. In his first message, in 1829, he called the attention of Congress to the subject, declaring "that it could not too soon be presented to their deliberation." It was again brought forward in his subsequent messages of 1830 and 1831. Our space will not allow us to enter into the details of the political contest which ensued. Mr. Biddle was, by his official position, placed in antagonism with his former political associates. In 1832, a bill for the re-charter of the Bank passed both houses of Congress, but was vetoed by the President. Notwithstanding the hostility of the Government, and of the dominant political party, the Bank maintained its credit throughout the commercial world

27

to the last moment of its existence. The charter expired by its limitation on the 3d March, 1836; and here ends the history of the last "Bank of the United States." Its name, however, was afterwards borne, with very different fortunes, by another institution. The stockholders of the late Bank received from the Legislature of Pennsylvania a State charter, by an act entitled "An Act to repeal the State tax, &c., and to charter a State bank, *to be called the United States Bank.*" There was at this time no man living who enjoyed a higher reputation as a financier than Nicholas Biddle. He was urgently solicited to accept the Presidency of the new bank. He assented, and continued at its head until March, 1839, when he resigned, and retired to a country-seat on the river Delaware, called "Andalusia," which his wife had inherited from her father. At the time of his resignation, the stock of the bank was selling at one hundred and sixteen dollars a share, with other indications of soundness and prosperity. Two years afterwards, however, it stopped payment, assigned its assets, and was declared to be insolvent. Whether this failure was attributable to causes incident to the financial condition of the whole country, and the anomalous position of the State Bank; or to measures pursued subsequent to, or during the administration of Mr. Biddle, were questions vehemently discussed at the time, and which cannot, now, be reviewed within the limits of this sketch.

The following succinct statement is from a biography of Mr. Biddle, by an eminent citizen of Pennsylvania, published in the last edition (1854) of the "National Portrait Gallery:"—

"The 'State bank,' called the 'United States Bank,' began and ended its career in a period of general expansion, over-trading, and over-banking. When the destruction of the Bank of the United States was decreed, it was the system of State banks—not a specie currency—that was put forward as the efficient substitute. To the State banks the public treasure was confided, and they were made the subjects of continued favor and laudation from the President in his messages, the Secretary of the Treasury in his reports, and the party presses that echoed the sentiments of the party leaders. The 'Globe,' the official organ at Washington, teemed with appeals to the State Legislatures to create more banks, and any tardiness in compliance was charged—as everything, almost, was charged in those days—to the influence of 'Biddle and the United States Bank.' 'The State banks,' said General Jackson, 'are found fully adequate to the performance of all services required of the Bank of the United States, quite as promptly, and with the same cheapness.' "By the use of the State banks," he repeats, in a subsequent message, 'it is ascertained that the moneys of the United States can be collected and disbursed without loss or inconvenience, and that all the wants of the community in relation to exchange and currency, are supplied as well as they have ever been before.'

"Under such vigorous stimulus the number of banks was more than doubled; the amount of what was termed 'banking capital' more than trebled; the notes of banks in circulation rose from 61,000,000 to 185,000,000 of dollars; loans and discounts were increased proportionally. The restraining influence once exercised by the Bank of the United States was scoffed at as an odious and obsolete oppression; and President Jackson, in an annual message, congratulated the State banks on the extinction of their former 'enemy.' State governments, too, caught the general contagion, and issued bonds, contracted debts, and entered upon vast schemes of lavish expenditure. In vain were warning voices raised. Daniel Webster declared in the Senate, 'We are in danger of being overwhelmed with irredeemable paper, mere paper, not representing gold and silver; no, representing nothing but broken promises, bad faith, bankrupt corporations, cheated creditors, and a ruined people.' Henry Clay predicted that, 'There being no longer any sentinel at the head of our banking establishment to warn them by its information and operation of approaching danger, the local institutions, already multiplied to an alarming extent, and almost daily multiplying, in seasons of prosperity will make free and unrestrained emissions. . . . . Inordinate speculation will ensue, debts will be freely contracted, and the explosion of the whole banking system will be the ultimate effect.' We recur now to these events not in a captious spirit of censure, but in justice to one upon whom it was afterwards sought to charge the consequences of a system which he always combated, against which he openly protested—the very opposite of that established and perfected by his efforts, under which the country so long enjoyed a sound and uniform currency, based upon and always convertible into gold and silver. In the perilous condition of things to which we have adverted, the United States Bank of Pennsylvania had even more danger to encounter than other State institutions. Its unwieldy capital was forced to seek investment in every part of the country, in stocks, loans, bonds, and like securities, which, when the crash came, went down, and carried the bank down with them. Whether its fate could have been averted by Mr. Biddle, if he had continued in the direction of its affairs, we do not undertake to decide. He had never been found unequal to any crisis; and his tact, and skill, and fertility in resources might have warded off some of the blows that proved most fatal. That his efforts could have availed in the later, as they had in the former trials of the bank, can neither be certainly affirmed or denied. Speculation upon what might have happened, if events had been other than they were, is mostly very fruitless."

After Mr. Biddle's retirement from the bank, he delivered two addresses before the Agricultural Society of Philadelphia County, of which he was the President, and discussed some topics of public interest through the press; he earnestly advocated the resumption of payment of the State interest, and the admission of Texas to the Union; but his health was broken, and he died on the 27th of February, 1844, of a disease of the heart, aged fifty-eight years. He had married, in 1811, the daughter of John Craig, one of the old merchants of Philadelphia, eminent for wealth, integrity, and public spirit; this lady, whose virtues insured the happiness of his domestic life, survived him for some years. His character was marked by great energy and resolution. Mr. C. J. Ingersoll, a political opponent on the bank question, in his sketch of the late war, says: "Nicholas Biddle was as iron-nerved as his great antagonist, Andrew Jackson, loved his country not less, and money as little." His manner was peculiarly attractive; it was not a display of artificial graces, but the natural expression of a genial nature and cultivated mind, and it had a powerful influence over those with whom he was associated. In youth, the beauty of his person was remarkable, and time dealt gently with it: he was fond of exercise on foot and on horseback, and though hospitable, his personal habits were simple and abstemious. He was a leading member of many societies and public institutions for useful and benevolent purposes, and his private charities and benefactions were as liberal as they were unostentatious. He was an ardent advocate of the improvement of his native State, and aided in the prosecution of the most important public enterprises. The Hon. Wm. F. Packer (now the Governor of Pennsylvania), in a speech in the State Senate, advocating the connection of Philadelphia with the Lakes, said: "This, sir, was the favorite project of Nicholas Biddle, of your city; and whatever may be said of him as a politician or a financier, all agree that on questions of internal improvement and commerce, he was one of the most sagacious and far-seeing statesmen in this Union. His fault was, if fault it be, that he was twenty years in advance of the age in which he lived. Sir, his towering mind enabled him afar off to

> —— 'See the tops of distant thoughts,
> Which men of common stature never saw.'

Had he lived and maintained the strong hold which he once had on the affections of Philadelphia, that city would long since have been placed, in relation to the trade I have attempted to describe, where New York and Boston now are."

His taste was formed upon the classic models with which his studies and travels had rendered him familiar; to it the city owes two of the finest specimens of Grecian architecture—the United States Custom-House (formerly the United States Bank), and the Girard College—the plans for which were adopted at his instance. He delivered many speeches and addresses, and his style was remarkable for purity, terseness, and vigor.—*Simpson's Eminent Philadelphians.*

NOTE II. (PAGES 350 AND 390.)

Clement and Owen Biddle, sons of John Biddle and Sarah Owen, were first cousins of Charles Biddle. Of Owen, the elder brother, the following sketch is taken from the Pennsylvania Historical Magazine, vol. iii.

Owen Biddle, of the city of Philadelphia, a great-grandson of William

Biddle, one of the proprietors of West Jersey, and for many years of the Governor's Council of that Colony, was born in Philadelphia in the year 1737. He was engaged in mercantile pursuits, and with his brother, Clement, signed the celebrated Non-importation Resolutions of October 25, 1765. He was a delegate to the Provincial Conference Jan. 23, 1775; member of the Committee of Safety from June 30, 1775, to July 22, 1776, and of the Council of Safety from July 24, 1776, to March 13, 1777; member of the Board of War March 13, 1777; of the Constitutional Convention of July 15, 1776, and, in June, 1777, Deputy Commissary of Forage. His name appears in the list of Philadelphia merchants healed by Robert Morris, who became personally bound for various sums, amounting in the aggregate to over £260,000 sterling, for purchasing provisions for the army at a time when there was great difficulty in procuring supplies. During the occupancy of Philadelphia by the British, the enemy destroyed his residence, (Peel Hall) which was on the site of the Girard College grounds.

He was an early and active member of the American Philosophical Society, one of its curators from 1769 to 1772, and secretary from 1773 to 1782, when he became one of the councillors, continuing as such until his death. He was one of the committee of thirteen appointed by the Society to observe the transit of Venus on 3d of June, 1769. These observations were made with eminent success by three members of the committee, Mr. Rittenhouse being stationed at Norristown, Dr. Ewing at Philadelphia, and Mr. Biddle at Cape Henlopen. Mr. Biddle died at Philadelphia on the 10th of March, 1799. His descendants have always taken a prominent part in the benevolent and business enterprises of the metropolis.

Clement Biddle was born in Philadelphia, May 10, 1740. Descended from one of the early Quaker settlers and proprietaries of West Jersey, he retained his connection with the Society of Friends until the commencement of the War of Independence.

In early life he engaged in commercial pursuits in his native city. Notwithstanding the discipline of the religious society in whose tenets he had been educated, he united, in 1764, in forming a military corps for the protection of a party of friendly Indians, who had sought refuge in Philadelphia from the fury of a lawless band, known as the Paxton Boys, who had recently massacred some unoffending Conestoga Indians, at Lancaster. These banditti, powerful in numbers, had advanced to within five or six miles of the city, threatening destruction to all who should oppose them, when the vigor of the military preparations checked their further progress. Scarcely had this local disturbance been quieted, when news was received of the resolution of the British House of Commons to impose certain stamp duties on the colonies. The feeling engendered throughout the whole country by this step, was nowhere deeper than in Philadelphia; and the consummation of the resolve of the Commons, by the passage of the Stamp Act, induced, in

that city, the celebrated non-importation resolutions of October 25, 1765;
one of the most decided measures adopted during the early part of the
struggle with Great Britain, for the preservation of the civil rights of the
colonists. This agreement was subscribed by the principal merchants of the
city; among them we find the names of Clement Biddle and his brother
Owen Biddle. The course subsequently pursued by the British Government destroying all hope of a peaceful adjustment, Clement Biddle embarked early and zealously in the defence of the liberties of America, and
was greatly instrumental in forming the "Quaker" company of volunteers,
raised in Philadelphia in 1775, of which he was elected an officer, before the
corps joined the army. Congress having, in June, 1776, for the protection
of the middle colonies, directed the immediate establishment of a camp of
ten thousand men, to be furnished by Pennsylvania, Maryland, and Delaware, on the 8th of July following, appointed Colonel Biddle the Deputy
Quartermaster-General for those forces, as well as for the militia of Pennsylvania and New Jersey, ordered to assemble at Trenton. At the close of
that year, Colonel Biddle took part in the battle of Trenton, and with another officer, was selected by Washington to receive the swords of the Hessian officers. He was also engaged in the stoutly-contested victory at Princeton; the battle at and retreat from the Brandywine; the attack upon the
British forces at Germantown; and during the winter of 1777-8 shared the
privations of the American army at the memorable cantonment at Valley
Forge. There, as Commissary-General under Greene, he rendered important services in several critical junctures, when the disbanding of the army,
from want of the necessaries of life, seemed almost inevitable. Many letters
from General Washington, written at this period, and now in the possession
of Colonel Biddle's family, attest his activity in the commissariat department, the urgency of the service he was engaged in, and the confidence reposed in him by the father of his country. He was again in action at the
battle of Monmouth.

After the war of the Revolution, he renewed, for a short time, his connection with military life, by serving as Quartermaster-General of Pennsylvania in the expedition, under Washington, to suppress the "Whiskey
Insurrection."

Colonel Biddle labored earnestly in the early political movements of the
patriot party of hi   . advocating effectively the revolutionary State Constitution of 1776, ,   .aming of which his brother, Owen Biddle, shared, as
a member of the Convention. After the organization of the Federal Government, under the Constitution of 1787, Colonel Biddle was appointed United
States Marshal for Pennsylvania. At a later period he engaged in business
as a notary public, and became well known in commercial circles for his
ability in adjusting marine losses. He preserved the friendship and enjoyed
the intimacy of General Washington until the close of the life of that great
man, and maintained with him a familiar epistolary correspondence until
within a few weeks of the General's decease.

Greene and Knox were also his warm personal friends and correspondents; and when the former was selected for the command of the southern army, one of his first preparations for the campaign, was an effort to obtain the services of Colonel Biddle as Quartermaster-General. By his marriage with Miss Rebecca Cornell, he had a numerous family. His sons have occupied prominent and honorable positions in their native city; of his daughters, one was married to General Thomas Cadwalader, another to Dr. Nathaniel Chapman, and a third to Thomas Dunlap, Esq., of Philadelphia.

His distinguished and useful career ended on the 14th July, 1814, at Philadelphia, in the seventy-fifth year of his age.—*Simpson's Eminent Philadelphians.*